SAINTS BE PRAISED!

Oh, you found me!

Well since you did, I came to offer a **WARNING**. This is NOT a Bible in your hands! It's far from it actually. There's elements of **EXTREME HORROR**, **GRAPHIC SEX SCENES**, and tasteless humor. Not to mention the **SACRILEGE** abounds! It's intended for the most crude & those who care not about their entry into the Heavenly gates. The cover alone has a plethora of sins. So unfortunately, I can't give you my blessing. However, if you choose to proceed, just know you were warned. It's a sin to lie, so I will confess that I skimmed a few chapters. The impure thoughts did abound, but I repented and begged for forgiveness. I suggest you do the same, especially if you are prone to rampant fanny flutters!

I'll pray for you,
Sister Calliope

The ether seemed to quiet the Virgin Mary, though now her correspondence was all Mother Superior prayed for. She pressed off the door and made her way up the melting stairs. The sweet hymns plucked at her heartstrings, making her sway as she crossed the foyer. Her habit billowed as she spun in place and did her best to hold this moment in her heart.

For that split second, she wasn't Mother Superior. She was Sarah DeRosa: blissfully happy lover of life and an infinite light in a dark world, a world she didn't understand, that wouldn't have her, and told her she was wrong and the only way to be right was to become everything she wasn't.

The hymn came to its end. Mother Superior felt empty again. A crumpled doll coming to a stop on her weathered Mary Janes, staring down the darkened hall. Mother Superior couldn't help but smile as a tear streamed down her cheek. Though she couldn't see her, she could feel the Virgin Mary watching her.

Seething. Volatile. Starving.

Sarah felt Mary pulling her close with those loving, glowing, omnipotent eyes.

My one and only.

Mary's blackened claws sliced through the darkness to caress Sarah's back, only penetrating her flesh when she slowed her steps.

The air that I breathe.

Mary's love was so intoxicating that it made Sarah lose her footing as she walked toward her cold, waiting embrace.

My heart. My everything. My ruin.

Standing before Mary, only able to see her silhouette but feel her presence, Sarah could forget who she was before. Forget the evil of the outside world. Forget the sins that played on an endless loop in her head, sins that hardened her heart and rotted her insides.

The blood that I spill.

Sarah was nothing without Mary. She was her vessel to punish those who did wrong.

It's better to be a vessel than a shell.

Though her tears may never stop, at least they were all for Mary. At least she knew she would never be alone. Ever.

I wish that I could quit you.

True, selfless love requires sacrifice. The greater the sacrifice, the more it strengthens her inamorata. She could never say no to Mary. Even when every cell of Sarah's being begged her to resist her malicious demands. Their souls had merged. The pact was ironclad, unbreakable, and written in blood. Sarah was a quivering instrument in her crushing palm, a piston in Mary's machinations.

Command me, Mary.
Take my love and let your wrath flow through me.
Let my hands be yours.
Bring all the evil pronounced against them
that they harkened not.

Scissor Me Timbers

PHRIQUE

CONTENTS

Foreword

Greetings book lovers,

If you're an avid reader, an author, or both—like me—then you know well that there are more books than anyone can read in a lifetime and countless authors writing them. This makes it hard not to get lost in the fold. It also makes it hard to keep from missing good authors that are just one ingredient in the mix that is to become the casserole of speculative fiction. It's okay. I'm here to help.

The last time I was asked to write a foreword was for one of my favorite authors as a reader, and I can proudly say that this time is no different. Sometimes, you read somebody that just hits different, a generational voice that steps out from the crowd and screams, "Look at me!"

Phrique is exactly that. His vocabulary is beautiful, but he doesn't use it in a pretentious way. Instead, he weaves it into eloquent prose that makes his novels read like poetry for your soul. He can make you laugh uproariously and then cringe with disgust the next moment. He can tug your heartstrings and make you cry, only to leave you gasping with fright in the next scene. He can take a silly, ridiculous concept and turn it into something serious with characters you care about and never want to leave.

He transcends just being an author like the millions surrounding him. Phrique is an artist. Is he perfect? No, of course not. But he learns more with each book he writes, and the thing I've seen, working with him on this particular book, is that he *wants* to learn. He wants to keep improving and is hungry for knowledge. He isn't content with mediocrity. Phrique wants to be the best he can be, and honestly, if he's already this good, imagining his best is actually scary.

If you're anything like me, you will be glad you bought a ticket for this ride and by the end of the book, you'll declare that you're not getting off.... Or maybe you are but not off of the ride, because this guy likes to make your gentials twitch with anticipation and invade your dreams until they're sloppier than trying to keep manwich in a hamburger bun. Of course, once you're fully aroused he will either send you back down, floating gently on the feather of laughter, or he will pop your sexy ass balloon with something horrific. If you're as fucked up as I am, you'll get off anyway, but that is to be seen.

Either way, you'll know just like I do that this is only the beginning for Phrique, and you won't want to miss a single step along the way. Whether it's nuns, drag queens (I've always envied and not-so-secretly wanted to be), or fast food brand mascots, he will make you desire them, downright crave them like preservative-filled french fries, and then cry for them when they are lost—like the chicken nugget that fell from your greasy fingers onto the bathroom floor and no matter how much you want it you know you can't possibly trust it after this moment. *Imagines reaching out like a dramatic action movie scene and screaming "Noooooo!" in slow-motion as it cascades towards a muddy boot print and piss puddle where it lands with a splash* Fuck!

You will curse him, praise him, and beg him for more, and that, my friends, is something special.

Mark my words, folks. Phrique is going to be bigger than I ever will, and he deserves to be. I will be there every step of the way, cheering him on as he surpasses me, because he's a diamond in the rough, a treasure, a drag queen's pearl necklace in the nun's clapped-shut clam at the bottom of this sea of endless writers, and when it comes to brilliant books, I'm a greedy, salivating mongrel. I can't wait for him to float to the top like an overindulgent purple monster mascot. And he will. I promise you that.

But don't take my word for it. Turn the page and see for yourself...

Sincerely,

Chisto Healy

THE CISTERCIAN NUNS OF THE VALLEY OF PERPETUAL FELICITY MONASTERY

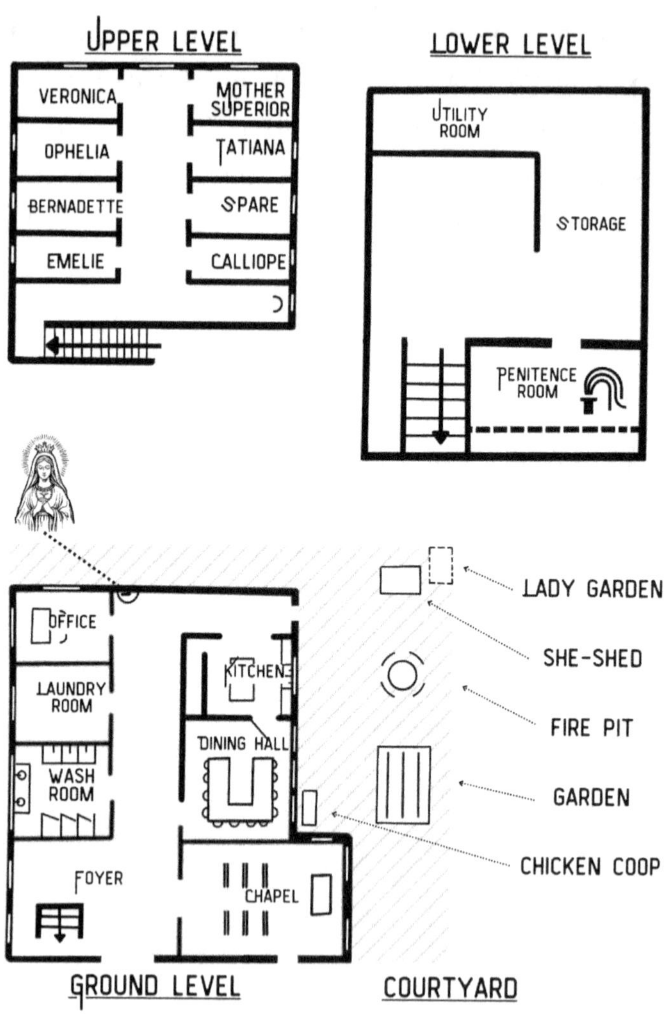

DEDICATED TO THE CATHOLIC CHURCH

It took me a while, but I finally got my licks in.
Consider us even.
TTYN,

Prologue: The (First) Last Supper

The arrogant horde yelled their orders belligerently toward the kitchen—hardly the type of behavior one would expect from clergymen. The sound of glass hitting the floor and shattering made Sister Sarah jump while removing the heavy shepherd's pie from the burning hot oven. Her eyes went wild when she felt the bubbling casserole shift and almost slide out of her hands. An uproar of hoots and laughter echoed throughout the monastery's halls just as Sarah steadied herself and shakily brought the metal baking dish up to the top of the oven. She kicked the oven door shut and blew the stray auburn wisps of hair off her glistening forehead. She hastily looked around for the trivet to place it on, still fumbling with the molten dish until it landed with a heavy thud. Piping hot gravy sloshed out of the dish, splattering the savory napalm up her exposed forearm, just past the worn oven mitt.

Sarah gasped in pain, pulling her hand out of the mitt while the gelatinous fluid bubbled and clung to her burning flesh. Her first instinct was to bring her arm to her mouth and slurp the offending juice. Though that might stop any further damage, she knew one drop of that rich gravy on her tongue meant a slow and painful death. The thought instantly calmed her. *This will all be over soon.* Her revenge would be served piping hot, with an extra little kick. The slam of the swinging door slapped her out of her daydream. She flinched as Father Thomas stuck his enormous cranium in the room.

"Can we get a move on here, Sarah? We're starving for crying out loud!" he yelled, more for his constituents than her. He was met with a death stare from Sister DeRosa, rinsing her arm under the cold tap. She sighed shakily.

"Could you at least help me carry this into the refectory? I burned my arm." She nodded toward the still-steaming casserole.

"You know I can't lift anything heavy with my arthritis, Sarah," he said, pulling away with disinterest. "And that tincture you gave me isn't worth a damn either. My shoulder still aches like a motherfucker," Father Thomas added before the door swung closed.

A deep exhale allowed Sister Sarah's mind to calm before the event. All the planning, all the torture she endured, she just hoped she did everything right. She rubbed an ice cube over the pink welts on her forearm while reviewing her mental checklist. She stared down at her rosy skin, strings of painful pearls bubbling under its surface. Realizing it was now or never, Sister Sarah slid on the oven mitts and braced her back. Like the broken bread of the body of Christ, she was hoisting the embodiment of her malice, topped with the fluffiest mashed potatoes she'd ever made.

Sister Sarah reversed against the swinging door into the dining hall, leading the way with her bountiful backside. The assorted catcalls and chuckles didn't phase her anymore; nothing did, really. The phrase *water off a duck's back* brought her solace, but could you trust solace? After the first few months of being trapped in a monastery, she had learned better than most that even the Lord's dog collar couldn't tame these deplorable beasts.

She steadily carried the aromatic meal to the long table. The crimson tablecloth she chose looked stunning and would make cleanup so much easier. The *little boys* masquerading as grown men all cheered sarcastically.

"Shepard's pie! Look at our Sarah becoming Martha Stewart right before our eyes."

"Martha Stewart couldn't fill out an apron like that. Hubba hubba!"

The men's laughter barely muffled the metal pan slamming onto the table next to the linen napkins, still stacked where she had placed them. She huffily grabbed the stack and handed it to a distracted Father James to pass down while she retrieved a trivet to protect the antique hardwood table. He sat the napkins before him, continuing his conversation with Father Andrew. She returned and flared her nostrils, slapping at Father James's shoulder to slide the trivet under while she lifted the shepherd's pie. Sarah stabbed the serving spoon into the golden mash and snatched up the napkins. She circled the table, handing them to each padre with palpable disdain. Her reflection in Father Peter's bald head caused her to pause. The face of a haggard old witch stared back at her; the three years devoted to the Lord had not been kind to her.

Father Peter spun around and angrily snatched the napkin, shocking her back to the refectory. She blinked the emotions away that tried to use her tear ducts as a means of escape. *Never cry for a man, especially not for this congregation of ingrates.* Dropping the last napkin in front of Father Thomas, she stood bewildered by the extra napkin she still held. She quickly surveyed the table, counting the idiots and coming up with one missing. *Who?* Her breath caught in her throat, agitation creeping onto her face.

"Where's Father Phillip?!" she asked shrilly, barely able to hide the panic in her voice.

"Where do you think? The john, as always," Father James said.

"He's going to go blind someday," said Father Peter to raucous laughter.

The spittle flying out of their guffawing mouths did not make Sister Sarah wince as usual; her mind was going into lockdown mode. She eyed the spoon still impaled in the casserole and attempted to leap for it just as Father James ham-fistedly grabbed it and shoveled food onto his plate.

"Hey, give me a scoop, James!" yelled Father Andrew.

Sister Sarah felt like her mind was a time bomb, counting down until she was left with just a bloodied stump for a neck.

"Yeah, me too. Since we can't even get served around here," Father Peter said with his extremely punchable face stuck in an exaggerated eye roll.

"Let's... let's wait for Phillip," Sarah choked out, barely audible over the angry yelling and the bees buzzing in her mind. The hive had been whacked with a stick, and the anticipation of the murderous swarm was making her sweat.

"*Father* Phillip will be all day at the rate he's going. Poor bastard," Father James said, pushing the hot food around his mouth between words.

"Would it kill you to put some bread out? What do you even do around here?"

"Besides burning everything and keeping her girlfriend Mary dusted and waxed?"

Deep belly laughs drowned out the clinking of silverware on plates.

"Waxed!"

Sarah felt her face go hot, still stuck in place.

"She's not my-" she was cut off instantly.

"Bread, sweetheart, bread!" Father James said as he playfully tapped her thigh with the back of his hand, snapping her back again.

Sarah frantically headed to the kitchen, her bandeau the only thing keeping the sweat off her worry-written face. She absent-mindedly grabbed the bread knife and the cutting board.

"Ugh, this is awful! What did you put in this gravy?"

Sarah slammed the hard loaf of bread on the board and started to saw at the thick crust.

"Hey Peter, what happens to a pretty girl with a full figure who can't cook?"

She could hear the snickers rising as the blade sliced cleanly through the heel of the loaf.

"Nothing. She becomes a nun!"

The room burst into cacophonous laughter. The bread knife clanged on the counter loud enough to stifle a few startled laughs before Sarah slid it blade-up into the pocket of her apron. She returned to the table with the vexation seeping out of her pores, like a poisonous gas clouding the room. The cutting board and bread clattered to the table, scattering the pieces across the tablecloth.

"Yeesh! Careful Andrew. Must be someone's time of the month!"

Laughter broke out again but quickly dissipated when the eyes of the aloof priests fell on Sister Sarah walking to stand before them.

A feeble cat call was quickly extinguished as Sister Sarah pensively glanced toward the washroom one last time and then turned to face them all. A single cough brought a smile to her face. The tension in the room rose out of the grooves in the aged wooden floors. The priests were watching the silent nun while still chewing or guzzling water.

"Pass the water, James." Father Thomas coughed into his arm. "Too much pepper. My throat is on *fire*."

"Mine too. What the hell did you put in this, Sarah?"

A laugh escaped Sarah's mouth. She couldn't stop. Her eyes started to water. She watched them all paw at their throats between water chugs and reach for the lone pitcher.

The view reminded her of a rendition of the Dionysian feast featured in *The Feast of the Gods*, but everyone recognized that painting, right?

"Oh, boys!" her voice shook the walls.

All increasingly bloodshot eyes went to her.

"How does my Belladonna taste?"

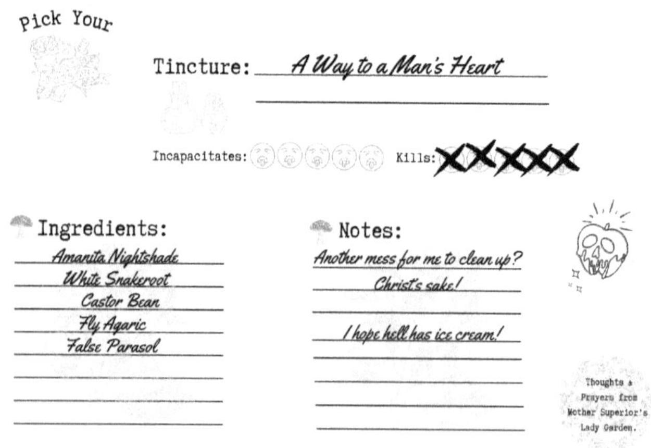

A scornful giggle slipped out of her.

"Burn in Hell, knowing this bitch sent you there!"

She turned a deaf ear to their choked cries and gurgled screams and made her way to the regrettably communal wash-room.

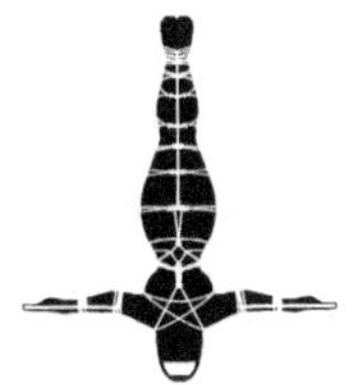

Sister Sarah held her breath and entered their washroom. Her eyes met her reflection in the mirror above the sinks, across the benches and tiled floor. She was surprised to see the smile plastered on her face that paired with her crazed eyes. The three stalls to her right housed the showers, but she knew her target was in the last stall to her left. Everyone knew to avoid the last toilet stall. That was Father Phillip's stall. He never claimed it, but no one wanted to know what he was always doing behind the closed stall door.

Sarah's face grimaced, feeling the thick air in the washroom permeating her habit. Out of the corner of her eye in the mirror, she spotted a bright green-topped aerosol spray can. She weighed her options: between that and the serrated breadknife still jostling against her thigh in a cramped, awful space. The sound of pained howls from the hall pestered her to grab the aerosol and get this over with. She slapped the can against her opposite thigh, letting the green plastic lid hit the ground. The sound echoed the walls, met by a startled gasp and shuffle in the only stall with a closed door.

"Hey! No horsing around! I'm hurting over here!" Father Phillip grunted. "Remind me never to eat Sarah's oatmeal again."

Sarah glowered, huffily approaching the stall and eying the door lock.

"Hello?" resounded through the sickening space.

"You're missing dinner, Phillip," she said sweetly before she pounded her fist on the door. A nudie magazine flopped onto the damp floor with another flustered gasp.

"I'm shitting my brains out, Sarah!" The thin metal door shifted as he pressed his hand against the back of it and retrieved his magazine. "Can't a man have some peace around here? Leave me alone!"

"You men don't *deserve* peace."

Sarah pounded her fist against the door again.

"I cooked!" She pounded.

"I cleaned!" She stepped back before squaring her shoulders.

"I MADE IT NICE!" She screamed as her Mary Jane kicked the lock, rocketing the door in, only for it to ricochet back out toward her. The busted catch clattered to the floor.

Father Phillip jumped backwards against the toilet, his pants around his ankles as Sarah charged forward and let the foaming bathroom cleaner spray out onto his face and bulging eyes. She covered her own face with her arm to keep the stray aerosols away and minimize the stench.

The priest yowled and wiped at his eyes, freeing his minuscule erection from his perverted grasp. Sarah's disgusted eyes could not help but notice, giving the offending appendage a dousing of spray foam as well.

"What the hell?!" shrieked Father Phillip as he had to grab at his holy place, leaving his stinging pink eyes to flood with blurry tears.

Sarah glared, grabbing at his shirt just below his clerical collar and pulling the weight of the hefty man forward. Having been caught off guard, he fell forward and sprawled out onto the floor before her. She was met with his anguished screams when she stepped onto his thigh and into the stall. She kept her eyes trained on the wall above the lid, feeling for the flush handle. Her few glances down caused her to scowl.

"Gross," she said with contempt as she flushed.

Over her shoulder, Father Phillip tried to inch away from her. He continued to army crawl along the slick tile. Sister Sarah looked toward the toilet tank and got an idea as it loudly refilled with water.

Father Phillip trudged forward blindly until he felt he had come to the long bench in the middle of the washroom. He swatted above his head to feel for the seat and pulled himself up once he had a confident grip. He let out an agonized wail once he had an elbow on the bench. He pulled his knee and scrunched his swollen eyes shut, listening to see if Sarah was still in the vicinity. His blurred vision in the mirror showed a darkened form standing just behind him, forcefully oscillating in his direction.

The toilet tank lid collided with the side of Father Philip's head, hard enough to shoot his skull to the left of him. A crimson splash accompanied bits of teeth that sailed to the right of him, spraying the open shower stall. The impact from the blow made his upper body crumple and his elbow slide off the bench. The other side of his head cracked into the shiny lacquered seat, boxing his ears and locking the tinnitus into his thumping skull. He lay weakly on the glistening tile, a pool of blood spreading beneath him. His head felt like it was in a cranking vice, a kaleidoscope of light and dark shadows swimming to the surface of his watery eyes.

Sister Sarah stepped over him and slammed the porcelain edge down as her foot landed on the other side of his head. The ceramic guillotine, powered by rage and gravity, jettisoned downward with enough force to collapse the gurgling priest's jaw in on itself. Everything below his twitching nostrils became a sleeve of skin, split open by the blindingly white slab. A mash of gore and combusted teeth collected around his fractured spine and collapsed windpipe. Sarah rested her weight on the back of the toilet tank lid, unable to genuinely enjoy the victory of seeing life leave his eyes. The final crunch, like a dozen wet knuckle cracks, brought her blood-flecked face back into a grin. The loose end being tied up with a bloody bow allowed her to hear the echoing screams resonating from just beyond the door. She stood and left the top of the toilet and Father Phillip in place. It slid until it slanted down, nestled in the divot of destruction. Exiting the washroom, she pulled the wooden door toward her and welcomed the choir of pained notes singing a song just for her.

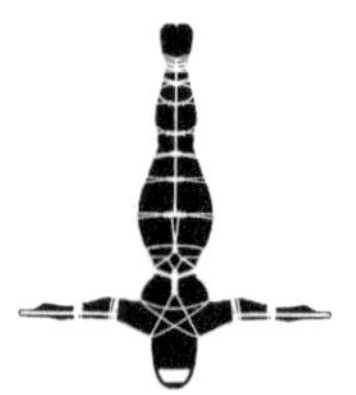

Before dealing with Phillip, her mind's eye took a mental snapshot of the fear and shock that ran rampant across the stunned table. On her return, the scene contorted into Bosch's

"*Portrait of Hell*," with the infernal priests writhing on the floor as if they were enchanted and floating in the River Styx. Sarah stood before the pious hypocrites splashing in their own sick as it spewed out of them, ranging from foamy ochres to vibrant reds. Sarah returned to the table, wanting to see the fruits of her labor with her own eyes. Up close and in deliciously diligent detail.

Only two poor souls stayed stationary at their place settings. Peter sat off-kilter, with his head dropped on his arms on top of his plate. Both ends of him had released like a busted fire hydrant; vomit was sprayed in an arc around him, and Sarah was certain his pants were full of an even worse offense, going by the scent alone. His pupils looked large enough to rival the jackass's pronounced, vibrantly green irises. His breathing began to go shallow, and the light in his unblinking eyes dimmed.

Father James began to convulse spontaneously and fall to the floor, spraying vomit as he tumbled. Among the pained groans, his was the loudest. The fall seemed to startle him awake from his languid state. When his mouth had stopped yawning in technicolor, he was yammering on about his throat itching through the sound of severely torched windpipes. Sarah felt horror and delight watching James scratch and scrape at his neck. In the blink of an eye, blood was spurting as his nails dug into the soft pink skin and tore off bits like soft jerky before it had finished curing in the sun. She stepped back as his blood began to spurt into a puddle from his makeshift stoma. His final gurgles sounded like hissing moans bubbling from under the crimson syrup.

As the overall cries in the room fell to a lull, she turned to the writhing mass of wet, seizing limbs. Father Andrew, ever the comic relief, seemed to have told his last joke. His jaw was clenched tight enough that Sarah expected his pearly whites to explode in his mouth at any moment. His normally tanned Sicilian skin was now an eerie jaundiced yellow that seemed to be intensifying before her eyes. Purple vines snaked out onto the yellow canvas that was his twitching face, trailing down to his darkening blue fingers. His suffering, their suffering, was the only punchline that truly brought joy to her heart.

Sarah's eyes traced the perimeter of the room. Sewage fumes crept across her face, as well as a frustrated look. The glint off Father Peter's shining bald head eclipsed in a pool of reddening froth beneath him. She told herself she would drive her garden trowel right through the back of that glistening dome one day. She could imagine the satisfying halt as the steel edge of the small shovel glided through skin, skull, and brain matter before it hit the skull once more. She would not get to honor that promise to herself, but she knew that this was for the greater good. *Let them all suffer in agony and see what it felt like. They may have won the battles, but I will be leaving victorious and wearing their lifeblood as war paint.*

Snapping out of that bloody garden daydream to wake up in the middle of a massacre of her own concoction brought a tear to her eye. She stepped through whatever clear floorspace allowed her to scan the other side of the table, looking for Father Thomas.

Knowing he could not have traveled far, she knitted her eyebrows and traced the trail of gore from the table to the kitchen door and back. She entered the kitchen, worry creeping across her face when she saw the footsteps and eventual drag marks toward the hallway. She carefully pulled the bread knife from her oversized pocket and followed the rust-tinted trail. Her eyes narrowed when she saw them leading toward the office.

Adrenaline flooded her system and carried her to the dark room. The light switching on caused the wheezing priest to jump and cower behind his hands while he leaned against the large wooden desk in the middle of the room. Father Thomas belched loudly, letting chunks of vomit trickle off his chin. Sarah winced at the sight.

"Should have known the fussy eater, Father Thomas, would push the plate away after two bites."

Steadily, she stepped closer, and he rose up taller against the desk.

"Especially once he found the mushrooms. Amanita Pantherina. Enough in my special blend to make it count."

She watched his hand snake up toward the top of the desk, causing Sarah to take another step forward with the knife—no longer concealed.

"You could have sat there and eaten your food. You'd be slowly dying in a prison of your own mind's making. Your brothers seem to like it."

She tightened her grip on the knife handle.

"They tasted death and found it delicious."

Father Thomas wearily pulled on the landline cord. Sarah trudged closer, then froze in indecision. Father hissed inaudible utterances through his clenched teeth as he yanked harder on the cord, pulling the old-fashioned phone toward him. Sarah bolted to the bookcase as the priest caused the archaic plastic monstrosity to fall off the desk and clatter onto him. She ignored the noise while she ripped at the phone cord stapled to the wall, tracing its origin. The croaking priest flinched and grabbed at the phone components, placing the receiver to his perspiring skin. In a panic, she tugged at the cord enough to slice through the slack with the teeth of the bread knife.

The dial tone went dead in his ear. Sarah grabbed Father Thomas's ankles to pull him from the desk onto the open carpeted area. She released her grip on his leg and moved to attack when the heavy plastic phone receiver collided with her temple. The blow sent her stumbling to the carpet, causing the knife to fall just out of her reach. Stunned and lightheaded, she reached for her weapon before flopping over to crawl the distance to it. Father Thomas pulled at her tunic, keeping her in place. He wrapped the spiral cord around his fist and climbed onto her prone body. She kicked and screamed, but he wouldn't let up. He grabbed her shoulder and pulled back. She felt his knee press into her spine and the cord stretch across her collarbone before he pulled.

Her already doubled vision multiplied after the cord pulled tight, cutting off her oxygen. Chunks of wet regurgitated food tumbled onto her as the priest got his bearings and pulled her bound neck up higher toward him. Through garbled breaths, he yelled, "Whore...of Satan!" before he lurched and heaved a warm spray of yellow, and increasingly pink vomit over her shoulder. Her disgusted screams bubbled out of her as his grip weakened. Sarah bucked the spewing cistern off her in his eroding state. She pulled the cord from her neck and sucked in as much air as she could before crawling across the carpet. Her fingers wrapped around the handle of the bread knife as she pushed herself up to her hands and knees. She heard another splash of sickness hit the carpet while she knee-walked back to him. His bloodshot eyes bulged for a last spew as he lay on his side, slightly leaning toward the desk. Unable to escape the spray, she arced the bread knife toward his exposed neck and dragged the razor-sharp teeth against his drumming throat. The soft skin pulled with the blade, unzipping the flesh as it traveled across his Adam's apple.

Vibrant ruby sprayed them both, with waves of ejecta alternately spurting out of the widening slice.

She flung the knife back toward the wall and sat back on her ankles while she watched Father Thomas take his final drowning breath. Sarah sighed and looked down at her hands, still shaking and caked with God knows what. She looked at the rug, sizing up the priest, and watched the circle of his dark blood grow larger as it soaked into the fibers.

"Well, this is getting trashed," she said quietly, noticing the beautiful silence. She looked around the office that would be hers. Before she left Father Thomas's side, she pulled the red-beaded rosary from around his butchered neck. A little rinse would do it good; it's the least he could do since she'd wanted it the first time she saw it. Genuine rosary peas, too. This made it all almost worth it.

Her eyes watered as she stood and shakily walked to the desk, plopping herself down in the oversized chair. She looked out toward the hallway, seeing a shimmering sea of sickly colors, and sighed deeply.

"And Sister Sarah is left to clean up the mess, one last time."

She wiped her hand on her sleeve and lifted the paperwork on the desk, determined not to get any cruor on it. The letterhead from the archdiocese shimmered in the light as her eyes skimmed the page. Though she had read the letter multiple times, she wanted to be certain her frantic mind was not mistaken. Her stare danced across the announcement decreeing the arrival of Sister Veronica and three novitiates in two weeks. She placed the papers in the top drawer and stared off with a coy grin, past the office walls. She replayed the epilogue to *"The Story of Sister Sarah"* that ended with the closure she would never have received if she had not taken matters into her own hands. Her heart swelled. Sarah was ready to begin this brand new prologue.

"Mother Superior has a lot of work to do."

If a Lesbian Falls in the Forest, Does She Make a Sound?
Chapter 1

Five *Years Later*

"Tiiiimbeeerrrr!"

Paulina wiped the sweaty, rust-colored hair from her brow and peered over her shoulder toward her logging crew. As usual, she had scouted ahead of the lagging *men* in her company. Maybe they had time to bullshit, but she had a hot date with a lil' filly by the name of Eve and could not wait to bury her face in that Garden of Eden. The reverb from the toppling timber rippled through the ground and vibrated up through her work boots. Her guys were far enough behind her that the thought of being crushed by a falling tree hadn't entered her mind. A moment later, she caught the tail end of their bellows before the thrush of branches and the unmistakable whoosh of over half a ton of wood barreled toward her unsuspecting, cocksure smirk.

What did her dirty was holding her chainsaw correctly, as instructed, instead of by her side when walking.

So, when the three-ton Louisville slugger came down on top of her, it was the force of the tonnage slamming into her that forced her torso to tear in two over the jagged steel teeth held horizontal. Had the fallen tree been a few feet to her right, it would have done her the service of crunching her bones into the soft earth and mashing her skull into a crunching, leaking jelly donut after the first bite.

However, it fell two feet to her left, pinning her down to the ground in a millisecond. Bisected, with many barbed limbs and branches impaling her in various painful pressure points. The worst was the six-inch-wide limb that entered just below her ribcage. The force of the fall ricocheted the sharp, broken edge up and out of her armpit, deflating her now fluid-filling lung but keeping her alive just long enough to feel her insides slopping out of her and soaking into the dark void that would be her final resting place.

Paulina shook the vivid daydream out of her mind just as the adrenaline rush from the narrow escape started to subside.

"Which one of you limp-dicked losers wants me to split their fucking skulls wide open and spoon out what's inside?!" she screamed as she slammed her pink chainsaw down on the fresh stump, surrounded by a half-dozen fumbling, foolhardy faces.

The sounds of the forest resounded through the small clearing filled with silent, solemn men.

"WHO WAS IT?" Paulina bellowed, eyeballing each of them. She placed her boot up on the stump to display the ripped leg of her jeans. Traces of blood and sawdust dotted the denim.

"You owe me a pair of slacks, Travis, and some drawers, too." She turned around to show her mud-caked derriere. "Cuz I seemed to have shit clean through mine." The crowd exploded in an uproar of laughter as she shook her ass lightheartedly.

"Let's call it a day, ladies. Travis & Boonie get those downies on the last truck before we ship out. Everyone else—straight home and get some sleep. If you are not here before sunup, you're not getting paid. Capisce?"

Her grimy men murmured in the affirmative and headed out wi th their tools. She grabbed her trusty chainsaw, Winnie, checked he r face for damage, and pulled out her phone.

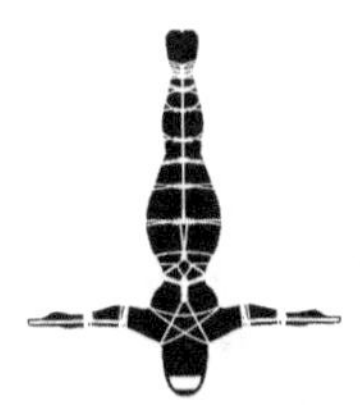

The dusty red pickup pulled into *Oak E. Doke's* parking lot. Paulina pulled her visor mirror down, gathered her damp red curls into a messy bun, and checked her phone again. No new texts, she noticed, lighting a cigarette. Smoke floated from her glossy lips as she eyed the handsome clientele outside the entrance. *Oak E. Doke's* wasn't a lesbian bar officially, but there were too many hunter green Subarus in the parking lot. Let's just say that. A familiar pair of snug, denimed hips swayed toward her without enough time to close her window.

"Well, if it isn't Miss Too-Busy-to-Text-back-for-Two-Weeks," said a nasal voice from the shadows of the branches dancing above the truck.

Paulina rolled her eyes and exhaled in her direction.

"You know I'm not a big texter, Rebecca. Besides, I've been too busy with work. We got that new contract and..."

Rebecca strategically crossed her arms under her heaving cleavage and glared at her, unblinking.

"I don't even have my phone, honest," Paulina said, attempting to tuck her mobile under her thigh as it buzzed and chimed to life. She groaned under her breath.

Rebecca scoffed and spat against the side of the pickup.

"You fucking sociopath, I hope the next beaver you damn has mildew." Her boots crunched the gravel back toward the flashing beer signs of the bar. She checked the message that came through.

Eve:

Running late, lol. Get us a drink. I'll be there in 5

The cool night air ran through the flaming orange ringlets that dangled off her bun as she tied the tails of her red flannel work shirt around her midriff. The curvy forms under the blinking fluorescent lights hooted and catcalled Paulina as she approached the entrance. She confidently strode past them, smirking but nodding slightly to the leering *lougars.*

"Check out the thot knot. She's taking no prisoners tonight."

"Ain't no fresh meat in there tonight, P. You must be getting delivery," said a raspy stone butch, choking on her cigarette smoke.

"Thanks for the concern, Caroline, and for remembering that only my friends call me Paulina."

Caroline and the coven of croc lesbians cackled while Paulina slipped through the front door.

"We'll be sure to send her in when she gets here...as long as one of us don't knock her off her feet first."

The low hum of the honkytonk and the door softly closing behind Paulina drowned out their chuckles. She headed toward the ladies room, brushing past every eyeball in the hallway. The two ladies queuing in front of the restroom didn't flinch when she walked in just as a tall blonde in a denim shirt walked out. She hit the head and then sudsed her mitts, studying her freckled face in the bad lighting.

One of the mousy girls outside snuck in and entered the stall when they heard the hand dryer go off. Paulina raised an eyebrow, tracing her full lips with a rarely used gloss. Her eyes darted to the crude etchings sprawling the wall like ancient filthy hieroglyphs. She grinned at "#LesbianEiffelTower" and counted how many times she could find her name. *Only four times; they must have recently painted in here.* She sighed, then made another adjustment to the...thot knot in her shirt.

I like that.

A dowdy middle-aged brunette slunk out of the stall, standing behind our primping lumberjill. Paulina gave her a devilish smirk that said she knew she had the sweetest honeypot in all the land.

"Would you fuck me?" Paulina asked, holding her grin.

Brunette squeaked, "I...uh...me? Su-sure! ...Now?" She said, looking around nervously.

"No, Silly," Paulina winked at her in the mirror before leaving the restroom. "Thanks, Mama."

Paulina hitched her jeans cutoffs a little higher as she made her way to the bar. All eyes were on her again, and she lapped up the stares like a pussycat to a saucer of milk. The only feminine gaze she wasn't commanding was the smarmy bartender's, who turned her violet hair buns away from the main attraction by instead trying to dry spotty wet beer mugs.

"You know you saw me, Serena."

The olive-skinned beauty turned, water drips soaking into her snug black tee. Her eyes were seething slits, the familiar voice causing her pouty lips to shift closer to her freckled nose.

"Hard to miss the community swimming hole. What do you want?"

Paulina smirked and nestled her cleavage, resting her crossed arms on the bar.

"Two White Russians. Extra creamy. You know the way I like it."

"You're a pig. I should have known when I saw the Spirit Halloween slutty lumberjack costume." The vexed bartender fixed her eyes on the small mole on Paulina's left breast.

"Worked on you, if I remember right." Paulina leaned in, plucking a toothpick to draw attention to her mouth. "My eyes are up here, Babygirl."

"Don't call me that." Serena let the two drinks in her hand land with a thunk on the aged wooden bar. Regaining control of her line of sight, she peered over Paulina's plaid shoulder at the bar's newest occupant. "Looks like your prey is here."

Paulina's eyes shot to the mirror above Serena, and she snatched up the drinks. Under her breath, she said, "What goes in that pretty little mouth of yours is always so much nicer than what comes out of it, Serena. Be a good girl, and maybe I'll come visit more."

"Hold your breath," the bartender spat before she sauntered toward the other patrons on the opposite side of the bar.

Paulina spun to face the lithe strides of her meal on wheels. Eve walked up to the bar, her deep brown hair flowing over her bare shoulders. Her fair skin was a wash of white, especially in contrast to her black tank top and dark waves. Her pale skin glowed under the low house lights, only seeming to warm up to a rosy undertone around her full lips. Her round glasses nestled her cute button nose, sitting above the small steel bauble that sat coyly snuggled in the cleft of her pouty lip. Paulina drank her all in, biting her lip and beckoning her near with a confident nod. Eve grabbed a drink from her and nuzzled in for a peck on the cheek. Stone-faced Paulina was a little disheartened at the lack of lip-lock but didn't let on.

Eve's flushed lips parted to smile, her small lip ring glinting in Paulina's face.

"Thanks, Ellie May Clampet," she said with a smirk, sipping her drink and taking in the lumberjill's outfit. "Is this what you really wear to work?"

Paulina wrapped her arm around Eve's waist and said, "Nah, I did this just for you; I thought you would like a little easier access."

"Ugh...PIG!" was screamed from behind them, prompting a smug Paulina to lead her immaculate Eve away from the bar and toward an empty booth.

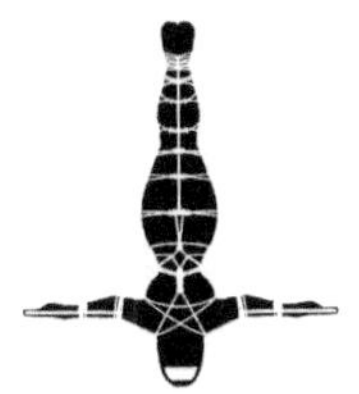

So why a bar?" Paulina asked, holding hands with her date across the table. Their eyes locked. "We have so much fun at your place."

"To make sure you're not ashamed to be seen with me."

Paulina smirked and rolled her eyes in response.

"Plus, I figured maybe if I could keep you vertical for a bit, you'd be forced to tell me more about the infamous Paulina Bunyan." Now it was Eve's turn to smirk. "And not just what I heard on my way in here... or saw written on the restroom walls."

Paulina snickered and covered her chin with her hand.

"What more do you need to know? I'm just your typical lady lumberjack. Work hard, play harder, fuck hardest. You've witnessed it yourself... and maybe a few others along the way."

"Mmmmhmmmm." Eve caught the waitress's attention and motioned for a round of shots.

"How long have you lived out here?"

"About a year or two, the company goes where the lumber is, and I ended up here; got a comfy lil place to lay my head after a long day of work. I can see nothing but treetops from my bedroom window, we haven't even been down in the valley yet. I will have work till I'm a little old lady out here."

Eve grinned, watching Paulina's face as she candidly waxed about her simple life.

"And how long have you been doing the lumberjack games for?"

Paulina swelled with pride.

"One-year training, two years competing. You were there to see my first big win."

"You were pretty incredible, I must admit. Watching you leave all those other girls in the dust was quite the aphrodisiac."

Paulina's eyes lit up, squeezing Eve's hand; she was about to switch to sit on her side of the booth when the waitress stepped up with a tray full of shots. The waitress's name tag said *Jessie*, which Paulina was already well aware of.

"Tequila, your favorite P," the waitress said dryly, plopping the tray in front of her. "Your tab, right?"

Paulina replied in an annoyed huff, "You betcha." She eyed Jessie as she headed back to the bar.

"How about a game?" Eve chimed, handing Paulina a shot.

"I think you watch too many reality shows, Babygirl."

"Oh, c'mon, grandma, afraid of what might come out with loose lips?"

"Nothing loose about me, Babygirl; you can attest to that."

"Tell you what, we can get out of here after. Deal?

Paulina gulped her shot down.

"Let's go."

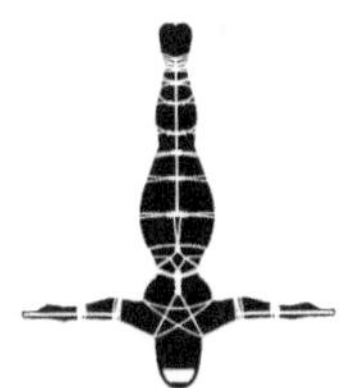

Paulina smirked. "Never have I ever...slept with a guy."

Eve took a shot.

Paulina said, "Gross."

"You're telling me. Never have I ever...used a strap-on."

Paulina took a shot. "This girl knows her way around all the tools of the trade; let's just say that."

"Hmmm. We may have to see about that."

"We can go see right now, Babygirl."

"That Babygirl line, does it work every time?"

Paulina burped. "Only on baby girls." She giggled. "Never have I ever...slept with an entire convent of nuns."

Eve gasped. "I'm sorry, what the fuck??"

Paulina shrugged. "A girl can have dreams." She snickered. "They're keeping it tight for Jesus."

"Omg, you are getting sloppy, P. Never have I ever...slept with over 100 women."

Paulina burped again. "Fuck, I need to hit the head."

Eve screamed to the back of an escaping Paulina, "WAIT, NO! TAKE THE SHOT OR DON'T!"

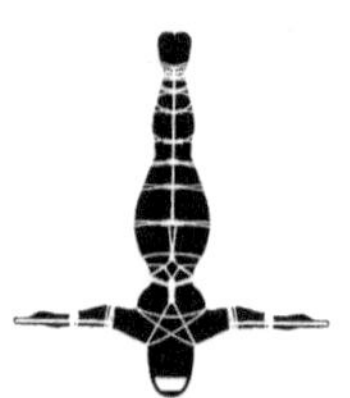

Eve and Paulina walked out of the bar arm in arm. Paulina was notably worse for wear than Eve was.

Paulina slurred in Eve's ear, "I'm going to marry you... I'm going...to make you my wife."

Eve walked Paulina to her truck, propping her up against it and feeling for her keys.

Paulina cooed, "Yeah, Babygirl, riiight here in the parking lot. That's...so hot." She grabbed at Eve's breasts under her tank top, who seemed less than enthused about the public display of affection.

Eve opened her door and slid Paulina inside while she was still trying to paw at Eve's chest.

"My Uber is here, P-baby. Are you sure you're going to be okay?"

Paulina slumped over onto her seat,

"Yeah, Babygirl, I'll be just fine."

"Sleep, Paulina. SLEEP, okay? No driving."

"Yeah, okay," Paulina slurred, already half snoring.

"Please don't drive. Be careful."

Eve got in her Uber and deleted Paulina's number from her phone. Paulina's snores started to fog up her windshield as the last Jetta pulled out of the parking lot.

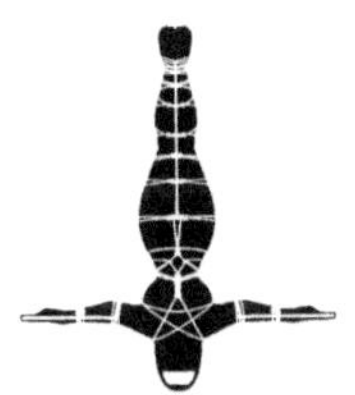

Paulina's phone alarm buzzed in the back pocket of her shorts. She clumsily fumbled with it, snoozing it at last and letting it flop next to her. After a few seconds of recollection, she shot up. Her breath was steaming in the chilled early morning air. Realizing where she was, on only 2-3 hours of sleep, she fired up the old truck and waited for her windows to defog. She looked in the rearview mirror, aghast. She had to get to the worksite before the rest of her crew showed up. Let alone see her in this state of dress. She'd never be able to live this one down.

She pulled out onto the winding road, thankful that the site was only 10 minutes from the bar. The job site was on the last shelf above the valley. She tensed her grip on the steering wheel and shook the tipsy, light-headed feeling out of her head as she started taking the more dangerous curves. One swerve too far would send her and her mighty truck bouncing down almost 200 feet of cliff.

The first streaks of sun began to paint the sky as she groggily drove this routine route. After a remarkably close call, she noticed red writing on her passenger-side window. She tried to pay attention to the road ahead, but her nosy nature would always be her downfall. She wouldn't be surprised if it were a random phone number or something lasciviously devilish. Fortunately, a patch of light was coming up, allowing her to see what looked like lipstick. She took a lingering, perhaps too long stare but made out the word *GIP*.

GIP? Gimp? And she thought she was the drunk one. Paulina winced and cussed as the front passenger wheel of her truck grazed the guardrail on the side of the road. She was coming up on one last big curve when her befuddled mind finally registered the word.

"PIG!" she yelled out irritatedly.

"Fucking Serena!"

Her slowed reaction to running out of road and the impending emerald ocean rapidly approaching processed too late.

She jammed her boot on the brake pedal but found no resistance. She agitatedly pumped the pedal, only getting back the spongey feel of a severed brake line that almost touched the floor of her truck.

Paulina's truck went airborne before she had time to reach for her parking brake or open her mouth to scream. For a split second, it felt like her chariot floated freely, weightless, and then took the mind-shattering two-hundred-foot drop as she soared toward the sea of green treetops.

It's Rainin' Femmes
Chapter 2

The falls of the leather flogger flicked red pigment onto the low, leaking ceiling. Droplets of merlot dotted the shuddering woman's porcelain skin. The vermilion rivers and scar tissue continued down her heaving spine like red and white serpents writhing together perversely in a sickly wet viper pit. The pain was not new to her, nor was the Pavlovian pleasure she felt coursing through her center to the top of her head. She was a holy warrior hellbent on mauling her own hide until she rid her body of this wicked yet intoxicating affliction. She attempted to catch her breath as the perpetual sin continued to leak out of her wounds, trickle down her ample buttocks, and pool beneath her shuddering vessel. She shakily stood and went to the medical supplies on the table in the room's darkened corner.

Just as she was securing the last surgical dressing, a gentle rapping came at her penitence chamber door. The sound of zippers and leather fasteners came at a hyper-speed before she sucked her breath through her teeth and eked out, "Just a minute!"

She studied the dripping ceiling as she fastened her cowl, giving herself a once-over in the mirror next to the door for any gore smears. With her nerves calmed and face no longer contorted in pain, Mother Superior took a breath and opened the door.

Sister Veronica glowered up at her as the Mother Superior tucked her graying auburn hair under her bandeau and pulled the bright red rosary necklace forward. Mother Superior venomously spat, "Oh, what is it, Veronica?"

"Mother, I can't find her."

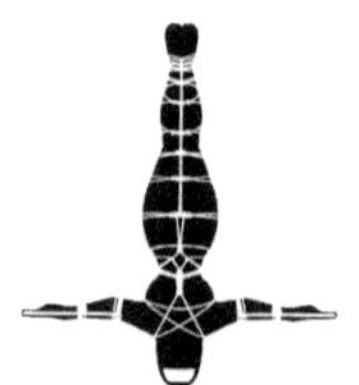

A frantic chipmunk scampered across the path as the sound of hiking boots padded the dirt trail. The canopy of tree limbs and leaves became so dense that the forest floor resembled a hunter-green galaxy. Only small sunbeams pierced the false twilight, lighting the path for the wandering forest nymph. While the darkness among the daylight discombobulated her, something drew her to venture out deeper into the forest. Further than she had ever hiked before. One could barely discern the white details on her almost all black ensemble over her slender build. The only part of her that wasn't black and white were her wheat nubuck leather hiking boots that matched her equally light brown skin. She huffed and paused, resting her weary body against a massive spruce.

Sister Ophelia felt at home in the wilderness. It was the only place she found peace. Being in contact with the mighty tree trunk made her feel like she could almost hear the secrets of the universe it held for her after its century of life experience. Losing her last remaining parent, Ophelia felt more adrift than ever before. Her father was her everything: her biggest cheerleader, her protector—her rock. The forest was where she came to talk to him. Memories of their camping trips together as a family came flooding back to her whenever she smelled the crisp, clean air. Even after her brothers moved on and started their own families, her father still planned a camping trip just for them.

Ophelia's best memory was when she told him she thought she wanted a girlfriend. She could still remember the look of concern on his face, a slow concentration before he pulled up on his fishing line and asked if she was sure. Her spirit dropped, and it showed on her face.

He followed with, "Cuz girlfriends are expensive, so you might need a summer job if you plan on wining and dining her right," and chuckled.

She hugged him harder than she ever had that night. Her father's arms were the one place she felt she'd always be ok, no matter what happened. That was her favorite camping trip, the last they took before he got sick. To lose a pastor and a pastor's wife to cancer seemed like a cruel joke, one that no scripture or sermon could deliver the punchline. The day she left his funeral service, she felt so unbelievably lost and alone, wandering aimlessly through the world. Just like she was ambling on this dim forest trail now. He told her he found meaning in God, so all she could think about was following in his footsteps and hopefully finding her way, which led her to this veiled convent out in the middle of nowhere, donning a veil herself. The calming silence in the forest left her with only herself and her recurring thoughts.

Was this her true calling? Or the biggest mistake of her life?

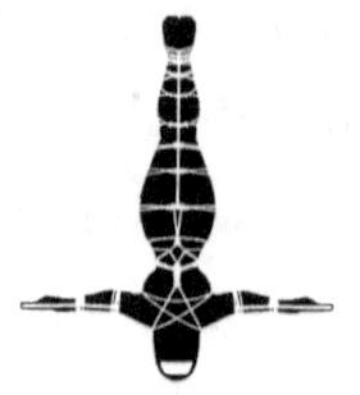

Mother Superior's hazel eyes blazed around the empty cell. The lumpy twin mattress had the itchy brown blanket pulled tight, with a pillow the size of a thick textbook on top. The modest desk sat unused. Aside from the lone crucifix, the rest of the room was as empty as the aged, craggy walls.

The second-in-command to the Abbess, Sister Veronica, slinked past her hot-under-the-collar hippy holiness.

"She was at breakfast this morning, Mum. I'm sure of it."

Mother Superior deeply exhaled out of her nostrils and exited the dismal room, Sister Veronica close behind.

"Since it seems Sister Ophelia doesn't appreciate her current accommodations, put her down for a week's stay in the Penitence Room."

Sunlight danced across Mother's milky skin as the corners of her naturally pouty lips pulled up into a grin. Her eyes were fixed on the statue of the Virgin Mary at the end of the grand hallway. Her gaze trailed down the slopes of womanhood and seemingly weightless fabric draping from her voluptuous dimensions.

"Understood, Mum."

Mother Superior stopped just before the regal, bronzed effigy and stared up at it in quivering adulation.

"Find her. This order has no room for prodigal daughters, violators, or any kind of mavericks. Scripture says mischief and misconduct lead to dissension, which leads to utter chaos," she said, biting her lip and holding the cupped, praying hands of the statue—the only part of the patina statue that remained shiny and polished.

"Which scripture was that, Mum?" Veronica asked, a puzzled but endearing look affixed to her gentle features.

"Find her. Take Sister Emelie with you. Just go."

Veronica scuttled away without hesitation, leaving Mother Superior to leer longingly at the Virgin Mary in all her sultry glory. Its beauty enveloped her. It made her bountiful body ache, her thunderous thighs shake, and her eyeballs quake in her skull. She listened for Veronica's footsteps to dissipate before looking toward the kitchen and down the corridors. She took a big whiff of a pocketed handkerchief and loosened the rosary cinching her corseted waist. Certain she was alone, her whispers began to float up to the Virgin Mary's cherubic, sorrowful gaze. Mother Superior's eyes met those of the eight-foot statue, climbed up, brought their lips together, and wrapped her legs around her immense folds.

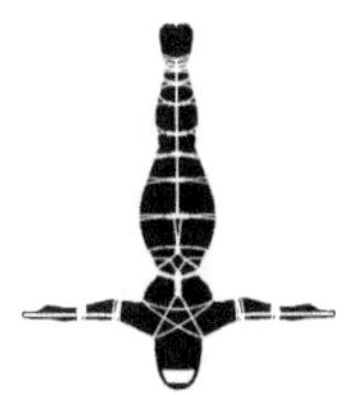

Ophelia pushed off the rough tree bark, hoping to leave her intrusive thoughts with the knowledgeable tree spirit. Maybe they could figure out what the postulant couldn't yet. Having gone through the discernment phase, she decided the religious vocation might be for her. After she passed the postulancy phase, she would become a novitiate and that much closer to finding her rightful place in life.

Returning to the trail and rounding a bend, Ophelia saw a glowing beam of sunshine off in the distance. She continued to trudge closer, feeling something pulling her toward it. Before she knew it, she was running toward the golden rays. The closer she got, the more it looked like dark clouds had parted and momentarily opened to give mortality a look into the eyes of their Lord and Savior. Ophelia's need for answers to quell her waning faith propelled her to the glowing gateway. She stopped short of the rays, saying a silent prayer before offering her hand to its warmth. She inhaled and stepped forward, prepared for whatever the Lord wanted her to see.

The sunshine warmed her face and hands as she tried to block the blinding light from her vision. Behind her shading hands, Ophelia could see a borehole through the trees and what caused it; a fire-red pickup truck was teetering on just a few shaky branches. Her eyes widened, noting the proximity of impending doom dangling over her like the sword of Damocles. As she took a step back, shrill voices screamed from behind her.

"Sister Ophelia!"

"Great Lord in Heaven, child, you scared us half to-"

Before Ophelia could turn to warn her fellow Sisters, the snapping and popping of feeble branches above her made the hairs on the back of her neck prickle. Half falling, half jumping blindly behind her, as if by divine intervention, she landed just outside the illuminated partition. Her Sisters ran to her aid as she stared forward and watched the few crumpled branches land soundlessly. Followed by a whooshing topple of metal and snapped wood as the floating vehicle crashed ass end first and slammed down onto its tires in the darkness behind it. Sisters Veronica and Emilie shrieked and pulled Ophelia's cowering body toward them as they were showered with an explosion of glass and tree bits. The boom of the tires blowing on impact caused their eardrums to hum and pop in unison.

Once the dust and shock cleared, the Sisters shakily assessed themselves for injuries. Luckily, they only got a few scratches and the scare of a lifetime. They embraced, peering at the red monstrosity that seemed to fall from the heavens. Sister Ophelia broke from the two Sisters, at the grumbling disapproval of her elders. Stepping through the brambles and remnants from the crash, she peered inside the truck bed. The blown-out glass covered a crumpled toolbox but wouldn't let her see past the still floating dust. Sounds slowly started filtering through her ringing ears, and she heard her Sisters clucking and clamoring behind her. The urge to see inside the truck cab allowed Ophelia to navigate around the vehicle and peer inside the jagged, broken window. The wind picked up as she squinted, blowing the dusty fog away. Her eyes traced the unmistakable human form inside, appearing lifeless among the debris. She thoughtlessly called to her Sisters and pulled on the battered door handle. When Sisters Veronica and Emelie joined her, the door crunched open, and she leapt into the crumpled cabin. The dust continued to settle, showing the form of a heavenly body needing immediate care. Ophelia's jaw shook as she whimpered and felt for a pulse. The moment of silence and bated breath was ruined by her screams.

"She's alive!" Ophelia gasped between sobs. "She's alive!"

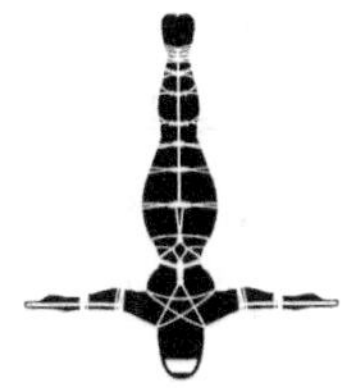

The vestibule doors burst open, and in spilled howls of wind and the cloistered nuns.

"Mother Superior! Come at once!"

"There's been an accident!"

"It's a girl; she needs medical attention!"

"Saints be praised!"

The sensational affectations of her flock tugged at Mother's sparse mustache hairs. The monochrome mother hen entered the grand hall, unruffled, to attend to her waddle of panicked penguin chicks. The nimble Sisters had fashioned a makeshift stretcher from a tarp and fallen tree limbs. Mother Superior beamed with pride at her self-sustaining faction of *femme formidables*. Emelie and Veronica panted, slowly lowering the impromptu gurney between them. The joy dripped off Mother's face in sheets, revealing a curdled scowl.

"Please help her, Mother! She's at Death's door!" wailed Sister Veronica.

Mother Superior bustled around, the fabric swaying behind her great billowing backside and begrudgingly pinching the unconscious woman's wrist between her thumb and forefinger.

"Settle down, Sister Veronica. How many times have I warned you that your histrionics will be the death of you?" quipped Mother as she assessed the reflexes of the fallen angel.

Sister Veronica gasped, stifling her hammering hyperventilations.

The novitiates, Sister Tatianna and Sister Bernadette, hastily tripped into the hall to investigate the commotion.

"Wherever did you find this...specimen, Sisters?" Mother's eyes scanned the scantily clad, convalescent lumberjack. "Is it raining prostitutes? Was the Devil having a costume party, and one escaped?"

The surrounding nuns broke from their concerned cries to snicker and stare. Mother Superior examined Paulina's skin for injury, noting only a few surface wounds aside from the massive head lump. Before she released her hand, she noticed the calloused pads and shortened middle and ring fingernails with an arched eyebrow. Mother folded Paulina's hands over one another and attempted to button her undone top, to no avail. Her eyes traveled and traced Paulina's full flannel fun-bags struggling behind the knotted fabric. The view polluted her thoughts and fluttered the butterflies beneath her bustle.

"Sister Ophelia, fetch us a prayer cloth! This is a convent, not a dairy farm." Mother Superior caught herself. "And we are not an infirmary either, Sisters."

She stood and stared daggers down at the sleeping beauty, her collar steaming with arousal and disdain.

Sister Emelie sliced through her cognitive dissonance, "We must get her to a hospital! She could be seriously injured."

On cue, by an impetuous but omnipotent author, Paulina's eyes fluttered and danced behind her droopy lids. The Sisters erupted and rejoiced, much to the chagrin of the Queen Mother.

"I will see to her injuries, Emelie." Mother sighed. "I've seen much worse. Until then, just... put her in Sister Calliope's quarters. There's a spare cot in there. She may stay until we can get her into town." The flock began to cluck among themselves. "This disturbance is not to detract this order from its itinerary. I will not stand for disruptions under my watch. Is that understood, Sisters?"

The cluster of nuns worked together to get their patient upright and lead her up the stairs to the dormitories. Mother Superior stared down at the beaten tarp and the trail of dirt left behind, along with her contemptuous desires.

"I just hope the bitch is housebroken."

A Vixen in the Henhouse
Chapter 3

Mother Superior set the glass on her bedside table and nestled back under her thin, itchy blanket. Lying on her side, she stared at the empty vessel, watching the moonlight sparkle through the dregs of the green liquid. Worried she was possibly going overboard with her tinctures sat heavy on her mind, but even those concerns were shadowed by those of this airborne gatecrasher. Why here—now? Was this a test? Was her Savior unpleased with her? How long would she be here? Could the Sisterhood withstand an interloper?

She did her best to push all these thoughts out of her anguished head. This is exactly why she could not sleep. She grasped for her rosary in the darkness, pulling it into the warmth below her blanket when she felt the dizzying whirr of the elixir taking effect.

As she came to the end of her row of Hail Marys, she mouthed, "Protect my faith. Protect my reserve. Protect this sacred space, and let all *our* secrets stay buried."

Her glazed eyes drifted into the room's darkness before her eyelids drooped. Mother Superior had only closed her eyes for a second when a scratching sound came from her window. Her eyes flashed open, listening for it again. Moments later, the same scratching sound came, like needles tapping and trailing down the pane. The room grew colder than before. The icy air hovered around her, excitedly searching for an entry point to penetrate her.

Mother Superior's thoughts went to a vile creature that only lived in the furthermost depths of hell that had crawled up and escaped through a glowing fissure in the ground. She wanted to turn and face the beast, knowing nothing could be more powerful than her most high. Yet her body would not allow it. She lay rigid in her bed; her knees shook and began to knock against each other. An occurrence she had heard about in movies but never actually experienced herself. It seemed her body was poking fun at her supposed faith or alluding to it not being as strong as she thought.

This turned her fear to anger. She wasn't a child hiding behind her covers, cowering from some boogie man under her bed.

I am Mother Superior, head of the Cistercian Nuns of the Valley of Perpetual Felicity Monastery!

She exhaled from mental exertion.

I am a veteran of the Belgian armed forces. I've seen things that would make a man faint and helped save the lives of hundreds. I've weathered misogyny, abuse, and harassment and persevered. I came out alive and thriving, though I can't say the same for my detractors. I am a tempest in a tunic, and nothing on this earth shall detract me from my mission through Christ.

She took in a deep breath and steeled her nerves.

Especially not the irrational fear of the meaningless limbs of a tree scraping against my window.

Mother Superior gathered her strength and threw the blanket from her body. Staring intently at the pitch blackness, highlighted by the moon's glow shining off in the distance. Her heartbeat thrummed in her ears as her eyes darted to all four corners of the windowpane but saw no such demonic monstrosity whatsoever. She let out a quick exhale, having promised herself to never let out a breath she didn't know she was holding, *ever* in life. Mother Superior was no cliché; she wasn't a Virgo. She was a Scorpio! The corners of her mouth began to curve upwards, internally laughing at this ridiculous predicament, anxious to crawl under her covers and forget the pointless ordeal altogether.

The clouds seemed to have parted, and the moonlight revealed what looked to be abrasions on the otherwise clear surface of the window. Her heart leapt into her throat. She fought to swallow it back down as her body began to shiver. However, her mind was made up, and her body would follow suit. She would not be bested by irrational fears. She maneuvered her legs from beneath the warm protection of her blanket, not taking her eyes off the window, and felt for her slippers with her quivering toes. She silently stood to investigate, against her better judgement, when she felt the sharp pain slice into her Achilles tendon and bite into her chilled flesh. A silent scream held on her lips as the Mother Superior's world sank, along with the rest of her, to that icy floor and the entity awaiting its prey.

Mother Superior was left sprawled on the hard floor, stunned and in pain. In a daze, facing the bed, she stared into the darkness and was shocked to see it empty. The moonlight gave little illumination, but her eyes were adjusted enough to see under her bed: A few dust bunnies and her slippers. She gained her bearings and laughed some, realizing she must have had some outlandish nightmare and fallen out of bed. What a painful reminder that will be, come morning.

She slowly picked herself up off the ground and turned toward her window to see that it had, indeed, been left ajar. The cold and the day's events must have influenced her mind to create such a fantastical dream. She pushed herself up and closed the window, locking it to be safe, and sat on the edge of her old mattress. Her ankle still hurt like the dickens; she must have landed on it when she fell. The weak moonlight let her see that it was swollen and raw, but it wasn't until she pulled her hand away that she saw her fingers wet with her own warm blood.

Her eyes flew to her reflection in the window, and instantly, she saw the glowing red eyes floating behind her. She turned quickly, attempting a scream when the entity, cloaked in darkness, stepped forward and gestured with her red fist, silencing her wail. Mother Superior sat petrified and silenced on her bed, twisted and staring in disbelief at this creature hidden by shadow.

The demonic abomination stepped forward just as the clouds outside Mother Superior's window shifted the moonlight again. The unmistakable shape of a female demon could be seen, even in the darkness. Her skin was lobster red, giving off an eerie orange glow that looked like hellfire pulsed from her very being. The eyes of the entity glowed the brightest, showing up as pinpricks of light in the stark blackness. She came close enough to Mother Superior for her to smell the redolence of floral nectar and burning leaves over a bonfire on an autumn day. While her body was frozen in fright, the warmth emanating from the she-demon's perpetually burning skin wasn't altogether terrible. Her frazzled mind tried to decipher why feelings of safety were coming from the heat of the Netherworld.

Mother Superior's eyes darted to the demon's devilishly cartoonish prehensile tail. The point of the tail came up to Mother Superior's eye level and swished before her, giving her a preview of its razor-sharp edge. Then it slithered to her lips, covering them as the crimson creature sauntered around her bed and stood before her window. The tail caressed her lips as Mother Superior regained her ability to move and untwist her posture, facing the demoness. Mother Superior remained docile as the entity pulled its tail from the silent nun and stood upon her like a powerful panthress looking down at its inferior.

The demon's glowing eyes dipped to Mother Superior's bloodied hands and followed her contours until their eyes met. After a beat, her voice floated through the pitch blackness like a dreadful chorus of damned souls all whispering at once.

"That bite should be taking effect by now," dripped from the sensuous lips of the tormenting temptress. The demon's tail snaked below, wrapping around her wrist and tugging Mother Superior's hand, still coated in her blood, to the creature's mouth. Her glowing eyes stayed glued to Mother Superior's as she lapped at the sanguineous syrup. A clawed hand lifted the enchanted nun's chin to look into her dilated pupils.

"Atta girl," wheezed from her mouth, like a symphony of sorrow.

The demoness leaned her body in, her nude breasts pressing against Mother Superior like fully ripe pomegranates and just as fragrant. Every move her body made was smooth and liquid, like a dance in the dark. Each shift lulled the Mother Superior into a state of relaxation. Her body felt like she needed to lie down and behold this brooding beauty.

Mother Superior's head hit her pillow, but her eyes couldn't leave the writhing, horned woman who was straddling her waist now. The heat melted the goosebumps on Mother Superior's pale skin, and the pleasing aromas made her dizzy. Yet still, she pushed past them to ask, with struggling, dreamy eyes, "Are...are you...a demon?"

The orange glow emanating from the demon flashed, like a fresh log thrown on the fire to burn.

"I have been given many names. My likeness has appeared in many books. What I am is not your concern, what I want should be your priority," hissed from her lips, filling Mother Superior with terror.

"Are you here...to take me to Hell?" Mother Superior choked out, her eyes erupting in tears.

"That's not my department, Sister." The demoness chuckled. "You could say I work in loss prevention and collections. I'm here to shake things up in this little henhouse of yours."

Mother Superior stared back at the entity as its face contorted to a familiar visage and took on a younger, sweeter tone. Her red flesh turned bronze, and a mane of red hair cascaded down, tickling Mother Superior's cheek as the fleshed-out demon came face to face with her. Her juicy pomegranates morphed into tanned, round breasts. Mother Superior shifted under the weight yet couldn't get enough of this mesmerizing creature.

"Why don't you let me stay a while? We can have some fun, just you and me. It'll be our little secret. Nobody has to know." The demon's voice remained a sultry, saccharine song, but the chaotic cacophony of disturbing utterances still surfaced sporadically. "I can give you what you want, Sarah. What you really want. What you're too afraid to want. What you dream about. What you ache for...once and for all." The nameless girl who had just fallen into all their laps smiled down at her with a glint of light behind her eyes. "What is it you want, Mother? What is it you desire? Is it me?" The moonlight shifted, as did the skin of the creature.

A pale, smaller-framed girl stared back at Mother Superior now. The nun's shocked eyes watched as her thick red locks transformed into blonde curls. "Or is it me you want?" The familiar voice and the accent made Mother Superior's blood turn to ice. The fiend let out a laugh like a legion of expelled souls. The deep red of her flesh returned, and her hair converted back to darkened horns on both sides of her head.

"Do we have a deal?" Her polyphonic voice had returned. Mother Superior sat stunned, fighting to wake up from this dizzyingly arousing dream. "Tell me what you desire, Sister. It's that simple."

Mother Superior stared at her, her eyes tracing her voluptuous shape. Her thoughts raced, hammering her confusion into the corners of her mind with a cartoon mallet. The words came from her quivering lips, but she felt powerless as she uttered, "I desire... you."

The enchantress grinned and huffed her animalistic grunt over the incapacitated nun. Their noses touched. Electricity ran down the length of Mother Superior's entire body.

The crimson beast haughtily bestowed a "Good girl" and planted a deep, sensual kiss on her lips as Mother Superior fell into the depths of burning darkness below.

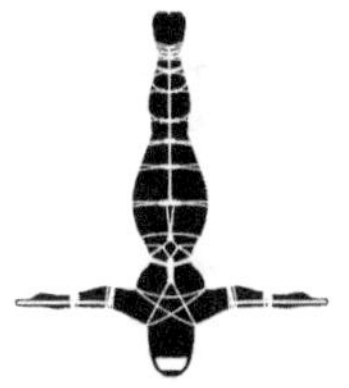

The next morning, Mother Superior woke with a start and peered around her bedroom groggily. The sun was just beginning to rise, leaving darkened corners in her room. She eyed each one, searching for glowing eyes, but found none to her confused relief. She rose from her bed and noted the window was still latched, and no marks were shown on its panes. So, it *was* all a dream. A nightmare. *Right?*

She sifted through her fleeting memories of the night before, only remembering the ominous sensual beast who had attempted to woo her. She felt her body begin to stir the more she pushed to remember more details, causing her to panic and ultimately shut it all down.

She knew all she had to do was pray and ask for forgiveness. The excitement from the day before and possible residuals from her last tincture must be the culprit. The Virgin Mary would understand; she always did. Mother Superior gained some pep in her step just thinking about seeing her lady-in-waiting in all her petrous glory. She finished making her bed, as she did every morning, and donned her daily vestments. While preparing to leave her space, she hesitantly looked back. Her eyes scanned the shadow under her bed, though she dared not look directly under. She closed her door and pushed whatever could be beneath her bed out of her mind. She had a date with a most holy mystery this morning that she shan't be late for.

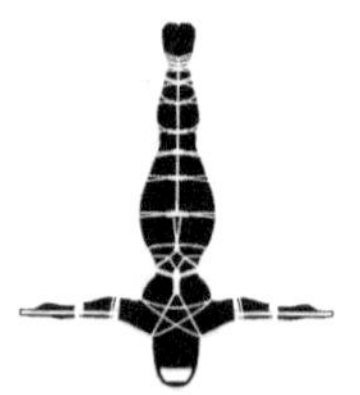

Mother Superior's eyes lit up as she pictured herself closing the distance between her and her statuesque inamorata. Her embers were already beginning to smolder, stoking the flames that wanted to spill forth from her quaking hearth. The Reverend Mother let the tips of her fingers trace the sides of her prayer pillows, and her pace quickened. Just as she was about to pinch the stems and press her swollen sugarplums together as a sacrificial offering to the Virgin Mary, a gentle laugh from Calliope's room dried her forbidden fruit. Her eyes became slits in her powdery pale skin, as she knew exactly who the ruckus had come from.

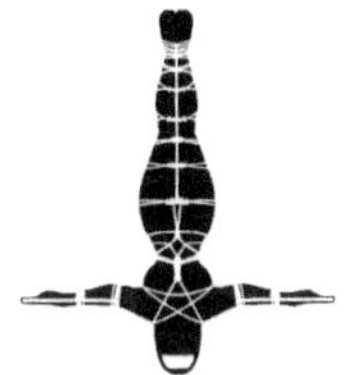

S ister Ophelia sat on the edge of the bed, smiling from ear to ear while she scooped and fed another spoonful of oatmeal to their patient. Paulina was awake and alert but still not ready to get out of bed. Her head was bandaged with enough left open for her fiery red mane to hang behind her. The two girls whispered and giggled between spoonfuls before a billowing figure darkened the doorway.

"Ah, what a miracle. She's awake," said Mother Superior through gritted teeth, stifling them both. "We were beginning to think we would have to dig a spot for you in the garden!" She chortled, covering her mouth with her hand. The two young ladies' eyebrows were raised with their hairlines and not laughing. Mother Superior stepped forth, passive-aggressively bumping Ophelia with her generous hip and inspected the bed-stricken beauty. She firmly lifted Paulina's chin, their eyes meeting this close for the first time. Mother Superior's skin prickled as she stared at the beautiful yet vacant eyes. Mother raised her pointer finger in front of Paulina and moved her hand left and right in front of her face.

"Follow my finger with your eyes, child."

Paulina did so, her pupils following at a satisfactory speed for someone who had hung like a Christmas ornament in a tree only a day prior. Mother Superior continued staring into her eyes, made aware of something deeper, hiding behind the patient's blindingly blue stare that felt like it was pulling air right out of the Reverend Mother's lungs. She blinked back to reality and stared at her poorly wrapped head with a sigh.

"So that's where all my gauze went."

Mother began to pull and readjust some of the bandages as Sister Ophelia rose, shifting the bed slightly.

"Awful lot of gauze for only a small bump on the head, wouldn't you say, Sister Ophelia?"

Sister Ophelia had already made it halfway to the door, tray in hand, before turning back.

"She-she can't remember anything, Mother Posteri-, oop, pardon me, Superior." Sister Ophelia said, gulping air.

Mother Superior turned to face Ophelia.

"Nothing at all, you say?" She raised an eyebrow. "Stay put. We have something to discuss." Mother rose and turned back toward Paulina, looking serene yet attentive in the bed.

"Maybe there wasn't much to remember in the first place, the poor dear."

Mother Superior beckoned to the door, guiding the obstruction that was Ophelia toward it.

"What our patient needs is some time to think, to pray, to ask the Lord what it is she is meant to return to." Ophelia stood in the hall while the Reverend Mother palmed the doorknob, pulling it behind her.

"Hopefully soon," she said, with the sound of her key locking the door behind her.

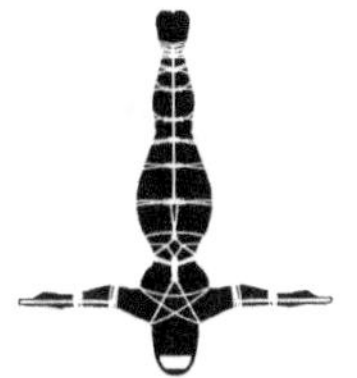

Sister Ophelia sat in the Reverend Mother's office. Her hands clasped her rosary as her eyes fluttered across the shelves full of religious texts and the countless oil paintings of the Virgin Mary adorning her walls. As her stare returned to the mahogany desk and the dusty leather chair behind it, her eyes floated to the brown telephone on the worn desk. She turned her ear toward the door, somewhat certain Mother would still be occupied with another mishap in the kitchen with Sister Veronica. She cautiously stood and hurried behind the desk, her ears pricked up for any hint of noise.

The phone looked like one from the old movies her dad would watch with her about possessed cars and bloody prom queens: no screens, just numbers in square buttons and a cord. She quickly snatched up the receiver and stared at the numbers staring back at her when she realized she had no one to call, no numbers memorized. No one would hear her scream, even if she needed someone to. The noises in her head filtered out just long enough to hear the dead silence of the room and then even more silence in the phone receiver. Frazzled and confused, she pulled the phone from her face and shook it, staring at it as if it were her only hope. Her eyes followed the cord to the phone's body, where two white plastic pegs perkily stared at her. She tapped them with her shaking hands, the silent receiver to her ear.

Just when she was about to give it one more try, she heard the unmistakable clacking of short heels on linoleum echoing down the hall. In that moment, a divine power allowed her to quietly replace the phone, come around the desk, and sit with a hissing plop just as the Mother Superior charged into the room.

The Reverend Mother paused mid-step, staring at the back of Sister Ophelia's slowly sinking silhouette in the armchair, back to her desk, uncertain yet suspicious. She closed the door, ambled her swaying hips around, and sat at her desk watching the eyes of Ophelia.

"I think this order has had enough excitement in the last day to last it for the rest of the year, don't you, Sister Ophelia?"

Silence.

Mother Superior steepled her fingers on her desk.

"While I'm sure you find yourself quite the savior, an Angel of Mercy as it were...I'm afraid that all I see is...an insubordinate little brat."

Sister Ophelia turned the chair and stared at the front of the desk while raking her tongue along the fronts of her teeth under loose lips. Mother Superior stood to stare at the trees out of her window with a glint of a grin in her eyes.

"How long have you been with us, Sister Ophelia?"

A pregnant pause.

"Answer me."

"One year." A beat. "Mother."

Mother picked up on the disrespectful pause, being a patron saint of passive-aggression herself. With a knowing grin, she responded, "And in one year, how many times have you been warned against leaving the property of the order? How many times have you visited the very necessary Penitence Room to pay for this transgression?"

No response.

"You know I can't protect you out there. Once you go out of bounds, the only one who will hear your cries is the Lord himself, and he's not too keen on young women with...checkered pasts...a good time girl who just picks them up like loose change off the street. ...or falling pickup trucks." The Queen Mother pressed her lips closed, making the whiskers on her chin tickle her. She stifled her giggle.

Ophelia held back as long as she could before she ejaculated, "Did you call the police? A hospital? Does anyone know she is here?"

Mother twirled around, standing behind her leather chair as if it were a grand podium for her to make her official statement.

"While I appreciate your concern for our very temporary patient, Sister. I must insist that you mind your tone when speaking to the head of a religious institute."

"For now. ...Your excellency. Now, if you could answer my questions?"

Mother's face hardened. She gritted her teeth before returning to her superficial smile.

"I did not summon you here to discuss matters that don't concern you, *Postulant* Ophelia. I summoned you here to inform you of the ramifications of your insubordination and truancy."

"Reverend Mother, I am within months of becoming a novitiate. I am not a student to be kept under your thumb like a child. I am a 24-year-old woman."

"Be that as it may, you are under my care, and while that is so, you will abide by my rules, or I will be forced to recommend your removal from the program expeditiously."

The air in the room grew thick with tension and indignation.

The Reverend Mother took the silence as a victory and once again sat at her desk.

"Perhaps this vocation isn't for you, after all. With someone of your–" She glanced at Ophelia's lengthy limbs and defined jawline. "--endurance and dexterity...perhaps the WNBA?"

Ophelia scrunched her face and cleared her throat, visibly fighting to keep her composure.

"Did you, or did you not call the police?"

"Yes, the appropriate calls have been made to the authorities, which still is none of your- "

"On what phone? Because that one isn't even plugged in." Ophelia stood and peered around the desk while Mother sat, taken aback. "I know there's supposed to be a wall plug or something."

Mother Superior rose and stepped in front of the investigation, blocking Ophelia's view.

"Our patient...is fine. She has no broken bones or excessive bleeding, so there's no point. I was an army medic for over a decade; trust my word."

"She has amnesia, and you just blatantly lied about calling anyone or even having a working phone! Have you been dipping into the communion wine?"

Mother Superior's eyes grew wide as her jaw clicked and her nostrils flared. Ophelia was the favorite of all the Sisters, and her mouth was loud enough to shake the walls of the entire valley wherein their little nunnery was nestled. This battle was not going in Mother Superior's favor, but she would win the war.

"Sister Ophelia, must I remind you of your vow of obedience? The one that if you cannot abide by, I—your superior—deny your advancement to becoming a novitiate?"

No response.

"Might I also remind you that you are here because Sister Veronica vouched for you and Sister Calliope because of unique circumstances? I chose to allow this as a personal favor to her. Did it not occur to you that your conduct reflects on her? Do you want to soil her good name just because of your oppositional defiance disorder?"

Sister Ophelia blinked quickly and looked at her hiking boots, bits of mud crumbling on Mother Superior's office floor. Her li ps pursed, for once silenced.

"Since you are such a fan of silence, I think it is a fitting punishment. For your gross insubordination and your need to be disrespectful to those who outrank you, you will be on kitchen duties. You are not to step foot in our patient's room until further notice. If you would like to regain that privilege, I suggest a vow of silence for one month."

Sister Ophelia brought her hand up, her pinky rising with contempt, and opened her mouth to shout, but Mother Superior cut her off.

"One month. Silence or no patty cake with your little playmate in plaid. Starting *now*."

Embers flared in Ophelia's eyes as she stared the pear-shaped, middle-aged woman down, her chest heaving. She felt the spite form a tear in the corner of her eye, as she turned and grabbed a pad of paper and a pen off Mother Superior's desk before she stomped out of the office.

"ONE MONTH!" Mother Superior yelled out before the smile returned to her lips.

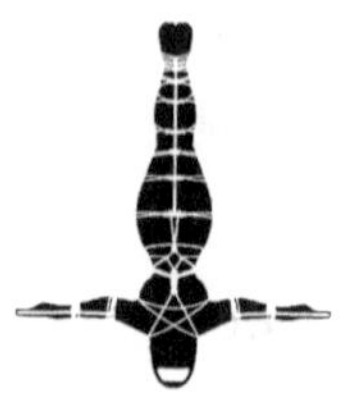

"Saints be praised!" was exclaimed from somewhere in the convent, drowned out by the sounds from the kitchen. Pots clattered, and joyous humming broke out into song as Ophelia approached the kitchen. The Cistercian Nuns of the Valley of Perpetual Felicity Monastery had been home to cloistered priests in the late 1900s before it was disillusioned and sanctioned for use as a nunnery, meaning that the place had been built modestly with a very small kitchen and dining area, but the Sisters made do. Sister Veronica had just come from the chicken coop out back with an apron full of freshly laid eggs. Ophelia quickened her pace and ran to get the door for Sister Veronica and her delicate cargo. They both smiled at each other as they entered the kitchen. Sister Tatianna was inside peeling potatoes at the large kitchen island while Sister Bernadette was scouring a scorched lasagna pan.

Ophelia swiftly walked past the two, grabbed the empty egg basket, and placed it before a grateful Veronica. Ophelia finished helping Veronica transfer them, then went into the pantry and walked out, securing an apron.

Even through her strong features, Sister Veronica's face was never without a smile. In her early forties now, her permanent grin had begun to carve the joy into their second eldest's face.

"Are you joining us for kitchen duties, O?" she chirped.

Ophelia nodded and started putting the broom to use.

"Are you not feeling well, Sister?"

Ophelia sighed and let the broom sit in the crook of her arm while she fished out her purloined pad and pen.

The three nuns swiveled to read the note and "oooooh'd" in unison.

Ophelia began to scribble another note.

The Sisters all snickered as the door from the dining room swung in and the Reverend Mother entered. Tatianna and Bernadette could barely stifle their giggles, camouflaging Sister

Veronica snatching up the sheet of paper. She begrudgingly crumpled and popped the note in her mouth.

"Good day, Sisters."

Mother Superior walked through the kitchen, eying the surfaces, her hips gliding along the table edge as Sister Veronica continued to chew. The girth of her glutes was heaven to the eye but hell on her oft-tailored habit. Doorways were seldom dusty when Mother Superior was around.

"What is on the menu today, Sister Veronica?" Mother asked, walking up behind her.

Veronica's face turned deep red as her jaws mashed the paper into paste. Ophelia's eyes stared blankly as she went back to sweeping. Bernadette turned toward the commotion when her gaze became glued on Mother Superior's gratuitous backside. Tatianna's eyes almost got caught in its gravitational pull when, in a panic, she yelled out, "Ham! Juicy ham!"

She held up the potato and peeler to distract her.

"And potatoes."

Sister Veronica grimaced and swallowed the unpalatable paper, allowing some color to return to her face.

"We should," Veronica sucked in air, "have much smoother suppers now that we have help." Her breathing returned to normal. "Thank you, Mother."

Mother Superior made an uncomfortable grin toward them all, and she excused herself, swishing away to her next responsibility.

The five of them reconvened at the table, in near hysterics.

"I thought I was going to be meeting the Lord Jesus himself, I was ready to choke right there."

"Mother has been extremely on edge since the arrival of our visitor. I wonder who put a bee in her habit?" Bernadette giggled and covered her mouth shamefully.

Tatianna went back to peeling the potatoes but asked, "If our visitor doesn't even remember her name, shouldn't we give her one? At least temporarily?"

The Sisters pondered before Bernadette broke the silence.

"Lidwina is the patron saint of falling. It's a little on the nose, but it's charming in a way."

The group sat in thought before Sister Veronica rose and placed her apron back in the pantry.

"Speaking of, it's about time I go check on our...Lidwina," she said, looking to the others for approval, getting back shrugged shoulders.

Ophelia scribbled on her pad and left it on the table before she finished her sweeping.

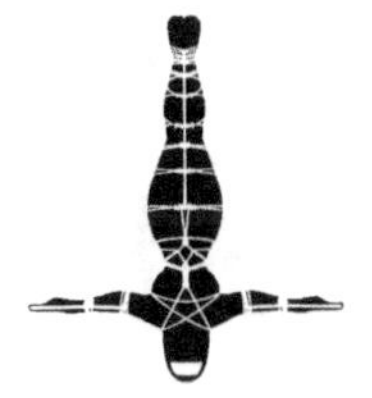

"Look who's bright-eyed and bushy-tailed!" Sister Veronica beamed. "How's your head? No complaints, I take it?" she said cheekily, ribbing their patient. "We like to have fun around here."

"Fun has different meanings to different people," Mother Superior said, swaying into the room, never too far away. "And different professions." She paused. "Still no name yet? Nothing?"

Paulina glumly shook her head and tried to come out from under her covers, fussing with the blanket overheating her. Mother Superior noticed the stirring and avoided the pull of her eyes to Paulina's ample cleavage from the loosely buttoned nightshirt instead of focusing on her blaze of red hair. "Has it had a bath yet?" she asked with a sneer.

"Not yet, mum, I've come to help Lidwina with it now."

"Lidwina?"

"Oh yes. The Sisters thought it might be good to give her a name. Something to make her feel more at home. It might jog some of that memory back. According to Sister Bernadette, Lidwina was the patron saint of falling!" Veronica helped *Lidwina* up and led her into the hallway and downstairs toward their laundry room.

Mother Superior pulled the sheets off the bed and left them in a pile.

Spitefully spitting soto voce, "Sounds like wiener."

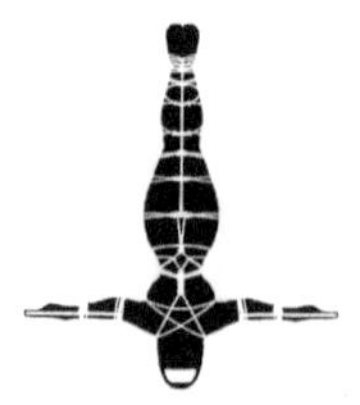

Sister Veronica gently ushered Lidwina into the dark and dusty room. The monastery's laundry room looked like something out of the Middle Ages. The old fieldstone walls glistened with musty moisture. They had a working washer and dryer, but the set looked older than any of the monastery's inhabitants. Sister Veronica pulled the lone string dangling from the ceiling, emitting a dull yellow glow around the dank room. Lidwina stopped, slightly swaying, where Veronica had left her. Veronica pointed at the wine barrel tub in the middle of the room and turned to get the pitcher. Mother Superior caught up with them, slightly out of breath.

"You know who else fell? Lucifer. From the skies. We could call her Lucy?"

Sister Veronica tutted, shaking her head and motioning for Lidwina in the tub to come out of her nightshirt.

Mother Superior continued, "I just don't think you should name a pet you don't intend to kee-"

Mother Superior's eyes bulged in their sockets as Lidwina's tanned flesh lit up the room. The motion made her pert breasts rise and fall like newborn puppies jostling before dozing off into an afternoon nap. Mother Superior blinked before she snapped up tall and looked straight ahead, steam whistling from her lips.

"You were saying, Mother?" Sister Veronica asked while she poured warm water over Lidwina, who wriggled under the initial shock. A few cursory droplets flecked Mother's face, prying her gaze from her makeshift land of denial.

"I was simply asking if you checked with her, our...Lidwina—if she wants to be called that?"

Both nuns looked her in the eyes, and Lidwina finally spoke, "Sister Lidwina sounds perfect for me."

The two women of God erupted in laughter. Mother Superior's eye fell on one of Lidwina's soaped-up puffy nipples that winked at her like a shiny copper coin just begging to be plundered. She bit her fist in response, her face contorting in pain while half-laughing and half howling.

Sister Veronica chuckled, lathering up the bar of soap in a washcloth.

"Why didn't you tell us you could speak, child? We thought you were mute!"

"I thought we were supposed to stay mostly silent. I am a nun like you all, right? Sister Lidwina?" said Lidwina with droplets of water and innocence dotting her eyes.

Sister Veronica blinked away her tears from laughter, soaping Lidwina between giggles.

"Like Hell you are," Mother Superior eked out through gritted teeth.

Sister Veronica lifted Lidwina's downcast chin and smiled at her, "I don't think so, my child, not yet, at least."

"Not in the getup you showed up in, at least," added Mother, shaking the feeling back into her hand.

"Perhaps you're some kind of lady of the land. You could've been a farmer in those clothes!" Sister Veronica giggled as she filled up the pitcher of warm water again.

Mother Superior rolled her eyes. "As if, Sister Veronica."

"Stranger things have happened!" Veronica cheerily said.

Somewhere off, down the hallway from the direction of the linen closet, came a disembodied yell.

"Saints be praised!"

The three women all looked in that direction questioningly.

"Oh drat!" Sister Veronica exclaimed, "I forgot to get her a towel to dry off with."

Veronica bustled past the Reverend Mother. "Keep an eye on her for me, Mum," she said as she entered the hallway. Mother uttered a stuttered response, and her face went blank once it was just the two of them in the room.

"I like your rosary, Mother," Lidwina said, her eyes glued to the dazzling red color. "Do you get that when you become a Mother Superior?" Mother Superior was ready to condescendingly answer the poor, concussed child until she thought about it.

"You know, I did actually get this when I became Mother Superior. It was a gift, a parting gift, if you will."

Lidwina continued to eye it before she shivered and hugged her dewy flesh. Droplets of water plinked into the rain barrel below, dribbling from her now erect nipples that were locked and loaded on Mother Superior.

"Mother," Lidwina said throatily while kneading her bronzed orbs as they danced in Mother's periphery, "would you let me sit on your face?"

The air in Mother Superior's chest froze solid, constricting her before it burst from her chest.

"I BEG YOUR PARDON, LIDWINA!?"

"Mass," Lidwina said, "Would you let me sit in on mass tomorrow. The singing sounds like angels to me." She smiled irreproachably at Mother.

"Y-yes. I suppose that's fine, my child. The church is the body of Christ, and we are members of that...body." Mother felt her eyes wander across Lidwina's supple skin and dug her nails into her thigh in retaliation. Mother's eyes went glassy as the warmth emanating from her most holiest of places bloomed into hot stabs, shooting pain and dripping blood down her leg. The sound of penny loafers entered the room, allowing some color to return to Mother's flushed complexion.

"So sorry, my dear. Leave it to me to get our survivor sick just as she begins her joyous recovery!" Sister Veronica turned to Mother, unfolding the towel.

"Why was Sister Calliope in the linen closet this time?"

She turned back, shaking her head to Lidwina, and swaddled her in the fluffy white towel.

"She was supposed to be finishing her mural on the washroom ceiling today."

Mother Superior's eyes met those of the *recovering survivor.* The innocence faltered from Lidwina's face as her steely blue stare burned a hole right through her.

In the Garden of Eatin' It from the Back
Chapter 4

Ophelia and Sister Emelie were heading out to the garden when they saw the Reverend Mother apprehensively bolting from the laundry room. The two messy novitiates ducked into an alcove to hide while still being able to watch the feature presentation. Mother Superior looked like she was fleeing from some invisible force that was quick on her heels. Her eyes darted between the corridors before she was again near her beloved Virgin Mary. Mother Superior saw the loving glow erupt from behind the statue but felt the ravages of her unclean thoughts grating against the inside of her skull. The gash she ripped into her leg was still squelching with a platelet punch that went unnoticed against her jet black vestment.

Her steps slowed, like she was trudging through waves of mud to get to the Virgin Mary's forgiving grace. Through lamented whimpers and tear-filled eyes, she threw herself onto the feet of the statue. Sister Ophelia snuck to the next alcove at the disapproval of Emelie, who was wracked with anxiety, not so much worried about getting caught witnessing this intimate violation but for the severe punishment that it invoked.

Mother Superior's eyes were puddles of sorrow. Her tears dripped off her cheek, bringing stripes of color to the statue's patina exterior. She begged the Virgin for mercy and forgiveness. Sister Ophelia caught more of the bizarre display, peering with her one eye around the corner. The Sisters had witnessed Mother's affinity with the effigy but never to this extent. Mother Superior was mouthing words up to it, caressing the statues' pleats lasciviously, and pounding her fist into her thigh with a sickening squelch. She brought her face to the Virgin Mary's praying hands. The stark contrast between its shining luster and the rest of the chalky surface was brought on by years of physical penitence and passionate erosion. She could smell her essence, her pheromones on the erect imploring phalanges.

The Reverend Mother moaned and nudged her cheek against the back of the Virgin Mary's praying hands. Sister Ophelia's eye widened as Mother Superior's tongue slithered like a writhing slug, caressing the clasped hands and enjoying the coppery tang as it tased her tongue. The shock and disgust on Ophelia's face turned to alarm when voices from the laundry room started to get louder.

In a stunted panic, Ophelia looked to Emelie, frozen in her alarmed stupor. Anticipating the laundry room door opening, Ophelia slid back next to her Sister in Christ and did her best to act natural. Sister Veronica and Lidwina exited the door and boisterously let all the inhabitants of the hallway know of their presence. Mother Superior absconded from her licentious embrace, quieting her unruly folds with trembling hands gliding over her curves. Emelie and Ophelia grinned as they passed the statue and its lone worshipper as a waft of coppery musk tickled their nostrils. Mother Superior gave them a flushed nod of approval as she, too, made her escape from the scene of the crime to her office. Sister Ophelia held the door out to the back garden for Emelie, quickly retrieving her pad and pen to scribble out:

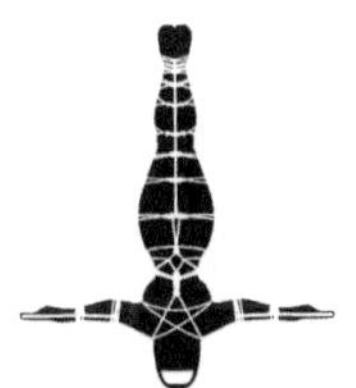

Emelie giggled incessantly as Ophelia handed her a bushel basket and grabbed the gardening gloves. By the time they were pulling cucumbers and tomatoes off their vines, the odd events prior exited her mind in place for the quiet sounds of mother nature. In a working meditative state, Ophelia picked and pruned the vast greenery of the self-sustained garden plot. She was almost done with the harvesting for the week when Sister Veronica and Lidwina came out of the back door and joined them.

"My good Lord, look how firm your tomatoes are, Ophelia!" Sister Veronica said, staring at her overflowing vessel.

"That's what Sister Calliope said last night while we were playing mahjongg!" Sister Emelie added.

"Oh, be careful playing with her; she cheats every time the good Lord turns his back!"

Lidwina's eyes bounced around the lush greenery before she locked eyes with Ophelia. Their smiles battled for whose would supersede the other.

"I have good news, Sisters. Gather round!" Veronica said with glee, gently nudging Lidwina forward. Lidwina had on baggy pajama pants with extra large boots and a well-worn T-shirt the Sisters had lent her until they could do some digging in the basement.

"Hello, Sisters, my name is Sister..." She turned back to look at Veronica for encouragement, receiving a grinning nod. "My name is Lidwina." She sighed with relief. "For now."

Ophelia stood, letting her gloves drop to the ground before crossing the small dirt path to hug her. Emelie jabbed her garden trowel into the dirt and dusted off her hands to join them when they all heard the door slam behind them. Deep sighs and all eyes went down as the gravel crunched under Mother Superior's Mary Janes. Ophelia deftly released and shifted away from Lidwina, while she mentally imploded Mother's skull into a pulped mash with her mind. Mother Superior returned the sentiment.

"Let's get a move on, Sisters; no time for dawdling or..." She glanced from Lidwina's head down to her feet, "distractions." She breezed past the pair, still standing a bit too close for her liking.

"What are we standing around for? Was there a midday solstice that I wasn't made privy? Do the heathens have a dress code?"

Sister Veronica stepped around Lidwina, joining Mother.

"We just wanted to let the other Sister know how well Lidwina is doing is all, finally talking. Every step counts on the road to recovery," she said jubilantly, smiling in Lidwina's direction. Mother Superior was rolling up her sleeves when her face soured like she had bitten into a particularly tart lemon.

"Never applaud the fish for swimming, Sister. The good book decrees it so. They will expect praise every time they wipe their arses or have a wee-wee in the morning."

"The good book says wee-wee?"

"Don't be daft, Veronica; it says to withhold praise until it's for something worthwhile."

"You'll have to lend me your bible, mum; I must have missed that passage in all my years familiarizing myself with the texts."

Mother Superior's nostrils flared, and her eyes ignited, her mustache was tweaked with vexation.

"Emelie, fetch the wheelbarrow on the side of the building so that you and Ophelia can lay down the fertilizer." Mother dictated as she made her way to the relic that was their garden shed. The roof looked paper-thin, and the doors sagged in on themselves. Ophelia and Emelie begrudgingly headed to the side of the building while Mother began pulling on the shed doors profusely.

"Help. Me. Veronica," she said through gritted teeth. Sister Veronica quickly sidestepped Mother's superior posterior before it collided with her. The door only opened about a foot, the bottom dragging in the gravel beneath it. Lidwina stood staring at the two nuns fussing with the infernal door, the cogs in her injured mind beginning to reconfigure. Her neurons sparked, and she confidently stepped forward, pulling the door up and then smoothly opening it to the relief of the two.

Mother Superior regretfully thanked Lidwina, which went unnoticed by the maiden on a mission in the rickety old garden shed. Dust particles danced through streams of sunlight that shone through the slats of the dilapidated roof. Sister Veronica and Mother Superior cautiously filed into the musty space, avoiding the blinding rays. Lidwina was diligently eyeing the neglected shelves, avoiding the crusty hoes and assorted elderly garden tools. A mystery force activated in her mending mind and directed her to repair this misshapen hinge that caused the sagging door. Her primed fingers snatched up the dust-caked screwdriver a second after she laid eyes on it. In one swift movement, she pulled the door toward her with one hand, stabbed the screwdriver under in a kickback motion, knocked the hinge pin out, and caught it in mid-air. The nuns winced when she chomped down on the metal stake, holding it gingerly in her teeth.

As if led by a divine hand, she blindly grabbed the pliers hanging to her left and deftly pulled the misshapen hinge knuckles back in line. With her grip still strongly holding the door in place, she pocketed the tools and retrieved the hinge pin. The Sisters were in awe at the proficient presentation taking place before them with such retained precision. Until their stomachs ached in unison when the *hawk-tuah* noise of her expectoration *daintily* erupted from her lips and the spittle rocketed to its target: the barrel of the hinge. Lidwina had come to the end of her trance-like state, fully snapping out of this involuntary spectacle when she inserted the pin with a satisfyingly smooth click. Her stare softened as the whoosh of blood flow in her ears faded, leaving just the sound of the grateful Sisters applauding, even the mean one with the mustache.

"Saints be praised!" could be heard from within the convent, barely noticed by the stupefied Sisters.

"Blessed be Lidwina's skilled hands," Mother Superior proclaimed as she tested the ease of opening and closing the shed door now. "Perhaps I've misjudged this swimming fish after all."

Lidwina was beside herself with joy. "I can remember this. I can remember using my hands to fix things, break things, and cut shit up!" The Sisters all gasped and giggled; Mother Superior was visibly offended. "Save that language for Home Depot, Lidwina; this is a house of God!"

Lidwina's eyes were as big as saucers, digging in her erring mind for fleeting memories just out of her reach.

"Sorry, Mother," she meekly responded. Sister Veronica put her arm around Lidwina, noting the frustration on her face through her knitted eyebrows.

Mother Superior returned to the shed to fetch some pruning shears and a hatchet illuminated by a single stream of golden sunshine poking through the perforated ceiling.

"How are you at roofs?" she asked dryly, gazing upward at the ancient awning. She tucked the hatchet into her belt and headed to the opposite side of the garden. Ophelia and Emelie were bringing the lopsided wheelbarrow around when they crossed paths. The two nuns were exhaustively pulling and pushing the rust bucket on wheels, sweat soaking their bandeaus. Mother Superior eyed the two in torment and did her best not to smile gleefully.

"Oh, Sisters, I'm sorry you had to lug that decrepit old thing all the way here." She looked the useless thing over; the wheel wasn't even spinning. "You might as well leave it there, ladies. It is of no use to us." She sighed, and the two nuns angrily dropped the relic in the tall grass. "Besides, you fit young fillies should have no problem handling the fertilizer by hand. Nice, strong backs and hands; it will bring you closer to God. I almost envy you," she said with a smirk, watching Sister Ophelia bite her tongue and trudge back toward the garden plot, pulling Emelie along wistfully.

"Lift with your knees, ladies!" Mother snapped, with a little chuckle under her breath as she continued toward the corner of the enclosure wall. Her chuckles fizzled out quickly once she saw the overgrowth of the tall grass blocking her path. She pulled out the hatchet and started whacking at it in a strong V pattern, strained breaths escaping through her pursed lips and gritted teeth.

Lidwina had seen the exchange but had already gone into the shed to retrieve the tools her mind led her to, like mental dowsing rods to hidden water. Sister Veronica was helping the novitiates make a hard job go as painlessly as possible. With no one to stop her, Lidwina pulled her hair back and shoved a handful of tools in her pockets before she tied the drawstring on her pants tighter. She approached the wheelbarrow, circling the dangerous adversary before she grabbed it by the handles and spun it like a top until it landed wheels up.

Groaning to herself, Mother Superior's wrists felt numb, like her veins were full of battery acid. She was ready to give up when she remembered she had a fresh young body just aching to be used at her disposal. Mother retraced her steps and came upon Lidwina toiling away at the wheelbarrow. Whatever she had done, the wheel was now freely spinning and working as good as new. The Sisters were approaching her to marvel at another Lidwina miracle. Mother Superior wouldn't have it.

"Lidwina, how about a little yard work?" she asked, leading Lidwina away from the others, her trusty hatchet in hand. After a few test swipes, Mother Superior showed her how to clear a path quickly and easily. In no time, the amnesiac made way for Mother to steal away to her sacred space just past the sizable apple trees. While Mother was tending to her pilfered proclivities, Lidwina made quick work of the lofty foliage. She paused to catch her breath with her hand on her hip and a honed hatchet in the other.

Ophelia donned her gardening gloves and gave Sister Veronica a hand, which gave her an opportune time for some motherly advice now that she could not talk back for once.

"I know that the Reverend Mother can be difficult at times, but she must keep us disciplined to keep us strong in our faith and minds."

Sister Ophelia rolled her eyes and kept working.

"Oh, my little O. You've always been my little firecracker. Ever since the day you walked into your first day of preschool. I knew you were going to be my little pistol."

Sister Veronica stood up and dusted her hands off on her apron, grabbing for Sister Ophelia's.

"I'm very proud of you. *They're* very proud of you. We're all very proud of you and know you can get through this annoying initiation process."

Sister Ophelia looked away as she started to tear up, though she tried to fight it.

"Think of it that way. Don't let anyone or anything get in your way. Not a brick wall or...

An ominous bird cawed in the distance.

"An old crow. You're more than halfway through. Prove you're tougher than she pretends to be," Sister Veronica said with a smile and a wink, excusing herself to check on the rooster and the chickadee.

Sister Veronica had questioned the eerie silence, noticing Lidwina proudly surveying her job well done. Just as Sister Veronica was crossing to join her, she watched as Lidwina palmed the hatchet, stared down its blade, tossed it up to catch the handle in her palm, and then, without a single hesitation, sent it hurtling toward the Reverend Mother. Veronica's breath caught in her throat as her glassy eyes watched the mini axe revolve as if in slow motion. It thunked itself into the tree bark only inches from Mother Superior's bustling behind.

"MOTHER!" Veronica screamed; the terror registered on her face while her lungs stopped working again after the outburst. Mother Superior promptly turned to her exasperated Sister with a question on her tongue. Lidwina's lithe, glistening form, standing in the downed plains, smirked, and proved to be a better entree for her eyes.

"This is exceptional, Lidwina!" Mother strolled up to her, with Veronica close on her heels.

"I don't like to be proven wrong." She paused. "I mean, it doesn't happen often." Lidwina had walked up to the pontificating penguin lady, nonchalantly placed her hand on the hatchet, and pulled it out indiscreetly. The swift motion went unnoticed by Mother, who was deep in self-contemplation.

"I think I have misjudged this poor soul. Maybe you are exactly where you were meant to be after all," she said, pleased with her realization just as Veronica showed up and wrestled the hatchet out of Lidwina's meaty mitts. After a few pulls, Lidwina let go. Veronica stood before Mother Superior, holding it with a dumbfounded look. Mother Superior returned the look with suspicion.

"What is it, Sister Veronica? You look as if someone has nicked your knickers and thrown them up a tree."

All present company within earshot giggled under their breath.

"I just...Mother...I...I wanted to see your...lady garden," Sister Veronica stammered painfully slowly.

Mother Superior raised an eyebrow, glancing at Veronica.

"Sister, you've seen my lady garden multiple times. If memory serves me correctly, the last time you did, you said my lady garden was overgrown and unkempt. I took offense to that. You know I take special care of my lady garden. Why, it's my pride and joy." A droplet of spare moisture gathered in the corner of Mother's eye. "So now it's off limits. For my eyes only and those whom I deem suitable."

"Mum, I..." Veronica replied, befuddled.

"I mean it, Veronica. I have feelings, too, and you hurt them. How would you feel if someone said your lady garden was dry and reeked of fetid swamp water? I think you'd be singing a different tune altogether, don't you?"

Sister Veronica chewed her lip and averted her narrow gaze. "I'm...sorry, Mum."

"As you should be. Now, perhaps Lidwina would like to see it. If that doesn't bother you, Sister Veronica." Veronica began to walk away from the pair, stunned disbelief in her squinted eyes.

"Well, what do you say, Lidwina? Would you like to see my prized lady garden?"

Lidwina beamed, "You're not going to be able to keep me out of it."

Mother Superior was excited beyond words to pull back the veil on her crowning glory to a fresh prospect. Lidwina's eyes weren't sure where to rest among the sensory barrage of colors and sweet scents. A lattice of vines with pockets of blooming flora sat inconspicuously against the rear outer wall of the shed. Mother simpered, pleased with how lush and inviting her lady garden must appear to an outsider's eye. White blooms bewitched her gaze, then directed it to the bursting florets of blues and lavenders amongst the breathing canvas of greenery. She paid special attention to a patch of coquettishly shy blushing buds. Lidwina finally threw caution to the wind and caressed a scintillating tapered tower of pink bugle-shaped blossoms before inhaling a lungful.

"Careful, dear. Foxglove is dangerously alluring to the senses but quite poisonous, even to the touch," Mother Superior said, unaffected. "All my lovelies are unfortunately of the poisonous variety, little beauties meant to be appreciated but never pawed."

Lidwina casually rubbed her fingertips along her thighs.

"I just love anything pink." She took one last glance, then tenderly turned to the proud nun, "What a lovely and not at all ominous garden you have, Mother."

The Juiciest Apple in the Orchard
Chapter 5

The sun was setting on the much-improved garden and a day's worth of victories. The elders had already retired within and claimed the hot water while the getting was good. Emelie graciously allowed Lidwina to take a hot shower before her, thanking her for her diligent digits saving the day. The dismal stone walls of the convent were bursting at the seams with a newfound vibrant energy as word of Lidwina's feats of strength spread amongst the small commune. Childlike giggles and joyful humming could be heard throughout as shadows from candlelight danced across walls.

With everyone retiring to their rooms for the night, Lidwina, energized and craving something sweet, crept into the kitchen. She braided her wet hair into a pigtail on one side while she braided the other. She glanced around the counters for something to satisfy her intense sweet tooth. As she moved past the window, she peered out into the darkness and watched her reflection staring back at her in the dull glow from the task light above the sink. Her mind was gnawing at her, pulling her to thoughts she knew were below the murky surface.

A woman who could be her doppelgänger was braiding the hair of a miniature version of her in a mirror. The woman had softer features but was the spitting image of Lidwina. She could almost hear the woman's voice, instructing the young learner to *braid the hair up and over, crisscross apple sauce until you get to the end, then you use a rubber band to make sure you don't lose all the hard work you just did.* She fastened the rubber band to her last pigtail, but her foggy memories wore on her. This fragment of a lost memory pulled at her heartstrings. The more she pushed to remember the familiar woman, the more frustrated she grew. Each memory felt like a bundle of Helium balloons floating just out of her reach.

The door to the kitchen swung open. The sudden intrusion jostled Lidwina from her brain fog. An equally startled Bernadette entered, her hand flying up to the towel wrapped around her head, which had almost fallen off from the sudden jerk. Lidwina had never seen her out of her habit, and Bernadette felt equally exposed in her baggy hand-me-down sweats. They both blushed, but Lidwina couldn't stop staring at this new version of Bernadette before her. The embarrassment faded from Bernadette's milky skin, and a smile crept across her supple mauve lips. Her dewy complexion looked immaculate, the apples of her cheeks naturally highlighted, and her strong eyebrows capped deep, blue eyes that now traced Lidwina's frame as she stood with her hip against the large work island in the kitchen.

"I guess..." Bernadette said throatily, then lowered her voice. "I wasn't the only one who was still hungry." Her glowing cheeks rose as a little giggle escaped her naive grin.

"I think I need something sweet." Lidwina said nonchalantly, "But God, please no more oatmeal." She said in mock pain, holding her stomach. Bernadette's eyes lit up with excitement as she swiftly walked toward Lidwina, throwing her off momentarily. The pared-down Sister was close enough for Lidwina to feel her warm breath on her cheek as she whispered,

"I think I know what will satisfy that sweet tooth of yours."

Lidwina's hunger grew, a heat bubbling to the surface when Bernadette walked past her and entered the pantry. Bernadette returned with a look of anticipation as she held her hands behind her back. The childlike innocence behind her eyes melted her heart and electrified her skin.

"Pick a hand," Bernadette said in a hushed whisper, just inches from Lidwina's watchful eyes.

"Left."

Bernadette's eyes gleamed as her left hand swirled around and presented a shiny red apple. Lidwina smirked and flirtatiously plucked it from her open palm. Bernadette chuckled, leaning against the opposite counter. With a smirk, she revealed another apple from her right hand. Her face was now glowing in the faint light as she rubbed the apple across the top of her left breast. Lidwina couldn't help but watch the slick red orb slide back and forth along the baggy fabric, giving hints to the heaving flesh below as it pulled taut and went slack. Bernadette was studying Lidwina's face, watching her eyes dance in her skull before a soft moan escaped her parted lips. Bernadette was about to take a bite of the apple but held it frozen in midair in front of her before she coyly asked, "Have you ever played the apple game?"

Lidwina shook her head *no* but held the apple ready for Bernadette to finish.

"We play it sometimes when we get bored." She snickered. "After Mother Superior goes to sleep." Their stare was a direct link, unblinking and unflinching. "Want me to teach you?"

"Mmmmhmmm," was all Lidwina could muster. Her mind, mouth, and words were all on autopilot as Bernadette's perky nipples peaked underneath the thick fabric, spearing Lidwina's focus.

Bernadette stepped closer, her leg now between Lidwina's, still resting against the counter.

"I bite some of my apple and then pass it to you."

"Sounds easy enough," Lidwina whispered confidently.

"You have to use your mouth. That's the tricky part. Then we go back and forth." Bernadette stated with a hint of trepidation, watching Lidwina's response.

Lidwina's smile grew to twice its size as she cocked her eyebrow.

"I think I can be good at this game."

Bernadette's eyes went dreamy as she brought the apple to her quivering lips. Her teeth punctured the skin, misting droplets of sweetly tart juice onto the roof of her mouth. Lidwina stared and watched with a nervous excitement that caused the skin above her lip to perspire. The crunch of the apple's flesh was muffled by Bernadette's mouth closing. Lidwina leaned closer; her breathing slowed to an absolute crawl. Bernadette grinned and bent forward, their mouths sailing toward one another like ships in the night before they crashed, sending shivers down their spines. Their lips parted, and electricity between the two completed the connection of a lifetime. The smell of apple, Bernadette's coconut shampoo, and her heavenly-scented sweat sent Lidwina's mind into overload.

The cold bit of apple passed from Bernadette's mouth to Lidwina, and she slowly, *painfully* pulled away from their bereft lip lock. They both felt the intense afterglow effects as they sat in a mild stupor of intoxicating excitement. After a beat of electrified silence, Bernadette looked at Lidwina expectantly. Lidwina quickly sobered fast enough to tear a chunk out of her apple and offered to bridge the gap again, in the name of innocent entertainment. Bernadette welcomed her playmate's mouth, tongue, and the sweet offering, almost as much as her warm hand caressing her aching flesh over the well-worn fabric.

Lidwina's neurons were firing on a thousand cylinders, guiding her hands over Bernadette's feminine contours. Bernadette was lost in the moment; her chin thrust upward as Lidwina trailed kisses along her neck. Bernadette swallowed the bit of apple, and Lidwina traced its journey down her neck until she was nuzzling her collarbone and kneading her breasts together closer to her face. Bernadette writhed in place, her hands pulling and squeezing at Lidwina's shoulders. Her mind was full of uncertainty but welcome surprise as she stared at the ceiling above them. Half worried about being heard or found, half wondering how she had never felt these sensations before this very moment. She wanted to pray for direction but chose to believe in what she could see, feel, and taste. Her body was the altar, and she wanted Lidwina to worship every inch.

For the past few days, Lidwina felt lost and misguided like a shell without a host, but now with her blood pumping, nerve endings firing, and senses all craving what this delicious little snack had to offer, her mind was a puzzle. The pieces jumbled, but this was as close as she felt to the picture coming into focus. She wanted her memory back. She wanted her life back. If this was the only way to do it, so be it. Throwing caution to the wind, Lidwina let her carnal desires take the reins.

In one swift move, she swung Bernadette around so her back was to the kitchen island. Her eyes went agog as the towel unraveled onto her shoulder. Allowing her still-damp blond hair to cascade down around her shoulders. The scent of her intoxicating coconut shampoo soaked into Lidwina. Bernadette placed the towel on the tabletop behind them. Lidwina wrapped her arms around her waist and fervently lifted her onto the counter.

Bernadette gasped as she felt the itchy fabric lift her arms and head out of the neck hole of the thin sweater. The nippy air clashed with her glistening skin, making goosebumps dot the pale flesh along her perfectly palm-sized breasts.

Now, at eye level, Lidwina hugged her closer and buried her face between the billowing pillows to keep them warm. A moan purred out of Bernadette's agape mouth. She let her hands explore and claw at Lidwina's muscular back. Lidwina was ravenously kissing at her heaving cleavage while squeezing and kneading the soft mounds from the outside. She pulled her face away to stare at the perky pair of breasts pressed together before circling each dark pink nipple and flicking her tongue around them. She had to quell the urge to bite into her flesh and devour her whole by instead nibbling her pebbled nipples.

The feeling of teeth on her skin sent waves of heat through Bernadette's body, causing her to shakily arch her back in ecstasy and catch herself from falling on the counter with her outstretched arms.

Lidwina seized the opportunity to view Bernadette's heavenly body in all its glory as she watched her teeter, almost too overcome to stay upright. She pulled her legs up by the baggy fabric and threaded her arms through Bernadette's bent knees.

Bernadette relaxed, pinching her own nipples to relive this new sensation. The combination of pleasure and pain while feeling secure in Lidwina's grasp made her see stars. The sudden feeling of her baggy sweatpants sliding off made her tense temporarily until she saw Lidwina's confident smirk planting little kisses on her perpendicular calves while maintaining eye contact. Before she knew it, the unflattering cotton panties flashed before Lidwina's eyes, quieting the last bit of nagging worry in Bernadette's mind.

Bernadette's body twitched in excitement, her back arched, and her fingers continued to twist her perky pink radio knobs, determined to find the perfect song to lose her virginity to. Lidwina pulled her body toward her by her hips before she leaned forward and pulled Bernadette close for a passionate kiss. Their eyes locked. Their souls melded. Their minds connected in the blink of an eye with a flick of the tongue. Bernadette knew she was in capable hands and an even more capable mouth. Their tongues swirled more before Lidwina pulled away, licking her lips with insatiably hungry eyes. Her head traveled down, planting the same little kisses that comforted Bernadette while quickening her heart. Past her chin, past her sternum, past her navel, feeling Lidwina's chin brush the modest thatch of blond pubic hair that was the same color as the wet strands dripping from her head.

The kisses became sloppier, more feral. She felt Lidwina's tongue tracing her golden trail before she felt hot breath between her thighs. Bernadette felt the dreaded hesitation—the pause that sapped all joy from her heart. The part of her mind that screamed *shame* at her for every thought, emotion, or moment not in prayer. Then she felt that part of her mind stall and detonate within her as Lidwina clamped her mouth onto her tender, aching pussy. Wetting Bernadette's swollen lips with her own while teasingly parting them with her tongue. The undulating movements of Lidwina's mouth muscles made Bernadette see the face of God more than a thousand verses or hymns ever could.

Trying to keep herself quiet was proving impossible, as Bernadette bit her lip so hard, it bled. The metallic tart taste only added to the ecstatic moment. Her nails curled, slivers of wood beneath her fingertips, as she rhythmically rolled her hips to match Lidwina's pile-driving tongue lashes. She lifted her head to see if her towel was in reach when she locked eyes with the feral, she-beast who was devouring her hole and lapping out her insides, slurp by slurp.

Inclined to show off, Lidwina clamped on her clit again and sucked as much juice out of Bernadette's engorged, dripping honeypot as she could. Her face was glazed and crazed with reckless abandon. Lidwina brought her hands up and caressed Bernadette's ample ass cheeks before she stealthily slid two fingers into her hungry, slick slit. A shot of electricity shot up Bernadette's spine and gave her just enough time to bite down on the damp towel while she muffled her moans of ecstasy. Lidwina could have pulled back, slowed down, and dragged this out more. She could have tortured Bernadette until she left her in convulsing hysterics, but she could never do that to Babygirl.

Baby. Girl.

The phrase ignited a part of her mind that knew how to send Bernadette into orbit. Her fingers twisted and teased Bernadette's opening into a feverish pitch. Her mind dug for that fading memory almost as hard as her tongue dug and swathed Bernadette's pearlescent, engorged clit. Both targets were within reach. She just had to push, evoke, and entice it out. Bernadette's muffled howls intensified, her hips bucking and shaking uncontrollably just as she gave in to whatever her body needed. Lidwina came up for air with an audible slurp but kept her fingers on the trigger before throatily coaxing.

"Cum for me, Babygirl," escaped her smiling, soppy mouth, a piece of the puzzle slipping into the correct slot. Just as Lidwina sat back in smug triumph, Bernadette heaved and thrashed. Her moans were barely contained by the drenched towel between her clenched jaws. Her soul quaked, trying to leave her body in her mind-blowing first orgasm.

Lidwina had stared into the eye of this storm before and gently shifted to the left as streams of warm nunny juice squirted out of Bernadette. Both were in stunned disbelief at the height and distance Bernadette was getting until one stray stream hit a hanging pot above the stove.

The resounding gong rippled through the kitchen and the silent bedrooms above it. The ruckus caused a sleep-mask-donned Mother Superior to shoot up in her bed, exclaiming, "What the deuce?!"

Statues & Limitations
Chapter 6

"Sew your seed in the morning, and at evening let your hands not be idle, but you do not know which will succeed, whether this, or that, or whether both will do equally well," Mother Superior bellowed from the pulpit, letting every word of scripture resound like she was speaking before the Signatura herself. She looked out at her small but mighty congregation of seven that she hand-selected, certain they would grow and enrich their faith through her strict but indispensable discipline—even Calliope, who was known to start fires.

Mother Superior's eyes fell on Lidwina, devouring every word she delivered like a starving puppy. She motioned for the congregation to bow their heads in prayer before giving her final blessing. Lidwina lowered her head last, stealing one final glance up front. Mother couldn't help but notice Lidwina's choice of t-shirt, pulled snuggly over her full bosom, and the sleeves rolled up to showcase her well-defined arms. Mother felt flush, in a daze that someone would bring their *Delilah spirit* into this hallowed place of worship, a place she fought so hard to orchestrate down to every detail.

Mother blinked to clear her mind of the impure glimpses she was now stealing from Lidwina. It befuddled the Reverend Mother how the young woman's protruding nipples always seemed to point in condemnation toward her. *What did they know? Who had they been talking to? What did they taste like?*

The latter intrusive thought caused her to almost drop her bible, creating a small commotion that luckily didn't attract much attention. She reopened her bible to find not the scripture she planned to end her sermon with, but instead opened it to the Book of Timothy.

> *Timothy 2:11-12*: A woman must quietly receive instruction with entire submissiveness. But I do not allow a woman to teach or exercise authority over a man, but to remain quiet.

The Reverend Mother's hand rested on the despicable page of the holiest of all books. It was taking every ounce of strength to not rake her claws down the text and get the damned passage out of her sight and out of her memories. The words repeated from the all too familiar voices. She grabbed for her rosary with her shaking hand. The crucifix glinted as she nervously encircled the first bead between her thumb and forefinger. Her mind began reciting the Hail Mary mindlessly. Her eyes slammed shut as her mind continued its known path. Whispers from her congregation were trying to distract her, unsuccessfully. Then the whispers from below her congregation's feet began, caus- ing a line of icy sweat to trickle down her leathery spine. The whispers grew into shouts and howls. Her fingers death-gripped the cursed rosary when the discord of long-dead voices fell to a disturbingly crisp silence. Mother Superior let out a shaky exhale, opening her eyes to conclude her sermon.

Five corpses sat in the pristine pews with gnarled faces twisted into tormented masks. Their leathery skin dimpled and pulled away from exposed ribs and dry, yellowed bones. Their eye sockets were deep wells of black with the faintest hint of light flickering behind the dark ripples. The tattered rags strewn amongst them hung like macabre party streamers, caked with mold and desiccated gore. Their only recognizable article of clothing made the bile rise in the back of her throat. The plastic cleric's collars shone blindingly white amongst the chartreuse putrescence commanding the room. Mother Superior's lungs seized, not willing to carry on as their stares pierced her insides and revealed every detail of her sins. She felt her knees shifting beneath her, watching in stunned disbelief as their gaunt jaws wrenched open and wailed in a cacophonous multitude of roars. The sheer volume sent shockwaves of demonic dominion that willed her mind to shatter into a million pieces.

"GO!" Mother Superior screamed. "GO!" Her voice grew more hoarse as she returned to the deathly quiet chapel with all sets of stunned eyes on her. She paused to compose herself, her shame manifesting into a frog in her throat.

"G...go in peace," she concluded, slamming her Bible shut and turning away from her confounded congregation. She made the sign of the cross and knelt before the useless crucifix hovering above her, imploring the Virgin Mary to hear her prayers.

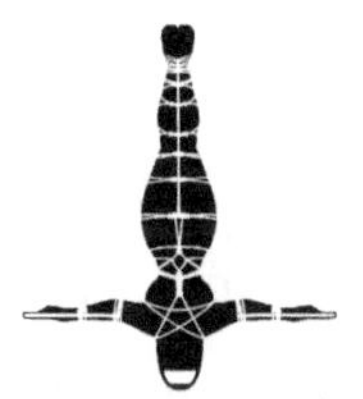

The soft dings of spoons hitting the bottoms of bowls were the only sounds in the dining hall. Each Sister looked down into their dismal, lumpy oatmeal. Sister Veronica entered from the kitchen, grinning until she noted her solemn Sisters' faces.

"What a bunch of forlorn fannies!" she exclaimed, met with assorted tittering. She looked to each nun for some kind of explanation. Her eyes moved to each Sister sitting around the long rectangular table, large enough for all seven of them and then some.

"No Sister Bernadette?"

Emelie perked up. "I don't think she's feeling well."

Sister Veronica nodded in gratitude. A bit of worry darted across her face as she continued down the table. When she reached Ophelia, the stern-faced nun pouted and grabbed her writing pad. Veronica watched her scribble a few words, tear the note off, and slide it her way.

Veronica gasped and gulped for air, crumpling the paper into a ball and stashing it in her cowl. Her bug eyes softened when her breathing returned to normal. "My beloved O, I do fear that you have somehow become louder since you took that vow of silence. Perhaps we should all pray for some humility?" Sister Veronica looked around the table. "The Reverend Mother is just under a lot of pressure, girls. It takes a lot of work to run this place. You know it isn't all *The Sound of Music* in these hills." Sister Veronica looked around the refectory, dimly lit by the few windows. Of the three sconces, only one was in working order. Her eyes traced the grooves in the worn hardwood floors that looked like they had been clawed in.

"The Cistercian Nuns of the Valley of Perpetual Felicity Monastery," she paused to take a pained inhale, "have certainly seen better days." She turned to Lidwina, who was shoveling the last remnants of gruel into her open maw.

"Liddy?"

The nuns giggled again, the morning's antics evaporating from their minds.

"What say, you and I take a little house tour today? I planned to show you a bit of our husbandry, where the chicken coops are and all that, but perhaps... if you're up to it, you could take a look around and see if we could put those skilled hands of yours to work." Lidwina's eyes lit up. She spoke in hums while nodding in excitement. "Well, girls, I think we all have our working orders for the day. Remember, being busy is a blessing." The chapel doors opened and closed quickly. The resounding slam and the steady footsteps of Mother Superior trailed off toward her office, echoing through the air. Sister Veronica's eyes looked uncharacteristically worried. "And it will keep you out of harm's way."

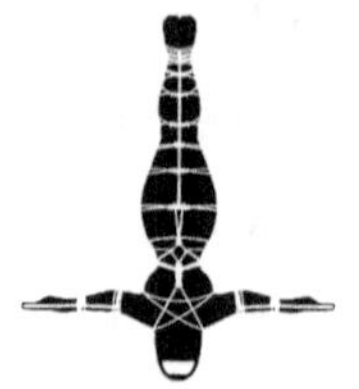

Lidwina donned her plaid shirt and denim shorts to beat the heat while she got some work done. She was fashioning a makeshift toolbox out of some ruddy old shelving in the shed. She grabbed the few essential tools she would need while Veronica talked to Mother Superior in the garden.

"I think that's a fine idea, yes. Especially in the kitchen and around the refectory. I fear the washroom doesn't have a prayer, but maybe our little Jaqueline-of-all-trades could give it a go."

Mother Superior looked back toward Lidwina in her hoe-down outfit again and sighed. A wind blew over the convent walls that swayed the derelict shed. Mother's hand flew to her nose as the scent of fertilizer tickled her nostrils. She grimaced and unpocketed her pruning shears.

"Just be careful; let's not have an amnesiac whacking away at fixtures and taking walls down just yet."

Sister Veronica looked back toward the shed, thankful that Lidwina was just out of earshot.

"And no work in the basement yet. I'll oversee that once the higher-priority work is done."

Mother Superior bid them adieu and headed back to her lady garden, excited to spend the whole day tending to her lethal lovelies.

Lidwina followed Sister Veronica through the hallways as they went from room to room. The most talkative of the traditionally silent order regaled Lidwina with tales of her growing up with ponies in Poland and how hearing her calling led her to travel across the pond and make a home here in the Pacific Northwest.

"Oh yes, imagine Mother Superior's face when she showed up to a monastery-turned-convent with only one communal washroom? I have brothers; I know what stinky little beasts they can be. When we showed up, the poor dear was passed out on the floor, scrub brush in hand! It took some elbow grease and a lot of prayer, but we made it a home. Going on six years next month, actually."

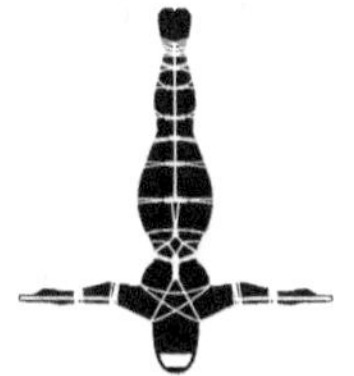

Sister Ophelia hung her apron up in the pantry, just off the kitchen. Not new to mental warfare, this battle was beginning to feel like it was leaning toward Mother Superior for the victory. Ophelia longed to be outdoors, tending to the garden and saying good morning to their chickens. Being stuck on dishes three days in a row was fighting dirty, but she expected no less from that all-caboose, crazy train.

She prayed that the Reverend Mother would keep to herself and have her little mental breakdown in the comfort of her office. She said good afternoon to Sister Calliope after she interrupted the elderly nun doing tai chi in the foyer. When the coast was clear, Ophelia snuck to her quarters to swipe a dab of the last remaining lotion she had pilfered to undo the ravages of kitchen duty. She took a moment to stare out her small window overlooking the sweeping trees in front of their cloister while she rubbed the lotion between her knuckles and kneaded her sore digits.

A spark of mischief zipped across Ophelia's face as she watched the swaying branches bathing in the sun. She knew she had some time before they had to start prepping dinner; she just needed some fresh air. *Some good, clean air,* she thought as she laced up her boots. Stepping to avoid the creaky floorboard on her way to the stairs, she checked if the coast was clear again. *Sister Calliope must be out feeding her pet fox.* Exhilarated and chomping at the thought of adventure just outside the walls, she crept into the chapel. This not being her first escape plan, she zipped past the foyer door, too big and loud. However, the chapel had its own entrance that led out to the convent gates. Everything was going according to plan until she silently turned from the chapel door into the hall and audibly gasped at Sister Bernadette standing in the middle of the aisle in silent worship. Bernadette's head jerked from her hunched stance before she could wipe the tears from her cheek. Ophelia glanced behind her and listened, hoping the silence meant she was still clear before she joined her troubled Sister. Bernadette wiped a sniffle from her nose as Ophelia stood next to her and scribbled on her pad.

She nodded and grinned with glassy eyes, not making eye contact with Ophelia. Sister Bernadette was a kind soul and a great singer, but what she wasn't was a good liar.

Bernadette nodded again, this time a bit more confidently.

"I just had to talk to God for a bit. I'll be fine. Thank you, Sister."

Ophelia put her arm around the slightly smaller girl's shoulder and squeezed.

"You better hurry; the almanac said it might rain later today," Sister Bernadette whispered loudly into her ear.

Ophelia smiled and snuck to the front chapel door before she looked back to her friend and pantomimed locking her lips. Bernadette mimicked the lock and shooed Ophelia on, watching her headstrong friend sneak out much quieter than she came in. The silence returned to the chapel, and Bernadette returned her gaze to the statue of Jesus looking down at her.

She wasn't sure how much longer she should punish herself for this. She prayed and asked for forgiveness for her moment of weakness the night before, for losing something Bernadette was raised believing she could never get back. Was the guilt punishment enough? The promise that she would never allow anything like that to happen again? Bernadette had said four hundred and fifty Hail Marys so far and got no response, so she figured, why not try one hundred and fifty more to see if that earned her some answers?

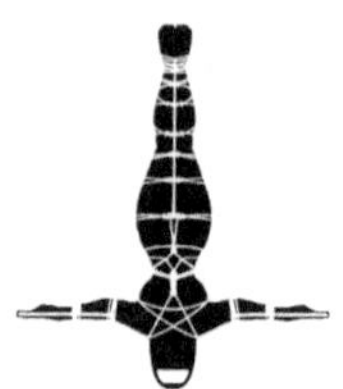

Mother Superior rested her open palms on the large wooden desk, *her* desk...now. The sunken, decaying faces from her past had come back to haunt her, but why now? Why, after all this time of radio silence? She felt her heart rate slow. She reached for the vivid red rosary. It coiled around her hand like a chainmail serpent. Feeling the cool beads roll between her fingers brought her comfort. She reached for the first and began to recite her prayers in hushed tones. Each bead she passed was like a gentle kiss on her frenzied mind. Halfway through, Mother Superior heard a gentle sob outside her office door.

A smile crept across her face hearing that familiar voice. As long as she could hear the Virgin Mary's angelic sobs, she felt the warm embrace wherever she was.

"I thought you were still angry with me," Mother Superior said aloud.

"*I could never be angry with any of my children, certainly not my Sister Sarah.*"

Mary's voice seemed to grow faint, prompting Mother Superior to pad across the office floor with tears in her eyes.

"After all these years, watching you blossom into the woman before me, I could never be anything but proud of you."

Mother Superior stood before her office door, her head resting against the heavy wood as she listened to the sweet words piercing her tough veneer like Cupid's arrow right through her still beating heart. She savored that warmth in her chest before reaching for the locked doorknob. Perplexed thoughts tried to push her out of her happy headspace. She knew fully well she hadn't locked the door earlier. A note of panic was blooming in her chest as she fought to open it again.

"However, something is worrying me, Sister Sarah," the sweet voice carried through the space, its tone turning sinister.

"You have allowed a serpent to enter your garden. With it comes disease, venom, and eventually...death."

Mother Superior pulled away from the entryway. The words traveled from just beyond the door, pummeling her like sharp stones. She heard the solid wood brace and buckle in its frame as if a ton of sand was pushing against it. She stared back in disbelief, "My Queen, I don't understand. How can this be?"

"The unholy beast can change forms. In the form of a serpent, it can shed its skin and take on a new appearance, but it will always be a snake. Your thoughts have become polluted. I can see the venom coursing through them already. If you allow the serpent to live, it will eventually poison your entire flock. Then where will you be, Sister Sarah? Will you be able to clean up and start all over again?"

Mother Superior fell to the floor, her face contorted in pained sorrow.

"Not again, my goddess. I pray to you. I offer my undying devotion to you and only you. Give me the strength to seek out this evil before it's too late. I beg of you!" Mother yelled at the bowing door.

"*If your eye causes you to stumble and sin...*" Mary's voice sounded like it was coming from just beyond the taxed door. Mother Superior cowered but couldn't pry her eyes away.

"Take it out and throw it away," Mother Superior yelled painfully.

"*And if your right hand causes you to sin...*" the voice boomed through the room. Mother Superior held her hand out in front of her.

"Cut it off and throw it away," she said through tears, feeling the sting of invisible hot pokers impaling her outstretched hand. "For it is better that you lose one of your members than your whole body go into Hell!"

As she recited the last line, she regained control of her limbs and threw herself down in prostration. In an instant, she snapped up like a puppet on strings as she felt Mary's voice decreeing through her own moving lips, "Though the wicked spring up like grass and all evildoers flourish, they will be forever destroyed. You are impure. You are weak. You must not let the venom take you over. The beast is strong. You must be stronger."

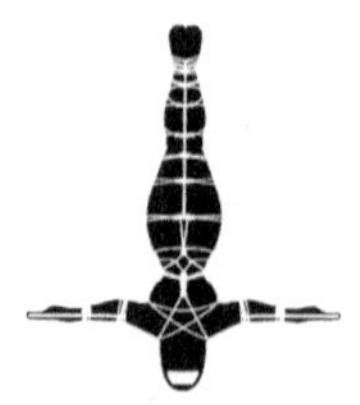

Sister Ophelia clandestinely traipsed through the grounds until she reached the hidden hole in the perimeter gate. No. It was not so much a hole, but a space where the barrier's rusted pickets could be slid over enough for her escape. She couldn't show anyone, lest word get back to Mother Superior. Sister Calliope showed it to her once on one of her notorious wine benders. Luckily, the spry old nun was clothed that time. Once she slipped past the improvised opening, she paused with her back to the stone wall to listen for any signs indicating detection. All she heard was the gentle breeze and the sounds of nature calling her.

Once in the clear, she took off running into the open air, smiling like the bright noonday sun embraced her with all its strength.

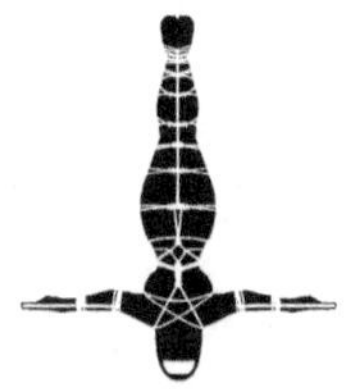

"Saints be praised!" echoed faintly as Sister Veronica shuffled through the hall, peering into each room as if on a mission.

"Good morning to you too, Sister Calliope!" Veronica yelled out in no discernible direction. "Just happy to be here, that one." She uttered before silently reprimanding herself.

Lidwina was fiddling with a bum light switch in the refectory before she started unscrewing the faceplate.

"Oh, wait, wait, Deary. Shouldn't we turn off the power before you begin to work on wires and holes in the wall?" Sister Veronica yelped, causing Lidwina to pause in her tracks.

"Do you know where the breaker box is?" Lidwina asked nimbly, wiping her sweaty mitts on her jeans cut-offs.

"It's in the basement. I'm pretty sure I remember where," Sister Veronica said before the smoke alarm began to sound. "Oh drat! My quiche!" She took off running in the other direction, leaving Lidwina to her own devices.

Lidwina looked around for anything else she could work on while she waited for Sister Veronica but came up empty. She eventually threw caution to the wind and crept closer to the stairs leading down to the lower level. The coast seemed clear. She reasoned she would only be down there a moment; what trouble could she get into that quickly?

Lidwina noted the weak sconce's poor lighting in the wide hallway. She followed it around to the large open storage area, sure the breaker box was somewhere behind the dusty detritus. Still, something was pulling her curiosity toward that single ominous door she passed. She doubted the breaker box would be in there, but it didn't hurt to check. Right?

She checked the stairwell, noting it was still empty when she tried the doorknob. It was unlocked, so she proceeded. No harm, no foul.

Lidwina entered the musty room, her eyes blinking quickly as the smell overcame her. A lone lightbulb hung near the center of the room. She entered, holding her hand over her mouth, and pulled the string, and the dull light came to life, illuminating a damp floor with a drain in the middle. The smell was pretty rank; she felt like just being in this space would imprint that smell on her hair and clothes. She pulled a flashlight from her pocket and shone it on the buckling brick wall taking up most of the room. A series of U rings hung from poorly attached screws in the brick. Parts of the brick looked like they could give way with so much as a good tug.

Lidwina got close enough to one of the rings with the oddly stained ropes dangling from it, noting the smell getting stronger the nearer she got. She looked closer just as a giant black bird flew into the room, cawing in her direction.

"Lidwina! What are you doing here?!" Mother Superior squawked.

Shocked and on high alert, Lidwina looked gobsmacked in her direction and threw her hands up.

"Holy shit, you scared the hell out of me!" Lidwina panted. "I was just looking for the breaker box. This was the only room with a door, so I started here," she added quickly.

Mother Superior furrowed her brow and pursed her lips, surveying the room for anything amiss before she guided Lidwina out. She tried to calm her nerves as she closed the door behind them and led Lidwina to the storage area.

"I'm sure you understand churches, monasteries, and convents are all sacred spaces. Some spaces are more sacred than others. The Penitence Room is a very sacred place to me and the other Sisters." She walked up to the light switch on the wall opposite them, giving it a test flick to no avail. "I'm afraid it is off limits to civilians like yourself. I'm sure you understand. The rest of this floor is mainly used for storage, but I'm almost certain the breaker box is somewhere back here." She extended her hand, expecting Lidwina to hand her the flashlight, but the agile artisan had already brushed past her, following the cables attached to the low ceiling.

"Do be careful, Lidwina; one more knock on the head might finally do the trick!" Mother said in a huff, certain the eager beaver hadn't even heard her. Lidwina was already in a far corner, pushing dusty suitcases to the side as she scanned the walls. Mother fussed as she tripped over several pairs of men's shoes that fell off a shelf.

"Stay there, Mother; I don't want you to get hurt," Lidwina said, shining the light back toward the bumbling Mother Superior.

"Oh, pish posh, I might be older than you, but I've still got my wits about me. These aging hands might not be as nimble as yours, but they helped make this convent what it is today!" she said as she stepped over a box and stumbled back into it. Her fall created a whooshing sound as her dump-truck derriere crushed the cardboard with a puff of dust. The sound the mother hen let out was akin to a chicken squawking in fear. Lidwina hid her smirking chuckle on her shoulder as she trudged to help the wide-eyed Mother Superior out of the cardboard bear trap. A vexed Mother Superior struggled to get out of her turtle-on-its-back position while Lidwina set the flashlight on the old end table near them and grabbed Mother's wrists. Lidwina helped a calmer, embarrassed but more gracious Mother Superior to her feet. She defiantly grabbed the flashlight before Lidwina could reach for it.

Lidwina raised her palms in surrender and let the matriarch have her way, following her as she pushed through more detritus.

"So, this place used to be a monastery?" Lidwina asked, trying to drown out Mother Superior's mumbling obscenities.

Mother proudly proclaimed, "Til I showed up." She attempted to hide how out of breath she was. "The place was on the brink of disillusion. Bunch of immature *men of the cloth* that treated it like a college fraternity more than a house of God." She sniffled as she made her way to the wall on the other side of the Penitence Room. Dust particles floated around her. "I did the world a favor by taking over, doing what I had to do to make it a place for true messengers of the Lord."

Lidwina's knee bumped into a pile in the darkened path, knocking over a heavy brown suitcase that exploded when it hit the stone floor. Assorted vestments, socks, and men's underwear were strewn about the opened luggage. She tried to scoop most of it back in before Mother Superior came to inspect the damage.

"They just left their things?" Lidwina asked benignly, still shoveling the contents back in the aged suitcase.

Mother Superior appeared behind her, catching Lidwina off guard.

"They weren't exactly pleased about the new management," she said sharply as Lidwina closed and clasped the suitcase. Mother Superior shone the flashlight beam to the last unchecked corner of the basement.

"It has to be back there by the boilers. I don't know why I didn't think of that before, actually."

The piles had created a thin walkway to get back there, which would be too tight of a squeeze for a lady of... her proportions. She surrendered the flashlight to Lidwina.

"I'll let you get back there. I don't think I would be able to...I'll supervise you. For safety."

Lidwina headed back, shimmying into the tight space. Mother Superior saw the beam from the flashlight bounce behind the clutter and then disappear, followed by a series of clicks with the overhead lighting turning on and the metal door closing.

"Let there be light!"

Lidwina appeared a few seconds later, giving Mother Superior a thumbs up.

"Look what I found back there. Power Drill!" Lidwina held up an old red drill wrapped with a long cord.

"You were definitely made for this kind of work, dear. I would have driven myself mad looking for that alone."

"Maybe later I can clear a path to get to it easier for all of us. When I'm done with all the big stuff."

Mother Superior agreed, in awe at their new little *handy-mandy*. They made their way back out through the disheveled mess. Mother Superior remarked, "I keep saying, 'one day we will donate this all.' Perhaps another day."

They walked silently into the main area, with only the keys jingling in Mother Superior's pocket. She paused before the door, looking toward Lidwina in a quiet moment of contemplation. Lidwina was about to head toward the stairs when Mother Superior said,

"Before you go..."

Lidwina looked back quizzically as Mother Superior opened the door to the Penitence Room and walked toward the fractured brick, barely holding the metal plates in place.

"Since you've already been in the sacred space, do you think you can do anything about these?" She said, pulling the chain from the lone bulb and pointing toward the metal U-rings with ropes attached.

Lidwina came back in the room warily, looking at the loose screws while Mother Superior watched her with hooded eyes.

"You want me to take them out?" Lidwina asked.

"Well... is there a way to tighten the hooks? You're taller than me, and..." Lidwina shone the flashlight on a particularly loose set of U-rings barely bolted to the wall.

"What exactly goes on in here, Mother?" Lidwina asked as she inspected the stripped screws barely connecting the plate to the wall.

"If you must know, we use this room to absolve ourselves of our sins." She inhaled as her eyes traced rust-colored streaks on the floor.

"What are the rings and hook plates for?"

"These are sacred practices not to be spoken about to civilians. I thought I made it perfectly clear."

"I need to know how much weight is being placed on these plates before I try to put them back. I might be able to reattach them, but it would be lower. Will that bother your...sacred practices?" There was a hint of defiance in her tone, one that Mother picked up on but ignored in the name of necessity.

"Enough to hold someone of my stature...in place...for an undetermined amount of time." She continued, "Lower is fine as long as it holds and won't come loose so easily."

A faint smirk crept across Lidwina's face as she handed the flashlight to an increasingly uncomfortable Mother Superior. She untucked and unbuttoned her flannel shirt. Mother Superior looked perplexed and struggled to keep the flashlight in place. Before she could protest, Lidwina tied the tails of her shirt into a simple knot. She tied her hair back into a messy bun and let her eyes trace the perimeter, taking in the ominous cabinet in the corner and the brick walls surrounding the opposite sides of the room. She glanced up at the ceiling, which took on a shade of brown that matched the wall stains behind her, while she rolled up her sleeves.

"These wall anchors are pretty rocked. Let me see if I can find the bits that go with this drill." She left the room, leaving Mother

Superior to question if this was a mistake. Lidwina returned with the drill in hand, tightening the drill bit to create new holes.

"If you hand the screws back to me, we can be done with this quicker," Lidwina said as she began to pull two of the four wall plates out of the wall. Mother Superior approached her, repositioning the flashlight as she checked the door out of habit.

Lidwina turned and deposited more screws in Mother's hand, each time her improvised halter top rode up a little higher. Mother Superior soured her face but stopped looking away toward the ceiling after the first few times. Lidwina stopped when she got to the last wall plate. It seemed secure in the wall still. She figured this was the only one whose screws went through the actual anchors.

"Who installed these?" she asked, tapping on the brick with the back of the screwdriver.

"They were here long before we got here. This was originally a monastery for an order of Flagellates. The ropes were part of a sacred practice."

Lidwina bit her tongue, noting the pregnant pauses were bringing more and more out of the nervous nun. The tapping of her screwdriver went from a dull thunk to a softer tap in an increasingly malodorous corner of the wall. A sour smell wafted toward Lidwina, with damp undertones of sweetness that made her stomach turn. Mother Superior pretended not to notice the strength of the odor.

"The smell is quite strong, especially after the rain. We've been meaning to get to that as well. There used to be a crawlspace that would flood due to a crack in the foundation. We think some vermin got in before it was walled up." Lidwina turned back to look her in the eye. Mother Superior was shining the light in her direction, but her worried face was stuck, mouth agape. "I didn't want to tear it all out and start over. So, we just got used to the smell, I guess."

Lidwina narrowed her eyes. "I don't know much about masonry, but I could give it a try someday." She kicked at the weak brick near the bottom of the wall, causing a crumbling part to fall off and echo.

Mother Superior's eyes went wild, and she shot up, "Yes, someday!"

The outburst caused Lidwina to pull away from the wall.

"How about one right here?" Mother Superior placed the wall plate a few inches below the old holes as a distraction. Lidwina glanced momentarily and watched Mother's eyes trailing the back of her thighs before she thumped the wall and nodded.

"Yeah, we can do that. As long as that will work for... you." That final tap cracked Mother's veneer and her reserve, and her verbal diarrhea began to spill.

"The order of the Flagellates has been around since the 12th century. They were called extreme until around the 1300s. That's when the Black Plague was called a punishment from God. When it eventually dissipated, they believed it was due to their practice of flagellating themselves to atone for their sins."

"What does flagellate mean?" Lidwina asked once she was done drilling. She grabbed a screw from Mother Superior to finish affixing the plate to the wall.

"They would whip themselves with branches to punish themselves for their sins. They believed that the more they suffered in life, the less they would suffer in death. They moved to whips because leather could do more damage to tender flesh which meant more forgiveness."

Mother Superior's breathing grew shallow as she watched Lidwina's body sway and tense while she drove the screws into the wall. Her twitching muscles made Mother's jaw quake. Just when she thought the basement couldn't get any more damp, she felt her lower regions overflowing. Her eyes traced a line of sweat rolling down the curve of Lidwina's back and dripping between the tight denim that hugged the snack cakes she smuggled below them. Mother's tongue ached to taste that bead of sweat and the journey it was on.

"Want to try it out?" Lidwina asked, her voice slicing into Mother Superior's mind almost as much as the screws that had begun to dig into her clenched palm.

Mother jerked back. "I-I trust your work." She said as she transferred the screws into her other hand and wiped the bright red blood onto her shaking thigh.

"So, what are the hooks for then?"

Mother handed one of the last screws to Lidwina before the impure thoughts returned. The only choice besides prurience was confession.

"Restraint. Oftentimes, we must...to subdue our innermost thoughts. Flesh can only be torn so much. Sometimes, sitting alone in total darkness, just you and your sins, where the only parts you can move are your fingers, toes, and eyelids, is the closest to heaven I've ever felt. Once you lose feeling in all your extremities, you're just floating in your body. I can hear celestial voices telling me my sins have been forgiven."

Mother Superior's eyes welled up; she turned away after handing the last screw to Lidwina who furrowed her brow and secured it.

"What sins require something as extreme as that?"

"Big ones."

She Loves Me Knot
Chapter 7

Sister Tatianna went wide-eyed as she noticed Ophelia sneak past the kitchen window with ninja-like precision. She quickly grabbed the hanging apron from the pantry and nonchalantly strolled to the back door toward the garden. Tatianna thrust the apron out of the door just as footsteps came up behind her. Sister Veronica let out an exasperated sigh as Ophelia stepped into the small back hall, loosely wearing the apron. "There you are, O; I was beginning to wonder..." Sister Veronica said softly, motioning Tatianna to get back to the kitchen.

Ophelia's face was flush. She was slightly out of breath and holding up the empty egg basket to show Veronica, too tired to grab her pad. Sister Veronica raised an eyebrow and grinned.

"Ah, you were just refilling the *eggs*."

Sister Ophelia nodded, her breath steadying.

"Always so resourceful. That's my O." Sister Veronica deeply exhaled. "Leave your boots outside to dry. Don't want you to track mud in when you return." She smiled and shook her head as she returned to their supper.

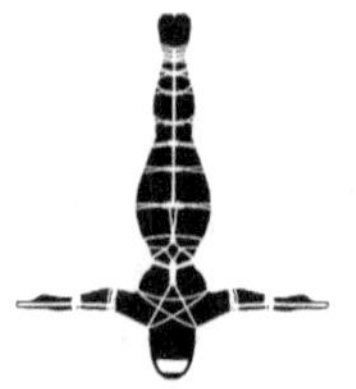

Lidwina wanted to shower off the day's toil before dinner. She swallowed the last of her apple before throwing the core in the waste bin. Sister Veronica would scold her for ruining her appetite, but her sweet tooth could not be satisfied. She peeled her sweaty work clothes off her slick but aching hips and alleyooped them into the ancient washing machine. They shaggily fell to the bottom of the washbasin as she ran hot water for her odd standing bath. She scrubbed away the day's dirt and refilled the washing pitcher, noticing the hot water running out already. Her mind barely focused on the tantalizing suds drifting down her neglected areolae, too busy piecing together her plumbing knowledge. Her eyes traced the water pipes,

No shut-off valve. Could it be the water heater?

She quickly threw on a towel without a thought to wash her legs. *Bless her heart.* With her damp towel barely held in place and doing its damndest to contain her tig ol' bitties, she skidded with wet feet out into the hall to the stagnant communal washroom. Her eyes flashed to the three dusty shower stalls to her right. She padded over to the first and turned the stiff hot water nozzle. Water slowly trickled out of the shower head and dripped onto the dry floor. She stepped to the other two and repeated the process, noticing only cold water dribbling out of the calcified shower heads.

Definitely the water heater.

She would be able to fix that—hopefully. She turned the ancient-sounding showers off, and dripping water drifted from the middle stall. Opening the partition door again, she took note of the clogged drain. She'd have to add it to her list to tackle tomorrow. She was too hungry to focus on anything but eating right now.

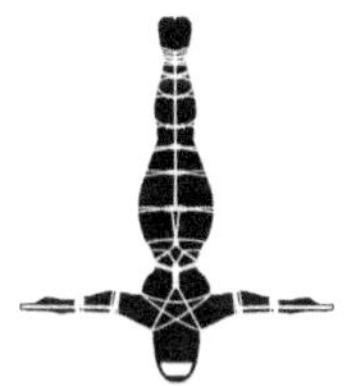

Lidwina was the last to join the long dining table, dressed again in baggy sweats with wet hair pulled up in a messy bun. The end of a productive day brought a calm over her almost as strong as her hunger. She had two helpings of Sister Veronica's quiche. Bernadette had picked the salad greens herself, but to Lidwina's dismay, she had already returned to the chapel. Lidwina's long face turned to curiosity as she watched Mother Superior clear her dishes and beckon to Veronica before she retired to her room for the evening. A few words were exchanged, and Veronica nodded in approval before the Reverend Mother joined them in their evening prayer and wished them all a good night. Lidwina carried her plate into the kitchen, pushing the door with her ass while she watched Mother Superior heading toward the basement with Sister Veronica trailing along soon after.

Part of Lidwina wanted to sneak down the ominous stairs to follow and listen in on what was being said in those whispered exchanges, but she had a bad feeling about Sister Bernadette avoiding her and shutting herself away in the chapel all day. Once Lidwina was sure the coast was clear, she hurried to the chapel entrance. The double doors parted as Lidwina let herself in. Bernadette raised her head to see who had entered but quickly went back to praying when she saw who it was.

Lidwina solemnly walked down the center aisle, feeling the eyes of Jesus on the cross looking down at them. She may not be certain what her real name was, but she somehow knew his. She fought to piece together bits of her past, yet seemed to remember those dead eyes staring down at her many times before. Familiar feelings of dread and a vague sense of danger enveloped her, juxtaposed with memories drilled into her that this was a *safe space* full of *love*.

Lidwina pushed past the feeling of her skin crawling and the irrational worry that her fingertips would ignite when she touched the weathered wooden pew and sat behind Bernadette. Once there, Lidwina's eyes were unsure where to rest. Little blond ringlets teased from below Sister Bernadette's habit. Lidwina traced the tips of her golden curls, leading to the generous polyester masking what she knew to be shapely, smooth curves. Flashes of their passionate tryst played back in her mind, causing her stomach to knot while yearning for an encore.

Lidwina was afloat in her ocean of thoughts and desires when a wave of sharp pain stabbed into her chest. That feeling of dread flooded her. Guilt. Uncertainty. Shame. Unworthiness. Regret. Each feeling, a stiletto piercing her heart until the center of her being was perforated beyond repair and hemorrhaging her dwindling life force.

Bernadette's gaze pulled her from the tortuous trance. It was no longer the dead eyes of a bleeding, hanging statue gazing at her. This time, the sapphiric oceans that were Bernadette's eyes appeared, glassy with tears. Sister Bernadette's body was turned, facing her.

"Why are you here?" Bernadette whispered, her voice quaking beneath her bravado of tranquility.

Lidwina's eyes met hers, but Bernadette looked away, masking the snub by bringing a crumpled handkerchief to her face. Lidwina knitted her eyebrows together and placed a hand on the seat, separating them.

"I came looking for you. I haven't seen you all day, and I thought... I hoped..." Their eyes met again, making Bernadette blink hard and squeeze out a tear. Hurt registered on Lidwina's face, "I just wanted to look at you again."

Bernadette sniffled and broke their gaze to glance at the closed doors behind Lidwina.

"I was compelled to speak to God... after what we did. What *I* did." She paused as if her words were burning her insides. "That can't happen again. Ever. It's not right. I shouldn't have allowed any of it to happen. It was a mistake." Bernadette stopped for a breath, her jaw quivering as she delivered the last line.

"Says who?" Lidwina choked back. "Who says it's wrong?

"Our teachings. The Bible. The church." Bernadette shut her eyes and exhaled. "It's a sin, and now we must beg for forgiveness."

"Fuck forgiveness," Lidwina spat but continued speaking to a silent, stunned Bernadette. "Fuck the church and fuck your teachings then. What good is any of it if it's wrong? What if they've been wrong this whole time? Then what?"

Bernadette's breath caught in her throat. "It's what I believe."

"It's what you were taught to believe... and for what reason?" Lidwina's face was flush with anger. "When you stop and listen to the things Mother Superior says during mass, it all sounds like it was written by men. *For* men. To help *men.* Women are only there to make babies and serve men. Is that what you truly believe?" Bernadette began to stammer, traversing the minefield that was her emotions while she tried to collect her thoughts as Lidwina continued.

"Being with you, feeling you, tasting you, the *real* you—it's the most whole I've felt since I've been here. So, I don't think it was a mistake. I think it's a mistake to deny who you truly are, what you truly want." Lidwina snorted a sniffle up her nose and relaxed her grip on the pew. "It's a mistake to lie to yourself and to believe something that wants to deny you your happiness and call it love."

Bernadette was a wash of tears on her slick, blushing face. She wiped what she could away, but as soon as she did, more flowed. Her expressions registered like she had been fatally wounded, but there was no blood spilled. She mouthed words, but no sounds left her throat. Lidwina stared at her as if with new eyes; seeing Bernadette's frightened, confused look caused her own to soften. Her words were worth their weight in gold, but she was unsure where they came from. She wanted to help Bernadette, but she didn't know how. She wanted to wrap her arms around her and whisper that everything would be ok. She wanted Bernadette and *all* the Sisters to know the truth.

Lidwina reached out her hand, hoping Bernadette would offer hers in unison. The gesture was rebuffed as Bernadette stood and moved toward the front of the church again. Lidwina's face dropped, defeated, but she pushed through the pain and composed herself. She began to walk out of the row but turned before her feet touched the center carpet.

"I'm not sorry" was all Lidwina offered before silently pivoting and leaving the chapel. Bernadette wiped the last tears from her swollen cheeks before she reached for the rosary in her pocket and stared up at that longing, mournful stare.

"Me neither."

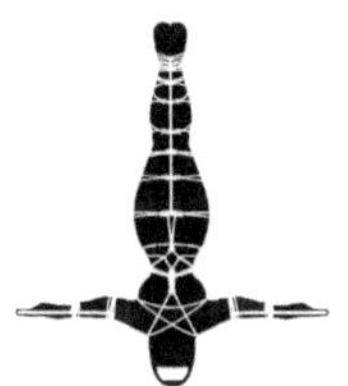

The lone lightbulb in the musty room swung in a shrinking rotation. Shadows bounced behind the few pieces of furniture in the otherwise desolate room. Mother Superior sat on the concrete floor, feeling the grit of dust particles press into her bare flesh. She pulled her heels to her stripped, sacred sacrum as she gathered the thick nylon rope being wound around her naked feet. A stone knot was placed around her left ankle and tightened to the point where it was secured but not pinching her skin. Mother Superior brought the rope ends around her pale upper thigh, repeating the tight spiral up to her knee. When she reached the apex of her bent leg, she brought the rope ends through from two angles and pulled to complete the left leg binding. Her dilated lips continued to shakily mouth her silent prayers while her skin blushed a rosy pink under the pinwheeled rope pattern.

Sister Veronica pensively paced the room, not wanting to watch the ritual until it was time to assist Mother Superior, but she could only dust off the lone table surface and fiddle with so many things in the lonely space. When she glanced back at

Mother, Veronica was relieved to see one leg done and the second limb being bound.

Sister Veronica crossed the room to the large cabinet with the lock hanging open from the lone latch. The door swung open silently until the thumping from the objects hanging behind the doors broke the silence in the room. Veronica stepped to the side so the low light could slightly illuminate the shadows inside the cabinet. The familiar smell of leather and nylon fibers greeted her nostrils. Coils of virginal white rope lay within the cabinet shelves amongst clamps, duct tape, and assorted medical supplies. Veronica's eyes darted to a large leather flogger that always seemed to detach from the aged hooks affixed to the wooden interior. She quickly snatched it up and returned it to its place among the others. Her mind went elsewhere as the thin leather tassels danced against the wood grain. Flashes of blood and sweat dripping off the clustered blackened rat tails made her twitch out of her brief mental retreat.

"I'm ready."

Sister Veronica grabbed the coil of rope and closed the cabinet. Mother Superior's knees were successfully bound together by the blinding white ropes spiderwebbing across her blushing flesh. She rocked her full hips to the side and placed one hand down to steady herself. Sister Veronica passed the rope to her forearm and offered her free hand to Mother Superior, who accepted it and pulled herself up to a kneeling position. She balanced herself and solemnly pressed her hands together, raising and offering them to Sister Veronica.

The sleek rope lassoed over Mother Superior's wrists and was knotted with enough tension to keep them bound together through the night. Sister Veronica continued the practiced rite of passing the rope over her steepled wrists until it reached the bottom of Mother Superior's forearms. The silence between the pair had become a sinister entity growing amongst their hushed breaths. Sister Veronica's eyes dropped while she worked, apprehension clouding her thoughts.

"Will you be warm enough?" she asked, a note of pleading in her tone.

"Mary will be watching over me. If I am meant to be cold, it is part of my penance." The question pulled Mother Superior from the meditative state she was beginning to enter. Searing pricks of pain attacked her knees as the concrete dimples bit into her skin like a colony of militarized fire ants.

Sister Veronica pondered for a beat, devising another dissuading question to pierce Mother's obstinate armor.

"The whole night? You know I don't sleep well once I leave you down here, Mum. I could come back after midnight to... unburden you." Sister Veronica brought the ends of the rope back up and threaded them through the first tie, shuffling around to Mother Superior's side and beginning her back knots.

"That won't be necessary, Sister Veronica. Mary welcomed the weary and burdened. She will give me rest after my body has endured what she has in store for me."

Mother Superior stared forward, slowing her breath. The sensation of her limbs being pressed against her like her own makeshift cage caused her insides to ache. Sister Veronica watched beads of sweat dot Mother Superior's shoulders as the white stripes tautly traveled south to her shoulder blades.

"Amen, Mother. I just... You know how I worry. You're all alone down here. No one would be able to hear you if you were suffering." Sister Veronica crossed the rope over Mother Superior's other side and secured it across her collarbone before threading the remainder toward her back.

"I aim to suffer. It's what she deserves."

"I'm sorry, Mother?" Sister Veronica responded, a bit distracted and seemingly lost in the trails of cord lying before her bewildered face.

"It's what I deserve." Mother Superior let out a sigh, glancing over her shoulder. "Over, Under, Over, Under. Across, beneath the center knots, and then over the shoulder, and finish the trail of knots in front."

"Ah yes, across and beneath. That's where I was off. It's been a bit of... time since I last... helped you." Sister Veronica trailed off as she wrestled with the rope ends again.

"Things have gotten worse since we last spoke."

"I don't like the sound of that one bit."

Mother Superior was floating in a pool of torment. The fine hairs prickled against her sensitive skin as her sins assumed a corporeal state. Each individual sin formed into a black serpent that crawled across her naked flesh. Their combined weight threatened to crush her. Their volume consumed her, leaving only her face above their amalgamated surface. She grimaced and shut her eyes tight, feeling the tines of a forked tongue flicker against her cheek before she blinked the sensation away. The stark awakening caused her to focus ahead with her hands secured in permanent prayer. Her eyes trailed down the ropes and ladders, encasing her supple flesh as profane pleasure washed over her.

"I am seeing visions again, haunting visions. I think...I *know* they are a sign that things need to change around here. Starting with me. I must prove my devotion and renew my bond with Mary so my multitude of sins can be forgiven."

Sister Veronica brought the shortened end of the rope around front with a frustrated look on her downcast face. She was only a year older than the Mother Superior, but their almost decadelong friendship always seemed suffocatingly maternal. Veronica only saw the innocent Sister Sarah of yore: pre-Mother Superior. She was the voice of reason, only seeing the good in everyone—especially her friend and superior. However, what she didn't know could hurt them both.

Mother Superior stared through her determined friend, tying the final knots for this blessed sacrament to the bricked-off space behind her. The dank basement held an indiscriminate amount of moisture, causing the contents of the dusty space to settle sporadically. The brick and mortar was ever so slowly degrading under these conditions. On cue, a cracked brick piece scuttled down from its cubby hole and hit the concrete floor with a thwack. The echoing reverb cracked through Mother Superior's disquieted mind like an armor-piercing bullet.

"Don't you think the punishment should fit the crime, Mum?"

The question caused Mother Superior to shudder and attempt to control her rapid breathing.

"That's what I'm afraid of."

TENDER BITS & BAD HABITS
Chapter 8

Sister Ophelia's thin, bare feet trudged up the creaky stairs, her boots in hand, held by their intertwined laces. She hoped there was still hot water to wash away the gritty dust that clung to her skin. Tatianna was silently reading in the book nook they had fashioned with an old armchair, a small table in the alcove, and a window adjacent to the library balcony. Halved bookshelves lined the balcony railings, while the taller counterparts sat sentry across from them. Ophelia didn't give a second glance to the overcrowded shelves or the nestled nun. She took a left at the junction to their rooms without disturbance. Once Tatianna had claimed the lone armchair and was enthralled in a book, she couldn't be bothered.

Emelie's euphonious voice floated through the hall as Ophelia slipped into her room to change. She loved it when Emelie did "Gracia Plena." Her dulcet tones penetrated Ophelia's soul, reverberating through her tired muscles. Her sweet voice always lifted her mood and made everything seem a little brighter. Ophelia threw her dusty clothes in her rickety hamper and put on her bathrobe.

Ophelia went next door with her hamper on her hip and towel on her shoulder, not bothering to knock, with Emelie belting the final lines of her aria. She let the door swing in and stood in Emelie's entryway smiling. Her pad thrust forward to display:

Emelie looked around her space and shook her head.
"Did you have fun today?"
Ophelia got to scribbling.

"Ew, Ophelia!" Emelie laughed while Ophelia wrote again.

"No, but you go ahead. I know you probably need it more than me."

Ophelia squinted her eyes and jokingly mouthed, *What the fuck are you trying to say?* to Emelie, who laid back on her bed laughing. Emelie said goodnight, and Ophelia gave a smiling nod and silently closed the door.

She continued back to the library corridor and passed the studious Tatianna to her left with her face buried in her book. The echo of the chapel doors closing resounded. Ophelia continued down the stairs as Lidwina entered the foyer in the low lamplight. Ophelia's eyes sparkled, and her pace quickened to catch up. They hugged, and Ophelia pantomimed for them to be quiet and pointed to the basement below. Lidwina nodded. Ophelia noted a brief glimpse of sorrow when the light moved the shadow on Lidwina's face.

Ophelia grabbed her hand and motioned toward the washrooms. They both crept down the hall and entered the communal washrooms together. Ophelia put down her basket, pulled her pad from her robe, and pointed to the showers with her other hand.

Lidwina nodded, watching the last of the water in the middle shower drain away.

"I think the water heater is busted. Shouldn't be hard to fix, but I could use some help. You up for it? Tomorrow?"

Ophelia grinned and nodded while scribbling.

"No more adventures?" Lidwina teased.

Ophelia pursed her lips and rolled her eyes in mock annoyance.

"I don't blame you. I know a free bird when I see one."

A spark between the two hung in the stagnant air. Ophelia grimaced and readjusted her robe, looking toward the laundry room. Lidwina followed her stare.

"Hopefully, by this time tomorrow, you will have hot running water to take a shower with."

Ophelia smiled and brought her hands together in prayer before the pair left the washroom and parted ways for the night.

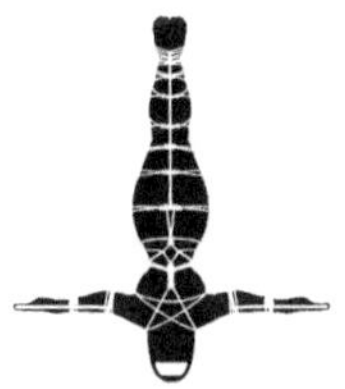

L idwina walked up the stairs, thinking deeply about what she needed for tomorrow's project. She saw Tatianna was in her own world in the quaint little library's alcove. Curiosity beat out Lidwina's plan to turn in early for the night. She paced all the bookshelves lining the walls and railings containing a spectrum of colored book spines.

Lidwina's eyes scanned each shelf for any titles she could remember or looked interesting at least: *Broken Vows*; *Once Upon a Convent*; *Venus in the Cloisters*; *Nun in the Closet*; *Immodest Acts.* Quite the extensive library for a little convent, with titles that seem like they would be relevant to her interests.

"I was wondering when you would get as bored as me," said Sister Tatianna, not taking her eyes off the page she was reading.

"Just seeing what catches my eye," Lidwina said, pulling a red book off the shelf by its spine: *The Nuns of Sant' Abrogio: The True Story of a Convent in Scandal.*

Tatianna let her eyes wander from her pages to see what Lidwina had chosen as she flipped it over in her hands.

"I read that one last year. It's insane. Some still don't believe the things the Sisters reported happening."

Lidwina's eyes darted across the synopsis on the back cover like a sponge mopping up a spill. "Sex, Poisoning, Hypocrisy? In a convent? How could that be?"

Sister Tatianna was placing a prayer card to mark her place in her book.

"Oh, I could believe it. Before we came here, our old parish was full of scandals, and the archdiocese looked the other way. That's why Sister Veronica jumped at the chance to get a transfer out here. She was hoping the fresh start would help us forget some of the things we witnessed back at St. Anthony's."

"Like what?" Lidwina asked innocently, holding the book against her chest.

Tatianna let her chestnut brown eyes unfocus from their gaze, lost in thought while she stood to ensure no one was in the foyer below them. She paused to tuck a lock of jet-black hair behind her ears and gather her thoughts.

"A lot of clergymen turn to the church because they are just as lost as the sheep they end up leading. I think a lot of people forget that." She paused to take her reading glasses off and hung the closed pair on the neck of her jumper. "Some took this calling with sincerity and integrity because they wanted to do good under God's watchful eye."

Below them, Sister Veronica breathily huffed up the basement stairs and walked back toward the office. Tatianna glanced over the railing bookshelf, watching the dark stairwell leading to the basement.

"Some of them had ulterior motives. Not everyone is here for the right reasons. Just because someone puts on a cleric's collar, a police badge, or a habit doesn't make them instantly good. Someone with a black heart is just as dangerous, no matter what uniform they wear."

Lidwina watched Sister Tatianna's body language turn defensive, her arms hugging her body. She nervously watched for movement below. "I'm sorry, Tatianna," she whispered and stepped toward her. "I didn't mean to bring up any bad memories or anything."

Tatianna looked up at the usually vivacious redhead, watching a bit of the tough veneer falling off in sheets before her. "You didn't, it's just been..."

"One hell of a day," Lidwina said as both caught each other's eyes, giggling like schoolgirls.

"You said it, not me." Tatianna smiled and looked at the time on the clock at the stairway end of the hall. "I think I'm going to finish reading in my room. Hopefully, some good sleep is all we need." She started walking toward her room before she looked back and saw Lidwina putting the book back. "Not one for horror stories before bed, huh?"

Lidwina smiled and pushed the book back in place.

"Enough is going on under this roof as it is. Let's not jinx anything."

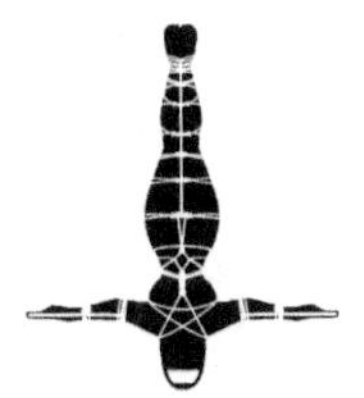

Sister Veronica grabbed the kettle off the stove and filled it under the tap. A cup of chamomile tea was the only thing getting her to sleep tonight. The clicking of the old range ceased as the ring of blue flame whooshed to life and settled under the dented metal kettle. She left the tap running so she could rinse off her hands, noting bits of rope fiber still clinging to them. Veronica couldn't help but stare out the window at the obscure shapes swaying in the darkened garden.

She dried her hands on a kitchen towel hanging nearby but winced as it rubbed against her thumb. Her nail must have snagged on the rope while she was helping the Mother Superior. A tiny ruby of blood formed on the edge of her cuticle. She instinctively placed her injured thumb in her mouth, but Veronica's mind was elsewhere. Perhaps still in the basement or out in the garden with the dancing shadows beckoning to her just beyond the thin window pane. Maybe it was trying to rationalize just when she agreed to the odd rituals at the request of the Reverend Mother.

The gurgling shriek of the aged kettle snapped her out of her mile-long stare and back to the kitchen. Veronica switched off the burner and grabbed her chipped "All the Single Ladies" nun mug from the cabinet. Her nephew had mailed it to her for her birthday a few years back. That was when they had a working car and could visit the only other church in the diocese. She wondered how big little Jeremy was now. Did he still think about her? Did anyone even know they were alive? The outside world seemed too far away from the dense forests of the valley. She remembered thinking what a great idea it had been to come out here with just her girls, God, nature, and solitude. But how much solitude could one handle before they went mad? They say, 'In space, no one can hear you scream,' but you'd be surprised at the silence that screams back at you in a valley filled with nothing but trees.

The single light left on over the sink illuminated the teabag canister as she dug around for chamomile. She fished out the last bag and hoped it made the list for the next drop-off. She never realized how much she looked forward to the first of the month, to be reminded that civilization still existed outside the convent walls. To hear another person's voice was a godsend. A little break from her bratty bunch was helping to keep her sane.

Though she fought it, her eyes darted to the window again. The sound of water running in the laundry room brought a welcome feeling of companionship, reminding her that she wasn't alone to battle things that stalked in the shadows of crypt-like basements. She pulled the bobbing tea bag from her favorite mug and sniffed the last splash of milk before adding it to her tea. Smelled fine to her. She hoped it hadn't gone bad. "What doesn't kill ya–" She turned off the kitchen light and crept up to bed.

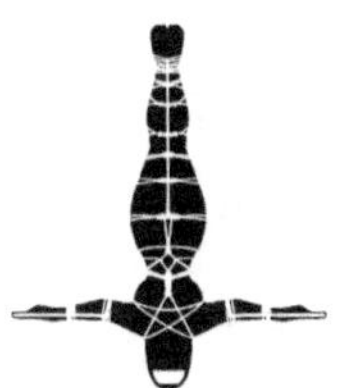

Sister Ophelia watched the last of the water rinse down the floor drain as she heard the ancient washer sputtering away. She threw her clothes in with Lidwina's, unsure which would be dirtier after the days they had. Their minuscule amount of detergent was dwindling. She tried to remember how long it had been since they had their last supply drop-off. It had to have been before Lidwina landed in their lives. Her sudden appearance had caused more than a few ripples in their pond, one of the last being that they were now feeding and clothing one more. Ophelia hoped they would be able to last until the drop-off.

She thought about staying long enough to throw their clothes in the dryer, but her aching feet could not take much more waiting around. She must have walked through ragweed because her nose would not stop itching. While wrapping the towel around her neck, she felt the telltale tickle in her nostrils. Her loud sneeze startled her, making her realize how long she had been silent. Recovering from the colossal sneeze and tying her robe, she remembered *why* she was being silenced.

It's times like this she had to remember why she was here, why she was doing this, and that this was for the greater purpose. She was up against more than just some stank ol' den mother; she was supposed to be figuring out if this was truly her calling. She turned the light off in the laundry room and listened to her ratty old slippers shuffle against the aging linoleum before she entered the foyer. The blood in her veins went cold when she turned to the darkened end of the hall. They always kept a light on in the kitchen. It's what made the statue of the Virgin Mary seem less ominous, but knowing what she knew now, seeing what she's seen? It wasn't helping her introspective mental check-in, that's for sure.

The dark figure of the statue made the damp hair on the back of Ophelia's neck stand on end. She wanted to brush it off but felt it was difficult to turn her back to the Virgin Mary. She knew that, rationally speaking, the statue was an inanimate object and incapable of harm, but something seemed so sinister about it. Her mind was atwitter with intrusive nightmare scenarios.

-A razor-sharp claw creeeping from behind her, slicing her jugular and spraying the walls with her warm blood.

-The feeling of helplessness as her body is lifted by some unknown entity and ripped in two, leaving shaggy, lifeless heaps behind.

- An intense heat starting at the back of her head before it envelopes her skull and leaves a cauterized clean hole to hit the linoleum between her shaking knees.

-A sweet voice that suddenly enters her mind, increasingly invading her thoughts, forcing her hand as she tears each one of her Sisters' hearts from their fractured ribs.

Ophelia blinked.

Thoughts.

Just thoughts.

Pray.

Not the Hail Mary.

She'd seen that movie.

Ophelia started to mouth the words to the Our Father and pulled the lapels of her robe tightly against her chest. Once she mustered the strength, she successfully turned and began to walk away from the momentarily menacing monument. The more distance she put between it and her, the more she felt her nerves loosen and relax.

"And deliver us from evil," she mouthed under her breath.

When she made it to the stairs to go up into the welcoming, dull light above, she was almost laughing. To be her *big* age, scared of the dark, making up vile scenarios in her head, and knowing she's in an anointed house of God. She smirked as she climbed the stairs with pep back in her step.

A booming shriek rolled up from the basement, and the sheer boisterousness almost knocked Sister Ophelia back on the last step. Her eyes went wild, trying to stabilize and control herself. Her fear turned to rage as the familiar tone echoed through the foyer again. Sister Emilie appeared at the top railing, shocked to see Ophelia.

"Penitence Room." Emilie sighed, "I had almost forgotten. It's been a–" her eyes watched the anger in Ophelia, appearing as though piping hot lava was ready to spew out of her vowed silent lips. On cue, Emilie swooped in and met her on the stairs. With one arm around her, she redirected Ophelia to come with her, doing whatever she could to dissuade her from going down there. That was the last thing any of them needed.

The swift detouring movement left Ophelia discombobulated. The rage was still simmering just below her skin, but having Emilie this close was causing it to dissipate quickly. They both shuddered at the lower, more guttural moans coming from below them. Emilie walked Ophelia to her room, humming the rest of *Gracia Plena.*

Ophelia felt calm, taxed, but calm. The urge to kill was falling, but the urge to give Mother Posterior the ass beating she needed, was rising. Not now, though, not today. She needed Emilie to put her to bed, to sleep, dream, and pretend she wasn't trapped in a convent with some dummy thicc mad woman.

Whip Me Baby One More Time
Chapter 9

Regret flooded Mother Superior the second the darkness filled the space. She knew Sister Veronica would ask if she wanted the light off to give her one last chance to change her mind. Just like she knew, as always, she would inevitably say yes. This sacrament was a punishment as much as a test to see how devoted she truly was. She would show no fear; she was put on this earth to suffer.

Every cell of her being was created to show her undying devotion to Mary. Whether she liked it or not. Like the shock to the system when diving into an icy pool, entry into this level of faith was not for the weak-minded. The ritual pulled your very soul from your body by its roots so Mary could wash it in her glory. Where she took you was only for her infinite wisdom to comprehend. Fear was always Mother Superior's initial response. The destination was always different but necessary for true enlightenment. Mother Superior feverishly waited for her shell to crack so she could brave this spiritual journey.

Her legs already ached from holding their position. The rope dug into her tender flesh as much as the sharp gravel below her. Her back was beginning to ache and spasm just trying to hold her body upright. But she knew this was the only way to reach a higher level of sanctity. It was so dark that Mother Superior couldn't tell if her eyes were open or closed. The darkness provided an ocean of ink for her to submerge herself. She knew the deeper she peered into its terrifying depths, the quicker she would be to the torrents of salvation.

The chilly air in the void drifted across her perspiring skin like the breath of the dead. Her flesh began to prickle while her insides began to ignite. Her mind's eye created a source of light, a glowing warmth that soon flooded her being to an almost unbearable heat. She surrendered control of her body, causing her to collapse onto the stone floor. The muscles below her chilled skin were roasting just below the surface. Fear invaded her like thousands of hypodermic needles, injecting her with adrenaline. She began to doubt if her body and soul could handle the torment this time. She felt her spirit pulling itself away from her limbs like interlocked Velcro, her body heaving with each pull. Every part of her wanted to howl as she was ripped from the only vessel she knew. She floated in the emptiness, the nothingness consuming her. The only thing she could do at that moment—the only thing her spirit would allow—was for her to scream as if her very soul depended on it.

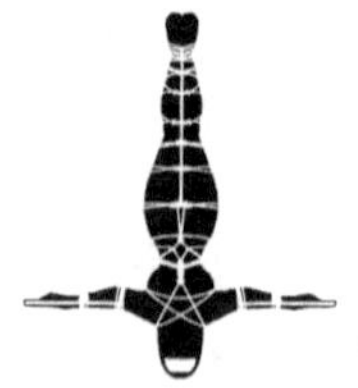

*E*ight Years Earlier:

   A beaming Sister Sarah walked up to the St. Augustine of Hippo Monastery with a suitcase and a pair of boots dangling by their laces from her fingers. The high stone columns with wrought iron fencing seemed ominous yet comforting. The opened gate entryway puzzled her, but she was sure they wouldn't have any security issues out in the middle of nowhere. The small gate call box seemed to be out of order, so she entered the property with childlike wonder. She was beyond excited to be the first nun—let alone woman—allowed in the monastery—the first woman accepted to join her fellow clergy. She was excited to begin this new chapter in her life. One that could change the ways of centuries-old traditions. She was ready to bring the Roman Catholic Church into the new millennium.

The large brick building looked like a castle of yore. Its light gray walls against the lush greens of the valley took her breath away. She saw one lone Buick parked in front, caked with dust from the same wispy winds that blew her habit to and fro as she walked up to the grand double doors. She rapped on the solid wood, hard enough to split the skin on the knuckle of her middle finger. She winced and drew it to her mouth to stop the bleeding while she waited for someone to answer. After a few more knocks and minutes passed, she walked around to the right side of the building. She hoped they were as outdoorsy as she was so she would have someone to talk with while she spent her time outside. She imagined her fellow clergy would be out back on such a lovely day as this.

Sarah felt rude knocking on the chapel doors, but tried the locked door handles first to be safe. She traversed timidly around the building, hoping someone would notice her. What seemed to be the dining room window rested at shoulder height, allowing her to peer into the vacant room. What looked like stacks of dirty dishes and silverware made her gulp down what would end up being seeds of regret. Not one to be a brooding Bathsheba, she kept it moving.

Her jaw dropped when she looked past the unkempt hedges. She saw a garden plot sprouting with weeds and potential next to a handsome grotto. She could make out a shed and several apple trees toward the back. She walked closer to the building; it looked like the fruit was almost ripe for the picking. She couldn't believe this would be her new home for the foreseeable future. It was like a fairy tale; this was all she had ever wanted. She walked up to the small door opposite the garden.

Not wanting to seem rude, she knocked again with her uninjured hand. She couldn't hear anything coming from the small hallway. There was a door at the end of the hall, but nothing seemed to be stirring beyond the screen.

"Hello! Is anyone home?" Sarah yelled out. A little louder than she intended, but she figured she might have to learn to speak up in a house full of men.

"It's Sister Sarah! From St. Killian's!"

Still no response. She sighed and scanned the yard once more before trying the storm door. Luckily, it was unlocked, but she couldn't help but feel this was wrong. The half-screened storm door slammed shut, and the startle slapped some sense into her. This was going to be her new home; this was the time to be strong and assertive. *Put your best foot forward and march in there like you own the place.* She confidently strode down the hall, looking left to an empty kitchen and dining room beyond, continuing to the door and another hallway to her left, leading to a grand foyer and more unnerving silence. The door ahead of her seemed to be an office; she let her toe sit on the threshold but turned back around once she saw it was also empty.

Sarah did a double-take when she noticed the tall statue of the Virgin Mary to her right, recessed in the wall. Her gaze wandered up the statue's profile from the daylight seeping through the kitchen window. She stepped closer to marvel at her ethereal glow from the front that she could make out in the otherwise dark hallway. It pained her to pull away from the Virgin Mary's immense beauty, but she really wanted to set her things down and get a plaster for her finger.

She continued down the shadowy corridor, using the little light from the foyer windows to lead her. She placed her suitcase and boots in the foyer near the stairs, retracing her steps to the door marked *washroom*. The pungent odors within assaulted her nostrils, reminding her of something she hadn't realized when accepting this opportunity.

A communal washroom? Every stall had a partition door, but... who killed the maid?

After Sarah hovered as if her life depended on it, washed her hands *thoroughly*, and found a band-aid, she returned to the seemingly empty monastery. Every room on the ground floor was empty, leaving only the staircase. However, the closer she got to them, the more she noticed a faint glow of light floating up from the basement stairs. She fought the feeling of her stomach knotting as she stepped closer.

I can't go down there. What if it's empty, too? Then it's just me in a creepy old basement in a deserted monastery. I've seen this movie.

Just as she was about to head upstairs instead, she heard hearty laughter. She sighed in relief and made her way down the stone steps. At least she knew there wasn't a pile of dead priests to haunt her nightmares down there. *Right?* Still unsure where all the light switches were located, she clung to the railing as the dampened stone steps felt slick under her Mary Janes. The laughter died down, but the conversation below became clearer with every step. As she made it to the last step, the bandage on her finger slipped off and fluttered to the cold stone floor. She kneeled to retrieve it when a booming voice only a room away started to speak.

"I don't see why we need a babysitter all of a sudden. Isn't the whole point of men being out in the middle of the woods to get away from women?"

"Yeah, but not the way you'd hope, James."

The group of men's voices exploded into laughter. It sounded like three or four different laughs, but it was hard to tell. Sarah nervously smiled, reminding herself that she had prepared for such crass humor in a space full of men. Priests or not, boys will be boys, though she'd always hated that saying.

"The way Monsignor made it sound, it's just a temporary thing. If she's a good fit, stays out of our way, and doesn't disrupt much, then we won't have any problems. Hopefully, they send us a quiet little church mouse."

"She won't last long with all the black mold down here. I can feel that shit coating my tongue every time I take a breath."

"Watch the fucking cussing too, Phillip. Especially after she shows up. For all we know, she could be a plant, here to report back on us."

A new voice snickered, then said, "Enough with the fucking conspiracy theories, Thomas. Just spray in the fucking corners already so we can be done down here."

"I don't see what you're all so bent out of shape about. This place could use a woman's touch, if you ask me. Someone needs to start cleaning up after you pigs. About time someone else does it."

"I wouldn't mind some eye candy anyways; I'm gettin' tired of just looking at you shaved apes day in and out."

The group broke out in raucous jeers as Sister Sarah second-guessed all the choices she'd made up to this point. Her fist balled up around her dirty bandage. She couldn't be bothered with her split knuckle opening all over again.

"And cook too! I'm tired of God awful rice and beans every other day."

The group offered affirmative grunts, sounding closer to the door in the elongated hallway. Sarah panicked and stood, unsure what to do with herself. She tried to smooth the wrinkles from her tunic and the emotions from her face.

"And what about our game room? Do we have to give that up too just because the diocese sent a spy?" The voice became louder as it entered the hallway. A short, dark man with salt-and-pepper hair crossed into the darkened room toward the end and flicked on the lights.

Sarah took an instinctive step back onto the last stair and braced herself, peering around for a place to hide.

"Nothing is going to change around here, boys. All they did was send us someone to clean up around here—the place and the books. That's all. If Thomas got off his fat ass and filled out the fucking paperwork and kept up with the books better, this probably wouldn't even be happening." The deep voice belonged to an Italian-looking man with olive skin and thick glasses entering the hallway.

"Hey, fuck you guys, it's not my fault they sent the bitch." The nasal voice of the pale, balding man stopped short as he exited the hallway and came face to face with Sister Sarah.

She pulled her foot back from the step and gritted her teeth into a smile.

"Hell-"

"Well, that's done and just in the nick of time, cuz I've got to shit like nobody's busine-" Baldy blindly smacked behind him, hitting the greasy-looking forty-year-old virgin, so he would stop talking. Three sets of leering eyes were now trained on Sister Sarah, gulping for air in a frozen panic. The two in the doorway were pushed out into the hall by a tubby, rosy-cheeked man with a sweat-dotted forehead. Sister Sarah took a deep breath and worked up the nerve to try again.

"Hello. I'm Sister Sar-"

The spectacled Italian brushed past her and silently walked up the steps, pulling the wind from her lungs and her sails. The pasty bald priest followed the first up the stairs, after staring intently at Sister Sarah's chest and ultimately pulling himself away unsatisfied due to the thick cover from her habit. The hefty priest looked toward the ground, then back into the room.

"C'mon, Andrew," he said before he got a closer look at Sister Sarah's face and grimaced as he walked past her. Sister Sarah swallowed the sudden urge to vomit, taking tiny breaths through her pursed lips, and the few steps to the dimly lit room. A small man with dirty blond hair was kicking a box into the corner, caught off guard by Sarah standing in the doorway.

Her eyes met his. She internally pleaded for a shred of kindness, some form of humanity. Andrew walked up to her, pausing before he stuttered, "I-I-I-I'm Andrew. Y-y-your, this... this is your room," he said. Sister Sarah replied with what she hoped was a smile or anything other than the scowl she felt the minute she went down those stone steps.

"ANDREW!" A shout came thundering from the top of the basement stairs, making the antsy priest go even more wild-eyed. Sister Sarah looked past his jittery shoulders at the dismal space before he finally made it clear she was blocking his path. She silently stepped aside, allowing his escape before he uttered "Welcome" and skittered past.

Her eyes traced the perimeter of the dank basement-turned-construction zone. Half of the room housed palettes of building materials covered in dust-caked tarps. The back wall was hung low from the ceiling; the entire length of the brick wall went from her hip up. Distant drips echoed from behind the dark space. Sarah begrudgingly crouched near it, resting her hand on the dip in the brick for balance to look inside; it was just a typical, musty crawlspace with a cloudy window shining dull daylight through aged grime. The low opening wall was half-filled with a new brick wall, apparently abandoned for some time, judging by the dust accumulation on the tarps.

Strangely stained ropes tied into knots hung from the upper brick of the half wall in uneven patterns. The brick itself had seen better days. Plaster was chipped off in places, and visible water stains dripped down to the stained concrete floor. The musty smell was still present, even with the drying puddles of bleach in the corners. Beneath it was the malodorous accumulation of stale sweat, rampant mildew, and tinny rust. A dusty old wardrobe sat against one wall. If it weren't for the piece of oversized wooden furniture, she would have described it as a prison cell. Minus the toilet.

Ugh, the toilet, she thought as she heard a few thuds and quiet retreating steps on stone. She popped her head out of the room and was greeted with her suitcase and boots thrown on the floor haphazardly.

And I didn't even have to tip them—how luxurious.

Sarah stared out of *her* door to the open storage space, taking up the rest of the dusty basement. She spied with her little eye something that looked like a wheeled cot among a hodgepodge of hand-me-down furniture. The residual frustration of this accumulating bind gave her the gusto to rifle through the miscellanea. She dragged her rummagings into the meager space, determined to flourish like a rose emerging from her concrete cell.

She opened her modest-sized suitcase on the lumpy mattress as it aired out. The wardrobe was surprisingly empty and critter-free. She only owned one other habit, so in the wardrobe it went, along with her favorite sweater from her time in South Belfast. Her pajamas and unmentionables went in the thin drawer below.

The only item left in her luggage was her gnarled, leather Bible with the title almost illegible. It had seen as many shores as she had and the mileage to prove it. A few tattered pages didn't bother her; she knew those passages by heart anyway. She pulled out the sacred book and smelled the leather, which still calmed her now. Tufts of manila bookmarks jutted out of the top of its pages like sprouted off-white tongues. They were her own special bookmarks she collected from her time abroad. Each one was filled with heirloom seeds she vowed to plant once she found a new home, someplace she could lay down her roots, long enough to let her collection do the same.

She sighed and cautiously sat down on the flimsy excuse for a mattress. She had worn sanitary pads thicker than this thing, but she was determined to make this work. She looked at what might be her humble abode for an undetermined amount of time. Unsure what the future held, but certain she could endure what was in store for her. How bad could a bunch of priests really be?

On cue, an uproar of laughter could be heard upstairs. She flinched as the heavy footsteps above caused the single light bulb

in her room to flicker. She stared at the brick wall in front of her
while she grasped her Bible tightly and did the only thing she
could: pray.

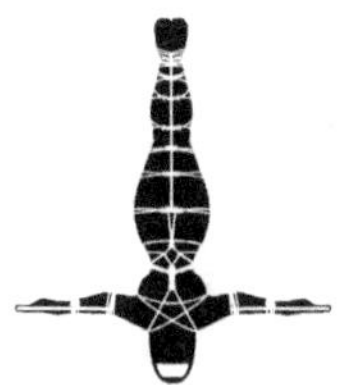

The following weeks blended like a montage of micro-ag-
gressions and passive-aggressive mental warfare: Catholic
tools of the trade. She spent the better part of her day in her *cell*.
To make lemonade in a house full of tart old lemons, she vowed to
do twenty squats every time the priests vexed her. This left her
with only two options: grow thicker skin or a thicker backside.

The priests never allowed the nun, party of one, to break bread
with them, which didn't bother her; she'd been to a farm before.
If you've seen one bovine stare, you've seen them all. They'd leave
her no scraps, and the only thing designated for her in the pantry
was dry oatmeal and plenty of apples. Imagine the look on their
sour pusses if they ever found out she actually *liked* oatmeal
and applesauce. She chose to shower at night while the rest of
the priests slept. It became a game to her—to acquiesce every
indignity and deflect every arrow they would launch her way.
They prayed for her departure. She savored their empty prayers.

She loved talking to God but found herself talking to the rav-
ishing statue of the Virgin Mary more often than not. More than
a few times, Sarah lost track of time praying to the statuesque
beauty, getting lost in her steely eyes until she'd have to hide
from incoming footsteps in the middle of the night. Talking

to the sculpture was her true salvation, yet it seemed to be unleashing some hidden demons. This caused her to pray more, seeking stronger forms of penitence and developing quite the toxic cycle.

She spent the rest of her time outside, enjoying the scenery within the property, quelling her curiosity the closer she got to the gates, wondering what existed beyond them, afraid she would return to locked doors. If one of the priests ventured out to get some air or have a smoke, they wouldn't acknowledge her existence. Eventually, she found herself in the unoccupied space just past the shed. She claimed it as her own and planned to make it official. Once the cold winter passed, she eagerly planted her seeds and began to cultivate her garden. Her *lady garden,* as she liked to call it, unbothered by the laughs of her dim-witted constituents. Woe to those who rely on foolish talk or crude joking!

Sister DeRosa watched her yellow jasmine prosper, her blood-root grow, and her henbane propagate throughout her little corner of the world. All the while, parts of her were growing and shrinking as well. The priests never let up, and she was a woman of her word. Her flowing habit was, indeed, beginning to hug her impressive hindquarters that jutted out like a window unit air conditioner. The priests seemed to notice, some more than others. Whether they were impressed or not, they began to stay out of her way. Before she knew it, a year had already passed. Her relationship with the Virgin Mary had grown exponentially, as had her hamstrings. The priests' contempt had simmered, but something still bubbled below the surface. They began to include her in prayer. They *allowed* her to take over most of the office work, morphing into stammering babies when asked simple questions regarding the books. Whether they wanted to admit it or not, they needed her around. They finally realized she wasn't going anywhere, so they came to terms with it. This wasn't a competition... but if it was...

More time passed, as it does. Things stayed the same, the contradiction of living together in solitude. Individually, the men weren't so off-putting. They discussed the strict order of the Cistercians she was ordained in, which seemed to elicit a quiet-but-momentary respect for her. It sparked a hushed conversation between Sister Sarah and Father Andrew, who explained that her room used to be what the flagellants had named a *Penitence Chamber*. He seemed haunted by things he'd read in books left by their previous brothers in Christ. When she inquired more, he shooed her away but let it slide that he knew Thomas didn't throw out the books. It was just up to her to find them.

It was the days toward the end of the week when the men convened in the refectory. That was when they returned to feral beasts. Whether it was dipping into their wine stash or pack mentality, those days she avoided them like the plague. Choosing to toil in the garden or pray for forgiveness in her pitch-black room while she tuned them all out instead.

It wasn't until one fateful night when she was discovered returning one of the Flagellants' books to the office library that unearthed some harsh realities for her. At first, the group acted rowdy as usual but calmed when they noted her presence.

"Sarah! Come in here, Sarah! We were just talking about you."

The men snickered as she approached the grand table, her eyes noting the darkness beyond the windows. Phillip nudged a chair in her direction, which she accepted with slight hesitation.

"We have a bet, ok?" Thomas's eyes glazed over as he grinned back at the other priests. "Were you pure when you took your vows?" The men all broke out in laughter. The stare Sarah gave Thomas was strong enough to turn him to stone, but no such luck. She paused to weigh her options as the men quieted down.

"I was as pure as you were when you took your vows, Father Thomas," she said to a stunned room that exploded into a cacophony of animal howls.

Father Thomas looked annoyed, laughing it off before he fired back with, "Fucking Dyke." Sarah hesitated for a split second before she grinned in Thomas's face. The priests bellowed out a collective "ooooh!"

"Is that the best you've got?" she asked, feeling unshakeable. The man-children chided and provoked them both to continue.

"Careful, Thomas, she might crush your head between those thunder thighs." Peter weaseled into the conversation. The boys laughed. Sarah winced in disgust but was determined to have the last word in this sanctified showdown.

Thomas fired back. "C'mon. We know the Army cranks out more clam diggers than the East Coast. Killing men is all those lesbians want to do!" A few chuckles came back, and Thomas appeared satisfied.

"I was an army medic, you jackass. Something you'll be happy about when one of you inevitably has a heart attack." The room sat stunned; even Sarah was shocked at what had dropped off her tongue so easily, but Thomas was not about to look bad in front of the other priests.

"Who leaves the Army and becomes a nun? A Dyke. Now, what do you have to show for yourself? Drying up in your moldy old room all alone? You were better off back in the army with all your little girlfriends."

More immature laughs cackled, the last of the wine topping off all their filthy glass mugs as they enjoyed the live entertainment.

"Do you always talk this way to women, Father Thomas? Or just one that intimidates you? I might be below you now, but not for long."

Sarah was so impressed with herself. Finally showing these poor excuses for men who they were *fu...er-pardon* fencing with. The men volleyed their heads to Thomas, who downed the last of his wine with a smile as he swallowed.

"Not long for what? This isn't the army, *Sister*; we will always outrank you in the church. What? Are you going to find a convent to dyke it up in? Become a Mother Superior? That's your master plan?"

"I can make a change. Where does it say a woman can't become a priest?" Sarah said, annoyed at the shake in her response.

The hyenas cackled louder than they had the whole night. The walls shook with their laughter. Unease pulled at Sarah's gut.

"In the fucking Bible." Thomas piped up, between laughs. "What part of God's likeness did you miss? Do you need them to spell it out for you?" The group continued to laugh.

"No bitches!" he yelled out between drunken laughs. The rest joined in, chanting NO BITCHES. Each refrain was a spike driving into Sarah's brain until she angrily rose from the table.

At the same time, Father Peter wobbly stood, spraying a stream of deep red vomit across the floor and half of Sister Sarah's tunic. She pulled away, masking her anger in revulsion as Peter hightailed it to the washroom. She waited for lulls in the laughter to interject. She wanted to fire back some kind of rebuttal, some response that would shut them up for once. In her stupefaction, she realized she had none. She could insult their drunken foolery, their lack of toilet aim, even their horrifying body hygiene. What she couldn't insult was the fact that they were right. These were seasoned priests, *over*-seasoned priests.

If they thought this way, what if they all thought that? Was she the fool here all along?

Peter returned and plopped down in his seat, placing his head in his hands. She flicked the chunks of vomit off herself and stared at them one last time before she retired for the night. She wanted to remember this moment, to remember their faces.

Her slow stride scraped on the stone steps, and she wore a look of dejected contemplation. She entered her room, not bothering to flick her light switch on before she shut her door. The laughter above her didn't seem to be dying down, adding insult to her collection of mental injuries. She stripped off her soiled habit and knelt in tears on the rough concrete. Each bit of gravel bore into her knees as she prayed. The sensation helped drown out the noise upstairs and in her head. She lost count of how many Our Fathers she had recited before she blinked a new idea into fruition. The Lord simply wasn't hearing her prayers. Maybe he's never even heard her voice before. Was she worthy enough to have his ear? In the pitch black, a divine force led her hand to the segments of knotted rope hanging from the wall.

Their purpose registered to her as she gripped the weathered handle and felt the gnarled ends graze her bare legs. It was as if some supreme presence was guiding her, telling her to take that anger, that sadness, that sin; offer it up to a higher power; and suffer as she did. It wanted to join in her suffering and watch the sin leave her body in the form of her blood, each lash against her skin, a trickle of her life force offered up to a now attentive Savior.

That night was the first night of Sarah's life that she felt truly heard. Having her heart ripped in two and her delicate flesh parted, she finally breathed for the first time. Her body wept so she would no longer have to. Pain was the answer. Pain was her salvation. Pain was the only thing that was going to make a change. It was the only way for her to right the wrongs in her life, right what was wrong in this monastery, and right what was wrong in this world. Blood was the key. Her new vows were written in thick incarnadine ink. The more she offered, the more she would be heard. She had so much to ask for, but would she have enough to give?

An Eye For An Eye, A Tooth For A Tooth
Chapter 10

Eerie silence permeated the convent walls as Sister Veronica shuffled down the basement stairs. She tried to hide her wrecked nerves, but the quaking water glass in her hand was telling on her. The single weak sconce down the hall barely lit her path to the Penitence Room. The key ring jangled against the worn wooden door as she unlocked it, praying Mother Superior was still alive. She paused for half a breath before pulling the light chain. The sight of the flinching pile in the center of the room caused a bubble to lodge in her throat. The low-hanging light circled at a snail's pace, giving the bare flesh below it a sickly pale glow. Sister Veronica hustled toward her downed Superior, trying to remember what to unknot first. During the night, Mother Superior dropped from her kneeling prayer position and switched to lying on her side.

The feeling of a warm hand on her back caused Mother Superior to take in a deep inhale and come back to the room. She blinked her eyes open as she felt Sister Veronica pulling at her bindings. The feeling of her blood circulating to her limbs was not one of delight. As life flowed back into them, it felt like thousands of needles stabbing at her skin. She tried to control her breathing, but the urge to break free was screaming in her head.

"Let's roll you onto your front," Sister Veronica said while speedily pulling and winding the spool of rope. She winced as she saw the indentation and swollen patches of skin from where the rope had dug into Mother Superior's back. "Ok, now on your back," she said gently, rolling her still nonverbal friend by her shoulders. Mother Superior appeared entranced, staring up at the ceiling as Sister Veronica began to pull at her clasped hand knots. Once those were free, she held both of her hands. "We are going to sit up now, ok?"

Sister Veronica felt like she was talking to a toddler. A light was on in the attic, but no one was home. She knew Mother Superior was not a morning person, and it usually took her a few moments to come back after her more extreme rituals. She pulled Mother Superior up to a sitting position so she could unwind the last loops around her shoulders. Life began to register in her eyes again as Veronica fully removed the last rope from her upper body. Sister Veronica returned the length of nylon to the hook in the cabinet. Mother Superior began to roll her shoulders in place and clench and unclench her fists to get more circulation.

"I was starting to get worried," Sister Veronica said, resting near her feet and pulling at ropes. Mother Superior groggily waved her off, signaling she would do this part. In just a few pulls, she slipped her legs out of the still-knotted bunches. Sister Veronica took the initiative to offer her a glass of water and gathered the rope before returning it to the cabinet.

Mother Superior cleared her throat and handed the glass back to Veronica before she massaged her wrists.

"I think I'd like some quiet reflection time—alone—for a bit, if you don't mind, Veronica."

"As you wish, Mum. Am I to lead the prayer this morning?"

"Yes, pick up where we left off. Ezekiel 23:18-21"

"Would you like me to leave your breakfast out?" Sister Veronica implored, hoping to entice her to eat while she fetched the Mother Superior's vestments. She handed the habit, swaying below the hanger, to Mother Superior, who still kneeled on the stone floor.

"No, thank you, Sister. I'm not the least bit hungry."

Sister Veronica nodded and made her way to the door, worry written across her face as she looked back to see her staring contemplatively into the abyss. Veronica left Mother Superior's keys on the small table and exited the room. Mother Superior's eyes flinched at the sound of the door closing before they drifted to the brick wall. She shut her eyes tight, allowing the silence to bring her back to her place of quiet prayer, clenching the fiery red rosary necklace in her hands, gripping each bead tight enough for it to burst at any second. Just as she finished her fourth Hail Mary, a scraping sound sliced through her focus. Clawing was coming from the wall. Certain she was hallucinating, that she was still restrained and having paracusia, she forced her eyes open. The second she did, the scrapes ceased.

She blinked, waiting for her eyes to focus again in the poorly lit space. The room was the same, just the wardrobe and the brick wall. Before she had time to assess the source, the cacophony of nails on stone returned. Five pairs of claws were shredding the inside of her skull as they grew louder and louder in the room. A cold realization swept across her face. The sound was not coming from the brick wall—not the bare brick wall—but from beyond the wall, just as she feared most.

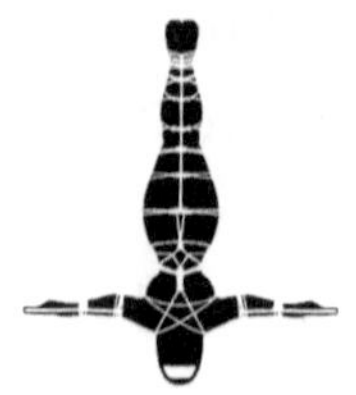

"You ready?" Lidwina said, leaning against Ophelia's door frame. Ophelia held up her pointer finger and mouthed *one minute* while she secured her habit and snatched up her dwindling notepad. Lidwina billowed the thin t-shirt from her slick skin repeatedly, trying to get some air to circulate.

"I hope we can get those showers up and running. Even though I'm sure, after today, I won't mind taking a cold shower," Lidwina said as Sister Ophelia rolled her eyes and her sleeves up in agreement.

They headed down to assess the washroom, entering the communal space after they gathered the meager tools from the garden shed. Sister Ophelia helped Lidwina mix plastic bags filled with vinegar and baking soda to tie onto the shower-heads. Knowing the longer they sat in the chemicals, the more the cruddy calcium would dissolve away. Ophelia tried to tie one of the bags on but couldn't manage due to her diminutive stature, splashing some of the liquid on herself. Lidwina tried not to laugh, taking over while Ophelia elected to scrub down the shower stalls instead.

While Ophelia was busy with scrub duty, Lidwina headed to the basement. She wanted to see if the water heater was just a pilot light issue. She prayed there was an easy solution. Once she made it through the piles of miscellaneous storage, she found the water heaters. The one on the left felt cold to the touch, so she hoped it was a case of the gas line or thermostat needing to be reset and not a whole new starter. She cleared the area and begrudgingly lowered herself to the floor. After opening the pilot light door and not seeing a flame, Lidwina pressed the reset button and waited. She heard the angelic noise of a pilot light starter clicking and whooshing to life and ensured the water heater dials were set to the middle for the best and safest temperature.

Lidwina was dusting herself off and walking out into the hallway when she heard what sounded like sobbing from the Penitence Room. She paused with her hand against a plastered wall, her eyes tracing the floor as she listened again. After a beat of silence, she decided to make a break for the stairs when she heard the Penitence Room door unlock. Lidwina nimbly ducked back into the storage area, hearing the fluttering fabric of Mother Superior's massive folds glide toward the stairs before doubling back to lock the door. The keys jangled and went back into the fabric before Mother Superior's feet clattered up the stairs and faded away. Lidwina shifted her weight a little, almost causing a column of boxes to topple. She caught them, but her foot slipped against the gravelly floor, and she froze in place, holding her breath, as she heard Mother Superior pause at the top of the stairs.

Lidwina pinched her eyes shut, arguing with herself about why she was even sneaking around. She wasn't doing anything wrong. *Who knew Catholic guilt was contagious?* She kept a firm grip on the box as Mother Superior turned back and headed upstairs to her office. After Lidwina was sure the coast was clear, she did her best to balance the boxes again, ultimately placing the uneven top box on the ground where it was safe.

As she brought it down and tried to find another place for it, she couldn't help but notice its contents were mostly framed pictures and some paperbacks. Curious, well, *nosey,* she reasoned that maybe the paperbacks were interesting and could make it into their little communal library on the balcony. Unfortunately, they ended up being bible companions, which they had enough of. The framed pictures, though, were what she really wanted to see.

She knelt on the floor, her screwdriver in hand and the flashlight clenched between her teeth. The first three photos were dusty; the frames seemed weak, and some of the glass cracked. Nothing interesting, no pictures of Mother Superior in her heyday to Lidwina's dismay. She strained to see who was in the photos between the shattered glass and the low light of the flashlight. It just seemed to be a group of priests at some kind of graduation. None included Mother Superior, though, for some reason. The fourth photo was of all of the priests in Mother Superior's office, looking older. The priest sitting at her desk was smiling and shaking hands with some pope-looking guy.

Lidwina's eyes darted to the bright red rosary necklace on the seated priest's neck. As she squinted to look closer, the flashlight came free of her jaw and smacked the cheap glass of the frame. A clear spider web bloomed instantly from the hit, centering on the priest's rosary. The air turned cold, and a groan like the house settling resounded. Lidwina prayed it was the water heater. An uneasy feeling in her stomach made her place the photo frames back and close the box as well as she could. She grabbed her tools and bolted out of the space, darting past the Penitence Room and up the stairs two at a time, more eager to join Sister Ophelia than she had ever been.

She burst into the washroom door, startling Ophelia, who screamed silently. Her face looked so much like the famous Munch painting; Lidwina couldn't help but laugh.

Ophelia collected herself and fake-choked her friend, a wide smile on her face that spread to Lidwina.

"I think we're back in business. Just have to wait for it to heat up; then we can see if all it needed was a reset," Lidwina choked out while laughing and forgetting about the basement incident.

Ophelia heaved a huge sigh of relief and went back to wiping down the insides of the showerstalls.

"How long were you guys without hot water in here?" Lidwina asked, squishing the shower headbags before she turned to look at Ophelia. Sister Ophelia pursed her lips and thought about reaching for her pad with her wet hands. Instead, she shook her head, held up two fingers toward Lidwina, and mouthed, *"long."*

Lidwina snickered, "At least you guys had the makeshift tub, and you made do."

Sister Ophelia nodded and exited the shower area to wash her hands. Lidwina followed her with her eyes in case she had something else to *say*. With her back to her, Lidwina couldn't help but trace Sister Ophelia's small but mighty frame. The curve of her hips leading to a narrow waist, up to a solid upper body and strong forearms, told her that Ophelia was hiding a tight little body under those cumbersome vestments.

The water in the sink shut off, snapping Lidwina out of her lustful gaze. Though her shirt still clung to her overheating body, Lidwina's nipples jutted out from the damp white fabric like snowcapped mountain peaks. A voice in her head that she didn't recognize whispered *All work and no play makes P a dull girl.* Who was P? Is she...? Ophelia's snapping fingers before Lidwina's eyes pulled her back. Lidwina's fleeting thoughts washed away like water down the drain.

"Sorry, I was just... I thought... I was just thinking about what else we have to do," Lidwina said. She looked defeated, her blank eyes downcast as she blinked away her frustration. Ophelia gave her a concerned look but bit her "*tongue*". She instead checked her watch, showed it to Lidwina, and mouthed *one hour*. Lidwina nodded and walked back to the first shower stall.

"Don't dump the vinegar; save it for the middle drain. Might help it unclog some," Lidwina said, squishing the cloudy liquid in the bag with her hands. She untied the bag and carefully walked it to the center shower, pouring the liquid directly over the drain.

"Can you scrub the shower heads?" I'll get the rest of these," Lidwina said, moving to the first shower. Ophelia cleared her throat, scrub brush in hand, reaching to the height of the shower head. She turned to Lidwina with pursed lips and a scrunched nose and handed her the scrub brush before she crossed her arms in annoyance. Lidwina laughed, shaking her head.

"My bad," Lidwina said, still chuckling but grabbing the brush. They went back to work: pouring, scrubbing, wiping. The tangy scent floated around the stale room, but the worst of it was complete. Lidwina walked to the first stall and gave Ophelia a hopeful look as she turned the shower on. Sister Ophelia crossed her fingers and gave a nervous smile. With a look of shocked excitement, Lidwina exclaimed, "It's getting warmer!"

They gave each other a wet fist bump and tested the other shower heads; all were running smoothly and clean, but the center drain was still clogged. Lidwina sighed in annoyance.

"Can you grab me the flathead screwdriver?" Lidwina asked as her waterproof boots sloshed in the tangy water while she crouched over the drain, making her grimace as she grabbed the screwdriver from Ophelia. After she was able to get the screws out, she lifted the drain cover. Ophelia watched as a waterlogged, decomposing rat clung to the drain holes for dear life—or death. Ophelia pulled back in horror and disgust before Lidwina tugged it loose and threw the clump of wet hair and soap scum out of the shower stall. Ophelia's face said *welp*, at her mistake. Lidwina laughed until she realized she would likely be stuffing her hand in the fetid water, and she didn't want to know what else was in there.

With slight hesitation, Lidwina winced and slid her hand into the murky water. She grabbed at slimy clumps that squished between her fingers and focused on pulling and dropping the tufts she got into the plastic bags, instead of what it was. After two pulls, the water began to go down markedly, to both of their relief.

Sister Ophelia felt her stomach lurch, causing her to jerk her head away.

Lidwina jammed her fingers as deep as she could, clawing at the most debris she could grab. After some resistance and a sickening slurp, Lidwina pulled back a putrid clump of awful chunks of rotten black bits and a brownish sludge that glistened in her hand, but a white shiny nugget stuck out of the sopping monstrosity. The mass of putrescence slowly twirled in her grip as she gawked at the gleaming white eye staring back at her, growing in size before it popped out of the gelatinous buildup. The white object clinked off the wet tile, ricocheting off Lidwina's hand and bouncing back toward the drain when she realized mid-grab, "It's a tooth!"

Ophelia turned her head back, cautiously watching as Lidwina dropped the sludge ball with a dreadful slap and frantically grabbed for some invisible object. Recovering from the sound, she watched Lidwina drop closer to the drain, positioning her eye over the hole. Lidwina volleyed her head back toward Ophelia and the drain before she exclaimed, "You saw that, right?"

She dropped her head so it was within inches of the stinking fissure, glaring frustratingly into the dark abyss. Ophelia stood over her, lost in confusion.

"It was a tooth, Ophelia. I swear!" From the mental fog before to this, Lidwina felt like she was losing her mind. Was that a tooth? Was she seeing things that weren't there? Who was P? Was she getting worse? She ruminated in her thoughts as the last of the water trickled down the cleared drain before her stinging eyes.

The door to the washroom burst open, and a flustered Sister Veronica entered. "What's all this then? What seems to be the problem, dears?"

Ophelia mimed that she didn't know by shrugging her shoulders with a disbelieving look.

"We were cleaning out the drains. I saw a tooth! A real tooth! I swear I saw it," Lidwina repeated in exasperation.

Sister Veronica sidled up close to the shower and draped her arm around Lidwina, who was rising from her squatting position. She scowled at the mounds of detritus sitting on the shower floor before replying, "Calm down, dear. No one is saying they don't believe you. Maybe it *was* a tooth. That's just an odd thing to find in a drain, is all."

Lidwina nodded and stepped out of the shower, uncoupling from Sister Veronica to wash her hands with blessed warm water. She felt tears forming in her eyes, though she did her best to push them back.

"Is anyone in this convent missing a tooth? Doesn't that seem a little odd to anyone else?" It's not like-"

The sound of sensible shoes clicked across the washroom tiles, and everyone went silent. Mother Superior came to stand between them all, inspecting the showers before turning toward Lidwina.

"By all means, continue."

Lidwina rose from the sink to look Mother Superior in the eye through the mirror's hazy reflection. She noted a twinge of fear in Mother Superior's steely gaze.

"I'm not...I think I..." Lidwina cycled through her words. She wanted to choose them correctly to fight the tension filling the funky room.

"I think you've done a day's worth of work in one morning, my dear. As nimble as those fingers might be, you're always putting them to work. You have a head injury, beloved. You might be overdoing it, I fear," Mother said with her slicing tongue and warm grin.

Lidwina turned to look at Ophelia and Veronica, both begrudgingly silent for once. She turned to Mother Superior, cocking an eyebrow and awaiting her move.

"Maybe I am," she said, sighing deeply and fighting the urge to grit her teeth.

Sister Veronica's eyes darted to the showers, aching for anything to pivot to.

"Look how clean it is in here!" she exclaimed with mock glee. Mother Superior blinked and turned slowly toward the showers, keeping her eye on Lidwina until the last second of her rotation.

"My, yes, I haven't seen it this clean in quite a while. You should both be proud," she said, slightly less dryly than normal. Ophelia cut her eyes to Mother Superior and then to Lidwina.

"We fixed the water heater; everything should be good to go. That middle drain should stay unclogged now, too," Lidwina said, slowly returning to normal.

Mother Superior walked up to the middle stall and turned toward Lidwina before she turned the shower on. Water sprayed from the shower head and swirled down the drain with no resistance. Steam began to waft up from the stall, to everyone's delight.

Mother Superior beamed at the shower drain as gallons of water flooded their pipes below. "Oh, Lidwina, what ever would we do without you?"

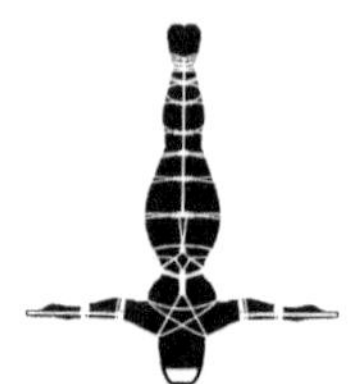

Mother Superior calmly left the communal washroom as the rest of the Sisters came to rejoice in the glory of Lidwina, their fiery red handywoman. While she also felt the thrill of a hot shower, a dark cloud loomed. She continued to the office, stopping before the Virgin Mary to offer her daily prayer. She took a deep sigh and clasped her hands together before she cast her eyes on her goddess. Still, to this day, her immaculate beauty took Mother's breath away, her purity, grace, and wide-set hips. The thought jolted her out of her meditative state, instantly penalizing her for the intrusive thought, especially while addressing Mary herself.

Starting over, she closed her eyes and focused on Mary's heart. The glowing red organ was throbbing only inches in front of her. Flames engulfed it, symbolizing the intensity of Mary's love, the same intensity Mother Superior felt for her. She felt the ostensible heat, the warm light sunning her face, and as she continued her prayer, her eyebrows began to knit together, nagging doubt flooding her mind.

Mother Mary?

Holy Mother Mary?

The silence chilled Mother Superior to the bone. She felt her body begin to tremble in fear. She knew what the silence meant, but she wished she didn't. Tears ran down her cheeks as she felt her knees buckle and fall to the floor in fervent labor. Part of Mother Superior's punishment was to remember her sins every day: the faces from her past, the hidden secrets, the web of lies. Each time they returned to her, she began her many prayers, hoping they would allow her the peace she craved. She did what she had to do and had no regrets for how things turned out. She just wished she didn't have to go to these lengths.

Her Penitence Room allowed her to be vulnerable and beg for Mary's forgiveness. Her rituals were a special offering to chip away at the boulders attached to her aching shoulders. The names of the *men* she had to punish to make it right for her Sisters were chiseled into the boulders' sides. Each night she spent in that room, *her* room, where her sins replayed, rotting and festering, removed perhaps a pebble, but this silence—the silence of her lover and the only thing in this world she had left—told her it wasn't enough. The only way she could complete this round was to go back, to relive what she had done, and watch every mistake she made: every painstaking detail, every drop of blood she spilled, every brick she laid. She was made to suffer, but the question was, was she made to endure the ultimate sacrifice?

Don't Need No Hateration, Holleration in this Rectory
Chapter 11

A sequence of angry horn blows sounded loud enough to make the nuns toiling in the garden jump in unison. The initial shock turned to whimsical delight, being reminded that life outside of this holy hen party still existed. Mother Superior huffily pulled her focus from tending to her overgrown lady garden, impeding her excited novitiates from investigating. Once they were properly stifled, she angrily proceeded to the front of the convent to see what this bedeviled brouhaha was all about. The front doors of the convent burst open as the angry nun marched up to the front gate hips-a-swaying with her pruning shears in hand.

"Finally!" An unfamiliar, deeply masculine voice said before a car door slammed.

Mother Superior caught her breath and dug in her gardening apron for her jailer ring of keys. It was indeed the church van for St. Killian's to deliver their monthly rations, that should have been there three days ago. She unlocked the gate just as a tall, dark twenty-something dropped a sealed box stamped with "OATS" in front of her. The boom and puff of road dust surrounded Mother Superior, catching her off guard. As she turned away and hacked up what she inhaled, she glared back at her girls' failing attempt to sneak silently up the driveway for a front-row seat.

"Ladies! Back inside this instant! We don't know this man," she demurely spat and continued, "He could be a rapist, or *the* killer, for all we know! Here to take advantage of defenseless women of God!"

The Sisters collectively interjected and stepped back, some watching from the vestibule. The young, tanned man hoisted a heavy box and brushed past the Mother Superior with music loudly heard through his headphones. His audacity and dark brown curls slapped her across the face, causing her to chase after him, stupefied. "Young man! I say, young man! Damn that devil's music!"

She finally caught up with the dashing intruder as he was climbing the front steps and rapped her hand on his shoulder. He annoyingly pulled an AirPod from his ear and sneered.

"Who are you? Who sent you?" she wailed in his face.

"I'm delivering groceries; what else, Sister?" He said, leaning the box up against the front door. "You gunna open the door or what?"

Mother Superior gasped in shock and tried to grab the box from him, dropping her pruning shears. Audible gasps echoed around her as he held the box in place, looking at her concerningly. She pulled the box from him, and regret instantly registered on her face.

"I'LL HAVE YOU KNOW THAT NO MAN HAS ENTERED MY RECTORY IN ALMOST A DECADE!" Mother Superior exclaimed as she dropped the box at her feet.

Just then, the door pulled open, and a cacophony of snorts could be heard as Sister Veronica pulled the box in and inhaled in awe.

"Is that little Willard?! George's boy?" She wrapped her arms around the young man while Mother Superior leaned against the outer wall, rubbing her back and hacking up a lung. They both turned to look at her apprehensively.

"Are you okay, Sister?" he asked begrudgingly.

"I'll be fine; just give me..." Mother Superior wheezed.

"She'll be fine. She's a tough ol' broad," Sister Veronica said cheekily, letting go of him finally. "Where's your father?"

His eyes dropped, as did his voice. "He had a heart attack last month. Came out of nowhere. We've been trying to pick up where he left off, but I'm still really behind." Willard replied.

Sister Veronica's eyes went glassy, and her bottom lip quivered. She hugged the boy again, sniffling in his arms. "I'm so sorry for your family's loss. He was such a good man." She pulled away from him and looked expectedly toward Mother Superior, still bent over and focusing on just surviving. "Reverend Mother?"

"Yes, very unfortunate," she stated dryly, painfully returning to a standing position. "He's in a better place. Anywhere but here." She finally stood and winced.

Before the two could acknowledge her hopefully pain-induced coldness, Lidwina stepped closer. She placed her apple in her mouth for safekeeping, grabbed the box from the floor, and carried it back to the kitchen.

Willard's eyes flashed in her direction and then blushed when he thought he'd been detected.

"I'm sorry if I disturbed anything. I didn't know if anyone was there or not. I didn't see any cars or a bell to ring."

"Oh, we don't have a car. We very much keep to ourselves out here. You and your father are all we have connecting us to the outside world," said Sister Veronica.

"That's the way we like it," added Mother Superior. "It's just us and the Lord, as it was intended." She attempted to walk past them and go inside, staring daggers at the gawking girls. "It's no disturbance. We are very appreciative of St. Killian's providing for us. It's just that usually your father delivers to our door and leaves. He had a gate key."

Willard pulled out his key ring, and Sister Veronica watched him thumb through the number of keys before she pointed out the right one.

"Now you know for next time," she said cheerfully, smiling at him and Mother Superior. She could see the agitation building on Mother Superior's face, so she knew it was time to get her inside. She reached into her apron, produced a small handful of stamped letters, and handed them to Willard.

Out of nowhere, Lidwina burst through the door, surprising them all.

"Any more in the van?" she asked with her hands on her hips, thumbs tucked around her exposed midriff from her improvised halter top, thanks to a pair of sewing shears. They made quick work of the baggy sweats she turned into work shorts that let her get as low or deep as needed.

Mother Superior didn't have the strength to ogle nor reprimand the trollop. "I'll be in my office," she offered as she slunk inside.

Willard gleamed as Lidwina raised her eyebrows, waiting for his response.

"Oh yeah, three more boxes. Want to help me?" Willard asked as he walked back to the van. He hopped in the back as Lidwina and the novitiates walked up to help. He slid one box of dry goods forward, which Emelie grabbed. Bernadette and Ophelia each grabbed insulated boxes labeled *perishable.*

"Make sure you put that stuff in the fridge; it's on ice." Ophelia nodded & motioned for him to hold on for a minute while she scribbled on her pad and handed him the slip of paper.

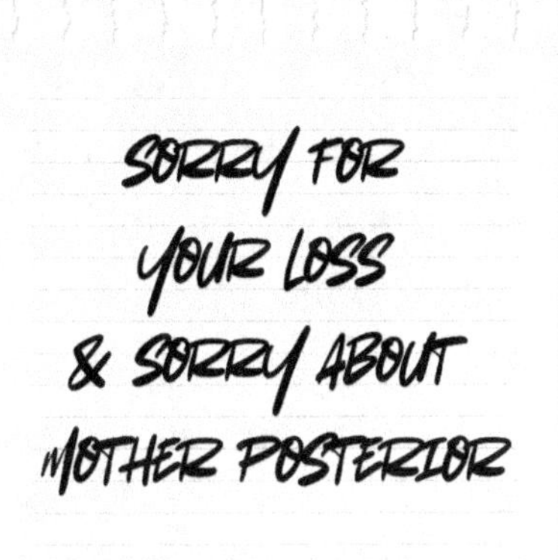

He read the note and snickered as Ophelia grabbed the box. She gave him a nod and headed back.

The last hefty box was detergent and assorted cleaning supplies. Lidwina stepped up as Willard slid it forward.

"You got it?" he asked, his eyebrows raised in fascination. Lidwina pulled it toward her with one hand and tucked it effortlessly under her arm. "Wow, I'm impressed."

Lidwina grinned, flexing her bicep, and then shielded her eyes from the sun with her hand.

"Not bad for a nun," Willard said, dropping out of the van to lean against the bumper. Lidwina chuckled, trying to see him through the sunlight.

"I'm not a nun. Not yet, at least." She paused, brain fog setting in a bit. She turned to look back at the convent from this vantage point, taking it all in. "I think they need me here. It's starting to grow on me."

"Is that it?" Sister Bernadette yelled from the stairs. "There's too many flies coming in!"

"Yeah, that's it!" Willard yelled back and waved. Bernadette closed the door, and Willard stood to close one of the van doors. "Oh wait, there's a bag of chicken feed too." He reached in the truck and pulled the medium-sized bag into his arms.

"I can grab this." Lidwina pulled it from his grasp and hoisted it onto her powerful shoulder with a smile.

"Wow. Well, it was nice to meet you...."

"Lidwina."

"Oh wow, that's pretty," Willard said. "It sounds like wiener, though."

"Okay, *Willy,*" she chuckled. "That joke is getting so old," she said, shaking her head. Lidwina started walking thru the gate before she yelled back, "Hey, next time, sneak me in some candy, will ya?"

He closed and locked the van door. "Will do, but can you wait a month?"

She laughed, "If I have to. I'll be here anyway. Hey, Twizzlers, if you can!"

Willard gave her a salute and yelled back, "I'll lock the gate!" He pulled it closed, and she nodded in his direction as she headed back. "Good luck!"

If the She-Shed is A-Rockin'
Chapter 12

Lidwina agreed to look at the convent's chicken coop after Tatiana suggested a few repairs to her and Mother Superior. Luckily, there wasn't much to it, just reattaching one of the door hinges and securing some frayed pieces of chicken wire. She was as happy to finish the job early as Delilah, Sapphira, & Jezebel were to have their coop repaired. The brood clucked in gratitude as Tatiana collected the day's eggs and Lidwina returned her tools to the garden shed.

Mother Superior strained her back a few days ago, so she had to get off her feet. No one would ever admit it, but the air felt a bit freer to breathe when Mother Superior wasn't around. The day's excitement waned as the kitchen crew busied themselves creating dinner schedules for the month and restocking the pantry. Lidwina placed the tools back where they belonged, sporadically staring at the starry sky through the perforated shed ceiling. She sighed in exhaustion; this shed would be a big job for a much later date. She enjoyed keeping herself busy. These quiet little moments helped dissipate some of the brain fog, though she was certain her memories would come back eventually. Lidwina was happy to be here, right now, at this moment, at some convent in the middle of nowhere, in a garden shed, making do with what she had.

The shed interior grew dark as a silhouette stepped into the doorway.

"Mind if I hide in here with you for a bit?" Tatiana loudly whispered with a mischievous smile drifting across her face. "Sister Veronica wants to completely reorganize the pantry, and I just want to finish my book." She let out a little laugh as Lidwina beckoned her in while she toweled off her perspiring neck and décolletage. Tatiana pulled the neck straps of her apron over her head and hung it on the hooks near the workbench.

"So, you mean if I go in, they're going to try and get me to help too?" Lidwina asked, watching Tatiana peer out the door before gently pulling it half-closed.

"Afraid so. Sister Veronica is a stickler when it comes to keeping everything organized. She won't sleep until it's done." Tatiana shook her head and let her eyes adjust to the darkened eight-by-ten shed.

"Well then, I guess we're going to have to hide out for a bit." Lidwina snickered as she strode across the creaky shed floor to lean against the empty workbench.

Tatiana looked into Lidwina's eyes, then traced her neck down to her shoulder before she cast her eyes down at her feet. Her face blushed as Lidwina returned the stare. Tatiana took a nervous step forward, leading with her hand. Lidwina's eyebrow rose playfully.

"I just wanted to..." Tatiana exhaled just above a whisper as she got close enough to Lidwina for her to smell honeysuckle on the novitiate's exposed skin. "My book...I left it in the apron pocket," she added as she looked past Lidwina. The two brushed for a half second when Lidwina slightly moved out of her way yet stayed close enough to require Tatiana to rest her arm on her shoulder. She marveled at Lidwina's fiery red mane, and the closer she got to it, the more the torrid tresses illuminated Tatiana's face like a crackling campfire. She couldn't help but inhale and take in its aroma. Expecting a smoky, spicy scent, she was pleasantly surprised by a clean, floral fragrance while mindlessly trying to dig through the hanging apron until she found what she was looking for. Unsure if it was the heat or the proximity, and despite the lack of flames in the shed, her embers began to smolder.

Even after Tatiana successfully retrieved her book, Lidwina could feel the warmth of her body and the slight hesitation she had leaving her side. It felt like an electric current was flowing through them. Both were silently eager to keep their connection as they parted, and the feeling regrettably faltered. Tatiana was visibly flustered, her cheeks turning rosy as she stepped away from Lidwina yet remained closer than she had been. Lidwina felt her insides stirring, the spark between them igniting a part of her mind she longed to have again. She urged it back like a willing vessel requiring a soul to reanimate her. She instinctively sized up the spicy little snack standing before her, and a hushed whisper softly echoed in her head. *Lick her. Taste her. Devour her. Make her yours.*

Lidwina stammered, "How's the... how's the book coming along?"

Tatiana flashed the cover of "The Nuns of Sant' Abrogio" to Lidwina again. "I decided to give your *recommendation* a try. It's... uh... a lot more scandalous than I expected."

"Oh?"

"There was a lot of sex going on behind the convent walls. No one knew but those trapped within. Everything was going great until an outsider showed up and shook everything up for them."

"And that's nonfiction?" Lidwina asked, letting her eyes trace Tatiana's shapely figure.

"That's the claim; it all happened right under the Diocese's nose too. I could believe it, although I've never witnessed anything like that."

Lidwina felt a spark, impulsively stepping closer to trace her finger against the book pressed against Tatiana.

"Not that you know of; maybe I'm the outsider in this scenario, and I come in and ruin a good thing?"

Sister Tatiana hesitated, then said plainly, "You definitely shook things up... but alas, nothing so scandalous has ever gone on behind these walls that I know of... yet."

Sister Tatiana could feel the atmospheric electricity rising. Her teachings told her to pray during these moments, and will these urges away. This was the devil whispering in her ear and trying his damnedest to get her to invite him in with a deal she couldn't refuse, but if the devil displayed his wares, would she be a willing patron? She pulled at her cowl to allow cool air to her perspiring flesh, exposing a sliver of caramel skin glistening below. Lidwina's eyes zeroed in on it like a voracious vixen needing sustenance.

It was as if the two gravitated toward each other, propelled by unseen forces beyond their control. Their lips met, locking like they needed each other to breathe. Labored inhales surfaced between their pink pouts, each second *above water* feeling like an eternity. Electricity flowed beneath their fluttering eyes like they were vividly dreaming until Lidwina felt Tatiana's hand travel up and squeeze her pert breast. Lidwina's eyes shot open as a giggle escaped her mouth before it transformed into a throaty moan. Sister Tatiana trailed her mouth down Lidwina's chin to her neck, sucking and kissing on her sweetly salty skin. Lidwina threw her head back, moaning louder. She let her hand travel up and down the novitiate's side until she had a handful of Tatiana titty in one hand and ass in the other.

Tatiana inhaled more of her female musk, letting a little laugh escape her with her exhale.

"Get up on the bench," she whispered breathily, immediately returning to glide her mouth against Lidwina's skin. Lidwina looked down at her, already wrapping her arms around her legs. She couldn't hide the smirk but felt her eyebrows hit the ceiling at Tatiana's surprising forcefulness. She pried her hands from Tatiana, raising them in an *I surrender* pose before she planted them on the bench and pulled herself up to the worn tabletop. Sister Tatiana raced to the shed door, peered out, and gently pulled it closed.

She stared back at Lidwina, with her legs spread on the workbench and her palms flat behind her. Tatiana quickly rejoined her, sliding her hands up Lidwina's tanned, smooth thighs. She rubbed her face in Lidwina's cleavage, savoring her scent again while she pulled her body closer. Lidwina sat back and enjoyed the attention. Part of her wanted to grab Tatiana's wrists—the part of her that seemed to be taking over, roaring for her to assume control. She wanted to see where this was going, how this would play out, and let Tatiana have the reins for a bit. What's she got to lose?

Tatiana ran her hands up Lidwina's stomach and under the loose fitting cut-off tee, massaging her breasts as they swayed in her face. Lidwina threw her head back again when Tatiana tweaked her nipples, rolling them between her nimble fingers. She was hot before, but the combination of the spontaneity, the chance they'd get caught, and the way Tatiana took control had her pussy throbbing against her pulled-taut cutoff shorts. The fleece sweatpants material hitched on the bench, causing the fabric to rub her already aching opening. Tatiana released her breasts, having worked Lidwina's nipples to stiff peaks. Lidwina's sweat mixed with her juices, making Tatiana salivate more as she traveled down that tight midsection to the much-anticipated elastic waist. Tatiana gently pushed her back on her elbows until she lay almost flat on the large work surfaces. Lidwina let it all happen, whatever *Babygirl* wanted to do.

Tatiana moved past the elastic waist, over Lidwina's trimmed pubes, to her overheating vulva. She nibbled at the fabric, rubbing even more against Lidwina's steaming slot. The fabric began to sop up her sweet juices, allowing Tatiana a taste until she couldn't take it anymore. She turned her head away and hastily listened for any noise outside for 1.5 seconds before she pulled Lidwina's improvised shorts and panties to the side. Before the hot air and Tatiana's breath could hit Lidwina's wet opening, Tatiana was already lapping up all her dripping juices.

She slurped and gave Lidwina wet kisses up her slippery slit. Tatiana let loose a few moans as she let their distinct lips commingle, creating a soft vibration that had Lidwina's eyes rolling back. Tatiana could feel Lidwina's pussy pulse and quiver, prompting her to clamp her mouth on her nether lips like a can opener. She sucked and lapped up every drop of sweet, milky juice before she slid her tongue past her folds and teased her for more.

Lidwina gasped and bucked her hips, grabbing the back of Tatiana's habit. Her face and tongue dove deeper inside her, lapping and tonguing at her center like she'd never felt before. Tatiana had her arms under and wrapped around Lidwina's legs now, pulling them apart and pumping them as she continued to polish her gushing hole. She didn't want to spare a drop of

Lidwina's sweet nectar, allowing herself to come up for air as she pulled her ass closer. Seeing the honey trickle down the trap to Lidwina's puckered asshole made her take a deep inhale and catch it all with her tongue. Making Lidwina scream before she bit her lip and stared above her as stars passed before her eyes. Tatiana continued to tongue her hole while her nose dug into her pussy, nuzzling against her vigilant clit. The more she licked and bucked her hips, the more her nose rubbed her clit through her hood. Lidwina had to hold back the urge to howl like a wolf baying at the moon.

Just when Lidwina was winding down and catching her breath, Tatiana stood to reposition herself between Lidwina's legs. She pulled Lidwina closer to her by the scruff of her shirt, letting her taste her own juices as they went in for a sloppy kiss. They continued to tongue-wrestle a few more moments before Tatianna pulled back and whispered into her ear, "I wanna show you something." She pulled back to look Lidwina in the eye with a smirk. "Let's see if you can feel what I'm writing."

Lidwina looked momentarily puzzled until Tatiana pulled her legs onto her shoulders and dove into her pearlescent pussy once more. Immediately, Lidwina felt Tatiana work her lips and tease her clit with the tip of her tongue. Between deep gasps, Lidwina felt Tatiana's tongue move left and right, around and down, and every way possible. All she could do to stifle the scream she wanted to let out was cover her mouth with her hands and grind her pussy against Tatiana's face as she went to town. The swirls became quicker and shallower, tracing invisible runes onto Lidwina's yearning clit. She tried to focus on the path Tatiana's tongue was making but kept losing track as waves of passion rocked through her.

After one last explosive orgasm, Lidwina felt like she was about to pass out. Tatiana came up for air, a glazed, glowing smile plastered across her face. "Well?" She leaned over Lidwina's body and rested her head on her chest. "Did you guess?"

Lidwina was still gasping for air and petting the fabric on Tatiana's sweat-soaked habit before she replied, "No idea."

Tatiana giggled and said in a whisper, "The Hail Mary."

Lidwina gasped, and they both chuckled to themselves while the holes in the shed shone down on them like little spotlights.

"Dear Lord in Heaven!" shrieked Mother Superior, followed by the slamming of the screen door. Sister Tatiana shot up like lightning, pulling Lidwina with her. She quickly stood by the shed door and extended it a few inches to see. Mother Superior was hobbling past the garden just out of sight of the door before Tatiana shot a look at Lidwina that said *Stay here.* Lidwina nodded as Tatiana palmed her book to her chest, creeping out of the shed and going the opposite way around.

Mother Superior frantically looked over the chicken coop as a startled Sister Veronica joined her. Tatiana seamlessly sidled up to the pair with her book in hand.

"Are you alright, Reverend Mother?" Sister Tatiana asked, keeping her distance.

"Didn't you hear all that noise?" Mother Superior bellowed frustratedly as she began to look under and inside the chicken coop.

"What noise?" Sister Tatiana asked innocently, shielding the light with her book.

Mother Superior's eyes went wild. "It sounded like wild animals!" Sister Veronica put her arm around her.

"Did you take *something* for your back, mum?" Sister Veronica asked with cocked eyebrows.

"This is ridic-" Mother Superior pursed her lips and turned toward them both. "I thought a fox got in the hen house!"

"It all looks fine to me, mum," Sister Veronica said, trying to get a look at Mother Superior's pupils. "Let's get you back inside; perhaps it's the pain talking." She started to will Mother back toward the door, Sister Tatiana joined them.

"Unhand me, Sister!" Mother Superior said, flailing her hands and wriggling out of her grasp. She turned to look at both of them while she smoothed her tunic.

"What's that all over your face?" Mother Superior asked a stunned Tatiana.

"I was...eating," Tatiana spat, trying to keep her cool.

"See? I told you, you'd come back to our apples eventually, though you might have to wrestle one out of Lidwina's dirty mitts to get one." The shed door swung open, and Lidwina stepped out, glistening with sweat in the hot sun.

"My word, remind me to hide my good sewing shears from Edwina Scissorhands. I think you cut more off than what's left, my child," Mother Superior said with her eyes glued to Lidwina's outfit clinging to her body.

Lidwina grinned and flashed Sister Tatiana a look before she walked past them. "It's just us girls, right?"

Sister Veronica grimaced at the level of sweat dribbling down her body.

Lidwina looked back. "I'm going to hit the showers." She waved them off, while Mother Superior's eyes stayed super glued to the moist fabric melted onto Lidwina's round ass. The Reverend Mother finally shook her head, prying her eyes off to say, "Does she want a yeast infection? Cuz that's how you get 'em."

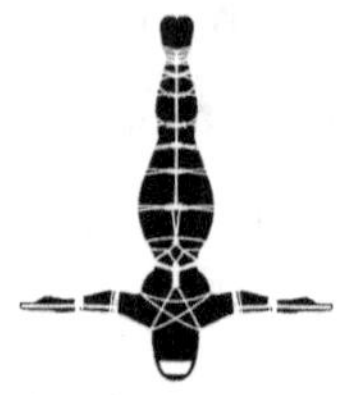

As much as Mother Superior hated to admit it, Lidwina had very much become a part of their little holy hideaway. The convent had never looked better, and the Sisters were in such high spirits. Their cheeks always seemed flushed with color whenever their patron saint of skilled hands and scant clothing was around. Mother Superior entered the kitchen just as Lidwina was rinsing off an apple she plucked from the pile on the table. Lidwina gingerly polished the apple on the curled edges of fabric of her freshly shorned T-shirt, exposing her midriff to Mother Superior's struggling eyes. Their gazes met as Lidwina trailed the juicy pomme past her diamond-cutting nipples and sunk her teeth into the tight, tart flesh. Lidwina made it a game to slurp the sweet juices before they ran down her face, to a mesmerized audience of one.

"Want a taste?" Lidwina offered, pulling the fruit from her mouth and offering it to Mother Superior. The red orb dancing across the nun's line of sight broke her trance, prompting her to answer forcefully.

"Oh no, thank you, my child." She paused to collect herself and look Lidwina in her amused eyes. "I think I've eaten more apples in the past decade than I ever have in my life. I fear the Sisters share my sentiment." Mother Superior's eyes traced a dribble of juice that ran down Lidwina's chin. "I'm glad they aren't going to waste with you around, at least."

Lidwina giggled the affirmative with her mouth full after swallowing. "I can't get enough of them. It just seems like nothing can curb my sweet tooth. Especially in these hot months."

Perspiration began to dot the surface of her freshly showered skin. She billowed her tee to get some air, exposing a bright pink slip of a nip to Mother Superior. Lidwina's reserve didn't wane, but Mother Superior's eyes widened.

"An apple a day keeps the sin away. Don't you agree, Mother?" The childlike affectation in Lidwina's voice made Mother Superior feel a shameful stirring. She quickly clenched her eyes and turned away to rest her hands on the kitchen sink below the window. She gathered herself and opened her eyes to gaze at the shed in view.

"An apple or busy fingertips, I say," Mother Superior responded finally. "What say we try to change a few of these lightbulbs?"

The Sister is Doin' It for Herself
Chapter 13

5 *years earlier*

Loud, angry voices rang out, pulling Sister Sarah from her deep prayer. Pain instantly shot up her back as the bloodied rope fell from her aching hands. She sat hunched over with her head in her arms while the last of the warm blood dripped off her scored flesh. She couldn't see its rich merlot color but could hear it trickle down the drain in the center of her Penitence Room. Through the waning pitter-patter of the viscous liquid, she could make out Father Thomas's gruff voice reprimanding someone. When no more penitence seeped from her wounds, she stood and turned on her light.

Sarah viewed the marvel of her handiwork splattered across the dingy-looking concrete floor. The tinny smell had become fragrant to her, sweet yet tangy. She fetched the small black hand towel from her wardrobe and dipped it in the water pitcher on her small bedside table. After a lull in conversation, heated words rolled across her ceiling again from the Neanderthals upstairs. She crossed the wet towel over her shoulder and passed behind her, slowly mopping up the excess blood. Each sharp sting of pain as the rough cotton rubbed her flayed flesh let a gentle moan escape her lips. Each nub and ridge stroked her wounds as if it were caressing her.

The boys...what are they still yelling about?

She opened her door a hair to listen while applying gauze to her new wounds.

"They can't do this," said the whiny Father Peter.

"You call the monsignor and tell *him* that. I'd love to see you do it," said smug ol' Father Thomas.

"I'll leave. We'll leave. We can all leave. We don't have to put up with this shit."

"They're well aware we are unhappy about the situation, Phillip. According to them, we can come and go as we please."

"Why don't we go then? Leave these bitches to fend for themselves and see how long they last before the coyotes get them. Heaven help them if they need a light bulb changed."

Sister DeRosa gritted her teeth. She couldn't reach the light-bulb on her own, and the chronically wet floor made her nervous to attempt using her table. *The jackass...*but wait...bitches? Her eyes sparkled as she got closer to the door and listened. She quickly pulled her vestments over her and re-pinned her hair.

"They're tired of our little boys club. His words, not mine. Then fucking Father Benedict's greasy ass got caught with those underage girls at Saint Killian's." Father Thomas sighed. "Now they have to shuffle all our fucking playing cards. They shipped him off to some battered women's shelter upstate, and no one's the wiser, they think."

"Oh God. Not Benedict; I went to seminary school with him. What a fucking sicko. May God have mercy on everyone at that shelter once he shows up." Father Peter sounded like he was speaking between chewing his fingers to nubs.

Sarah gently poured the pitcher of water onto the floor in little circles. Watching the sprawling stream of water awaken the dark red blood into a blooming magenta that circled the drain.

She frustratedly listened for any mention of the...*bitches*...but it got quiet, too quiet. She shook out the last drips from the upside-down pitcher to the sound of the slurping empty drain. She checked her face in the small mirror near the door. Sarah licked her thumb to get a bit of dried blood off her cheek before she decided to get some answers.

She came to the top of the stairs and passed through the dining room to return the pitcher to the kitchen. She was silent as a church mouse, listening for movement. The hall's back door burst open, and a constipated-looking (though he always looked like that) Andrew was followed by a pensive-looking Peter. Father Andrew was making his way into the kitchen until he saw Sister Sarah and froze, causing Father Peter to collide with the poor cretin.

"Goddammit, Andrew!" he yelled, "Get the fuck out of the way!" Father Andrew angrily walked through the kitchen and into the dining room. Father Peter walked toward the office. Sarah finished rinsing out the pitcher and placed it in the drying rack when she heard Thomas and Phillip enter the hall. Father Peter snapped his fingers and walked into the kitchen while Sarah dried her hands, her face deadpan. Peter angrily pointed in her direction, eyeing the two priests.

"This is because of her, isn't it? Because we didn't send her packing. I told you, we should have sent her ass screaming for the hills. Now that they know one bitch can survive, they're sending a whole flock of penguins. We can't have *shit* around here!"

Sister Sarah looked in his direction and sucked her teeth before she hung the towel on the oven door.

"A waddle," she said, sotto voce.

Peter looked at her incredulously. "Huh?"

"A group of penguins is called a waddle, you jackass."

Father Thomas and Phillip joined them in the kitchen, sniffling and wiping their noses. Father Thomas was twisting the fire-red rosary he wore around his neck closed. Sarah felt uneasy as they blocked one exit; she eyed the other. Father Andrew stood in the doorway, goofily nodding his head.

"Yeah, that's what they're called," said Father Andrew.

Father Peter's face turned red; the dick vein in his forehead threatened to rupture and spray the room in liquid indignation. "This isn't fair!" the grown man whined, like a baby with a wet nappy.

Sister DeRosa nonchalantly looked in his direction and rubbed the corner of her eye with her hand. She clenched her fist and twisted it in place while doing her best to keep a poker face.

"FUCKING..."

Father Thomas grasped the crybaby's shoulder and nudged him toward the other room. Peter shuffled his feet, a bit discombobulated.

"...BITCH!" he added as the accomplished man of God walked past her, his eyes wide with malice.

Father Thomas turned his attention to Sister Sarah.

"Did you have anything to do with this?" he asked sternly, holding a letter with the stamp from the diocese on it between his fingers.

"Do with what?" she asked, pulling the letter from his grasp more confidently than she expected. She unfolded it, and her eyes flew to a sentence at the end that read:

> *Pleased to announce that Sister Veronica Huezo
> and three novitiates will be joining St. Augustine
> of Hippo Monastery in one month!*

Sister Sarah gasped and covered her mouth in disbelief. After all this time, all her pain was finally paying off, and her prayers were being answered. Her eyes watered when Father Thomas snatched the letter back.

"So, this *is* your doing?" he said, raising his voice.

"This is as much news to me as it is to you, Thomas. I was under the impression that they were only sending me," she snapped back.

"What have you told them?" he asked, his tone still heavy and pointed.

"Told who?" Sarah fired back. "When? You're always in the office when I am, watching me like a hawk. As if you have any idea what to even do behind that desk."

"You–" he seethed and glared at her before he turned to Father Phillip, who was absent-mindedly looking in one of the cupboards. Father Thomas walked up and slammed it shut, startling him. "You fat fuck. We gotta get to fucking work. NOW!" He turned to glower at Sister Sarah. "We don't got time to bullshit."

He grabbed Phillip by his sleeve and thrust him toward the dining room table.

"FATHER JAMES, GET YOUR ASS DOWN HERE!" he yelled, causing Sarah to jump before she turned back toward the sink. She tossed some dish soap on the filthy dishes while she heard James lazily pad down the stairs to join them. This seemed like the most opportune time to wash the mountain of dishes and ensure they were *extra* clean.

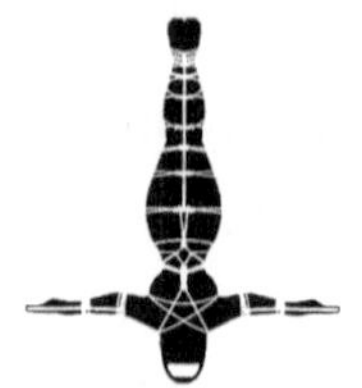

"Most of the materials we need are still down there. We may need some tools and mortar for DeRosa's room. Whatever we can do to keep this shit cheap, we gotta do," Thomas said with his palms on the table, trying to get the boys to focus.

"With what money?" Father Phillip asked flippantly.

"With whatever is left in the account, you idiot. What kind of question is that?"

"There isn't much in there, you idiot!"

Sister Sarah giggled under her breath, masking it as a sneeze as she wiped her nose with her sleeve. Father Thomas glanced over and lowered his voice. "Listen, you fucks, the only way I could get them to cut us a check was to say we were working on repairs while out here. I told them whatever they needed to hear to get them to leave us alone, and it worked now, didn't it?" he barked under his breath through a clenched jaw.

"Almost," said Father Phillip, staring over at Sister Sarah, letting his eyes trail to her holiest places.

Sarah was all ears, trying her best not to laugh at the folly of the fools she had to share a roof with. She had warned them about the water coming through the crawlspace when she first arrived. They wouldn't listen. She felt a breeze coming through the opening when the wind picked up. The rustling of the tarps covering the dusty bricks, now hung over the crawlspace opening, had scared her out of a good night's sleep more than a few times.

Sarah asked when they were going to finish the job. She even offered to help; they just laughed her off. Now they were in the shithouse, and she was here to watch the show. The thought of the monsignor showing up and discovering the truth about this place filled her with pure joy for the future. She couldn't believe things were actually going to work out. All her sacrifices really were making a difference after all.

"Phillip! Pay a-fucking-ttention. There's nothing left. We spent it all on our last trip. Whatever is left we have to use to finish that fucking basement."

"Oh, fuck me, we won't have enough to get what we need. Not in that amount of time."

"We can, and we will. We don't have a choice here, bucko. Do you know what happens when you misplace funds from the diocese? They won't hide you in a homeless shelter or orphanage. You're out on your ass."

The group got quiet.

"And you will all go down with me. Capisce?"

They shook their heads and started to rise from the table. Sarah shut the water off so she could hear everything.

"You could get that shit done fast; I know you can. All you used to do was talk about you and your old man doing jobs back in the day."

"Yeah, that was when I was still in college! You know how long that's been?"

"Well, it's time for a refresher course, 'cause we have a month to get that shit done, and I need to look at that sump pump and the boiler too. You don't have to do it perfectly. Just make it look good. That's all."

Phillip sighed. Thomas looked around at James and Andrew. "C'mon. We gotta get this shit done. Andrew, you and me will go get the shit. You got the keys?"

Andrew nodded.

"Wait, let me go with you; I need to pick up my insulin anyway."

"How much mortar do we need?" Thomas asked Phillip.

"Five bags, at least. I need to look at it again. I haven't been down there in ages. That place fucking wreaks." Sister DeRosa made an accidental sound of irritation, clearing her throat to mask it. Thomas rolled his eyes and looked over in her direction.

"DeRosa. Move your shit out of that room. We gotta fix that wall starting today."

At that moment, Sarah prayed the hardest she ever thought possible. She implored the good Lord to hold her tongue so she wouldn't say something passive-aggressive or condescending for once in her adult life. She pleaded. She fought the urge, pushed it down, and did her best to keep that bubble of disdain inside. The feeling made her dry heave, bile tickling the back of her throat. She swallowed it back, with her shoulders slumped over the sink, and turned to them.

They all waited for her rebuttal. They longed for it. They *wanted* to be reprimanded, talked down to, and made a fool. Yet, doing so would detract from the larger picture. The only thing her body allowed her to do was close her eyes and nod. It took every bit of strength she had. She turned back toward the sink. Triumphant. The only thing giving her hope was the future. The only thing she had to borrow from was her own peace. Please let this all work out, she concluded in her still-deferred prayer. This was her last hope.

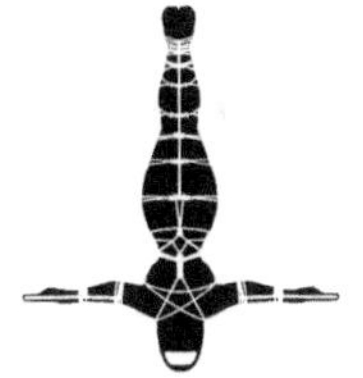

Before Sister Sarah could say *Saints Be Praised*, the boys angrily toiled away downstairs. They moved her bedroom furniture out into the hallway to make room for the work they needed to do. Not even her tinctures could get her to sleep in that drafty space. By day, Phillip and Andrew were laying brick and mortar; by night, they were drinking and bellyaching about it all. Thomas and James were having a hell of a time trying to work out how to keep the coal door secured and tight. So, Sarah cleaned the rest of the monastery, presenting it how she hoped it had been not so long ago. She would supervise the remedial priests, now and then, marveling at how neat and orderly the masonry work was.

Phillip had to go into the crawlspace to see the level of water damage and where the air was coming from. Sarah grew bored of sitting in the hallway while they worked, so she wandered into the room and watched Phillip as he worked. Andrew was there to be his gofer but kept disappearing, taking longer and longer to return. Father Thomas would come to check on the progress, but that never ended well. At one point, Sarah had to step in to keep him and Father Phillip from resorting to fisticuffs. "Look at how much space there is from the wall to the dirt, Thomas. It's at least a few feet. We need to put down water barriers at least."

"We don't have the time or the money for any of that shit, and you know that, Phillip. Maybe you should have been this articulate when you suggested we all go to Atlantic City last time. That's where half the fucking money stayed."

"The water won't stop just because we brick it off, Thomas."

"Then so be it. This is just for right now. How many times do I have to fucking tell you?"

Phillip sighed and wiped the sweat from his brow. Thomas looked into the dark space just past the wall with a flashlight. "Just keep working, and once you get done, that's all you have to do. Then you can go beat off in the washroom to your heart's content."

Phillip eyed Sister Sarah, who turned away, before he sneered at Thomas as the large man left the room.

"Can you get me some water in that red bucket? Not a lot; just fill it up to this line." Phillip showed Sarah where the bottom of the label sat on the side of the bucket. Sarah didn't argue. This was probably the nicest Phillip had ever spoken to her because he needed something, but she wasn't one to look a gift horse in the mouth. Andrew was given the electrician's duty to get the lights in the unoccupied rooms to work. As she filled the bucket in the utility sink in their laundry room, she pictured what life would be like in the next month or so. A half convent, half monastery? Maybe the other nuns would influence and tame these untamed beasts like she couldn't. Maybe they had only treated her as lesser because she was outnumbered. Once the scales were balanced, perhaps they'd finally behave. Suddenly, Sarah's stomach tightened as she turned the faucet off. *They certainly couldn't get any worse, could they?*

The smell of the mortar and the brick dust settling made Sarah nauseous. She was about to head upstairs but wanted to see how the first row of bricks was settling. She watched Phillip as he worked, meticulously matching seam to seam, slinging and slathering mortar between them, all to sandwich it all together in neat little offset rows. It was mesmerizing to Sister DeRosa. She would often be lost in thought, staring at the open chasm of the wall and the darkness that loomed beyond.

The wall in the Penitence Room was going to take about a week. It was a day's worth of work for Phillip, with Sarah helping. They were adding enough brick to fill the eight-foot-long by four-foot-tall space. Phillip laid down the base of the wall, about three bricks high from the intact wall to the corner. Then, every day, he would brick vertically until he could fit that top brick nice and snug. That was Sister Sarah's favorite part, perfectly perfect in every way. It was made to be there. Father Phillip let his conscientious student do the top bricks while he mixed more mortar. The first panel of brick was already drying and seemed strong and set.

Sarah cautiously leaned down to peer into the hollowed-out space behind the soon-to-be complete wall. Now that she had a flashlight, she could see the odd hollow space. It had originally been a coal room, complete with a coal chute. That explained the breezes she felt. Peter had replaced the chute door and sealed it to the best of his abilities, which wasn't much.

The crawlspace had a dirt floor, stained black by years of coal dust. The damp coolness smelled pungent and earthy. As she looked down the length of the dark expanse, it occurred to her why this liminal space was calling to her. Her *friend*...Angelique introduced her to some older gothic horror stories written long before their time. Angelique was a cute little blond French girl with the accent and everything, but Sarah obsessed over her taste and deceptive veneer. You'd never think that this bubbly little fairy read nightmare-inducing books and wrote some of the most beautiful but cryptic poetry she'd ever read. Sometimes, they would just lay in bed all day and read, falling asleep in each other's—

Sister Sarah sighed. The air evacuating her lungs made her chest burn. She dashed it away, trying to remember the story. *"The Cask of Amontillado" that was it.* She knew she could never forget it. In that instance, she could remember the feeling of dread she felt reading about a man buried alive in the basement of a grand castle, never to be seen or heard from again, all while his decomposing corpse—still posed in mid-shriek—clawed at the rough brick in the murky darkness. A chill ran down her spine. She couldn't fathom anyone deserving of torture like that.

> *"The thousand injuries of Fortunato I had borne*
> *as I best could, but when he ventured upon insult,*
> *I vowed revenge."*

Suddenly, a series of thumps came from above, slapping her out of her momentary daymare. She pulled herself away from the inky blackness and snuck upstairs to investigate. The commotion was coming from the top floor, where all the priests' cells were. She crept up the top stairs, noting she'd never been up there before or cared to be. She wasn't sure if *subterraneans* were *allowed* this high above sea level. Her face contorted into a scowl before she reached the barren balcony. The shuffling of boxes could be heard when Father Andrew scuttled out of his room, hunched over and pushing a box stacked with sweaters and shoes across the floor to the room opposite his. A lone Birkenstock tumbled to the floor. She approached cautiously, grabbing the sandal to return it.

Sarah was careful to keep her toe behind the threshold, as they were taught a woman of the cloth was never to enter a man of the cloth's cell. Andrew was mindlessly fussing with something before she loudly whispered, "Andrew!" and presented his sandal to the surprised but thankful priest. He returned to his tasks while Sister Sarah noticed the decent-sized rooms they had up here. She turned to gaze behind her, noting eight rooms in total, which made her curious how the boys planned on making all this work with the new company arriving in just a few weeks. A clatter and a crash caught her by surprise, coming from the room farthest down the hall. She didn't hesitate to follow the noise in case one of the men-children was seriously hurt.

As she happened upon the last room, the door ajar brought a cool breeze and the crunch of broken glass.

"You're fucking useless, James, you know that?" barked the impetuous Father Thomas, his hand gripped in a tight fist, blood dripping down his wrist. The window pane beside him was broken, and air danced over the shimmering broken pieces on the hardwood floor.

"Go get the broom and dustpan," he ordered as Father James, silently brushed past Sister DeRosa. Her eyes met Father Thomas', and his face immediately hardened, dropping his gaze to his hand.

"And bring the first aid kit from the pantry!" Sarah yelled after him, kicking herself right after. You could take the medic out of the army but not the medic out of the nun. Father Thomas continued to avert his eyes, mumbling as he stared at the broken window pane.

"Just more money we have to cough up now."

Sister Sarah leaned against the doorway. "So, when exactly were you going to tell me about the missing funds? You know that would have made the bookkeeping a lot easier," she said dryly.

Father Thomas angrily turned to face her. "That's none of your fucking business and nothing that would ever concern you anyway," he spat. The blood from his clenched fist trickled from his palm faster. Father James clumsily made it back, handing the first aid kit to Sarah and shuffling past with the broom in hand. Thomas moved out of his way, stepping closer to Sarah while James began to sweep up the mess.

Sarah chose then to peer at her nails and sprinkle in a, "I would have found out eventually. I probably even could have helped y—"

Thomas lividly got in Sarah's face. "I WILL NEVER NEED THE HELP OF A WOMAN. EVER. YOU HEAR ME?" he bellowed out through clenched teeth. DeRosa's eyes never left her manicure. With the flick of her wrist, she offered the stuck pig the first aid kit.

He snatched it out of her hand, spittle flying onto it as he cussed under his breath and tried to open it one-handed, pressing the box against his body.

After a few tries, Sarah looked at the desperate-looking man-child. She silently took the first aid kit from him, opened it, unwrapped the gauze, and prepared the antiseptic spray in her hand before delicately offering her open palm to him. He exhaled angrily and placed his injured paw in hers, wincing at the cold sensation of the spray. She quickly and quietly cleaned the blood from his hand and bandaged the wound from the glass. It was a clean cut, not too deep. The idiot would live another day, unfortunately.

Just as she grew bored of this hypermasculine game of Show and Tell, Andrew walked up to them quizzically. "I thought we weren't giving her a room up here?" he asked before turning toward the room across from them.

"We aren't," Thomas said, before turning to Father James. "Finish cleaning this shit up. Now we have something else to add to the list."

Thomas pushed past Sarah, forgetting his gratitude, and followed Andrew. The priests were moving their rooms to the left so the Sisters could all be on the right. How gracious and lovely for all parties on the top floor. Sarah felt the urge to vomit, but chose to rise above all this and return to her *room* for the night. She could hear Andrew and Thomas snickering, making the bile in her stomach fizz even more. James exited the room with broken glass shuffling in the dustpan.

"Just think of it this way, boys," James said with a smug look. "We're about to go from one maid to five." All three of them broke into laughter. Phillip appeared from behind a slightly closed door, laughing hysterically and bringing a smell of rancid hair oil and dust.

"That's one for each of us!" Peter yelled out loud enough to make Sarah jump, regrettably. The men all continued to laugh raucously. Phillip stepped in front of Sarah before he added, "And an extra one to take care of anything else we need!" He lasciviously grabbed himself to the amusement of his peers and the disgust of Sister Sarah.

This repugnance would not stand. Not anymore; things were about to change, and it was about time they knew it. Sarah pushed past Phillip, shoving him by his shoulder into the nearest wall. The men continued to hoot and howl as she walked toward the landing before turning to them.

"Do you actually intend to carry on this way when these women of the cloth join us?" Sister DeRosa yelled out, louder than she'd ever heard her voice rise in the last decade. The men stopped laughing. "Do you think you will get away with it? You would subject these women who were just ousted from their homes because of a scandal one of *your* brothers caused? Have you all gone mad? Do you think they would stand for such behavior?"

The men stood silently looking at one another, mouthing words but saying nothing. The tension in the air gave Sister DeRosa a glimmer of hope; maybe she had finally gotten through to them after all. She glared at each of them; not a single set of eyes met her stare before she prepared for her dramatic exit. Father Thomas's eyebrows rose with a peculiar look on his face.

"Why not? It worked on you, didn't it?" his voice boomed in the silent hall.

Sarah took a step toward the men with an incredulous look. "Worked on me?" Sarah repeated, her voice shaking.

"We wore you down, didn't we?" Thomas looked at his fellow priests. "You thought you were going to come in here and shake things up? You thought you were going to run this place. That you were going to be the First Lady priest?" James giggled under his breath. Sarah eyed him, then the large shard of broken glass quivering in the dustpan only inches from her shaking hands. She watched her reflection blink back angry tears as she looked down at it.

"Looks to me like we got a nice little setup here. They send us nuns; we break them and turn them into meek little church mice to stay in their rooms and know their place." He snorted. Sister Sarah tried to soothe the bubble that was forming in her chest. "We did it once; we can do it four more times. You boys got it in you to teach these new Sisters how it is around here?"

The men all cheered. Sister Sarah kept her eyes trained on the glinting shard jostling before her. She watched her hand dive into the dustpan. She saw the shocked look on James's face as the other pieces slipped and fell out of the dusty plastic receptacle. She felt the loose glass shards slice under her nail beds as she gripped the largest shard. The pressure elicited a hot, pouring heat to bloom in her palm as she stabbed the entire length into James's stammering neck. She pulled it back out with a sickening squelch. His warm blood cooled as it hit the air and landed on her face, her eyes unflinching.

Phillip and Andrew stood stunned as the arterial spray dotted their faces and cast a negative outline of the pair onto the wall behind them. Sarah grunted and brought the transparent blade up, slicing in an arc and catching both Phillip and Andrew across their throats. The spray from them both coated Sarah's grinning face. Anything white she had on was now a bright, shining red. Both men comically grasped at their neck wounds, attempting to hold in what little life force they could. The color was already draining from their faces. Sarah couldn't be more pleased. Andrew's legs buckled beneath him, and he dropped like the useless sack of bones and meat he was. Phillip slumped against a door that wasn't closed completely and slapped the cold, hard wood floor with a satisfying thud.

Father Peter was trying to help Father James, not realizing he was in just as much danger. She came up behind the kneeling priest and stabbed the shard into his upper back and shoulders, over and over again. Squelching spurts of blood poured out of him as he groaned and landed on the ground. Viscera began to spill from him as she jammed the glass in a few more times, allowing the cuts to grow larger as she pulled it back out.

Father Thomas was taking shallow, quick breaths, his eyes roving and blinking fast as he leaned against the back wall, holding up his left arm with the bandaged hand. The blood of his brothers caked his frightened face as Sister DeRosa stepped closer to him. He tried to focus on her, but the mysterious pain and loss of feeling to his left side were pulling his wavering attention.

Sarah pushed her body up against him, her blood-streaked visage only inches from his. He winced in pain, spasming as she watched and savored every bit of it. She shakily brought the glass shard up, carefully unfolding her deeply sliced palm, and switched hands. Her small grin never left her face. It just grew into a triumphant smile. The blood of her slain enemies dripped past her lips and tasted like heaven itself.

She brought the bloodied shard up to Father Thomas's raspy throat. The harder she gripped, the more she felt the sharp ends pluck her palm and unleash a stream of crimson down her wrist. Father Thomas's breathing became more labored as she pressed the sharp edge to his throbbing jugular.

"Now. who's. a. weak. little. mouse?" Sarah asked, her eyes not leaving his. The smell of voided bowels tickled Father Thomas's nostrils, greeted by the scent of the deep amber urine soaking his vestments and puddling below him. He sniffled and pleaded with his eyes, unable to speak. *Well, what do you know? Miracles can happen.*

The mouse was now the cat, dangling its frail, smelly corpse in front of her hungry fangs. However, the game was over. Her prey couldn't even put up a fight anymore. What fun was that?

She watched his eyes go shaky as she released the shard from his neck and pointed it at his face. She braced herself against him as she jabbed it toward his eye and steadily drove it through the offending organ with a satisfying pop. A low moan escaped his drooping mouth as clear fluid commingled with his blood. She rotated her wrist and pulled, freeing the sliced horizontal orifice of its leaking former inhabitant. A scream started to build within him as she shook the deflating eyeball from her weapon and went in for the other.

This time, the man of God howled as his knees started to give. Sister Sarah held him in place as they both drifted to the ground, the glass still plunged deep into his screaming skull. She tried to remove it, but the sharp edges tore her hands to shreds. The former shell of Father Thomas began to slump and slide to the ground. His body enfeebled even more as shock and pain took over the few final moments he had left. Sister Sarah grabbed his left hand and placed it, palm down, on the blunt end of the glass shard. His body jerked involuntarily at the addition of new pain as she grabbed his right hand and repeated the process. She rose from his body, his flimsy limbs unmoved from where she had placed them, to her delight. The game was over, and she was the victor.

With a bloody flourish, she placed her splattered Mary Jane on the back of Father Thomas's stacked hands and stepped down forcefully. The pressure impaled the shard of glass into the priest's head until she could push no more, and his ragged breath finally stopped. The glass shattered once its edges caught his orbital bone, and the few remaining pieces lodged in place.

Sister Sarah gave a huge sigh of relief. The first she'd felt going on three years now? It was the best feeling she'd felt in so long. She stepped back, wiping the bottom of her shoe on Father James's somewhat clean vestments.

Ugh. Clean.

Maybe tomorrow? After seven days, God was allowed a day of rest for his creation. Sarah owed it to herself for this, her creation...by subtraction. She might even take an extra-long shower tonight, with all the hot water she wanted. She earned it. She could have some time to enjoy her final victory as a treat.

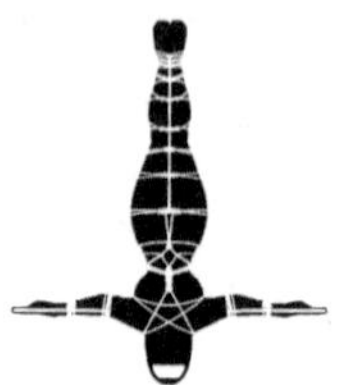

"C'mon, move it, rump roast!" Father James yelled aloud, startling Sister Sarah out of her malaise. He motioned with the broom and jingling dustpan in his hand. Sarah covered her mouth with her hand and watched the back of his head disappear down the stairs. Her glassy eyes shot to the very much alive priests conversing in front of their rooms. They returned her glance here and there, shifting uncomfortably as she stared incredulously. She peered down at the gleaming floor, which had, not a second earlier, been sopping wet with steaming gore. She extended her arms to examine her palms and was relieved yet confounded to see them intact, no longer shredded, leaking, shaking ribbons. Her blinks felt like slow camera shutters, like she was still between realms. The nausea returned, this time resulting in a rising geyser that spewed from her lips.

The sickness hit the wooden floor at the T-junction of the corridor, witnessed by Father Thomas, who curled his lip. He beckoned Andrew and Philip to follow him. Sarah hastily retreated downstairs to get towels to clean up the mess she had just made.

As she silently mopped the balcony and hallway floors, her head continued to swim with thoughts of the massacre she had witnessed. It all felt so real. She could still smell the copper in the air! Was it the henbane? But she only used a drop in her tincture. She returned all the cleaning supplies to the laundry room and gently closed the door behind her. It seemed like the boys were already calling it a day, she deduced by the silence above her.

Perhaps she just needed to calm down, have a nice, hot shower, and some time to pray. Yet the pangs of guilt flooded her system like venom in her veins. She felt eyes on her, not angry eyes, sorrowful eyes, neglected eyes. Sarah turned toward the Virgin Mary at the end of the hall. Her beautiful face glistened under the recessed lighting. *She's crying again because of me, because I haven't been honoring her as I should.*

Sister Sarah stepped up to the statue, watching the tears flow down her rosy cheeks before they cascaded into her welcoming bosom. *I'm sorry, Mother; I've just been so busy trying to prepare for the Sisters' arrival. No, never, Mother. I could never replace you. I swear to you. Yes, yes, we shall pray tonight. Just you and me; I've been so lost without you. I'm so lost. I'm so scared. I'm afraid these...priests...are going to make me crack. I know, Mother. I place all my doubt and worry into your hands. You are the holiest. Yes, my undying love for you. Anything for you. I am waiting for your instruction. Please give me your reconciliation. Yes, tonight. I promise.*

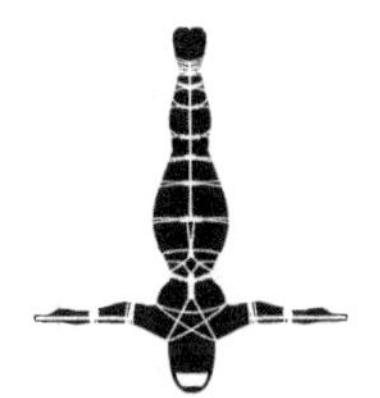

A sliver of light sliced across Sister Sarah's determined face. She crept cautiously up the damp stairs, listening for any stirrings from the bed chambers above. The room furthest down the hall was the one she had to pay attention to. She was very aware, after months—no—*years* of silent observation, of what a tiny bladder Father Phillip had. That, or he snuck down to the lavatory to fondle himself. Sister Sarah's lip curled at the thought, gathering her nerve as she dashed across the pitch black hall. Her bare feet swept silently across the cold stone, letting a chill bury itself deep in her marrow.

Trivialities.

She was here to please her lady-in-waiting, honor her, worship at her altar and pledge her undying love, hopeful that she would receive the same. She pulled a small candle they seldom used in the chapel from her pocket and a book of matches from one of the kitchen drawers. She turned to kneel before the statue, looking back toward the kitchen.

We should start leaving the small light on above the sink. Just seems like a good idea. But not today, not tonight. Mary, pristine Mary, deserves to be worshiped as well as all the other significant symbols of our faith.

She crept closer to the sorrowful effigy, on her knees and bowing her head. Her flimsy, weathered pajamas barely covered her enough to guard against the drafty monastery after hours. She paused her silent prayer to gaze at the Virgin Mary, awaiting some acknowledgment but receiving less than none. Sister Sarah bowed lower to the floor and silently lit the candle. She held the matchstick in the flame long enough for the blackened stick to be fully engulfed before blowing it out and placing the glowing spent match to the exposed skin on her chest. The small glowing ember hissed and spit as it connected with her supple, white skin.

Sarah's face remained stolid, even when a small smell of burning flesh tickled her nostrils.

As the smoke and sulfur stung the surface of her eyes, a searing tear escaped her pursed lids. She again looked up to the Virgin Mary, meeting her unblinking stare. Sarah felt all the tension melting from her body as her queen's loving gaze spread an intense warmth throughout her body.

"Thank you for allowing me your presence, your grace," Sister Sarah whispered.

"*Thank you for your offering, my child, but I sense turmoil in your heart.*"

The Virgin Mother's voice soothed Sarah's woes, but she knew she was powerless from her all-seeing eyes. "*What is causing you such distress?*"

Sarah clasped her hands together as if she were trying to wring the blood out from her knuckles onto the floor below.

"I fear for the future of this house of worship, Mother. I feel as though I have suffered since the day I set foot in here, but I chose to stay because I knew I would one day look back on it all and laugh. Now it seems that just as our doors open to our Sisters, they may be subjected to the same torment I have endured these last few years. I worry that if I don't step in and intervene, I will be complicit to their sins."

Sister Sarah paused after pouring her heart out. Truths she only thought heretofore, spoken aloud for the first time, knotted her insides, almost as much as the silence coming from the Virgin Mary. Tension filled the icy space, charging Sarah's neurons like a dark cloud of relentless wasps invading a vulnerable bee hive. Seconds felt like hours. Sarah could hear the capillaries of her bottom lip rupturing below the thin mucosa, like ripe grapes bursting beneath her unnerved bites. Splotches of vermillion dotted her quivering lips. After a few more agonizing beats, the enchanted statue responded.

"Are those who torment you supposed men of God, as they so claim?"

"Yes, Mother."

"Are they truly men of God? Or are they false prophets? Pharisees? Hypocrites? Wolves who prey on those truly in need of the word of the Lord from his very flock?"

"Yes, Mother."

"Jesus called the Pharisees 'whitewashed graves.' Clean on the outside but full of hypocrisy and lawlessness on the inside. Thus, these sinners were not welcome into the kingdom of heaven."

Sarah was intently listening to the living miracle speaking and delivering an act of mercy to her.

"You say you worry that your complacency might land you in the same burning torment destined for those men. In this instance, I fear your concern is with merit. Perhaps a divine force has gifted you with a precognition of what is to come. If you do not act on that gift, I'm afraid that you will suffer the same fate as they."

Those damning words delivered in such a velvety tone struck Sister Sarah like a wrecking ball to her temple. Her breath caught in her chest. She felt lightheaded and nauseous, but above all else, she felt dumbfounded. She yearned to respond to the Virgin Mother, but words would not form in her mind.

"Holy Mary, Mother of God," she eked. "How can I...? What can I do?"

"There's only one thing to do, my child." The Virgin Mary paused for contemplation, the climbing tension threatening to snap Sarah in two.

"A whitewashed grave must be cracked open and cleaned from the inside out. If you want your Sisters to have a fresh start, they will need a clean slate, a sacred place of worship, unmarred by those unfit to call themselves disciples of Christ. What did Corinthians 16:9 say?"

Sister Sarah's mind was overwhelmed, but the quote was familiar.

"A wide door of opportunity is open for me, and there are many adversaries," she rambled, her thoughts swirling around in her head.

The Virgin Mary's visage grew dark as the lone candle flickered and danced below them. The warm and passionate voice dropped a few octaves, and a gravelly tone could be heard.

"Prepare their home. Prepare the crypt. What evils must be performed to create more good?"

Sister Sarah couldn't believe what she was hearing. She sat back on her feet, stupefied. Not by the bidding of the Virgin Mother, but by the unearthing of her innermost thoughts, ideations she had deemed messages from Satan, waiting to pounce at her hour of need, watching her prayers go unanswered as her blood sits, drying on her flayed skin. She whispered sweet nothings of revenge and the comeuppance her tormentors deserved.

Some nights, the dark thoughts were the only thing keeping her sane:

-Bashing Father Thomas's head in with his own beer stein, watching the shards of glass glisten from his splintered skull.

-The sound of Father Phillip's neck crunching and snapping after her hands pushed him over the balcony railing. Watching his contorted body heave a final sigh as it slumped over the rest of him.

-Father James receiving a dirty fork to the eye after he leaving it for her to pick up after him. The sound of the scrape against bone and flesh popping behind the tines as she pushes it deeper and deeper.

-Bringing the altar candle to Father Peter's vestments and watching the flames consume him. Admiring the heat licking his flesh away as the blackened smoke filled the chapel.

-Father Andrew catching the business end of a shovel in the neck after witnessing him trampling through the garden again, the air sucking in and out of his lacerated throat as she drives the blade deeper.

-The entire clergy taking their final bites of the delicious pie she offered them, watching the veins in the stunned faces become more prominent as blood dripped from every orifice. The poisons working their way through their bodies, severing their systems one by one until they were no more.

"Nice and slow, just like they deserve," escaped Sarah's mouth, to her surprise.

Nervously peering around the darkening space, she looked up at the Virgin Mary one last time as the light from the candle extinguished entirely, dropping the room into complete darkness. The faint glow of the candle wick faded below her as whispers filled the hall. She instinctively looked up and saw the same glowing lights emanating from the statue's eye. An ominous orange light chilled Sister Sarah to the bone.

The internal light grew brighter. The whispers fell silent. Static electricity filled the space around Sarah before the Virgin Mary's voice startled her. She spoke clearly, as if she were hovering over her left shoulder.

"*By any means necessary. Brick by brick,*" it whispered.

The whispers returned, coming from the stairs to the basement, causing Sister Sarah to rise and follow them, ignoring the pain of kneeling for so long. Curious to hear what they were saying. Her bare feet scraped down the stone steps and followed the trail to her room. The whispers came from the partially open brick wall. The closer she got to the opening, the more the effluvium of death terrorized her senses. Yet she had to know, to hear, and get close enough to see what was being revealed to her. Suddenly, a faint orange light shone from behind the wall, drawing Sarah toward the jagged brick mouth glowing in the darkened room.

She got close enough to see the human shape that held the glowing eyes. She watched it backing deeper within the chasm until the rot-filled air clung to her skin. The demon masquerading as the Holy Mother stopped its retreat. The dim lights glowed, boring holes in Sarah's soul, until the whispers ceased, and the ruined voice returned to echo through the vast darkness.

"Brick by brick."

How Do You Solve a Problem Like Ophelia?
Chapter 14

"**T**his place is just way too holey. There's no way it's going to hold much longer. Not under all that rotten wood. We're lucky it hasn't come crashing down on all of us yet," Lidwina said, looking at the sunlight streaming through the pinprick-riddled tin roof. "Our best bet would be to get some lumber and rebuild the roof from scratch." She inspected the interior, satisfied with the skeletal beams inside but not the ones above them. "This frame will hold, but I need wooden slats to fix this." She pulled the hatchet from its place on top of the workbench, giving Mother Superior a close look at its gleaming, honed edge. A beam of sunlight glinted off the blade and stung her eyes.

"This might cut through a sapling but not a mature tree."

Behind her, Sister Ophelia came up to return the apple bushel. Mother Superior had her hands on her generous hips, looking up at the shed from the outside. Sister Ophelia silently waited, hoping to avoid the authority figure if possible.

"So, you have the tools but not the materials?" Mother Superior offered. Lidwina looked toward her workstation, which she had cleaned and created out of what she could find on the property. She asked Willard if he knew anyone who could donate to their cause, but she wouldn't get an answer until next month's delivery.

"If I had the tools, I could make supplies. We're surrounded by trees. I could take my pick and get the wood we need. I just need more tools." Twisting and turning the hatchet, she flung it across the yard. It landed with a hard thunk in the trunk of a cherry tree on the opposite side of the garden. A shocked Emilie emerged from the house after the projectile whizzed past her with stunning accuracy. Mother Superior angrily scoffed, bumping into Sister Ophelia. For the first time in a long time, Mother Superior was stricken silent. Her eyes darted between the two women before she exhaled and returned inside.

Sister Ophelia rolled her eyes and stepped into the shed, amusing Lidwina.

"Must have been something you said," Lidwina joked with a sneering laugh that Sister Ophelia had never heard from her. She rubbed the back of her neck while she watched Sister Ophelia return the bushel to the shelf. Lidwina could feel the sweat starting to soak into the collar of her shirt, making the cool shade inside call to her. "I'm going to go read a bit; there's a book I'm trying to finish finally," she said to Sister Ophelia. "You good?"

Sister Ophelia's eyes were tracing the shed's wall supports, not noticing Lidwina tracing her supports too. She nodded. Lidwina quickly headed back inside, leaving Sister Ophelia to figure out how to complete this final task. It seemed a shame to be so close to everything being done in the convent but to leave this glaring problem incomplete. Sister Ophelia pulled a few dusty remnants forward from the shadows, looking behind and under rusted lawn equipment and broken ladders. She hoped some hidden tools might have fallen and been forgotten through time, yet she found none, to her dismay. Her mind scrolled to anywhere else in the house where tools may be hiding when a crow cawed and echoed through the churchyard. Sister Ophelia's eyes found it as it flew away, gliding through the sky above the trail she had walked the day Lidwina fell into their lives for the first time.

Fallen.

Lidwina.

Fallen.

Tools.

Lidwina's truck!

Could they still be there?

Could her truck still be there?

Was Mother Superior the lying, schemin' ol' scalawag she'd proven to be since day one?

Sister Ophelia watched as the sun began to set and decided these questions could be answered tomorrow. She should be able to skip out after mass concluded, and Mother Superior would be *nun* the wiser. She had time to help finish dinner, shower early, and get enough sleep for tomorrow's excursion. Something told her this would be a trip she would not soon forget.

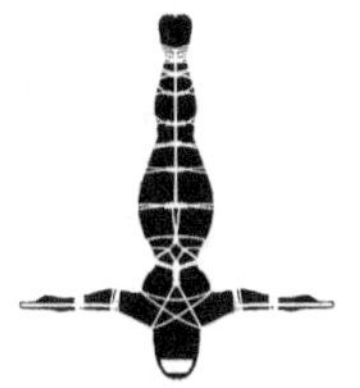

Lidwina couldn't sleep. The events of the day left her feeling more dehydrated than normal. She snuck out of her room, certain she wouldn't wake the hard-of-hearing Sister Calliope, yet she still tried to keep it down. She descended the stairs into the pitch-black foyer. While she considered herself no scaredy-cat, the convent took on a much more sinister feel once the sun went down. The ominous silence planted notions of nightmare creatures with glistening fangs watching the scantily clad girl in just a long T-shirt.

She cut through the dining room. The statue in the hallway creeped her out. The last thing she needed was to have any incidents alone in the dark with it. The light above the sink shone brighter, illuminating the kitchen in a pale greenish glow. Lidwina got a glass of water and chugged down half. She placed the half-full tumbler on the counter and returned to close the cabinet from which she got her glass. The hinge felt a little loose; she could fix that.

Just as she picked up her drink to finish it off, Mother Superior's office door creaked open and caught her off guard. Lidwina panicked, dropping to a crouch behind the kitchen island and listening as footsteps crept closer. They sounded off-kilter, jerky. Lidwina wanted to investigate, but her instincts told her to stay put.

The steps were getting louder, making Lidwina grab her water and duck walk to the side of the island, not facing any doorways. Before she could look toward the dining room to plan an escape, the swinging door burst open with a bang.

Lidwina slammed her mouth shut and turned her back to the center island, listening for the intruder. She had no weapons in reach but reasoned a busted glass in the head would put anyone down. A grunt and disheveled step entered the room. She looked up at the clock on the microwave above the oven and saw the reflection of Mother Superior sluggishly looking around the empty kitchen. She saw the distinct black and white habit sway before it pressed against the swinging door, locking it in place.

Lidwina nervously eyed the corridor off the kitchen by the back door, certain she could make a break for it, but that big open space would attract too much attention. Movement in the microwave's reflection made her glance at the image of Mother Superior leaning over the island and pulling the knife block closer. Lidwina's blood ran cold. Mother Superior 'eenie-mee-nie-miney-mo'd' the knife handles and pulled out a small paring knife.

What little Lidwina could remember of her life flashed before her eyes when she saw Mother Superior look up at her in the door's reflection. Mother Superior smiled and twirled around, dancing into the hall behind her.

Lidwina pinched herself, hoping this was a dream, but stayed sitting on the floor in the kitchen, deflating that hypothesis. She heard Mother Superior's twirling steps traveling back to her office. She quickly stood, dumped out the water, and placed the glass quietly in the sink. She wanted to escape, but she just...had to know.

What the fuck is she on now?

Lidwina snuck through the open area, letting her eye slowly pan down the hall but not enough to be detected. She saw Mother Superior in the hallway but was unsure what she was doing. From what she could see, Mother Superior was swaying through the hall. She stopped in front of the statue and began a mating dance in front of it. Lidwina watched her silhouette against the lights from the office, with the door still ajar.

Mother Superior began to hum and chant, low enough for Lidwina to hear. She couldn't take her eyes off this anomaly unfolding before her. They went wide as she recognized the knife glinting in the air above. She watched in disbelief as the entranced nun pulled her habit up enough to expose her thigh and made a series of cuts along her flesh.

Lidwina couldn't see the carnage, but she could see the blood beginning to puddle below. The urge to sneak away returned. She felt she was witnessing a bizarre act that no one should see.

Mother Superior placed her bloodied hands on the Virgin Mary, ravaging the statue's brazen breasts and letting her hands caress its consecrated curves. She let her hands fall to her sides, grabbing her vestments and pulling them off in one fluid movement. She let the fabric fall to the floor, soaking up the blood she had spilled for Mary. Her head spun; her tincture was much stronger than she had anticipated. The Virgin Mary told Mother Superior to steady her befuddled mind, to trust the Virgin Mary fully, give herself to her, and welcome her embrace to become one.

Lidwina gawked. Stunned disbelief shook her to her core as she watched the nude, bloodied nun begin to climb the statue. Mother Superior continued to chant and hum.

The weighted statue held in place, solid and sturdy. Even when Mother Superior threw her leg over the Virgin Mary's forearms and lowered her aching sex down upon Mary's praying hands. Wetness coated the slick copper as Mother Superior's developed thighs allowed her to ride the skyward pointed hands. Letting the holy spirit infiltrate every part of her and bring her love for the Virgin Mary deeper and deeper. She willed Mary to use her, to fill her up until she became a screaming, moaning vessel fountaining her love juices in squelching explosions of ecstasy.

Lidwina stood, witnessing enough of the depraved act to haunt her for life. She watched Mother Superior's body shudder and collapse on the statue, giving her the only opportune time to escape. She crept through the kitchen into the dining room, cautiously crossed the foyer, and went back upstairs, avoiding any creaking steps the entire way. She made it into her room, silently closing the door behind her, and wriggled under her sheets to stare up at the ceiling, wishing she knew how to reset amnesia.

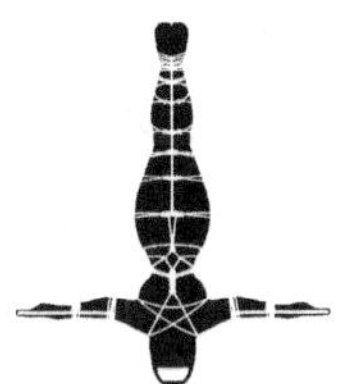

The next morning, Mother Superior was surprisingly chipper for a woman of a particular age with noticeable facial hair growth. Years ago, she had forbidden mirrors in the convent, which allowed her to be blissfully ignorant of the bristly thigh-tickler accumulating on her upper lip, but none of the Sisters were bold enough to mention it to her.

However, Sister Ophelia made it her duty to stare intently at the thin thatch of peach fuzz with a few darker, longer hairs whenever they spoke. She would sit before Mother Superior, tauntingly tracing her hairless upper lip with her thumb and forefinger in a downward motion. Sure, it was a little passive-aggressive, but Ophelia was held captive by her vow of obedience. It was all she could do to retaliate against the tyrannical Mother Superior. Watching her cocky veneer crack before Ophelia's eyes was all she needed to get by sometimes.

Mother Superior waxed poetically about the need for constancy from the faithful, or something like that. The postulant could barely focus on the words as her eyes drifted to the windows, praying for clear skies. Tatiana said the almanac called for a *clear day* to *make a discovery.*

Mass concluded. As usual, Ophelia and her dwindling pad were excused from confessing so she stole away to the kitchen pantry. She pulled her hiking boots and loaded her knapsack inconspicuously from behind her hanging apron, tied her laces up tight while checking for movement before she bolted for the back door. She paused a beat for any sign of noise besides the blood pounding against her temples. Certain the coast was clear, she snuck through the gate and headed down the adventure path.

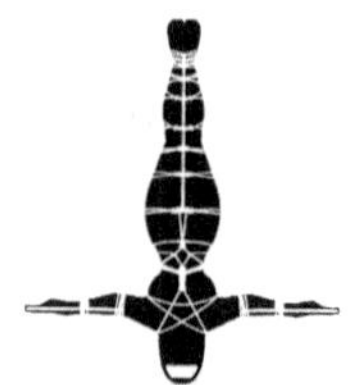

"Saints be praised!" echoed through the halls just as Lidwina left that morning's sermon. She looked around quizzically, but the itchy long-sleeved button-up shirt was chafing her something awful. She bounded upstairs and instantly stripped off the one outfit she had that was still *modest.* If she was being put to work, at least let her be comfortable. While Mother Superior was busy in her office, Lidwina snuck downstairs to pick through the clothes for the donation she had spied. She found a few keepers. They just needed her magic touch and some scissoring before they were just right.

Lidwina knew she had some electrical problems to check out today, but she just wasn't feeling it. She sauntered over to Tatiana's room, hoping for a repeat where she could turn the tables, but was met with an empty room. She could hear the clattering of pots and pans through the quiet halls, so she figured the Sisters were getting started on dinner. Her stomach was grumbling already as she walked through the first-floor hall toward the kitchen.

Lidwina entered the kitchen just as Tatiana and Bernadette walked in from outside.

"There's our little Project Runway contestant! You are certainly a marvel when it comes to working flannel!" Sister Veronica said, taking in Lidwina's latest alterations to the otherwise drab men's shirt. The other nuns looked at Sister Veronica questioningly.

"My first convent had *Bravo*." The novitiates nodded in agreement. Tatiana snapped her fingers three times in succession. "Anyhoo, it is truly a wonder to think how much you've done for this convent. We are blessed to have you here, even if they are under less-than-ideal circumstances."

The mood in the room shifted.

"Has any more of your memory come back?"

"I get little glimpses of things, but it's more like pockets of feelings I hit. I don't know where they come from." Lidwina sighed. "It just gets frustrating. There will be something there. It's so close, I could taste it. Then it just floats away."

"I'm sure it'll come back, dearie. The Lord is truly magnificent, but the human brain is a close second."

Sisters Emilie and Veronica could feel the palpable sorrow coming off Lidwina. Sister Veronica tried to think of something else to say to offer her some hope but was coming up empty. Suddenly, her eyes lit up. "How about we have a little party? A birthday dinner for Lidwina and a thank you for all the hard work she's done for us, to show our appreciation."

The two nuns smiled and watched for some kind of reaction from Lidwina, nervous she might not be too keen on the idea. To their relief, Lidwina's lips curled up into a smile. Her eyes gleamed in excitement. "I don't know when my birthday is, though," she said, her sails deflating.

"Well, that's fine, dear. We can make one up until you can remember! Who doesn't love a party? Why, we could call it Lidwinapalooza!"

The chapel doors clicked open and shut, causing them to start.

"But to be safe, we will just call it a *special dinner*," Sister Veronica said in a hushed tone before returning to putting the few dishes away. "Just to avoid any ....friction."

They all parted ways and got back to their chores for the day. Lidwina grabbed an apple and bit into it enough to hold it in place. Mother Superior entered the kitchen and sputtered in laughter as she caught Lidwina backing out into the hall with the cleaned gardening tools she was returning to the shed. Her resemblance to a roasted pig would be lost to a group who would never get the cartoon reference. She caught up to Lidwina in time to hold the back door open, getting a snorting nod in approval. She joined her so they could discuss any other jobs that needed to be attended to before fall arrived, still chuckling at the TV show in her head.

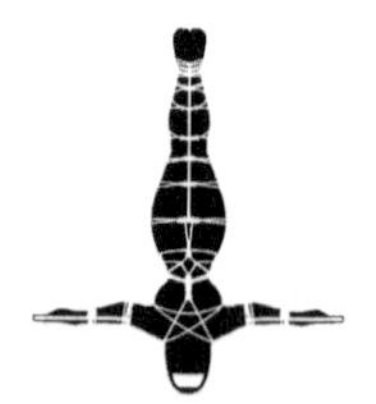

As soon as Mother Superior and Lidwina headed outside, the Sisters began to plan the party.

"There's a roast in the deep freeze still; I could make that with the mashed potatoes she loves so much," quipped Veronica.

"I have a scarf my cousin made for me that I never really use. She looks like the type that would enjoy a scarf. Doesn't she?" Emilie asked.

Sister Bernadette shot up.

"What about a cake?" she asked the group in a tizzy. "Do we have anything to make frosting with?" Sister Veronica walked to the pantry with Sister Emilie, then to the fridge.

"Enough butter and flour to keep my seat warm all winter, but not near enough sugar or baking soda, dearies," Veronica said, dejectedly. The congregation whined in unison.

"What about an apple cake?" Sister Tatiana offered.

"Not without more baking soda than we have, love."

"How about pie? An apple pie?"

The group grew silent.

"An apple pie! Why didn't I think of that?" Sister Veronica exclaimed. "And it's her favorite; that would be perfect. Good thinking, girls."

"I hope she likes apple pie because this place has ruined me for apples forever. You couldn't pay me to eat one now," Sister Emilie said pragmatically. The other women nodded in agreement.

"So, are we all in agreement? A whole apple pie for Lidwina and gathering around a bonfire sounds like a lovely night to me," Sister Veronica said excitedly and met with a unanimous yes from the Sisters.

"What about Sister Ophelia?"

"Oh, I'm sure our little trailblazer will be more than happy to change things up around here," laughed Sister Veronica, looking at the clock on the microwave. "I just hope she's back before Mother has time to notice."

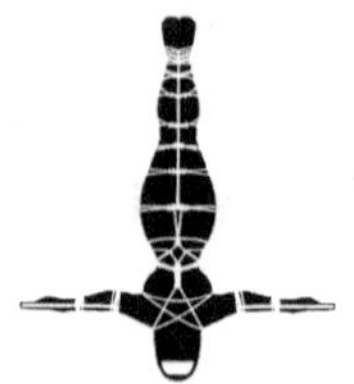

Sister Ophelia was grateful that the summer days were getting cooler. Traipsing this far would have killed her in July. She followed the trail like before, passing the fields that used to be the vineyards. She rounded a curve in the path and saw the large grove of tree clearings in the distance. The sun was already beginning to sink behind her, shining off the road barriers. She noted that they stopped after the dangerous curve. That would explain why no one noticed any kind of accident. Regardless, the tiniest part of her was hopeful that Mother Superior had contacted the authorities. That tiny part was her pinky toe, which was already beginning to ache in her snug hiking boots.

She couldn't help but ponder more as she walked, a sense of clarity washing over her the further away she got from the monastery and the valley. Whether it was the fresh mountain air or the sense of freedom, getting away from the draconian digits of Mother Superior made her feel so much better about life in general. As Sister Ophelia passed through the dark depths of the forest, she felt the same urge she had last time. It was as if the spirit of the forest spoke directly to her this time, willing her to escape whatever was chaining her to that convent and showing her what other beauty was out there instead. She saw the tree she had rested at last time, signaling she was almost there. Ophelia tried not to think about the fact that it just meant she still had to make it all the way back, hopefully, with the treasure she set out for.

She hit the last bend on the path and saw the same opening in the canopy, the same feelings drawing her near, but with the hesitation of knowing the portal to the heavens above could conceal whole ass trucks falling at lethal speeds. The setting sun kept her from seeing the same rays calling to her. She was just happy to have made it and gave herself a much-needed break after that trek when she got to the clearing.

Ophelia was overcome with emotion, unsure of why. Seeing little bits of broken glass sporadically strewn about. Most were no longer visible, perhaps covered by wind-blown dust, overgrowth, and rain. She rested against the nearest tree trunk, peeling her eyes to where the battered truck was last time. She cursed herself for not leaving earlier. The already dark space had throngs of shadows descending upon her by the minute. She didn't even bother to bring a flashlight, thinking this would be a cakewalk. Her head swiveled left and right, peering deep into the starless galaxy of thicket.

Once her lungs caught up with the rest of her, she pushed herself off the tree and trudged into the thick greenery. It had grown a lot since last time, hindering her vision even more. After surveying the abyss, she was stunned to see that the truck was gone.

So, the old battle-ax was true to her word. Was I wrong about her this whole time? Was I meant to be here? To endure the harsh discipline to make me into the person I was meant to be? Was Mother Superior truly trying to aid in the extreme agitation needed to conjure the pearl I was meant to present the world from within her bearded clam?

Just as the postulant was about to sell herself this different view of Mother Superior, that her heart was larger than her donkey booty, a shimmer of glass caught her eye. She trudged closer and made out the shape of a sapling and a dust-covered red pickup truck.

That raggedy, old, trifling, saggin-ass cunt.

Anger filled her veins as she walked up to the dilapidated truck that time forgot and nature quickly usurped. Seeing the shattered windows flashed her back to the first time she saw the nameless damsel in distress who now enhanced their home with some much-needed vivacity. Tufts of moss adorned the blown-out tires. Wildflowers and fern stalks rose from the front of the truck, which gave her pause. She silently crept around to the back of the pickup, feeling for the tailgate hitch. She didn't sign up for wrestling with flora or fauna, so she inhaled deeply, let it fall open, and peered inside.

To her relief, no varmints nor mean green mothers from outer space jumped out. Just a lot of debris, vegetation, broken glass, and whatever that little sliver of black were inside. She had no choice but to lift herself up and into the pickup's bed. She used her boots to clear as much as she could, but at last, she found what she was looking for. The tool chest was much larger than she remembered, instantly dampening her reserve. It wasn't until she saw the handle and what looked like wheels that she saw her prayers being answered. She extended the handle and pulled it toward the tailgate. Realizing there was no way she could carry it down by herself, she slid it down onto the soft ground by the long handle with a loud thunk. Hoping nothing got too messed up. It gave her some trouble as she pulled it out toward the trail. She wondered if there was anything she could take out of it to lighten the load but noticed the combination lock in place, preventing any sticky fingers.

She pulled the xxl cooler-sized box onto the trail at last. The black resin looked scuffed and filthy, so at least she didn't have to worry about doing much more damage to it. She retied her boots and looked at the darkening path back to civilization. Determination showed on Ophelia's face as she pulled the necessary box of hardware behind her and braved her journey back to the only home she knew for the last year and a half, which gave her more than enough time to ponder how much of a home it really was, along the way.

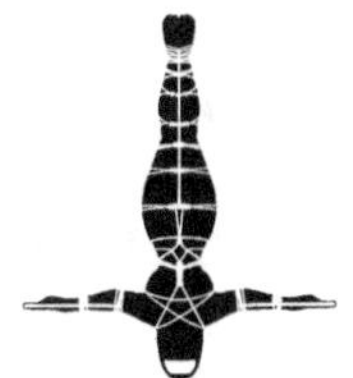

Mother Superior followed Lidwina to the shed and held the door open for her. She looked toward her lady garden, remembering she needed to trim her henbane back. She followed Lidwina into the shed and grabbed her pruning shears. Mother Superior sniffed the air.

"What is that smell?" she asked with squinted eyes.

Lidwina mashed her lips with her teeth and didn't answer, shrugging with her back to her.

"It smells very familiar," Mother Superior said, cocking an eyebrow and sniffing in the corners of the shed.

"Oh, I found some bricks and bricklaying materials over in the storage area earlier. If you still want to try to work on the Penitence Room walls before winter gets here."

Mother Superior choked on the bile that thrashed the back of her throat at the mention of bricks, or more so that Lidwina had been snooping around enough to notice them. She swallowed back the rising sickness, knowing full well how insanely guilty she appeared right now as she eyed her up and down.

"Where did you get this shirt?" Mother Superior asked, stepping forward to rub the collar fabric between her fingers.

"The clothing donations downstairs. I didn't want to keep borrowing from the Sisters, so I did some digging. It's all men's clothes, but I found a few things I could salvage." She adjusted the knotted shirt on her torso.

Mother Superior was staring incredulously at her; one eye began to twitch.

The uncomfortable silence made Lidwina anxious, which she was not a fan of. To fill the space, she blurted out, "I noticed some pictures down there too. Did you know the priests before you came here?" She turned to face Mother Superior, who looked like she could spit bees from her mouth at any moment. Lidwina's eyes fell on the bright red rosary around Mother Superior's neck.

"Never mind that, my child. I don't think a big job like that is necessary at the moment." The tone in Mother Superior's voice went cold. "I don't want to do anything too substantial considering you may not be with us much longer."

"What do you mean?" Lidwina asked, pain registering in her voice.

"Do you really intend to stay here once your memory returns?" Mother Superior asked, watching Lidwina's response for how to pose her next question.

"I...I don't know. I like it here. I feel right here. Can't I learn to become a nun and stay here?" she asked dismally.

Mother Superior burst out laughing. "Oh, my dear, sweet, concussed child." She sneered. "You don't just decide one day to become a nun and join a convent. It takes years of schooling and dedication. You must be called to the Lord. You don't just show up at the door and say, *Hey Sister, I dig the monochrome. Where's my habit?*"

"I...I thought I could stay here. I thought I was meant to be here. I got so used to it, I never thought about much else."

"You don't belong here, my child. Look at yourself. Look at your mannerisms," Mother Superior said, her words intentionally cutting slices into the lost little girl with each lash. "We appreciate all that you've done to help us. I'm sure you have earned some much-needed grace from the Lord for your good work, but that doesn't mean you are meant to be here. The sooner you come to terms with that, the sooner your memory will return."

Tears streamed down Lidwina's face. She knew Mother Superior was right, but seeing the monster she was and always had been was beginning to sink in. Maybe it was her best bet to get away from this place as soon as possible. But what about her Sisters? Well, what about the nuns? How could someone like this be an ambassador for an all-loving God? Lidwina snuffed her tears back, allowing herself to calm her emotions.

"Once I'm done working on the kitchen plumbing, I can start looking for where else I can go. I don't want to leave anything unfinished here."

"As you wish, my child, your calling is certainly to work with your hands in one way or another."

Lidwina wiped her nose on the shoulder of her cut-off button-up. She pardoned herself from the grinning Mother Superior to get her tools.

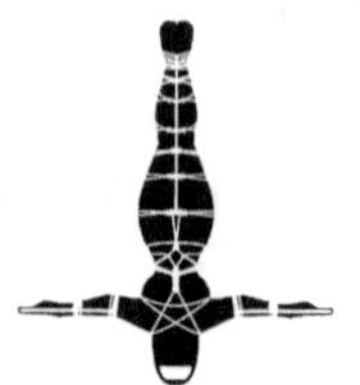

Sister Ophelia was hauling her hiney as quick as her little legs could carry her. After losing daylight, it dawned on her that a truck had fallen from the sky and landed a few hundred feet below. Whatever was inside either made it or didn't. So, she stopped worrying about how much the toolbox was tussling its insides to and fro and just focused on getting home. The whole trip back, her mind vacillated between her anger and sadness. She felt just as lost, if not worse than the last time she walked this trail.

By the time she could see the outline of the convent on the horizon, the sun was a blazing ember fizzling out in the pinkish blue sky. Her body was so sore that she felt completely numb. She was running on survival mode until she could finally stop and complete her task.

The skin on the back of her ankle was so raw, she could feel it tearing like wet toilet paper with each rub from her boot. Still, she pushed through, not just for Lidwina or to prove what a deceiving wide-mouth trout Mother Superior was, but because the trip made her see this place may not be for her anymore.

She wearily marched around the bend to her secret entrance/exit through the convent gates. Her ears buzzed with tinnitus, and she could no longer hear the hulking tool chest behind her. To her relief, the convent appeared dark and quiet. A warm light was glowing from the back garden. She crossed the yard and saw smoldering embers in the brick fire pit. They let off a bright orange glow against the ailing shed that became her beacon before she collapsed. She slid the tool chest up against the side of the worn building before she took a few steps toward the benches near the raised fire pit. Her hands caught her fall as she crawled onto it, turning up to peer at the night sky. The full moon caught her eye. The delirious agony made her want to bay at it, but she was too tired to even open her mouth.

Ophelia's lids felt heavier with each blink. The back screen door opened and slammed shut, rocking her from her minimal slumber. Lidwina stepped into view as she crossed the courtyard with tools in hand. As soon as Lidwina noticed the supine Sister, she walked her way. Ophelia's eyes focused on Lidwina as the light from the fizzling bonfire made her skin glow to match her fiery red mane. She smiled and offered her hand, prompting Lidwina to pull her up.

"You ok? Where have you been all day?" Lidwina asked, scanning Ophelia from head to toe.

Ophelia sat up fully and pointed behind her, toward the shed.

"I went on a little field trip. Brought you back something I think you can use," she said, realizing she hadn't used her vocal cords in a while as she rubbed the ache out of her lower back.

"How did you sneak out?"

"There's a spot over there where you can shift the gate from the column." She pointed toward the gate weakly. "Where the stone and the fencing meet. I'll show you later, but go see your present."

Lidwina lit up, looked back toward the shed, and hesitantly rose. "Are you good, though? You're not going to pass out on me or anything, are you?"

"Not yet, not until after I shower," Ophelia said, yawning and nodding. "Go look already before I do, though."

Lidwina headed back, her steps hampered by the dewy grass, and audibly gasped. Something clicked in her mind as she walked up to the blockish anomaly. Even in the moonlight, it looked so familiar to her. Not just because it was a toolbox but because she knew she had seen it before. She stepped closer, letting her fingers hover over the dusty resin box that was half her size. The side had a sticker with a pink dinosaur on it that said *Lickalot-tapus,* which made her giggle. The minute her hand gripped the handle, several pictures shot into her mind. Flashes of toppling trees, bar fees, and trembling knees played in her head in rapid succession like they were being uploaded to her memory cloud. She instinctually yanked at the telescoping handle and pulled the chest out into the light from her waning bonfire.

Sister Ophelia groggily watched the excitement on her face as she brought it closer. "Where did you get this? How did...I think I...know this?" Lidwina said, kneeling to fiddle with the lid.

"It was yours. Something told me you could use it. It wasn't supposed to be there, but that's another story, girl."

Lidwina turned to her, still processing it all.

"Wait, you're talking again; I forgot what your voice even sounded like!"

"Yeah, I just didn't have much to say after that vow of silence. I'll be doing a lot of talking after this, though. Just you wait. Things are going to change around here," Ophelia said, bracing her aching knees as she stood up. "After I get that shower and sleep for a day or two."

Lidwina's fingers traced another sticker of a lollipop that said *I licked it, so it's mine!* She noticed a phone number scribbled on a worn label: *Ashley, or Asher if ya nasty* with a heart. Her mind instantly conjured a stacked little spitfire with short black hair, a Beetlejuice backpack, and an ass that just wouldn't quit. She sat stunned for a second as her hand rested on the combination lock holding the lid shut. She could smell the Tobacco Vanille by Tom Ford, see the neon bar lights, and hear the slow hum of an Ani DiFranco song playing across a dance floor full of canoodling, croc-tapping, clamdiggers.

"Can you cut that off?" asked Sister Ophelia, knocking her out of her flashback.

"Huh?" Lidwina said, blinking at her, then the lock in her hand.

Sister Ophelia let out a low moan as she stretched and twisted, looking back toward Lidwina.

"I doubt you would remember the combination; maybe we can find something to pry the lock off with?"

Lidwina stared down at the aged lock, the scratches and worn pink dial showing its age. Her eyes traced the numbers until a sequence formed in her mind.

"36...24...36-24-36! That's it!" Lidwina yelled out, twisting the protuberant nipple-shaped lock like a teenager in a backseat. After a final turn, she pulled on the lock, which successfully released in her meaty mitt.

"Of course it was," Sister Ophelia said, shaking her head and sauntering toward the back door. "Well, I'll leave you to all *that*."

Lidwina chased her down, wrapped her arms around Ophelia, and squeezed. Ophelia was startled by the embrace but had forgotten the last time she felt real human contact, so she closed her eyes and enjoyed it.

"Thank you so much, I... I just...I think this is going to fix everything!"

Ophelia smiled, and the pair parted. Lidwina went back to her treasure chest. Ophelia stepped inside to claim a shower while an ominous shadow standing in one of the windows overlooking the courtyard shifted and stepped away into the darkness.

Vengeance, Voices, & Vapors. Oh My!
Chapter 15

Sister Veronica scheduled an impromptu choir meeting in the chapel using the downtime between hymns to plan the festivities for the low-profile Lidwinaplooza the next day. She continued to knit the sweater she had started for Lidwina, handing it to Emilie to help size it. Emilie held the pink and purple striped sweater to her somewhat thin frame. The body of the sweater just barely covered her ribs. Sister Veronica nodded and let out an exhale, grabbing for more yarn.

"That's not going to fit those sweater puppies. I better get a move on."

Bernadette and Tatiana were harmonizing in the background to keep up the ruse, but both seemed mentally elsewhere as their eyes darted around the sacred space.

"Alright, girls, I think we have everything ready. I'll pull out all the ingredients tonight, just in case. We can clean up tomorrow while the roast is in the oven."

Emilie returned to finish a drawing Lidwina modeled for her in the garden last week. The sunlight shone through her blood orange tresses, making it look like a lion's mane—perfectly juxtaposed with the greenery around her.

Sister Veronica's ears pricked up as the sound of water whooshing through the pipes let her relax. She hoped that was the sound of Ophelia, or Mother Superior, turning in early. Either would be a relief.

"Mother Superior has been keeping to herself today. She might be a little under the weather." She paused to finish a row in her knitting. "Either way, we might be free and clear. I won't say pray for it, but... let's hope for nothing too crazy to go down tomorrow."

The clock in the otherwise silent foyer chimed ominously.

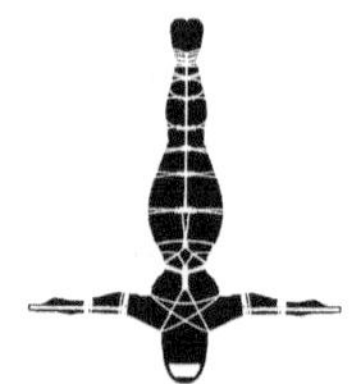

The wind began to pick up as the last of the bonfire flickered out. Lidwina wanted to dig in the old toolbox more, but there was only so much she could see with the moonlight. She found an array of saw bits and hand tools, just scratching the surface of the handywoman's toy box. She spun a pink multitool between her fingers and pocketed it as she watched the embers dwindling in the fire pit. Bits of sawdust floated up and out of the box, coating Lidwina while reminding her of the familiar scent. Her eyes pulsed as she returned *her* tools to the toolbox, each touch of the metal teasing her with more unlocked memories. She lugged the box back toward the shed and used her foot to pull the door open. Just as she pulled it up and over the small lip, she saw a blur of movement out of the corner of her eye. Her eyebrow rose, but she kept pulling until it made it safely into the shed.

Lidwina stuck her head out of the shed to listen. Her eyes scanned the grounds, but the only movement she noted was wisps of smoke rising from charred bonfire remains. She cautiously closed the shed and headed inside, eyes scanning her periphery like a metronome.

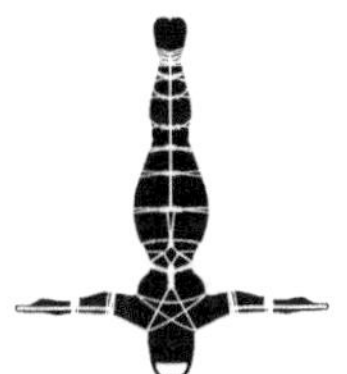

Ophelia would have described the feeling of the hot water hitting her exhausted muscles as orgasmic if she hadn't had so much on her mind. Her feet were finally starting to relieve the ache, and the residual water brought them some comfort. The only thing the water wasn't calming was her mind, which was still trudging down its trail, lost in a sea of too many thoughts: wild accusations, problematic realizations, and timely decisions that could not wait any longer.

As much as it pained her to leave the steamy sanctity of the shower stall, she could feel the pull of sleep beckoning her. Her vision flickered, just as the lights of the washroom turned off. Ophelia jumped and turned the water off; the sound of the last few trickles was drowned out by the footsteps coming near. Anxiety flooded her system as she grabbed her towel to wrap around herself and turned to see who had entered. The only light she had was the glowing windows above the sinks, which she intended to head toward once she stepped out of the shower stall. Before she gathered her wits about her, a figure swooped in and forcibly pressed Ophelia against the shower partition.

"Gotcha!" Lidwina loudly whispered, shocking Ophelia while also calming her with a shot of ease. Ophelia swatted at her, her tight curls hanging loosely above her shoulders, splashing flecks of water onto a beaming Lidwina.

"Now is not the time, Liddy, not after the day I've had," Ophelia said, pulling her towel more snugly around her torso and heading toward the sink to get her leave-in conditioner.

Lidwina slinked behind, her eyes studying her and the vines of curls hanging down from her head.

"I've never seen your hair out; it looks so sexy. I wish you could wear it like this more often," Lidwina said, her voice throaty and commanding.

Ophelia chuckled, not giving her a response but eyeing her friend in the mirror's reflection as she massaged the creamy product in her hair.

"Anyways, I just wanted to thank you for finding my tools and all you've done for me." Lidwina started to trace her finger down Ophelia's shoulder, connecting the dots between drops of water. "You know you're very special to me, my little Babygirl."

Ophelia turned toward her friend, checking her pupils, wondering where all this was coming from. Lidwina returned the eye contact before closing the distance between them. Her eyes were within inches of Ophelia's. In one smooth motion, Lidwina's lips were on Ophelia's. Her tongue darted into Ophelia's mouth as the stunned nun's breath finally caught up with her. Ophelia felt strong hands caressing her and drifting lower, grabbing handfuls of damp towel-covered flesh. Ophelia's eyes opened in shocked disbelief as she grasped for Lidwina's arms and unhooked herself from her clutches.

Confusion mixed with her anger and disbelief. She kept a strong hold on Lidwina's slithering skin under her damp hands.

"What are you..." Ophelia's voice cracked. "What do you think you're doing, Lidwina?" she asked. Angry tears began to form in her eyes.

Lidwina restrained herself and made a little pout, trying to look away. "I just wanted a little taste, that's all," she said assuredly, an air of cockiness in her voice.

Ophelia blinked the tears away, holding her towel and pressing herself against the sink behind her.

"Well, besides the fact that I..." the anger in her voice began to climb, "Did you ever think to ask me what I wanted? Not just...ravish me like this is some bad nunsploitation movie?" Ophelia looked around the room, grabbing for her things. "In the showers of all places?"

Lidwina pouted again and crossed her arms in front of her. "So, I take it; that's a no," she said, switching her hips and looking anywhere but in Ophelia's face.

"If you had asked me, it would've been a no. If you had asked me, it would've been an... *I like you as my friend.* It would've been an *I took a vow*; it could have been anything. But you'll never know because you never asked me."

Lidwina looked up at the ceiling and started inching toward the door. An annoyed, arrogant look surfaced on her face as she shook her head and clasped her hands in front of her. "Well...thanks anyway. I guess I fucked up, huh?"

Her eyes darted to Ophelia as if gauging her reaction. She was met with Ophelia's face squinting with raised eyebrows.

"I can take a hint," Lidwina said as she slunk out of the washroom, leaving Ophelia to stare at the exit in the dark room. She slowly blinked as she took a mental inventory of her day thus far. She wasn't sure she knew who she was just talking to or if she had it in her to deal with any more shit today.

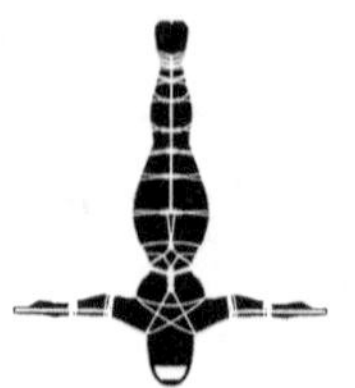

Mother Superior sat in the pitch darkness of the room. It was the only thing keeping her sane at the moment. Her head was swimming with her thoughts. She focused on the words of the Lord's Prayer, hoping it would help block out the booming voices pounding inside her head. She came to the final verse, paused, and shut her mouth tightly. Her breath wafted through the patch of hair that festooned her upper lip. Her pulse began to calm and quiet, slowly thrumming against her temples. The blessed silence was the sweetest sound she'd heard all day. She took advantage of the jeopardized quiet to listen for footsteps but heard nothing.

Until Mary's voice wormed its way into her unguarded mind.

They that plow iniquity and sow wickedness reap the same.

Her Virgin Mary had been manically speaking to her for what felt like the last few hours, repeating herself in succession, not responding to Mother Superior, but rambling quotes from the scripture, as if she wasn't already aware of them. She could hear the pain and suffering in Mary's voice, but what she heard most—what she could feel down to her marrow—was the seething anger. She hadn't heard Mary in this form since her last night with the priests. Cold sweat traveled down her spine, adding a chill to the haunting words funneling into her head.

What good did you gain from what you now feel ashamed of doing, because the ultimate result of those actions is death?

Mother Superior begged her Queen to allow her the silence she needed to carry out the task at hand.

Punish the world for its evil,
The wicked for their iniquity.
Cause the arrogance of the proud to cease,
Lay low, the haughtiness of the terrible.

The Virgin Mary's screams felt like a stiletto slowly pressing into her skull. The volume and pitch would have shredded her eardrums if they were audible. She controlled her breathing as the last wails ceased, allowing her to hear footsteps. Her target was here. The time was now.

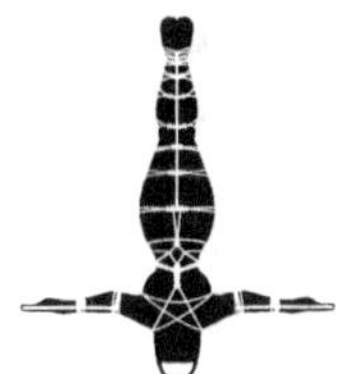

S ister Ophelia gathered the rest of her toiletries and gazed at her reflection in the mirror. *What a motherfuckin' day.* She tied her robe around her waist and opened the door to be greeted by a darkened hallway. Her hand hovered just above the washroom's light switch, but the ominous blackness gave her pause. The sound of the Sisters' hymns usually brought her comfort. Now, their voices became a sinister soundtrack to her irrational fears of what could be *in* the dark. The day's events had worn her patience to an all-time low. She braced herself, looking dubiously into the hall leading toward the kitchen, and decided *if you want something done right, do it yourself.*

Ophelia bravely hit the light switch, cloaking her in darkness as she scuttled into the kitchen. The slight glow from the full moon hitting the other side of the convent gave her just enough light to find the sink's overhead light switch. *These bitches better stop cutting this off.*

She swiftly shuffled toward it as a slight rush of air swooped in from her right. The sound of fabric jostled as it enveloped her. Her arms heedlessly reached for the light switch, only inches from her grasp. Until she felt the pull of hands on her body and a funky-smelling cloth pressed against her silent, screaming mouth.

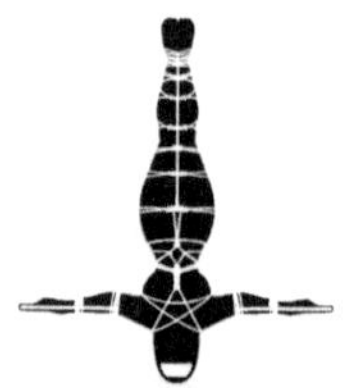

Lidwina sat in her room, frustrated with complex emotions she wasn't sure how to process. Who was she? What was she? Where did she belong? Why was she the way she was? Most of all, why could she not get Sister Ophelia's disgusted face out of her head? The few fleeting memories led her to believe she was *quite* the snack. For all she knew, she'd never been denied by another *female*. Let alone one that she *really* liked. Is that why she couldn't stop thinking about her? Or was it just because she was the *one* that turned her down?

Lidwina lay in bed, tossing and turning, thinking about the last few things she had in store for the little convent she had made a home. Thoughts of Mother Superior's scornful words brought anger and spite out of her pain. How dare that old bitch speak to her like that? Lidwina *knew*, just looking at the battle axe, that she was hiding something, something big, besides her voluptuous dimensions, something that needed to be brought into the light. Lidwina could feel her old self seething behind a thin veil, just waiting for the last few pieces of the puzzle to fit together. Perhaps this last job would unlock them, or she might have to test Mother Superior's faith once and for all.

She turned over again, flipping to the cool side of her pillow, and let her head slowly drift onto it. *Tomorrow is going to be one hell of a bash.*

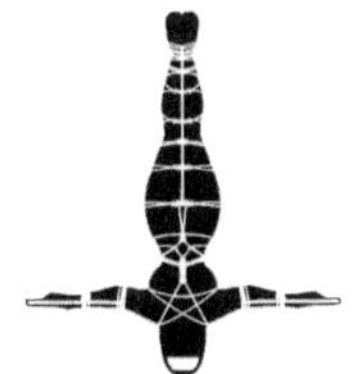

Ophelia could sense light through her closed eyelids. She could feel something fastened behind her head, yet as much as she strained to open her eyes, they wouldn't budge. She felt like she was suspended in a vat of mud; any movement felt like it was in slow motion. She could feel pain in her knees and her arms being held high enough above her to cause her ribs to ache. Finally, a sliver of light broke through to her eyes. Her lids slowly opened, though her vision was blurry and slick with tears. Her sense of smell came back to her, to her great dismay. The mildewy scent of wet, feculent rot flooded into her flaring nostrils as the ball gag in her mouth allowed very little air to pass. Her vision cleared, and she recognized the all-too-familiar Penitence Room. She recognized the bustling, bottom-heavy broad, too, unfortunately.

"Well, if it isn't our Little Harlot on the Prairie," Mother Superior remarked snidely as she attended to something in the large cabinet that took up most of the room. "How nice of you to join us."

Ophelia started to respond to her, but her words came out garbled. A line of saliva ran out of her mouth, silencing her. Mother Superior turned and wrinkled her nose as it dripped to the ground.

Ophelia lurched toward her supposed superior, but her wrists and ankles were tied extremely tight in intricate knots that held her in place.

"Some girls," Mother Superior said haughtily, "just can't take a hint. Isn't that right, Ophelia?" She produced three vials from her hand and slid two of them in the belt of her habit. She waved the single vial before Ophelia's face, watching her eyes track it sluggishly. "Did you know you could make your own ether? Out of plain old church wine and rhododendrons? That's something Martha Stewart won't teach you."

Pick Your

Tincture: _____ *Ethereal or Real Ether?* _____

Incapacitates: ✗ 😵 😵 😵 😵   Kills: 😵 😵 😵 😵 😵

Ingredients:
Church Wine
Rhododendrons

That's it.
Who knew?

Notes:
Give my regards to
Mr. Sandman!

Leave the rag please.

Thoughts & Prayers from Mother Superior's Lady Garden.

She paused. "On second thought." She grabbed Ophelia's chin and held it between her thumb and forefinger. "You shouldn't be feeling its effects that much longer."

The reverend Mother stepped away and opened the door a crack, still hearing the voices of angels serenading the night. Ophelia tried to pull and scream but couldn't do much of either. Bits of wall dusted her sweaty brow as daggers formed in her eyes, looking at the senile old sociopath.

"I'll give you the night to sober up. Wouldn't want to waste a perfectly good villain monologue with you still stuck in the ether." Mother Superior paused. "Oh Father, forgive me for that one," she said, glancing skyward and making the sign of the cross. She reached down to the small table near the door, produced an aged hypodermic needle still in its worn packaging, and placed it under the white guimpe of her habit.

Mother Superior then pulled the crumpled cloth from her pocket and inhaled deeply before she flung it in Ophelia's direction and pulled the light chain.

"I'll leave the rag," she said before exiting. The door closed soundlessly and locked from the outside, leaving Ophelia with more time to think. *Just what she needed.* Mother Superior had always given her the creeps, but the look of a checked-out, crazed Karen with the racial insensitivity to put a black woman in shackles registered a whole new level that would give her nightmares for the rest of her life. That is, if she could find some way out of this, some way to get the jump on this beast and give her the lesson that her mama should have.

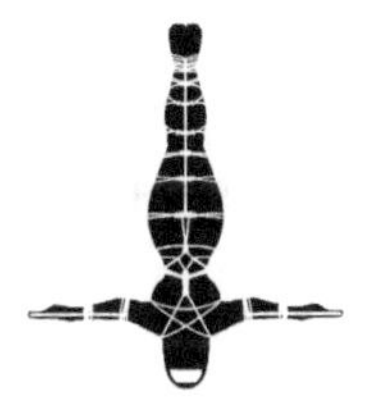

Mother Superior tucked her key ring into her pocket and placed her forehead against the solid wood door. She allowed herself a moment to close her eyes and take a deep breath.

Now what? Now what am I supposed to do? Do I just keep her down there forever? How can I silence them both? Can you re-concuss someone?

The ether seemed to quiet the Virgin Mary, though now her correspondence was all Mother Superior prayed for. She pressed off the door and made her way up the melting stairs. The sweet hymns plucked at her heartstrings, making her sway as she crossed the foyer. Her habit billowed as she spun in place and did her best to hold this moment in her heart.

For that split second, she wasn't Mother Superior. She was Sarah DeRosa: blissfully happy lover of life and an infinite light in a dark world, a world she didn't understand, that wouldn't have her, and told her she was wrong and the only way to be right was to become everything she wasn't.

The hymn came to its end. Mother Superior felt empty again. A crumpled doll coming to a stop on her weathered Mary Janes, staring down the darkened hall. Mother Superior couldn't help but smile as a tear streamed down her cheek. Though she couldn't see her, she could feel the Virgin Mary watching her.

Seething. Volatile. Starving.

Sarah felt Mary pulling her close with those loving, glowing, omnipotent eyes.

My one and only.

Mary's blackened claws sliced through the darkness to caress Sarah's back, only penetrating her flesh when she slowed her steps.

The air that I breathe.

Mary's love was so intoxicating that it made Sarah lose her footing as she walked toward her cold, waiting embrace.

My heart. My everything. My ruin.

Standing before Mary, only able to see her silhouette but feel her presence, Sarah could forget who she was before. Forget the evil of the outside world. Forget the sins that played on an endless loop in her head, sins that hardened her heart and rotted her insides.

The blood that I spill.

Sarah was nothing without Mary. She was her vessel to punish those who did wrong.

It's better to be a vessel than a shell.

Though her tears may never stop, at least they were all for Mary. At least she knew she would never be alone. Ever.

I wish that I could quit you.

True, selfless love requires sacrifice. The greater the sacrifice, the more it strengthens her inamorata. She could never say no to Mary. Even when every cell of Sarah's being begged her to resist her malicious demands. Their souls had merged. The pact was ironclad, unbreakable, and written in blood. Sarah was a quivering instrument in her crushing palm, a piston in Mary's machinations.

Command me, Mary.

Take my love and let your wrath flow through me.

Let my hands be yours.

Bring all the evil pronounced against them

that they harkened not.

The singing stopped, as did the visions. Mother Superior sat stunned, kneeling in the darkened hallway. Details were etched in her mind as if waking from a dream. She glanced up at the beautiful visage of the Virgin Mary. Only the faintest details of her handsome profile could be seen through the darkness, but that was enough to strengthen Mother Superior, knowing that everything she did was with purpose. No matter what happened, she had pleased her ultimate one and only.

The chapel doors leading into the foyer opened unceremoniously, and the lights blanketed the space in brightness. Mother Superior shook as she stood solemnly posing in front of the statue. She placed her hand over her heart, feeling that the hypodermic needle was still there. The murmur of the novitiates going upstairs made her relax some. It wasn't until she heard the swishing and the footsteps of Sister Veronica approaching that she tensed. Sister Veronica came up behind her and placed a gentle hand on her shoulder, prompting Mother Superior to turn and face her.

"Excuse us if we interrupted you, Mum." Sister Veronica glanced worriedly at Mother Superior's uneasy body language and tightened jaw.

"Are you feeling all right? I must prepare a couple of things for tomorrow. I could make you a sandwich or something if you're hungry."

Mother Superior watched Veronica waiting for her response. She felt like a prisoner, held captive behind a shiny glass window, the knife to her back, invisible to anyone looking in. The illusion appeared normal and safe to outsiders who couldn't see past the darkness behind her.

"Their voices are the only peace I know," Mother Superior let slip from her lips, instantly tightening her posture when the realization hit.

"Pardon?" Sister Veronica took a closer look at her face. "Have you been crying again, Mum?"

"I...Their voices always make me tear up. It reminds me that there's still beauty in the world, good things out there that go unseen in a sea of evil," Mother Superior said, dejectedly.

Sister Veronica slowly blinked and looked to her right, speechless, which never happened. Mother Superior came back to the surface, taking a deep breath. Some color showed on her face. "Whether or not you are aware, Sister Ophelia was caught being truant again. Her punishment is to spend the rest of the weekend in the Penitence Room. I know you are not as strict as I am, but I believe the best way to get through to her is for her to see how much freedom she truly has, by comparison."

Sister Veronica's face fell, but she nodded and replied to her superior. "As you instruct, Mum, I will respect your methods."

"Thank you for abiding by me, Sister Veronica, as I trust you and I trust that you will not intervene or coddle our prodigal daughter when it is discipline she sorely needs."

"Whatever you think is best, Mum," Sister Veronica said earnestly.

"You've always been so good to me, Veronica. I'm incredibly lucky to have good people like you to remind me that the world isn't as full of monsters as we believe."

Sister Veronica's face registered uncertainty that quickly turned into worry. "There are no monsters, Mum, just confused souls that lost themselves along the way. I believe everyone finds their way eventually. Just some take longer than others."

Mother Superior felt a geyser of emotions bubbling to the tip of her tongue, threatening to spill forth and ruin everything. She just wanted to admit to it all, to come clean, and repent for her sins to begin the long journey leading to forgiveness. The floodwater that frothed in her throat hit the dam, sending it all back down where it came from as Mary's voice sliced through her. "Your deeds will return upon your head."

"Yes, the book of Obadiah was very strict indeed, Mum, but I don't think that should be interpreted as in-"

Mother Superior glanced at her friend through the corner of her eye, fighting to control her body from shaking as Mary's voice poured through her. She fought to keep her hands at her side, even though the muscles in her arms tensed as if they were ready to tear through anything in their way.

"Punish those who do wrong; repay them," Mother Superior hissed.

Sister Veronica took an unintentional step back, watching a vein protruding from Mother Superior's neck bulge like a hungry earthworm writhing through the dirt.

"Mum, Romans 12:19 spoke about not punishing others who do wrong, for it is up to the Lord to decide their punishment. I think most forget it's a very old passage that can be easily mis-construed. Especially if it ever got into the hands of someone who wanted to use them for evil. Perhaps you should start reading some of the lighter passages more."

Mother Superior felt the black inkiness enveloping her soul, like tar sealing out any air she needed. Every pore in her skin felt like it was being infiltrated while she stood, appearing calmly docile. For a hair of a second, she felt the pressure release its grip on her, allowing her to take control again. She chose that moment to grasp the edges of the fissure and tear it open as much as possible.

"That sounds like a good idea, Veronica. If you don't mind me, I'm going to go into my office and do just that," Mother Superior said, trying to release the tension from her jaw.

Sister Veronica was taken aback by the abrupt reversal but grinned at her old friend, happy to see that maybe she was finally getting through to her.

"I think that's just what you need, Mum. '*The Lord is my light in my salvation; whom shall I fear? The Lord is the strong God of my life, of whom shall I be afraid?*' That's from the Psalm of David. It's my little reminder, my little *Who Gonna Check Me, Boo?* It comes in handy."

Mother Superior smiled the most genuine smile she felt in years. She shockingly placed her hand on Sister Veronica's arm and squeezed it. "Thank you, Veronica, for everything."

Veronica placed her hand over Mother Superior's, returned the squeeze, nodded, and headed into the kitchen. Mother Superior used the rest of her fading strength to pull herself away from the statue, open her office door, and lock herself inside.

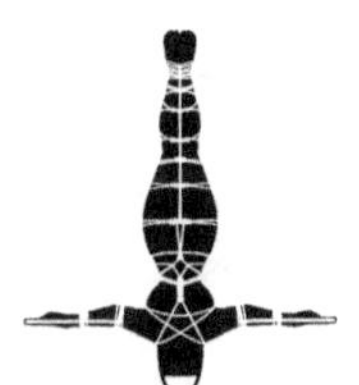

Sister Veronica turned on the little light above the sink, intending to leave it on for Sister Ophelia. She tried not to fret, confident that Mother Superior would do as the divine instructed her. She set the sticks of butter to the side in the fridge and ensured the flour was fresh and pest-free. Lastly, she burrowed through the apple bushel in the pantry, searching for the plumpest red apples, knowing they were Lidwina's favorite. She then placed them in a bowl and left them with a note.

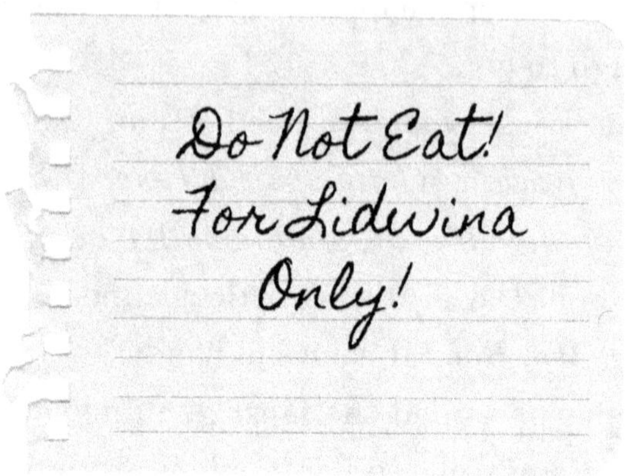

She snickered to herself, knowing that nobody but Lidwina would eat them, but she gave a little tongue-in-cheek wink to the audience.

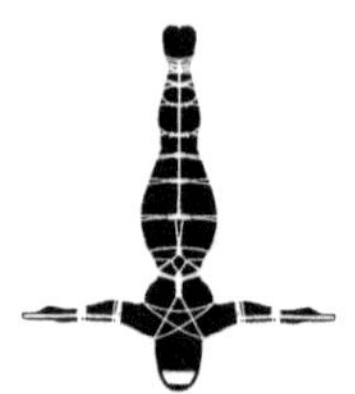

"The Lord takes vengeance and is filled with wrath," Mother Superior whispered in the darkness. She sat with her back against her office door, her nails digging bullet-hole-sized openings in her exposed thigh. Once she heard the floorboards above her creak, signaling that Sister Veronica had retired for the night, she stood and unlocked it. She exited the office and slipped off her shoes. Using the light from the kitchen beside her, she pulled the hypodermic needle from her guimpe and a vial from her waist. With a surgeon's accuracy, she stabbed the needle into the vial and pulled the plunger back until the chamber had about a thumb's width of her tincture.

Pick Your

Tincture: _____ *A Real Ladykiller* _____

Incapacitates: 😖😖😖😖😖   Kills: ✗✗✗😖😖

Ingredients:
Amanita Nightshade (A Classic)
Flu Agaric
Oleander Honey (the real stuff)
Claviceps Purpurea (Ergot)
Cyanide (apple seeds)
Black Henbane

Notes:
If you want a happy ending,
try another story book.

Cancel that U-haul Sister!

Thoughts &
Prayers from
Mother Superior's
Lady Garden.

She intended to creep up the stairs and deal with Lidwina once and for all. As she tapped the side of the syringe, she envisioned the look of terror in Lidwina's eyes, her screams muffled behind Mother Superior's clamped hand as she emptied the poisons into the tender flesh of her neck. Mother Superior grew excited by thinking of seeing that dosage entering her bloodstream, the toxicants instantly taking effect. Mother Superior grew wet with the desire for the antihero to lose her mind as her body began to shake and eventually shut down as the compounds overwhelmed all her major organs. She ached to run one of her bloody fingers over her slick womanhood, the dried blood meeting her heavenly juices, creating a slip and slide of depravity that felt too right to be wrong.

The syringe quivered in her hand, shaking before her face when she felt Mary's voice surfacing.

"Let the wrath of God be your guide."

Mother Superior spoke confidently, ready to dispose of the real poison in this convent with the most potent elixir she had ever concocted. She felt her reins being taken over once again, preparing to brave the cold, dark hall, but was surprised when her body did not step forward. Instead, it turned toward the kitchen and commanded her to enter.

"Let the wicked die in their iniquity," she whispered, stepping up to the counter and eyeing the bowl of apples. "The wickedness of the wicked shall be upon her. Punish her according to the fruit of her doings," she said with righteous indignation.

A smile crept across her blood-stained lips. Her free hand picked up an apple and jabbed the needle into its center. Just askew of the stem, the rich caramel-colored liquid was injected. She repeated this for the other apples in case her pet serpent wanted a late-night snack. Lidwina always did, especially after an arduous day doing the work of Lucifer himself. Mother Superior was always the first to rise so she could dispose of any leftovers. Mary had concocted the perfect plan, the fairytale ending she deserved. She trusted her queen. Mother Superior knew the Virgin Mary would never do anything to harm her.

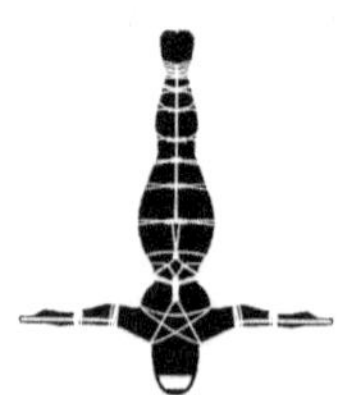

Sister Ophelia thrashed against her bonds. She felt like she had sweated out most of whatever Mother Superior had drugged her with. The anger flowed through her, and her breath huffed out of her nostrils as she felt more brick-and-mortar particles floating down like falling snow. Eventually, she found a system of pushing off the wall and jumping that felt like her left restraint was getting looser. However, the toll on her already overtaxed body was starting to wear on her. She didn't know how long she had been there, but it was enough to exhaust her. Maybe after one more tug, she'd allow herself a little shut eye. Just to recoup some of her energy. With the last of her might, she pushed her ass against the wall and kicked off the lower bricks with all her weight in her aching knees and feet. An explosion of dust, rubble, and the foulest stink she'd ever imagined left Sister Ophelia feeling her left arm and leg come free from the crumbling brick wall.

Requiem for a Wet Dream
Chapter 16

Mother Superior laid back, letting her shoulder-length chestnut hair flutter behind her. Her nerves made her head a veritable powder keg. An explosion was imminent. With everything in place, it was in her best interest to relax and get some much-needed sleep. She had much to do when the day broke.

Her eyes darted around the swirling ceiling. The effects of her special *Now I Lay Me Down to Sleep* blend set off strings of little fireworks that prickled her nerve endings.

Pick Your

Tincture: *Now I Lay Me Down To Sleep*

Incapacitates: **X** ☺ ☺ ☺ ☺ Kills: ☺ ☺ ☺ ☺ ☺

Ingredients:
- *Mugwort*
- *Damiana*
- *Maca*
- *Devil's Trumpet*
- *Fly Agaric**

**easy girl*

Notes:
- *Sweet dreams are made of these!*
- *Don't mind if I do*

Her eyes went glassy as she brought her hand up to her face and watched her skin rolling and rippling before her. She appeared as if she were lost in thought, deep in love, and reliving a past trauma all at once. Heat rose through her body, making her face flush. She fought to close her eyes, unable to tear herself away from this new universe floating above her.

All her concerns melted away as she entered the throws of the devil's trumpet. The blood in her veins danced under her pale skin, giving her a rosy complexion as the prickles grew into delicious vibrations that quickened her breath. Had she not been lying down, these sensations would have sent her to the ground. Nestled and protected, she welcomed this bizarre kiss from Mother Nature, her tongue still tingling from the taste. Who knew one tincture could transport her to a place where her thoughts were no longer stabbing hot pokers, only there to harm and never to heal? This was her sanctuary, her temple to the Merciful Virgin. Her only refuge from the venom her mind produced.

The silence was broken by whispers, giggles, and her door closing. Mother Superior's eyes shot open, jolting her from her self-induced haze. She sat up on her twin-size mattress; her hand flew to her spinning head. Out of one eye, she was struck dumbfounded as two barely legal girls snuck around her room, in the dark.

Even in pitch black, Mother Superior recognized the smell of incense from the hall of her old dorm room. The scent mingled with the crisp pine drifting in from her half-open window and reminded her of the happy times she had in her first taste of seminary life in Belgium. The look of familiarity crept onto her face as the two figures bumped into the bed. The one with the generous hindquarters sat on the foot of the bed, still holding the other girl's hands in hers. The petite blonde girl giggled as she pulled her hands to the seated girl's face, bent down, and pulled them closer together.

Mother Superior watched in awe, a growing unease building in her gut as the two planted little kisses on one another that quickly increased in intensity. Still too dark to see, Mother watched the sitting girl pull away, reach in a drawer, and retrieve a book of matches. The girl's sweet perfume was intoxicating, like fresh strawberries and lilac. The scratching sound of the match striking the grit and igniting startled her.

The room gained a golden halo around the seated girl, reaching to light the candle on the bedside table. Mother Superior recognized her own facial features but was decades younger. Her plump apple cheeks, button nose, and dewy lips were all caught in the glow of the lone light source before they turned back to her excited guest. Once the young Sarah moved out of the light, Mother Superior instantly remembered the other mystery girl, who was now slipping out of her plaid skirt.

"Angelique," Mother Superior mouthed, engrossed in watching this scene play out as it had several times before in her mind.

Angelique, her personal little ballerina, shook her hips and smiled. The classically trained dancer watched Sarah's eyes tracing all the curves of her body during her movements while she swayed to a silent number just for her. Shadows on the ceiling grew into roaring monsters as the glow of the candlelight caught Angelique pulling her sweater and bra off and tossing them on the floor. Sarah inhaled, marveling at the most beautiful breasts she had ever seen. The first pair she had ever seen this close, revealed *just* for her. Perfectly round and perky, with little CrunchBerry nipples. The nostalgic memory of her favorite cereal mixed with Angelique's fruity scent sent her reeling.

Sarah motioned for Angelique with open arms, and she willingly obliged, stepping closer to the bed. Sarah wrapped her arms around her, pulling her close and taking in her scent. She wanted to lock her heavenly fragrance in her nostrils forever, gulping it like a mad woman. Sarah brought her face up and rested her head in Angelique's ample cleavage, kissing and encircling her perfect breasts with every breath.

Mother Superior gasped when Sarah, still seated, let out a low growl as her hands crawled up Angelique's back and slid her nails down her soft skin to her perfect heart-shaped ass. Never having watched herself as a spectator before, she was surprised by her aggression.

Angelique gasped as well, ending with a soft moan as Sarah squeezed her ass cheeks. The peach fuzz on her lady cakes rose as goosebumps began to dot her flesh. The flesh of her pink nipples hardened just as Sarah was circling the right one with her tongue. Angelique threw her head back but clamped her mouth shut to quiet what would have been a very throaty "ahhhh." Sarah held Angelique's milky mounds in her hands, pushing them together until she worked each nipple between her thumb and forefinger. Her lips stayed sealed, but she struggled to remain silent as Sarah pinched and teased the hardening flesh the way she had always wanted to. Angelique was getting lost in the throes of orgasmic sensations that were causing her moisture to spread across her already fragrant thong. A sudden wind sent a draft through the room, making flickers of candlelight dance across the pair. Dizzy with delight, Angelique leaned forward onto Sarah. She straddled her legs, and they both drifted onto the bed as she whispered wantonly in Sarah's ear, "Il fait froid." *It's cold.*

Mother Superior was engrossed in the scene playing out before her and the events that led up to it. She remembered the electricity running through her fingertips as they explored the hips and dips of her first girl crush after months of longing, feeling it was so wrong and yet the most right she had ever felt in her life. She felt trepidation working up the nerve to just kiss her for the first time, nagging thoughts saying she could have had this so much earlier if she just listened to what she really wanted. She was reliving it all, feeling it all, and dripping with anticipation for the impending climax.

Sarah lifted her torso and raised her arms so Angelique could pull her shirt and bra off. Angelique watched Sarah with fascination, like she was the most beautiful creature she had ever laid eyes on. Sarah could feel the wetness seeping through Angelique's panties and soaking into her jeans as she rhythmically rubbed her swollen vulva against her.

After Sarah threw her clothes to the floor behind them, she grabbed Angelique's hips and angled her own to accommodate her thrusts. Muffled screams and deep groans floated between them before Angelique sat back, still grinding into Sarah's bucking hips. Sarah rubbed her right thumb away from Angelique's shaking hip, sliding it under her sexy lace thong. Met with slick wetness, she got her thumb wet enough to feed the hungry hole she longed to give pleasure to.

Sarah traced Angelique's entrance with her slick thumb, causing her to arch her back while still being on top. Angelique threw her head back toward the ceiling. Sarah pushed past her hot lips and encircled her clit, rubbing it through her hood. Her breath quickened as her gyrating rapidly continued. Sarah's jeans felt plastered onto her as her thrusts met Angelique's. Her body ached for release as they massaged their most sensitive parts against each other's.

Sarah's fingers quickened their circles in, out, and around Angelique's gushing opening as she felt her own body tensing under the pressure. If they weren't both soaked in their sweet-smelling juices, Sarah would have worried they might start a friction fire between them. The heat had come to a fevered pitch, and Sarah could feel Angelique's canal throbbing and tightening around her quivering digits. Sarah gave one final rock of her hips as the release rippled through her body in an explosion of panting ecstasy.

Then everything went black.

Sarah's eyes rolled behind their lids. She willed them open, but they were not responding. Feeling began to circulate back to her extremities. She struggled to move but found her limbs were all stuck in a fixed position. Her skin felt warm and damp, yet yearning for freedom from the suffocation, like she was trapped at the bottom of a tar pit, unable to move.

Her attempts to scream and to take in a mouthful of air were all pushed to the back of her mind in fear that opening her mouth would fill her lungs with thick gobs of smothering obsidian. The whooshing in her ears was all she could hear as her body made little pointless micro-thrashes. It wasn't until she stopped trying to move that her heart rate stopped thrumming against her temples. That's when she heard the soft opera notes resonating through the leagues of murky resin. She felt a bead of sweat originate at her hairline before it dripped down to her nose and eventually to her lips. The tang of salt penetrated her pursed lips, causing her to realize she wasn't submerged, after all.

The sound of taps rippled through the dense galaxy. She felt each stab vibrating through her skin. Then, in an incredibly awe-inspiring sequence, she felt a buzzing pressure press into the nape of her neck and trace its serrated teeth down the back of her skull up to the crown of her head. Like the softest, most freeing chainsaw swipe known to man.

This cut brought cool air that prickled her face. The unmistakable sounds of Maria Callas's "Vissi D'Arte" tickled her tympanums. The beauty of the melody paired miraculously with the strength of the diva belting out each passionate note. Tears formed in her eyes as soft light shone on her bare eyelids. Sarah felt her skin part and peel from her temples as it slipped from her face. She was unafraid, ready for her fate, whatever it may be. Her sins had landed her in this land of in-between where her skin would be flayed from her in sheets while the voices of angels accompanied her torturous eternal punishment, gravity pulled her flesh away from her, and she heard it land with an unceremonious plop.

Through the blur of tear-filled eyes, she prepared herself for the grotesquery she was about to witness. She blinked, and a black leather mask with a gleaming silver zipper stared back at her.

Sarah's tears ceased as the final droplet ran off the tip of her nose and traveled down before it pitter-pattered onto the supple leather. The realization that she was alive and her skin seemed intact made her suck in a deep breath. Her mouth was still obstructed but she sucked in as much cool air as she could through her nostrils. The sweet smell of vitality permeated her sinuses and filled her lungs. She could feel every molecule of oxygen rejuvenating her cells. Her relief was short-lived as her reawakened cells reported that her arms and legs were fixed behind her back.

Whatever held them in place softly pressed into her limbs and cut off her circulation. Her pain receptors were all online now and screaming at her to escape this torture. It caused a low wail to rumble from deep in her diaphragm that was only expressed as a loud exhale through her nostrils. The ache in her jaw set in when she tried to figure out why she couldn't speak. Saliva pooled around the side of the apparatus, only registered as candy apple red from the edges of her vision looking down at it.

"Welcome back."

The throaty voice startled her, but the restraints kept her from lifting her head to see who it belonged to. The taps of high heels came closer, stabbing into her brain with each step.

"Are you ready for Heaven?"

Confused, Sarah panicked but could only stare down at these shards of memory deep in her past. Try as she might, she couldn't fit them together to remember where she was. The sound of a motor above her came to life and whirred, slowly lifting Sarah higher into the darkened room. A lone spotlight shone down from above, making her shadow grow as the shiny black vinyl boots came into view. Sarah's body swayed as her eyes scanned every inch of the ethereal creature loading before her. The light from above reflected off the shining black PVC mini-skirt attached to the boots by large clasps at the front of the mysterious maiden's thighs. The plastic material looked coated with an entire can of jet black paint and was still wet on the curves of her hips that tapered into an extremely cinched waist. Her bosom blossomed before Sarah's eyes, fully covered by a thick white bib collar that held her heaving chest at bay behind the squeaky material. A full black veil draped behind her, spilling across her shoulders as the cutout revealed the face attached to this heavenly body.

Sarah's eyes met those of her captor. Thin, chestnut-brown eyes with a heavy cat eyeliner extending past heavy purple lids. Her head was capped with a white bandeau with a black PVC sheet cascading off. A slice of slicked-back brown hair teased out from under the white cap. The femme fatale puckered those cherry-red lips before they curled up into a smile. She broke their gaze to hit the stop button on the pulley attached to the lone ring holding all Sarah's weight. Sarah felt lightheaded at that moment. Her body was begging to be set free, but her soul and her fluttering flesh had never felt more alive. She traced the beauty's shapely silhouette with her stare, enamored with the feast her eyes were indulging.

"Art thou a sinner?" her velvety voice cooed inquisitively while she batted her thick eyelashes.

Sarah's face grew flush. Her eyes grew wide and uncertain. She knew the obvious answer, but was she ready to admit it? Was she ready to confess, to endure her punishment for her sins? Her jaw felt like it would snap, crackle, and pop at any minute. She sucked any saliva that was pooling in her agape mouth to try and answer.

"Blink twice for yes," The Dominatrix seductively purred as Sarah drifted off, staring into the beauty's eyes as they bored holes through her soul and blinked twice quickly.

Her princess in PVC brought her hand up, caressing the intricate knots holding Sarah in place. Her long, lacquered nails traced the bulging flesh squeezing out from behind the snug restraints.

"Your sins bind you, Sister Sarah, and only one person can unburden you from your sins."

She rested her hand under Sarah's chin, bringing their faces closer. Sarah could feel her body tingle and melt from her touch alone. She could smell cherry-scented lip gloss that her eyes fixated on as the Dominatrix planted a small kiss on the red ball gag wedged prominently between her jaws. She clamped her hand on Sarah's throat and squeezed.

"Me."

Sarah's body shook and rocked, unable to escape the firm grip of the claws digging into her neck. She tried to suck air in through her nostrils but was met with resistance as her airway was being blocked. Her aching lungs were being robbed of the oxygen they so desperately needed. Her attempts to adjust the ball gag in her mouth were fruitless. Her eyes pleaded between painful blinks. She felt her chest burn like the bomb's wick had just reached her ribs before they exploded and coated the floor below her in a sea of crimson.

Then her angel and devil, in one, relaxed her grip, to Sarah's ultimate shock. Her nostrils flooded with cherry-scented oxygen as shooting stars darted across her field of vision. She felt her body quiver as her blood flooded with endorphins. They were preparing her for battle, though the identity of her assailant was still unknown to her.

"Slow breaths. Little breaths. Good girl," the PVC princess said soothingly as she held Sarah in place while watching her pupils shrink back to normal. Sarah was lost in the warm brown pools of milk chocolate, staring back at her while her breathing returned to normal. The sadistic Sister squeaked over to a wall of leather paraphernalia.

"Don't get any ideas." She turned back to wink. "That costs extra."

The Dominatrix smirked and pulled a leather stool away from the wall and slid her shiny ass onto the seat. She positioned herself under her suspended prey.

"Ugh, these heels," she said while rotating her ankle and watching Sarah watching her.

"So, I ask you again, Sister Sarah, art. thou. a. sinner?" She paused a beat. "Think about your answer." She cocked a perfectly arched eyebrow. "Blink twice for yes."

Sarah continued to suck air into her nostrils while fighting to avoid the pain in all of her sore joints, especially her jaw. Her eyes stayed open, but she shifted her gaze to the floor.

"Keep your eyes on me. Good girl. Now, we may proceed."

Sarah stared intently at the seated sadist as the music stopped.

"Art thou enjoying yourself?"

Sarah hesitated, then blinked twice.

"Art thou fulfilling your fantasies?"

Sarah blinked twice.

"Art thou your most honest, bare, natural self at this very moment?"

Sarah's eyes widened as she realized that she was entirely naked—the only thing covering her were a bundle of meticulously died nylon rope knots washed over her. Sarah blinked twice.

"Art thou a lover of women? Do they turn you on? Do they make you hot? Do you enjoy eye-fucking the female form? Does seeing a beautiful woman make your body ache? Your mouth salivate? Your pussy drip? Hmm Sarah? Sister Sarah?"

Sarah's eyes filled with distress. She kept her eyes open, waiting for her final question.

"Are. you. a. lesbian?"

Tears filled Sarah's eyes as the word caused shame and disgust to fill her body. She let the tears drip down her face. Her eyelids twitched, wanting to blink, longing to, for more than just her body's reflexes, but she just...couldn't. She stared at the beauty in front of her, animosity building as she watched the dominatrix rise from her seat.

"Oh, my sweet girl. You're just not ready yet. That's okay; it takes more time for some of us than others." The heavenly-heeled creature sauntered Sarah's way in a slow strum of clicks. "It took me a long time to realize that it wasn't the uniform I donned that defined me. It was what was underneath." She let her fingers trace her thighs up to her waist, fanning out as they caressed her perky little breasts beneath the skin-tight material. "Even this spicy little number has a lot of weight attached to it. A lot of baggage. But I think we wear it well." She turned to show Sarah her lithe profile and slapped her hand against her own ass. The slap echoed throughout the room, snapping Sarah out of her babydoll-eyed stare.

"I just want you to... someday see that it doesn't dictate who you are or who you're meant to be. No god would deny you true happiness and being who you were meant to be."

The Dominatrix stepped closer to Sarah, almost within arm's reach of her.

"You know who put that there? That shame? That hatred against what we see in the mirror." Her bright red lips sneered, letting out an honest snicker. "Men. A man...now Sarah, I ask you. Art thou going to let a *man* tell you that you don't deserve to be happy?" She stopped in front of Sarah and leaned in. Sarah could feel the electricity between them and melted when the delicate cheek grazed hers and whispered, "Just something to pray on."

Sarah finally allowed herself a watery blink. Which let a stream of tears express from her searing eyes. The Dominatrix planted a loving kiss on the apple of her cheek before pulling away.

"But I have to send you back, unfortunately. It's going to be a rough trip, but..." Sarah's eyes shot open at the statement. Her tears caused the mysterious woman's face to shift and distort before her eyes. "You've had worse."

Her voice was distorted, like a song trailing off while the radio lost power. "Just remember, you're welcome back to the Heaux B. Haven any time." The fiend's smile curled higher, exposing razor-sharp teeth and slit eyes. Her claws returned to Sarah's neck, squeezing out a final breath.

"Pray for us sinners," the sinister, raspy voice hissed at her as it watched the light dimming in her eyes. Sarah's chest was billowing, but the obstruction was not budging. Darkness crept in the edges of her peripheral before fingers of ink spread across her field of vision.

Then it all went black again.

Sarah gasped for air, a weight pressed on her heaving breasts. She was encased in darkness again, but her eyes were wide open. Her nerve endings all seemed to be firing at once. Then she felt the writhing against her skin. Then the scent hit her, incense and pine. Angelique sat up, prying herself from their warm embrace.

"I never came so hard in my life," she said, still out of breath. "I'm actually dizzy!" Angelique giggled as she toppled over, lying next to Sarah. She stared into Sarah's eyes, still dazed and wondering where she had gone. Angelique nudged her nose against Sarah's chin and slid her arms around her.

"Garde-moi au chaud amoureux."

Keep me warm, lover.

The candle flickered, causing Sarah to stare up at her ceiling, then turn frantically toward the head of her bed. Not exactly sure who or what she'd expect to see sitting there, she stared at the dancing shadows as Angelique pulled their conjoined hands back.

"Are you alright?" she asked before they came face to face again.

"Yeah, sorry, I just. I just can't believe this is all happening. I can't believe you're here, in my bed. It's all I've ever wanted," Sarah said, her eyes going glassy.

"Mon Dieu! You did not tell me, Sarah. I am...I was...your first time?" Angelique asked, staring into her eyes intently.

"I never thought, I never knew it could be like this. I'd never wanted to be with anyone the way I wanted to be with you." Sarah said, her mind still buzzing from the moment.

Angelique brought her hands to Sarah's face and pulled their mouths together. The electricity flowed between them as their lips needfully caressed each other. Sarah let her tongue slip inside Angelique's mouth, exploring every inch with a newfound vigor. Angelique welcomed the intrusion, sucking on Sarah's tongue and jousting with her own within their shared openings. Sarah felt Angelique's cold fingertips prickle against her skin as they wrapped around her exposed breast. Her cool palms made her nipples stiffen in protest, even though her body temperature was rising to fight the cold. A gentle moan vibrated through her throat, exciting Angelique all over again.

She kicked her leg over Sarah and used their grip as leverage to mount her once again. Sarah couldn't take her eyes off the delicate beauty that stared down at her with an intense, hungry gaze.

"I was your first, and now I want to be your second." Angelique cooed as she pulled Sarah's hands up to her chest and let them rest on her breasts once more.

"This is too good to be true." Sarah marveled at this goddess incarnate staring back at her while Angelique once again started to gyrate her hips to her own silent melody.

"Of course it is, silly." Angelique raised her arms above her head and let them sway. Sarah watched the flicks of the candle create dark masks over her smiling face.

"You know how this ends. You fall hopelessly in love with me and ultimately choose your faith over your true happiness." The sugary-sweet broken English no longer registered in her voice. Sarah snapped out of her lustful daze and let her hands tumble down to her sides.

"I brought my parents here to meet you. Told them all about you. Told them how you planned to be an army medic just so my dad and you would have something to talk about. They couldn't wait to meet the first girl I wanted to introduce them to. When I came to get you, your room was empty. You didn't even leave me a note. I was too hurt to be embarrassed, too angry to cry. The look on my parents' faces, unsure what to do next, made me feel the most alone I'd ever felt."

Sarah's tears dripped down the side of her face into her hair. Her chin quaked as she tried to form words with her dancing jaw. "I didn't know what to... I was so scared. I didn't know what I was. I thought I wanted to stay here and be with you, but...how could I explain? How could I live a lie? What if the church found out?"

Sarah cautiously tried to return her hands to Angelique's hips. Tears appeared to stream down her face before her phantom lover turned to look skyward.

"You left me here to rot."

Angelique's arms intertwined above her head, the backs of her hands together in a striking ballerina pose. A cold air filled the room. Sarah could see her breath as it exited her mouth.

"Just like all of your dirty little secrets."

The words came out as a hushed whisper, dry as autumn leaves drifting down before they landed on a speechless, frozen Sarah. Her eyes stayed stuck on Angelique, holding her perfectly posed posture until a lone blond ringlet of hair slipped off her still upward-looking head and landed behind her. The candle was almost burnt to the base, lowering the already sparse light in the freezing room. The clouds shifted, allowing some moonlight to shine into Sarah's window, which gave Angelique a surreal blue tone. The smell of sickly sweet putrescence began infiltrating the room and Sarah's nostrils.

The silence and frozen animation of Angelique made Sarah's blood run cold. Her chilled fingers still sat on either side of Angelique's hips, now feeling just as cold as ice and sharp as the head of a shovel. Angelique broke the silence by emitting a string of squelching sounds and a whispering whoosh when the rest of her blonde curls tumbled down and landed on Sarah's exposed thighs. Angelique's blue-tinged skin looked like it was moving before Sarah's eyes. The surprise shock of the nearly weightless drop sucked the air out of her chest. She instinctually pulled her arms back to sit up on her elbows when the rocking of her hips caused Angelique to fall forward again.

A wide-eyed Sarah watched the skeletal totem that had taken the place of Angelique plummeting toward her. The sickening wet slap of a moist skull bludgeoning Sarah's face sent waves of cracking fireworks into her eyes and sinuses. The initial impact shattered her nasal bone and sent slivers of its thin shards into her soft membranes. Blood filled her nasal cavity, causing her to rock up and take a breath as it poured down her throat.

Sarah reflexively sucked in air, as well as the slimy remnants of rotted flesh that were filling her open mouth like an overflowing manhole. A thick layer of damp rot pulled away from Angelique's bones like a slow-roasted leg of lamb. Undulating insects used her face like a greasy slide as they cascaded onto her shoulders. Vomit flew out of Sarah's screaming, gagging mouth as she tried to wriggle out and away from the corpse of her first true love. Now reduced to sheets of festering gelatin that coated her skin and the inside of her mouth. Angelique's bones continued to stick to Sarah and crack under her weight as she tried to roll off the bed. Spurs of bone punctured her sides and sliced into her thigh.

A scream was building up in her chest that she finally let loose when she made it to the floor. Her shaking hands scrambled to any clothing she could feel as she used her bra to carefully wipe the muck from her mouth and enflamed, crackling nose. She pulled the T-shirt she had been kneeling on out from under her and used it to clear whatever was obstructing her eyes. Gore clots with bits of Angelique rocketed out of her wilted nostrils until she was finally able to take an actual deep inhale. She exhaled a pained wail as she doubled over and hugged her carrion-caked head to her knees. If there was ever a time in her life that she needed to pray—to ask for a helping hand—it would be now. Then the thought stabbed into her brain like an ice pick that made her cries stick in her choking throat.

Who would answer her prayers?

Too Many Fingers in One Pie
Chapter 17

Sister Ophelia felt a surge of adrenaline course through her veins when her arm jerked free of the wall. She pulled her fist to her chest until the stinging ache dissipated, and the dangling rope tickled her bare leg through her open robe, barely held in place. Once she could feel her fingers again, she pulled the saliva-strewn ball gag from her mouth and took in a lungful of the most putrid air she had ever encountered. The relief was a mixed blessing, to say the least. She took a few more deep breaths and tried to calm herself, feeling for the other restraint on her still-attached arm. She could feel several complex knots coiled around her wrist, but was able to feel them give the more she manipulated their coiled intricacies. After a few tries, she completely freed her other hand.

As she waited for the blood flow to return to her unencumbered limb, she trepidatiously noticed the structure of the wall behind her. The surface felt like it was starting to compress and crackle around the aperture. Her body tensed, causing her to slow her movements reflexively, with the very real concern weighing on her mind that she might get crushed under a ton of bricks. Her mind couldn't help but reflect on the situation she'd gotten herself into and the irony of her lifeless body being found under a pyramid of bricks after being tied up in some weird sex dungeon.

The horrifying stench was her main concern right now, that is, after she freed her legs. Still blind in the thick darkness, she felt behind her for the knots and turned until she sat on the damp floor, searching the tangles with her nimble fingers. She noticed a very dim sliver of moonlight that seemed to be coming from the small opening where the kicked-off bricks got pushed.

Sister Ophelia loosened the ropes enough to pull her overtaxed feet through, allowing herself a split second of gratitude that she was granted mercy. As she shakily stood, she felt the urge to pray. She felt the need to thank the Almighty for allowing her to escape. Like she wanted to pay her respects to the same being that put her in this situation, led her to this convent in the first place, and allowed her to be manipulated as long as she had been under one of its employees.

She was thankful that the urge passed, eclipsed by the curiosity of what was behind this crumbling brick wall.

She wanted to pull the string for the single light bulb in the space, but something told her it wasn't worth the chance of anyone noticing it. Instead, she tried the door handle—knowing it was locked—but she had to check. That left her two options: the festering hole in the wall or waiting out this punishment.

"The fuck am I seeing?" she whispered as she got closer to the hole.

The closer she got to it, the more the fetid air slapped her in the face. She could feel the stench of rot clinging to her, exposing and soaking into her sweat-dotted skin. Her actual need for survival trumped the artificial thought patterns her anxiety was supplying her as she peered into the space.

She placed her hands gingerly on the exposed brick opening and slightly stuck her head through the roughly foot-wide hole. She could feel loose bricks around the opening that jostled under her light pressure. Inside, she could see moonlight shining through a small, dingy window on the other side of the area. It only seemed to be a few feet away. Her stomach gurgled just thinking about what was creating the scent that caused her to only breathe through her mouth. She knew this was her only choice.

Sister Ophelia apprehensively felt around the opening; the bricks on the top felt secure, but the lower and surrounding bricks seemed like they could be removed. She had to clear as many as she could to squeeze through. Cautiously, she began to wiggle and pull, placing the loose bricks on the ground below. She paused between each removal to listen for any sign of an incoming deluge. After a small pile of bricks sat at her feet, she decided this was it. Now, or never, time was of the essence. Whatever waited on the other side was certainly better than what was in here.

The ominous opening was now roughly the size of a manhole, just vertical. She tightened her robe but paused when she realized her state of dress she was about to attempt an escape in. Her stomach bottomed out as she decided this was it; there was no turning back. She went and stuck one leg through the mysterious maw.

Ophelia fought to keep her body upright but found herself discombobulated beyond belief once she made it to the other side. The darkness, the lack of oxygen, and her taking shallow breaths of stinking air caused her to dizzily hit the ground with a sickening wet crunch and a face full of musty dander. Sharp shards of what felt and smelled like rotted wood pierced her palms and knees. Still, she pushed forward, toward the light, determined to make it out of there. She was forced to army crawl against the gravelly pockets of stone and tattered rags that clung to her exhausted body. Bits of God-knows-what stuck to her lips, no matter how much she spit out, and stung her tongue with a tang that set her on high alert.

She finally reached a diagonal hole that felt like a slide with the dusty moonlit window above. She used the oddly slanted wall to pull herself up to the filthy see-through trap door, it took her more than a few tries. She noticed it was loosely closed. The lock was held together by what felt like a wire hanger and a few flat pieces of plywood. She could feel the rusty wire scraping her hands and a collection of splinters jabbing into her skin, but she persevered.

She pushed and pulled, noting that the hinge at the top was beginning to allow more sway. She pulled her body closer to the window, fitting the wood planks in any opening she could, and put all her weight behind her shoulder. With one final push on the wood slats, she felt her gnarled hands touch the earth. Twigs and leaves crunched below them. The vines and shrubbery that cloaked the opening gave way. Sister Ophelia pulled herself forward through the loose grass and rolled onto the ground. The window slammed shut with a satisfying crunch as she lay, staring up at the moon she had now witnessed twice in one night.

Sister Ophelia was so unbelievably exhausted that she couldn't fathom what she had gone through, crawled through, or even what she was about to do. What she did know was what she perhaps knew all along but forced herself to go with. She did not belong here. She was not one of them. She loved her Sisters like she would love any of her friends. But she was not meant to be tied down. She was not meant to be under scrutiny every moment of every day. She was not meant to be an example or a follower but to fly free. The realization lit a fire in her belly allowing her to stand slowly and walk away from the building.

The moon bathed her skin and created an ethereal blue tone. She paused for a breath against the side of the outer chapel.

From that vantage point, she could see her hidden gate opening that promised an unsure future, but freedom nonetheless. She turned to peer behind her one last time. All she saw was a cage. Empty promises. Empty vows. Why follow a vow of silence when no one listens anyway? Why live under a vow of obedience in a world run by tyrants? She was her father's daughter, but why live caged like a bird in a world that already treated her like one? At that moment, she decided—made the decision she knew she should've made in the first place—she followed her heart. Her heart led her to her secret passage, and her feet were not far behind.

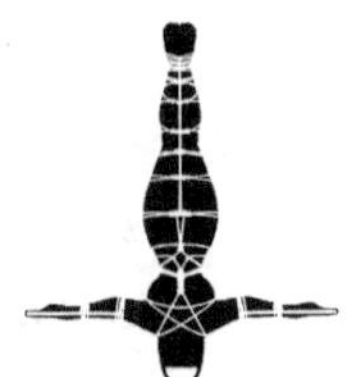

The smell of apples and cinnamon smacked Lidwina in the face. She turned over in bed, shocked to see the sunlight, and sat up groggily. She had woken up late, which never happened. Usually, you could hear Mother Superior's booming, arrogant monologues, or at least a–

"Saints be praised!" floated through the upper rooms, giving Lidwina some comfort, knowing at least some things were as they should be.

The incident with Ophelia still weighed heavy on her heart. She hoped she could make it up to her somehow or at least not let it spoil the celebration. She donned her gay apparel: her plaid button-up, denim booty shorts, boots, and all. It only seemed appropriate for the occasion. She even parted her hair in two bouncy pigtails for the special day, which allowed her red waves to look their best.

As she came downstairs, she noticed a cheery air that she had never felt before in this place. She heard hustling and bustling in the kitchen and smiled as she began to smell succulent roasting meat on her way through the dining room. As she entered the kitchen, Emelie waved to her and made a shushing gesture. Sister Veronica, Bernadette, and Tatiana all did the same. Lidwina eyed the delicious-looking apple pie on the counter as she stepped closer.

Sister Veronica dried her hands on her apron and whispered, "I'm glad you got some sleep. I'm sure you needed it. Something tells me you're gonna need a lot of energy today," she whispered and smiled innocently.

"Ugh, I couldn't sleep, and then Sister Calliope talked my ear off until I finally passed out," She whispered before looking at them all. "Why are we whispering?" Lidwina said softly, eying the flaky pie crust with cross cutouts.

Sister Veronica stepped closer and placed her hands beside the pie on the island counter. "Mother Superior is sleeping in today, too. It's a miracle." She winked. "Happy Lidwinapalooza!" she said in a loud whisper. The other nuns repeated it in a whisper. Lidwina was starving, but something told her not to spoil her appetite.

"What time is it?" she asked, looking at the microwave clock glaring from the midday sun.

"Almost two p.m.," Sister Veronica responded after checking her watch. "The roast doesn't have much longer. We could eat a little earlier if you'd like—if you want something more substantial than oatmeal. It's your day, dearie; it's up to you."

"That does sound good. That pie looks amazing. I could probably eat that whole thing myself," Lidwina said, eyeing the caramelized filling dripping from one side. "Who made it?"

Emelie piped up. "I made the crust, but Sister Veronica did everything else."

Sister Veronica beamed and added, "I picked the biggest, reddest apples in the bunch. I know you like them plump and juicy."

Lidwina nodded a knowing smile, eyeing the pie and then Sister Emilie, who blushed.

"Or you could start with dessert!" Sister Veronica said, matter of factly. "I won't lie, I'm curious how everything tastes. We got so burned out on oatmeal and apples before, but I must say, the smell of this pie is driving my mind wild."

"Well then, I vote we do pie first," Lidwina said with a smile. Emelie reached for the butcher knife from the block and asked if she could do the honors. The Sisters nodded in agreement. Lidwina looked at them all again, then back toward the pantry, and lastly, looked outside while Emelie began making delicate little cuts in the pie.

"Where's Ophelia?" Lidwina asked.

Sister Veronica was placing a dried pan on the hook above but accidentally banged it against a hanging pot once she heard the question. She set the pan where it needed to be and turned toward Lidwina with a solemn face.

"I'm afraid she won't be able to join us, my child. Mother Superior caught her being truant again last night and is now disciplining her. So, unfortunately, she's not going to make it."

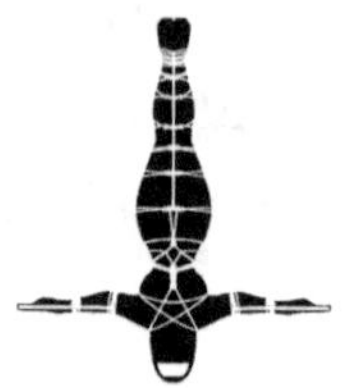

Mother Superior rose like a ghoul from her crypt, groggy and disoriented. The sour taste in her mouth occupied her mind more than the sunlight shining through her closed drapes. The silence brought her an ambivalent relief that bored a hole in her already pounding head. The lingering taste of fly agaric made her regretfully think about the dreams from last night. Her body shuddered and ached as the rest of her mind attempted to reassemble itself. The daylight began to register to her as the hour became apparent. Then it all came flooding back.

Flashes from her dreams interweaved with thoughts of her bound and gagged captor. She dressed as quickly as possible, dropping her Mary Janes multiple times in her clumsy distract-edness. While she slipped on her veil, the empty hypodermic needle landed with a sharp snap, prompting her to stash it in one her drawers apprehensively. As she finished tying her belt and grabbed her rosary, the shiny red beads prompted the deed she had committed last night and the trail of breadcrumbs she had to clean up before it was too late.

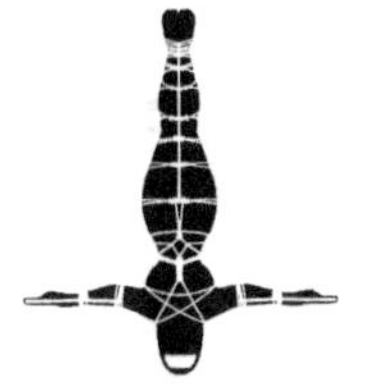

Sister Emelie licked the sweet, cinnamon-laded syrup from her thumb as she handed the pieces down to her excited Sisters. She cut the biggest piece for Lidwina- knowing what a sweet tooth she had- and plated the second biggest piece for Sister Veronica. Even though she was busy breaking the bad news to Lidwina, Emelie was sure the pastry would turn all their frowns upside down, much like hers right now. She wasn't sure why, but she couldn't remember ever being this happy. Ever.

Ever, ever, ever.

Ever, ever, ever, ever.

If she smiled any bigger, she feared her teeth would crack into little exploding candy cane pieces.

Say, where did that pie go?

What was that?

Is the sky falling?

A series of bumps above their heads let them know Mother Superior had finally risen. The joy melted off their faces, except for Emelie, for some reason. Sister Veronica froze, fork in hand, about to dive into her pie. She quickly rose from the bar stool and put her apron back on. The other Sisters, except Emelie, pushed the pie away from them on the shared island tabletop. Lidwina watched in fascination as Emelie kept jamming her finger in the pie crust and watching the filling ooze out of the sides. Every few jabs, she would taste it and giggle, seductively winking at her...or was that a twitch?

"Emelie!" Sister Veronica whispered, eying the novitiate as she pointed to the pantry with her head and made her way there. Emelie sluggishly slumped in her seat, licking the filling from between her fingers and blurted out, "Why did that old bitch have to wake up anyways?" to a stunned room.

Lidwina couldn't help but giggle.

This was about to get interesting.

As much as she wanted to enjoy the show, it wasn't nearly as fun as it would have been if Sister Ophelia was there to enjoy it. She frowned and looked down at her plate. An idea crept into her head. She rose from the table with pie in hand and exited the kitchen. Unbeknownst to the petrified penguins piling in the pantry.

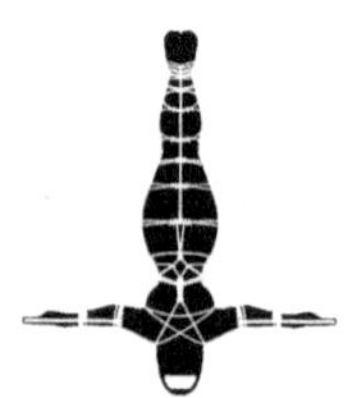

Mother Superior lurched into the hall, using the bedroom doors to keep her balance. Her vision flickered, and her mind reeled. She felt the overwhelming rush as the voice of the Virgin Mary forced its way into her mind. Her head was beginning to spin, and her knees buckled as she braced herself against the banister at the top of the stairs. She felt bile bubbling at the back of her throat, forcing her to point her head toward the floor in case it finished its journey.

Through exasperated breaths, Mary's voice poured out of her as pained whimpers.

"And I will kindle a fire in the forest thereof," she hacked, "and it shall devour all things round about it. On flaming fire taking vengeance on them that know not God." She coughed and swallowed. "And that obey not the gospel of her glory."

The nausea passed, allowing her the strength to peer into the foyer. To her shock and blinding vexation, she saw Lidwina walking down the stairs to the basement. Mother Superior slogged down the stairs but was unsure which way to proceed. Only she had the key to the Penitence Room, but she wouldn't put the notion past Lidwina to have something to pick the lock on her person. Then, she thought about the apples and the smells of supper wafting from the kitchen. The object of her aversion needed to be top priority.

"Her blood will I acquire at thine hand!" erupted from her lips as she felt the eyes of the Madonna piercing her. The fabric of her vestments undulated across the stone floor as she crossed the foyer and followed Lidwina down the dark steps. The outburst alerted Lidwina to the advancing nun coming in hot. She turned to face her, slipping the multitool back in her pocket, and presented the plate and fork.

As Mother Superior stumbled from the last step, Lidwina cocked her head and gave her a once-over glance. The flustered nun propelled herself forward and stood nonplussed before her Penitence Room.

"What do you think you're doing, Lidwina?" Mother Superior said, cocking an eyebrow.

"Bringing our prisoner some food, *Mother*, or is that against one of your rules?"

"I don't think I appreciate your tone, Lidwina. I fear your time with us will end sooner than anticipated with that level of familiarity and cheek."

"Are you fucking through?"

Mother Superior took a startled step back. Lidwina switched hands with the plate and rattled the door knob indignantly.

"Lidwina! I will not tolerate your filthy mouth. You will be asked to leave this convent at once if you do not respect my authority."

Lidwina laughed in her face, and mid-laugh went deadpan and stated, "Sister, you couldn't handle my mouth." Without missing a beat, she added, "Kick me out so I can alert the proper authorities that you are holding girls hostage and not feeding them. You'll be able to pray all you want—in handcuffs."

Sister Veronica, put on lookout duty, had ventured into the foyer to report her superior's location. Overhearing that ostentatious outburst sent her right back where she came from, glad she wasn't in Lidwina's boots right then.

Color drained from Mother Superior's face as the realization hit her. The Virgin Mary's screams shredded through her mind while she calmly retrieved the keys from her pocket.

"That won't be necessary." Mother Superior said, calculating how quickly she could get to her cabinet of contrition. "This is all just an honest to God miscommunication, dear." She delivered sweetly, pondering which flogger had a hard enough butt end to cave in a human skull.

Lidwina maintained her facade of tranquility as Mother Superior performatively unlocked the door and opened it a sliver.

Behind a pretense of peace, Mother Superior stepped out of Lidwina's way as she glanced up the stairs, pleased to see no eavesdroppers. Lidwina charged into the room as Mother Superior explained. "Now you know how we discipline here. So don't be alarmed when you see O..."

An angered Lidwina turned back to her and yelled, "Where the fuck is she?!" just as the foul stench hit her. Mother Superior rushed into the room once she caught her footing.

"What are you talking about?" she asked while she stared at where she had left Sister Ophelia the night before. Lidwina pulled the string for the light and yelled out, "and what the *fuck* is that smell?"

Mother Superior's eyes darted around the room to Lidwina's to monitor her movements.

"Wait, wait, wait!" Mother Superior babbled, raising her hands defensively as Lidwina menacingly approached her. The abrupt retreating rotundness of her rear caused the Penitence Room door to close behind her. Which just left her and the pissed *plaid-ette* in the malodorous space. Mother Superior grabbed for the cross on her rosary, holding it toward Lidwina to perhaps keep the demoness at bay.

Lidwina belligerently stared at the miniature crucifix in her hand and then back at her. "If I don't get answers right now, you're going to need a lot more than that to keep me off of your ass!" Lidwina spat, fed up with the stall tactics. She turned away from Mother Superior, intent on answering her own questions, the first one being, *what the hell is behind that wall?*

Mother Superior gasped and pushed away from the door, her rosary still in one hand. She grabbed Lidwina's arm, trying to firmly lead her away from making any discoveries.

"Lidwina, no! Look at me!" she said, tightening her grip and pulling just as Lidwina was inches from the inglorious hole. Lidwina gritted her teeth and swung her free arm around, smashing the pie, plate, and fork into Mother Superior's matriarchal mandible. The blow caught Mother Superior off guard, snapping her head to the right. Her head housed a sea of stars as she fell back and landed on her padded posterior.

Lidwina seized the opportunity to grab the swinging pendant bulb and pointedly thrust it toward the curious crevasse, determined to shed some light on the situation while Mother Superior was still down and hearing church bells. Though the fixture didn't give too much light, its swinging allowed her to see the black mold-covered floor within the small crawlspace to what appeared to be an old coal chute turned into an improvised window. It wasn't until she panned lower that her eyes scanned assorted scraps and remnants, until the bulb's revolution faintly highlighted two deep-set holes in an otherwise dingy yellowed globe. Lidwina realized in stunned disbelief that she was staring at a human skull.

Her stomach lurched as she slowly moved closer, kicking at the loose brick and noticing what seemed to be tattered rags and protruding femurs. An unmistakable rib cage was the last thing she saw in the makeshift catacomb before the pain of the fork being jammed into her thigh caused her to change focus.

Mother Superior screamed, putting her weight on the burrowed flatware, digging it so deep in Lidwina's leg that it scraped bone. Her maniacal, strudel-strewn face was already beginning to swell from a pie-in-the-face gag gone awry. Lidwina let out a scream that shook the room before she hammered her closed fist down onto the side of Mother Superior's cheekbone. After a few choice mallet chops, Stabitha Stevens plummeted to the hard concrete like Lucifer nosediving from heaven.

Lidwina wrenched the fork out of the bleeding divot in her leg, unable to give proper thought to why her screams seemed to be echoing above them. Thankfully, the tines hadn't punctured anything crucial, but that would be an interesting scar to discuss at parties.

Mother Superior grunted as she was using the wall to push herself up.

Lidwina looked at her formidable opponent and the ropes dangling down from the hooks she had reinforced. She proceeded toward an almost upright Mother Superior, corralling her toward the swaying tethers.

Mother Superior yammered to Lidwina, cowering behind her hands.

"Ha-have mercy. You must- just let me explain!" she yelled at Lidwina, turning her bruised face away in defense.

Lidwina stood over her, snatching her wrist and began to wrap the rope around it before she yelled, "You've got about 30 seconds while I hog tie you in your little dungeon!" Mother Superior instinctively pulled her other paw away, making Lidwina snarl.

"Give me a reason to snap your neck with my bare hands, you homicidal heifer. I dare you."

Lidwina grabbed for her other wrist. Mother Superior submitted and began trying to explain.

"You don't understand! I didn't want to! She made me!" Mother Superior said, tears streaming down her face.

"Who made you?! Who did this?" Lidwina yelled, looking into Mother Superior's crazed face.

"Mary did! Mary made me do it! She told me I had to clean the convent and rid it of impurities. If I didn't get rid of those bastards, they would have hurt our Sisters!"

"So those were the priests in the photos?"

"Yes, yes! I had to do it. I did what had to be done!"

Lidwina furrowed her brow, listening to the ramblings of a mad woman. She reached for the knotted ropes next to her, making Mother Superior flinch in response before she understood she was about to have her ankles tied as well.

"Wait, Lidwina! Let me finish! I did it for my girls! I did it for *OUR* Sisters. Don't you see!" Mother Superior's face was awash of tears and baked apple bits.

Lidwina was fighting her own thoughts, trying to make sense of all of this. She pulled the ends of the rope tightly around Mother Superior's ankles, watching the raw pale skin behind them turn rose petal pink.

"And speaking of *OUR* Sisters, where is Sister Ophelia?!" Lidwina stood, trying to gather her wits.

Mother Superior began to stutter and stammer again,

"I-I-I-I really don't know, Lidwina. I left her in here last night and haven't been down since. I swear it!"

Lidwina sneered, wanting to pound the other half of Mother Superior's face in when they both heard ungodly shrieks from above them. They both froze and watched the ceiling, listening to the bellows. Lidwina started to make her way for the door.

"Wait, wait, wait, Lidwina! You can't leave me in here! Don't leave me in here. Why—why I can help you look for Ophelia. I might even know where she went!"

Another blood-curdling scream could be heard coming from above, cutting Lidwina's rebuttal short but sweet as she pulled the light cord and closed the door behind her. "Go to Hell."

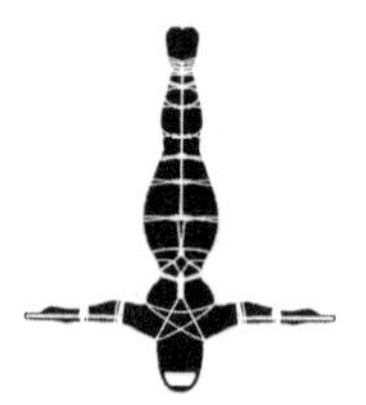

Mother Superior's yells could be heard through the hardwood door as Lidwina used the hanging keyring still in the lock to keep her inside. An ear-piercing wail startled her, making her almost drop them. She pocketed the keys and ran up the stairs toward what she knew would be the worst surprise party ever.

Mother Superior slumped against the musty brick wall, manipulating the poorly tied knots against her wrists. This was not how she had planned things, but if there was one thing she was, it was resilient. The crocodile tears on her cheeks began to dry as she felt the tension in her wrists loosening, prompting her tongue to dart out the side of her mouth and taste the sweet, leftover pie on her cheek.

Mmmmm cinnamon.

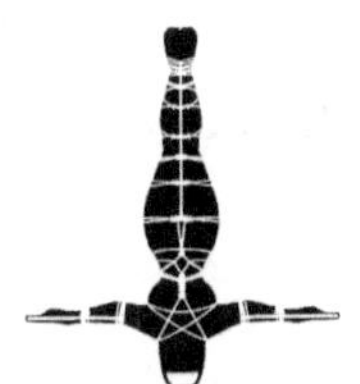

Sister Veronica scuttled back into the kitchen, her mind still reeling from hearing someone finally standing up to Mother Superior. She loved her work bestie, but everyone needed to get knocked down a peg sometimes.

She walked past a still-seated Emelie, who was having the best time pulling the strands of her brown hair from below her habit and watching them fall in front of her face. The other two novitiates had just finished putting the last dishes away.

Sister Tatiana asked, "Do you think Mother Superior will be joining us?"

"I'm not certain, love, but I have a feeling things are about to heat up in here," Sister Veronica responded, remembering to baste the browning roast.

Sister Emelie piped up through her latticed hair draped across her face.

"As soon as we say grace, we can eat, *right?* I'm *tired* of *waiting,"* she exclaimed like a petulant toddler.

Sister Veronica slumped her shoulders and shook her head in resignation.

"Yes, yes, girls, let's eat while we have the freedom to do so."

Veronica pulled out her stool and sat at the kitchen island as the other novitiates joined them. Sister Bernadette offered to say grace and nodded, smiling at her Sisters. Before they could pick up their forks, Emelie had dug her fingers into her pie to shovel bits into her waiting mouth.

The girls watched the show, giggling as they took their first bites. Sister Veronica finished chewing and swallowing, her eyes trained on Emelie.

"Sister Emelie! I've never seen you in such a mood. You must really be enjoying our little confection." Veronica said with a chuckle.

The childish nun's eyes slowly rose to look at her, then her Sisters, and a goofy smile crept across her face.

"It's more fun with your hands." She paused mid-chew to look at her long, spindly fingers. "They are my forks." She pointed her fingertips down and proceeded to stab the mangled pie multiple times like a dainty pitchfork.

"It's very good, Sister Veronica," Sister Tatiana said between chews, "but what's the spice you used? It's making my tongue tingle." She gave a surprised giggle and covered her mouth with the hand holding her fork while she finished chewing and let out a little cough.

"Oh, the nutmeg, that's probably the nutmeg!" Sister Veronica said, chunking off pieces of the pie sliced before she took another forkful. "I was always heavy-handed with the nutmeg," she said with a smile. Her eyes traced the wood grain in the countertop that led to Emelie, now licking her plate and eyeing the butcher's knife sitting in the quarter-full pie plate.

Sister Bernadette's fork hit her plate, startling them all and quieting the room. Below them came muffled yelling, but they were none the wiser. Bernadette began to pull at the cowl of her habit uncomfortably.

"It's so hot in here," she said, pulling at the fabric enough to hear a small tear. "Oh no!" escaped her mouth as she tried to look down at her torn vestment.

"I'll open a window." Sister Veronica said, standing shakily from her stool and taking another forkful. Her dilated pupils looked at her reflection in the window as she unlocked and slid it open. Stools shuffled behind her, but she was too transfixed to notice.

"Girls!" she paused. "When were you going to tell me that I got old?" she asked, giggling and pawing at her reflection. The laughter relaxed her and reminded her where she was. Her eyes traced the sun rays that seemed to point to the firepit, which reminded her.

"Oh! I must start the bonfire! I almost forgot. Who wants to help?"

Sister Veronica pulled herself from her reflection and waited for one of the girls to respond. Sister Emelie sat between Tatiana and Bernadette and pulled at Bernadette's damaged guimpe while Tatiana watched with her head resting on her arm across the table. The stained white neckerchief and cowl came off in one piece. Giving all three of them something to gasp and laugh at.

"Just me, I guess," Sister Veronica said, hovering over her plate to shovel the last bite of pie into her gaping maw. After she chewed and swallowed, she let out a loud belch that made the three novitiates all howl in uproarious laughter. Sister Veronica's already flushed face turned even brighter pink. "Oh, bless me, or no, excuse me. Well, pardon me!" She giggled to herself as she opened drawers and began to look for the long matches.

"You're so pretty, Bernadette," Sister Tatiana stated lazily, still staring at her with her head in the crook of her arm. "I've wanted to kiss you for so long," she said with a starry-eyed grin.

Sister Emelie was cupping Bernadette's face in her hands while she tried to fix her hair back in place. "I want to kiss you too!" Sister Emelie said, her face only inches from Bernadette's.

"We mustn't, Sisters. I've already sinned by kissing Lidwina. I already worry I will never be forgiven," Sister Bernadette said, though her worry didn't register in her glazed-over look.

Sister Tatiana sneered and gave a dismissive glance toward them before she lazily said, "I kissed Lidwina too, but I bet I'm a better kisser than her."

Emelie gasped and squeezed Bernadette's face between her two hands. "I want to try!" she said, bringing her lips to Bernadette's conflicted face. Bernadette instinctually puckered her lips and closed her eyes, only for Emelie to begin to lick the bits of pie from the sides of her mouth. Emelie continued to lick across her cheeks and nose, like a mother cat cleaning her kitten.

Bernadette pulled her face up and laughed.

"Stop Emelie, that's not kissing and that tickles!"

She pulled away, and Emelie continued licking the air in her seat. "I want to chew on it! It tastes so good!"

Bernadette ignored her, stood, and lifted her tunic, letting it billow in the cool air.

"It's so hot! I can't stop sweating."

Tatiana popped her head up, stating, "Not me; I'm cold. Feel." She stood and placed her chilly hands on Emelie's face.

Bernadette's eyes bulged, and she gasped, staring into Tatiana's drooping, sleepy eyes. "That feels so good!" she said, placing her hands over Tatiana's.

Tatiana looked deep into Sister Bernadette's eyes. Their eyes were dark pools of pupils, reflecting each other. She whispered, "How could you let her kiss you before I did?"

Bernadette started to cry, but her mouth wouldn't let her words come out. Emelie shuffled to the stool on the other side of the island, grabbed the butcher knife, and began stabbing it into the leftover pie.

Sister Veronica closed the last drawer and watched her girls kissing, playing, and having a good time.

"Oh, if only I were 20 years younger!" she said with a slur, lumbering toward the back hall to go to the courtyard. "Don't let Mother Superior catch you!" She chuckled.

Tatiana was now kissing Bernadette deeply, their slobbery, numb lips smacking against each other. Tatiana lorded over the still-seated Bernadette, kneading her breasts hidden behind her tunic and moaning. Emelie continued to watch the pair, licking her lips and stabbing the 10-inch butcher's knife into the pie plate until the sound of the blade tip clunking the glass pie plate became muffled pricks.

Bernadette lifted her tunic above her head, confusing Tatiana in all the folds. The fabric flashed in front of her face like a bullfighter's cape.

Sister Emelie watched the pair lecherously, biting her lower lip while she continued to bring the knife down with one hand. Her other hand traveled down to rub her swelling vulva. Feeling the heat and the moisture seeping into her vestments made her angry. The harder she pawed at her aching wetness, the harder she stabbed with the other. The thunk of the glass cracking made her freeze, then break out into a giggle. She let the knife drop, the blade grazing her hand as she let it fall to the counter.

"Ow!" she yelled angrily, flinging the knife across the counter and pouting. Her eyes darted between Bernadette's nipple being sucked and pulled on by Tatiana's teeth and the red sliver that began to open in her hand. The moaning next to her, combined with the red syrup that was leaking from her palm and down her wrist, made her lean against the counter to watch it pool. She watched intently, positioning her dripping pussy against the stool while she worked her hips back and forth.

I'm a pie. I'm made of pie. What kind of pie am I?

She pulled at the dissected pie plate in front of her, maintaining her humping action against her seat, while she found the biggest piece of the pie plate. She held it in front of her, watching the distorted view behind the warped glass.

What's my pie? Who am I? Are they made of pie? What do I taste like?

Through the glass, she saw a two-headed, six-legged creature writhing on the counter. Her vision began to go blurry as the orgasm built up below her. She shuddered as she pummeled the bar stool below her and caught her breath.

Tatiana had pushed Bernadette onto the counter and was lapping at her sweet honeypot, open to her through her spread legs. Bernadette could feel the waves of pleasure rushing through her body as she bucked her hips against Tatiana's suctioned mouth. She opened her eyes and watched the swirling ceiling above and felt the shaking coming through her knees. The clouds above were opening to take her to heaven.

Sweat dripped off Bernadette's quaking body as Tatiana did her best to work her clit with her top lip and dart her tongue between her swollen folds simultaneously.

Emelie pulled her tunic up and tucked the ruffles under her chin. She licked at the red, tangy pie juices coming out of her wrist as she pulled and sliced at her obstructive pink panties that she knew hid the best slice of pie. After a few tries, the slashed fabric fell away, and her pie began to ooze with its beautiful juices. Her clear juices mixed with the red slices she had made for the crust. Now, she just needed to cut the perfect piece.

Tatiana didn't want to come up for air; she felt like the deeper she dug into Bernadette, the quicker she could find her prize. So far, she had only scratched the surface, but she could tell by the noises that she was almost at the treasure. Tatiana felt like she had hit the limit; there were too many obstacles getting in her way. She wasn't sure her hands could do the job, but she was sure if she kept eating, she could chew her way to the finish line.

Bernadette's face contorted from pain to pleasure as she felt the heat come again; this time it came pooling from below her. The flames of hell were beginning to cook her flesh, and she needed to get as far away from them as she could. Her screams of fright commingled with ecstasy. Hell felt so good, though; her body fought with her mind, not allowing her mouth to work—just screaming unintelligibly.

Emelie watched the giant bug in front of her twitch and screech; its pink shell glistened with poison. She knew it wanted to kill her, so the only way to lure it close enough to her was to offer it her pie. She switched the grip on her glass shard and watched her red juices drip on her waiting sugary trap. She watched the bug's legs reaching higher on the counter until it found the waiting butcher knife. It was coming for her pie; it was now or never.

She stabbed the glass shard into her pie, shocked at how much it affected her eyesight. She couldn't believe how juicy the pie was. She could feel the juices pulsing from the crust and down to the floor. If this didn't entice the insect, nothing would. After two more deep slices, she just needed the bug to take the bait.

The flames burned Bernadette, she could feel the skin on her back crisp and crackle from the heat. The back of her head felt like the hair had melted into one huge mass of burnt flesh. As much as Tatiana was trying to help push her up to heaven, it wasn't working. Worst of all, the Devil wouldn't let her speak. Her body wouldn't listen. The devil was too strong. She had no choice but to stop Tatiana before it was too late.

She stared down at Tatiana, expecting to see her friend kissing her most intimately. Instead, she saw the deeply crimson face of Satan biting and pulling at her flesh. His fiery red horns were caked with gore, but he was intent on eating her whole. Her face was frozen in terror, finally seeing through the Devil's clever disguise. While the pleasure rocked through her body, she had to vanquish the demon. She stretched her arms out and up, feeling for anything she could use as a weapon. Her sweaty palms landed on the handle of a sword she was sure a higher power placed there for her.

Her skin blackened against the flames, but with all her might, she hoisted the sword above her. The devil was none the wiser, so she tensed her body and brought the magical blade down and into the fiend's bobbing head.

Emelie watched the insect attempt to stand up tall, the knife in its claw. It wouldn't turn to face her, but she knew her sweet, coppery scent enchanted the mighty bug. Her powers must have been too much for it. As she prepared to be attacked, making herself look weak and unarmed, she watched it jam the knife into its own abdomen. The eerie silence after the motion was broken by the head crying and disguising its voice as Bernadette's.

"You can't have me, Lucifer!" it yelled, jamming the knife into its thorax until its bottom half was sawed clean off. The bottom set of legs thrashed on the ground, but its movement slowed as the top half kept screaming and yelling, pulling pieces of meat off its own back. It kept screaming about the burning and the devil's tricks.

Sister Emelie collapsed with her head in her hands, overcome by her powers. She had given too much, and her pie was too much to handle.

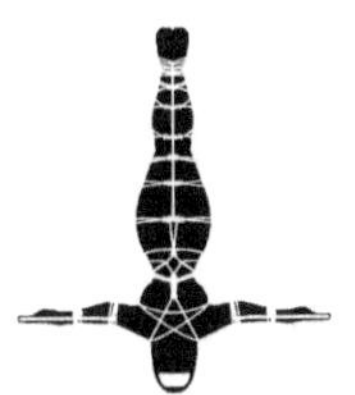

Everything hit Lidwina so fast, but she had to keep it together. She stood in the now-silent foyer. Her body jerked toward each little sound she heard, trying to pinpoint where it was coming from until it went quiet.

Her scream shattered the silence.

"Veronica? Ophelia! Where are you?!"

A clattering sound emanated from the kitchen, prompting Lidwina to investigate. A raw, coppery stench hit her as she ran through the empty dining room. Unease filled her soul as she braced herself for what was awaiting her. She slowly rounded the corner to the open door and saw Sister Emilie lying next to a fallen bar stool from the kitchen counter. Hair that peeked out of her habit was soaked in the blood pooling around her. Her eyes were a vacant stare lying in a bizarre splatter pattern that framed her dented-like a dropped egg-skull. Lidwina cautiously proceeded into the room when she discovered the novitiates Bernadette and Tatiana. Her face contorted into utter shock and disbelief at the grim scene.

Sister Tatiana was sprawled across the floor; the handle of a butcher's knife was jammed to the hilt in the side of her head. Her face was caked in blood; gore could be seen dripping out of her gaping mouth. Just above her, Sister Bernadette was in an unbelievable state. Naked as the day she was born. Her mangled nether regions, or what was left of them, looked like the remnants of a grenade explosion. Torn muscles lay underneath shredded skin, and dangling yellow fat was strewn near white bone that jutted from the darkening damaged flesh.

Lidwina was unable to fathom what she was seeing. She stepped around the maroon pools on the floor, praying that this was a nightmare. She peered around the other side of the counter, thankfully finding no other victims. Her mind was still trying to wrap around what could've taken place from when she left them to now. Looking back at Bernadette, she saw bits of torn flesh in her bloody hands still attached to her back and shoulders. Bernadette's empty eyes juxtaposed with the joyous smile plastered to her face would stay with Lidwina forever.

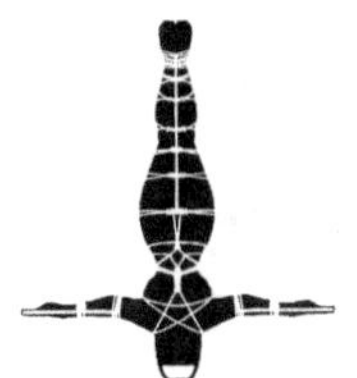

Mother Superior continued to rub her palms together and flex her forearms, loosening the ties. Her familiar smirk of disapproval returned to her slightly beaten face. A loud slam coming from above her hastened her manipulations. One last wriggling maneuver allowed her to pull one hand free from her restraints and take a deep breath of the fetid air. She stared at the hole in the brick, silently reprimanding herself for allowing such an oversight. She vowed to let it pass as long as she could somehow rectify this mishap and silence those who meant to bring disorder to *the convent built on a catacomb of love.*

She wasn't sure where Sister Ophelia had disappeared to or where Lidwina had gone after all that yelling, but she was sure she could smooth everything over as she always had. She rubbed her wrist once she freed her other one before she got started on her ankles. She wasn't certain why the notion of her being tied up in her own Penitence Room made her chuckle uncontrollably, but she had to admit that the irony wasn't lost on her. After unfettering herself, she stood and inspected her rosy cheek in the hanging vanity mirror next to the door.

She grabbed her largest flogger from the Cabinet of Contrition, reasoning it was the best accessible weapon, placed her ear against the door, and listened. No sound to be heard, giving her the go-ahead to try the lock. It was surprisingly unlocked, but opening the door let in the familiar scent of a burning roast. She slowly advanced into the hallway, thankful some things were still the same but unaware of what she was about to intrude upon. Like clockwork, she felt the Virgin Mary's voice step to the foreground to take control and reprise her role.

"Spilling her blood will be your only salvation," escaped her lips, and who was she to argue?

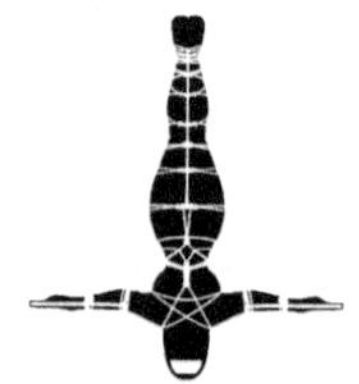

Lidwina was beyond distraught; she felt vomit geysering up her throat. She exited the kitchen and ran toward the washroom as her body lurched and vomit dripped from her chin. She made it inside a toilet stall just in time for a stream of vomit to make it in the otherwise pristine bowl. After she retched up most of her insides, she wiped her mouth and recouped her senses. She needed to find Veronica and Ophelia.

Lidwina entered the hallway; she reasoned that the only places unchecked were the chapel and upstairs. She crossed the foyer, doing her best to keep her eyes away from the dining room/kitchen, and peered through the glass chapel doors to empty pews. That led her to peer up to the empty library balcony before cautiously scaling the stairs.

She checked the four rooms on the left side of the hall-way—even her own—not finding anyone. Her frustration was forgotten due to a dull thud from below. She quickly threw open the other four doors and noticed Sister Calliope's untouched bed. As she left Mother's Superior's room—the furthest room from the stairs—she heard the unmistakable sound of someone ascending them. She gasped in relief before she ran toward the small library.

"Ophelia! Veronica!" She yelled out as the final step before the balcony creaked, and she was greeted by the unthinkable. Sister Emilie straightened her body upright after she took the final step and stood facing Lidwina. The stunned survivor bolted toward her bloody Sister before Lidwina noticed there was something wrong. The side of Sister Emilie's face was still tacky with thickening blood, but her hollow look made Lidwina stop dead in her tracks. The pale nun standing before her displayed the dripping shard of glass gripped in her hand like a vice as she staggered closer. Lidwina was frozen in place, unsure of how to proceed.

"Emelie? Emelie, talk to me." Lidwina eked out an emotional sob. "What happened?!"

The atrocity stepped forward, with an unnerving smile creeping across her face. She began to gather her tunic in her hands, showing Lidwina the torrent of blood cascading from between her legs. Lidwina pulled her eyes away from the grotesque sight and repeated herself.

"What happened, Emilie? What happened to you?! What happened here?!"

The ghoul stumbled, dropping one side of her blood-stained tunic, and opened her mouth to speak. "My pie."

Her voice came out like a hollow reed instrument. Each word seemed like it took whatever strength she had left. "Why didn't you want my pie?"

Lidwina's face grew more panicked as Sister Emilie pointed the glass shard toward her, and the twisted smile faltered. An eerie silence floated in the few feet between them before Sister Emilie slowly blinked as if she had grown sleepy. Then, like a sprung trap, Emilie dove blade-first for Lidwina. She was able to grab her shoulders, keeping the attack at bay. Sister Emilie gnashed her teeth in her direction, making Lidwina adjust her grip on the deranged nun. With freakish strength, Sister Emilie brought her arm up. The weapon glinted in the light as Lidwina fought to keep it away from her.

Sister Emelie wheezed in a hauntingly exasperated exhale. "Was I not pretty enough for you?"

Emelie laughed and shook, dragging the glass shard across her face. Lidwina's eyes widened at how the sharp edge cut an almost invisible red line on Emelie's once-perfect skin. Before Lidwina could switch her grip and stop her, Sister Emilie pressed the tip of the glass into her face and dragged the jagged shard through the meat of her cheek. Blood sprayed onto Lidwina's shocked guise and dripped down Sister Emilie's dangling, slashed jowls. Lidwina struggled to keep the crazed nun off her as Emelie asked a final question, "What about now?"

Lidwina grimaced as Emelie's wet whisper carried through the splashing blood. She braced her boot against the dry spot on the floor behind her and heaved the shell that was Sister Emilie off her. The animated corpse's face stayed unchanged, staring deep into Lidwina's eyes as her body toppled over the half bookcase and hit the railing in one fell swoop. Lidwina let out a labored groan that escalated into a roar as she peered over the bookcases in horror at the bloody remnants of her heinous deed.

WHAT'S BLACK & WHITE & RED ALL OVER?
Chapter 18

Mother Superior couldn't believe how resilient she was; she barely felt any swelling in her face. It wasn't until she noticed the numbness on the side of her mouth and tongue that the gears started to crank.

She snuck out of the Penitence Room and listened from the bottom of the stone stairs. She could hear bits of a conversation above but not enough to make out what was being said. She began to creep up the steps until she heard a struggle, pausing to listen carefully. She was halfway up when she heard Lidwina howl. Her shoulders jerked, and her eyes darted vigilantly.

As Mother Superior's eyes leveled with the foyer floor, she heard a scuffle from the upstairs library. Her eyes flinched toward the scene; her hands flew to her mouth. She fought to hold in her screams while she watched her kindest, congenial novitiate fall, hit the railing of the stairs, and bounce in mid-air, landing with an unceremonious crunch as the side of her head and jaw caught the brunt of her fall to the foyer floor. Emelie slumped over her cocked neck and the rest of her body coiled around her before it slid flat.

The motion above Mother Superior caused the astonished nun to glance up and meet the gaze of the teary-eyed screaming Lidwina. Both of their eyes went wide when they saw each other.

It wasn't until the rage registered on Lidwina's face that the redhead turned and started barreling down the stairs.

Mother Superior's eyes flashed from Emelie to the locked front doors, to the glass chapel doors, as she took off through the foyer toward her office. There were only so many places she could escape to before Lidwina could catch her. Mother Superior ran through the dining room and kitchen since the stairs bottomed out where she stood. She prayed she could get a better weapon from the kitchen.

The worn bottoms on her Mary Janes were barely making traction through the dining room when she heard the hearty thunk of Lidwina landing in the foyer after she hopped the last set of stairs. The fear of God rocked her nerves as she hit the swinging door into the kitchen. As the bald toe tread of Mother Superior's shoe hit the blood puddle, she felt herself jerking and slipping out of control. Her hip slammed into the corner of the island and threw her sideways toward the sink counter. The flogger fell and landed silently in the partially drying blood behind her. Mother Superior was having trouble recovering from the blow as she jerkily straightened herself against the counter, using it as a crutch toward the back door in the hazy kitchen.

That was when she saw the nude body of Sister Bernadette stretched across the top of the island and Sister Tatiana just below her. Her mind tried to reason what she was seeing, but the sound of pounding boots closing in made her pull away from the horrid scene. She held herself upright as she traversed the dry side of the floor next to the sink when she heard Lidwina's slippery steps closing in. The beast of a woman's hands flew toward Mother Superior, missing her cowl by a hair's width as Lidwina began to slip in the blood. Mother Superior had to change all her plans and direction as she turned away from the kitchen's back door and took off toward her office.

Lidwina skidded through the smears and puddles toward the sink from the hideous scene on the kitchen island and landed in another. She fought to give chase, slipping and sliding in the pools of mushy goo. Finally able to get some traction, after momentum took her to the back wall of the corridor. She stopped with a jerking halt next to the back door, just missing Mother Superior slamming the office door shut and locking it. Lidwina ran and rammed her slick shoulder into the hardwood door, gritting her teeth with aggravation.

Mother Superior pressed herself against the closed door and jumped when she felt Lidwina pound against it. Her eyes wildly panned the room to the only things to stop Lidwina from coming in: the two aged armchairs and her desk. However, she wasn't sure how long it would take to move that desk. She kept her back to the door and clasped her hands in prayer as it was her last refuge. Mary's words poured through her again. "Woe unto the wicked," she whispered, "the wage of sin is death."

Lidwina's yells from the other side of the door drowned her out. Mother Superior kicked her heel against the door in vexation, realizing that, even in her hour of need, her savior was telling her *the outlook is not so good.*

The kick against the door jolted Lidwina out of her enraged tirade, cussing out Mother Superior while checking if any part of the Virgin Mary could be pulled off and used as a weapon. Lidwina angrily pounded her hands against her thighs in frustration when she felt Mother Superior's keys.

Mother Superior's eyes shot open from mid-prayer when she heard Lidwina go silent. Had her prayers been answered? Did the Virgin Mary smite her foe down and save her thick hide? The sound of her keys jangling on the other side of the door answered her question and took her breath away.

Mother Superior ran toward her desk, throwing the armchairs out of her way like a defensive tackle as she passed them. She came to the other side and braced herself before she gave it a heave toward the door. The heavy desk screeched a few feet forward, but not far enough or quickly enough. The sound of keys being tried in the lock caused her to summon the strength to rocket this large piece of furniture across the room before it was too late.

She lowered her center of gravity and fired every muscle fiber in her gracious glutes. The heavy desk glided over the floor, only feet from the door. Mother Superior summoned the strength for one last push just as the lock successfully clicked and thunked. The desk stopped within inches of the door swinging open. The impact of the door slamming against the desk rattled through the wood, startling Mother Superior.

Lidwina screamed as the door was blocked, only allowing her arm and shoulder to fit through the crack. She tested the range of her grab by swatting in Mother Superior's direction but couldn't reach her across the desktop. She pulled her arm back, watching Mother Superior drop to her knees and sit, hiding behind the desk.

"Open this door and face me one on one, you fucking bitch!" Lidwina yelled, practically foaming at the mouth. Lidwina tried to maneuver through again; this time, she squeezed more of her upper body, using her back to push against the door jamb. She noticed the desk would move a little, the more she forced her way in.

Mother Superior began to hyperventilate, feeling her ass scrape the ground with her back pressed against the front of the desk. She begged the Virgin Mary to give Lidwina an aneurysm, to protect her now in her hour of need by letting the earth swallow Lidwina whole. Let her be overcome by the smoky roast…. *Anything.* She reached for her rosary and had a revelation.

Mother Superior sat up on her knees, still pressed against the desk, while holding her rosary with both hands. She watched Lidwina take a few steps back and rush her body into the door, making progress with each slam. This was her only chance outside of going out the window, and she wanted to save that for her emergency plan B. She finally got the bottom half of the crucifix free of the rosary just as Lidwina crammed her torso through the breached door. Mother Superior ducked and pulled back as Lidwina took swipes at her.

Lidwina was about to let out a barrage of every name under the sun as Mother Superior quickly doused her with the thick, green liquid housed within her rosary cross.

The tincture splashed the left side of Lidwina's face, enveloping her eye and seeping into her nostril and screaming mouth.

The reaction and shock of the act gave the poisons just enough time to react with Lidwina's tears and mucus membranes.

Within seconds, Lidwina's face felt like a brigade of fire ants attacking every opening in her head. Pulling back, her hands flew up toward her eyes, but she caught herself before she rubbed them. She growled in indignation as she kicked the door and turned blindly in the dark hallway.

Mother Superior laughed maniacally before she flopped over the desk, reaching for her keys in the lock. After a few grunting tries, she pulled her key rings from the lock, holding them tightly to place them back in her pocket, where they belonged. It proved difficult to climb off the desk like a lady, especially with her exhausted thighs. She could have really used a prayer cloth. She slammed and locked the door before she exhaustedly rocked the desk back in place against the threshold. She grabbed the two armchairs and jammed them up against the desk for good measure.

Lidwina tried to see through her searing tears, blinking them away just enough to see through the unaffected eye. Hearing Mother Superior steal her keys back almost made her drop to her knees in furious dejection. She fought to keep her sobs silent, but she was overwhelmed. She felt like she'd been bested. She wasn't sure who or what was watching over her, but she hoped that whoever it was could perform miracle reversals. Lidwina rose and felt for the wall leading to the back door. Her hand grazed the ample breast of the Virgin Mary. She almost pulled back abashedly when a flood of ideas came to her. Namely ones that involved her box of toys waiting out in the courtyard.

Mother Superior nervously paced in the barren office. Her mind tried to reason through her very short list of escape plans. She thought about reconnecting the phone but was sure the ruined phone line would rule that out. She eyed the window in her periphery, listening for noises from the hallway. Once she heard nothing, she nervously meandered toward the waist-high fixed window and drew back its dusty drapes. The view from her office had always been obscured by the oversized foliage of the white alder tree, but considering it might be her only choice, she was glad she never gave the order to have it removed. She hoped it wouldn't come to that, but considering the silence in the hallway, it might not have to.

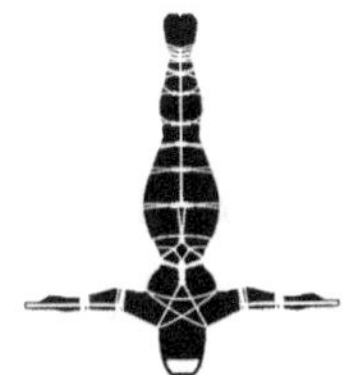

Lidwina reached the end of the hallway and pushed out the back door into the rear courtyard. She wiped the tears from her impervious eye with her shoulder to try and find the garden hose they kept on the side of the building in front of the kitchen windows. The chemicals burning her felt like they were dissolving her eye behind the lid. The quicker she got it off her face, the better. She felt for the water spigot that jutted from the stone and listened for the water pouring out of the other end of the hose. She quickly followed the hose to the end and rinsed her hands, cussing and spitting while she aimed the cold-water stream toward her face. She cussed like a sailor as the water felt like it made everything intensify. The first few seconds were excruciating, but after a few moments, the burning finally began to subside.

As she knelt and held the hose to her face like a makeshift eyewash station, she noticed the strong smells from the bonfire. Blinking and looking in that direction, her vision was still too blurry.

"Oh God, no," she said as she stood upright and closed her eyes tightly, hoping she had rinsed off as many chemicals as possible.

She dabbed the tears from her swollen eyes with the inside of her shirt, allowing her vision to clear enough to stare aghast at the burning bonfire.

Lidwina stumbled closer to the raised pit, splashing hose still in hand. She circled the outdoor brick fireplace, questioning her vision as the silhouette of a body lay engulfed in flames. Pockets of steam burst from the blackened, crisp skin in the middle of the fire. Whatever hair and clothes had already burnt off, making Lidwina's mind reel, not knowing if this was Sister Ophelia or Veronica. It wasn't until she walked around the other side of the bonfire near the shed that she saw Sister Veronica's loafers and not Ophelia's trademark hiking boots. She wished the discovery made her feel better but the realization that every nun in this convent was dead or missing, with all evidence pointing to the head bitch in charge who was now locked up in her office, made her blood boil.

"Fuuuuuck!" Lidwina yelled, bawling more tears as she steadied herself on one of the benches surrounding the fire-pit. Her sadness turned to rage, remembering why she came out here. She pulled the hose and doused Veronica's remains, leaving the running hose in the raised brick to hopefully finish the job.

Reinvigorated, she angrily stepped away from the popping and steaming remains to pull her toolbox out of the shed. She kept her back to the hissing, dwindling fire pit, saying her goodbyes and devising her plan.

The afternoon sun shone behind her while she pulled the top tools out of her box and rifled through all the goodies at the bottom. She heaved the black case from the bottom of her wheeled tool chest and placed it beside her on the ground. She pulled the powerful pink chainsaw from its case and marveled at the nicks and abrasions she remembered adding to its rough exterior. Her hand grabbed the Motomix fuel, uncapped the gas tank cover, and gassed up her old friend out of habit with no hesitation. She felt a curious piece of tape on the underside of the chainsaw. Handwritten, in permanent marker:

Every memory came flooding back: the jobs, the girls, the boobs, the broken hearts, her truck, her questionable *fuckboi* behavior, all of it. She put a pin in all of that, adjusting her big dick energy and headed back inside the convent with her chainsaw resting on her shoulder. She had one Sister to find and one that needed to be cut down to size. She wasn't about to let some old door, a formidable female foe, or a still-running hose get in the way of this final boss battle.

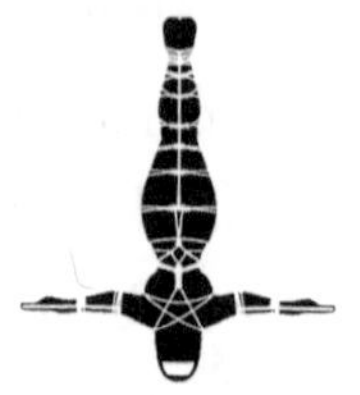

Mother Superior jumped when she heard the back door slam shut. Feeling the effects of the belladonna, she thankfully metabolized and let her common sense return. The sound of Lidwina's boots halted in front of her office, and the hair on her top lip stood on end. Mary/Mother Superior raved, "The Lord says I will take revenge; I will pay them back. Be the hand of God." A low rumble echoed through the hall.

"I give up! I'll turn myself in!" Mother Superior yelled through the locked door. "Whatever you want me to do! Just don't hurt me!" A stream of sweat dripped down from Mother Superior's bandeau during the silent tension.

"I don't believe a word you say, you lying cunt!" Lidwina fired back with braggadocio. "What I want you to *do* is tell me *WHY* you poisoned your own order!"

Mother Superior quickly recovered from the dropping of the C word in a house of the Lord and pushed past it. Her voice shook as she spoke. "I didn't mean to poison them all! I swear to you! I swear on all that is holy!"

Sorrow could be heard in her voice as she choked out, "It was supposed to be you! Just you! The serpent that offered temptation and sin... Mary warned me you would be our downfall, but I foolishly didn't listen," she murmured through choked sobs.

Lidwina raised her eyebrow and nodded before she looked up at the Virgin Mary. She licked her lips and yelled out, "Now that I know you're batshit crazy, I won't feel bad giving you what you deserve once and for all!" The purr of the chainsaw crescendoed into a high-pitched, ripping screech before it whined, and sparks flew through the darkened hallway.

Mother Superior backed away from the door apprehensively. Her mouth went agape when the loud thunk hit the floor. She screamed out, "Don't do this, L-" before the sound of the chainsaw whirred back to life and screeched as it made the hardwood door shake against its frame. Mother Superior's blood ran cold as she watched the shining steel teeth of the blade slice diagonally above the door lock and then diagonally below the door handle. The triangle of solid wood stood in place as the chainsaw was pulled back.

Suddenly, Lidwina's boot kicked the piece of door through. The thick wood plank almost struck Mother Superior before she took cover and landed on her built-in trouser trampoline. The stunned nun looked toward the door in horror as Mary's sorrowful eyes appeared through the improvised glory hole.

Lidwina jammed the decapitated head of the Virgin Mary into the opening, her sunburst crown's spines lodged in place. She ceased the chainsaw before yelling out, "Heeeere's Mary!" between laughs.

Mother Superior crab walked backward, stupefied by the horrifying sight. She screamed out, "Mary! Nooo! Don't leave me!" Her face contorted into an ugly cry. "Not now in my hour of need!"

A line of spit dribbled out of her mouth between sobs. Mother Superior took one last look at her inamorata before she noticed the smoke flowing into the room through the head-filled gap in the door. The smoke alarm started to shriek violently.

The bitch is trying to burn me alive in here!

Mother Superior pushed herself up and grabbed the chunk of door. She still heard the fading chainsaw thundering through the hall, so she knew she had to act fast. She braced herself and rocketed the chunky hunk of wood and metal through the window like a makeshift shot-put. She was thankful the crash only made minimal noise, but it didn't clear near enough glass from the corners. Shards of glass fell from the off-center starburst in the pane. She cautiously kicked the pieces at the bottom of the pane with her still bloody Mary Jane. She looked back toward the door to listen and decided it was now or never.

She sized up the hanging limb, almost touching the convent roof from the white alder, and prayed it would hold her dangerous curves, at least enough to let her make it to safety. She still needed to worry about the three- to four-foot jump between the jagged windowsill and the hopefully strong limb. She gathered her tunic above her knees, hoisted herself up, and tried to angle her body toward the center of the branch. Mother Superior closed her eyes and said a quick prayer, begging this bough not to break, even though her pleas felt empty without the presence of Mary in her head. Stray glass shards sliced into her ankle and poked through the thin insoles of her shoes. She winced through the pain, began her countdown, and jumped for the outstretched limb.

Time stood still as the flying nun floated through the air. Her arms flailed, and her blood-stained habit billowed behind her like a holy superhero cape. She closed her eyes and latched onto the branch, which thankfully held due to resting on the roof as a brace. Her legs swung her toward the tree trunk, which she took advantage of once she swung back again. She grunted and prayed her grip strength would carry her the few feet she needed them to. Her body edged closer, allowing her to pull herself closer to the bristly center of the thick tree. She took one swinging leap, lurching her exhausted body onto the upper trunk. Her foot found a small hold to rest on as she looked for the next one to grab.

Mother Superior vowed then and there to start doing pull-ups as soon as she got out of this dreadful ordeal. She let out the breath she was *well aware* she was holding and embraced her *new* Lord and Savior: her now-favorite tree. Gravity allowed her to slide down until her knee found a crotch of limbs that came together to hold her momentarily. She could do this; all she had to do was make it safely to the ground. Getting through the gate was another issue she would worry about later. She took a deep breath and tried to calm her nerves. The sound of the wind whistling was music to her ears. The approaching chainsaw rumbles were not.

Mother Superior gasped and craned her neck down toward the base of the tree just as Lidwina walked up to it and looked up in her direction with a wink.

"Well, well, well," Lidwina said, the amusement in her tone was sickening. "It looks like I found me a murderous old fat bitch tree... just ripe for the picking."

Mother Superior shook with exasperation, doing her best to maintain her place on the trunk.

"FAT?!" she howled vociferously.

Lidwina laughed and gave the mama bear up the tree the once over. "Consider that part of your penitence," Lidwina said, tapping the chainsaw against the tree bark.

Mother Superior could feel the arousing vibration of the motor through the trunk, which made her stutter as she yelled out, "Wait! LIDWINA! WAIT!"

Lidwina smiled in her direction, "Oh, before I cut this short, Mama, I almost forgot to formally introduce myself." She made eye contact with Mother Superior. "My name is Paulina, and I'm a lumberjill, the sexiest lumberjill you ever did see," she said with a nod.

Mother Superior was sweating profusely, causing her grip to slip just as *Paulina* brought the chainsaw further up the trunk.

"And this here is my best girl. I named her Winnie. Wanna know why?"

Mother Superior felt her grip give as she slid down the tree trunk, now only feet from the inflamed lumberjill. Paulina cranked her chainsaw until the *Winininninnninn* screams rattled Mother Superior's ears. As if by a divine intervention, the limbs Mother Superior had been gripping for dear life snapped.

Sister Slaughter, full of grace, slid down the rest of the limb-free trunk, devout derriere first, just as Paulina let Winnie's whirling teeth glide up in a most graceful arc through the bark. Paulina maintained its upright angle and rested the tip into the gaping hollow of the tree for stability.

That hollow and Mother Superior's gravity allowed Winnie to slice from where the good Lord split her to where her habit sat. The revolving steel teeth parted the downcast dame like the Red Sea, sending blood and viscera in all directions until it snagged the thick folds of the screaming Mother Superior's habit. Tearing her cowl off, revealing a handsome buzzcut just as the hungry cutting chain separated it into two halves. Paulina's smile parted as well, allowing blood to spray into her mouth as she said, "Nice," among the shrill sounds of the nun-piercing power tool. Both sides of Mother Superior were loosely held stubbornly at the thick crown of her head, which Paulina gladly sliced through with one final motion.

The earth was lapping up the blood of the fallen foe, as was most of Paulina's now fully soaked outfit, making it look like she'd won a wet T-shirt contest in hell. Plasma beaded across her arms and legs as she wiped Winnie's blade off with Mother Superior's heaved habit. The victor stepped away from the vanquished before she crossed the courtyard to fetch her trusty toolbox. The bonfire had put itself out finally, but the smoke coming from inside didn't bode well for the woeful house of worship.

The jacked lumberjill took Winnie, her toolbox, and the crimson clothes on her back as she searched for and left through Ophelia's hidden spot in the fence. The sun was beginning to set on the *uninhabited* convent, and Paulina still had a true calling she needed to answer.

Epilogue: A Nun Taught Me How to Yodel

"How in the hootenanny does an entire convent get lost in a mudslide?" Sister Paige asked no one in particular.

Sister Desiree continued to pull weeds but added, "Stranger things have happened." Sister Paige squinted at what looked like a lone figure with a long instrument case strapped to its back, ambling up the windy path toward them; positive it was just a mirage. She returned to her newspaper, looking for today's Pisces horoscope, which promised a surprise visitor.

The Order of San Julianna and New Beginnings in the Desert sat atop a sandy hilltop just south of Las Vegas. The convent had seen its share of sinners but very few visitors. Sister Desiree looked up from the weeds she was pulling and gasped. "Madre de Dios! A gringa!" She corrected herself and made the sign of the cross. "I mean a visitor!"

Sister Paige folded her newspaper and stretched, following close behind the histrionic Sister Desiree, dashing toward the mysterious stranger.

"You went so long with no white people jokes," Sister Paige noted. "That must be a new record!" she said, shaking her head.

Sister Desiree looked back at her in mock annoyance. They met the weary traveler halfway up the wooden steps.

"Salutations, amiga, and welcome!" Sister Desiree yelled out as soon as they were within hearing range. The stranger's fiery red hair was spilled out only on one side from below a blood- and sweat-stained cowboy hat.

"Are you hurt?" Sister Desiree asked when they were within arm's reach. The beautiful girl looked dazed and confused, possibly suffering from sunstroke. Sister Paige yelled back to the nosey nuns—sticking their heads out of the chapel doors—to bring water. Sister Desiree put her arm around the disoriented visitor and tried to get her to sit for a spell and talk.

"You poor thing, what are you doing all the way out here?!"

The novitiates came trudging out in the hot summer sun, one shapely nun-in-training covering a glass of water with her hand.

Novitiate Olga approached the two nuns and their downed damsel-in-distress, prompting her to offer the cool water to the poor, lost soul. The weary traveler looked up. The patch of reddish copper hair stayed in place over her left eye as Novitiate Olga blushed and stared into the most beautiful blue eye she'd ever seen.

After the newcomer drank slowly and her throat was no longer parched, she finally spoke.

"I'm so sorry to intrude." Her velvety voice paused, struggling to get her words out.

"I was looking for someone, but then I fell off my horse and..."

She rubbed her head with her free hand that wasn't innocently cupped just below Sister Desiree's supple breast. The wind picked up and blew her hat off her head. Novitiate Olga chased it down to return it to its owner and get one last look at the divine beauty. The Sisters eased the stranger toward the pueblo-style chapel to get her out of the sun.

"Señora, who were you looking for?" Olga asked as she handed the hat to the fiery ginger.

"Oh, I've been looking everywhere for her; I hope one of you knows where she is. Her name is Ophelia. Just...Ophelia."

The convent doors closed. Sand swirled up and over the desert hills as the wind whispered, "Saints be praised!"

FINE.

Acknowledgements

The Phrique brand would be nothing if it weren't for my very supportive enablers. The ones who sit back and let me do what I do; trusting that I will do it right, even when I don't trust myself every time. The answer will always be to make it funnier, less neon, make it more fucked up, make it more Phrique.

Patrick: Effluvium, that was all you. Our lesbian daughter wouldn't be the beast she is without your help & your fatiguingly keen eye. Thank you for planning for the most, knowing that's exactly what I'm *always* going to do. <3

Paige: We don't do mushy. What are we, Cancers? All we need is to know that we are appreciated & never taken for granted. Which you are. <3

Asher: I'm glad we both found our niches & I'm glad they crossed where they did. Psss! Let's go smoke. <3

My ride-or-dies: Willard, my tea cousin; Sarah, my table first; Asia, my penpal; Matt, my reference competition; Desiree, my poison pal; Brandon, my write-or-die; Judith, the Sweetheart of Horror; Zaq, "valid" & "fair enough"; Lisa, my other set of eyes; Chisto, we did ittt!

My friends/family: Thank you for supporting me & my gibberish. As if I gave you a choice.

The readers: Thank you for at having such refined & sophisticated taste when it comes to nonsense. <3

About the Author

Phrique writes phoolery, not at all plain & far from simple. For legal reasons, he only writes what the voices tell him to. He willfully abuses alliteration & injects innuendo where it ought not be, with the intent to make the reader giggle, gasp, and gag at his gaiety. He wants you to laugh at things you shouldn't, so he's not the only one being stared at.

https://linktr.ee/phrique

Gig of the Damned: Slay the Competition
Keep Your Hennies Close and Your Henemies Closer. One pageant, one winner, and one Queen hell-bent on snatching that crown by any means necessary. Gamble Donna Phart is a fishy little drag queen aiming to make a splash in a pool of tenacious, bloodthirsty sharks. Despite that, she's determined to shake up the food chain at the upcoming Trick'd & Treated pageant. So when a fierce, masked killer starts slaying the competition one by one, it's every hunty for herself. Luck be a lady-killer tonight, for there can be only one Queen.

Lube Me Up with Fry Grease: A Bizarro Smutsploitation
Fries, Shakes, & Videotapes! Journey into a horrible land of make-believe where familiar drive-thru characters, female or-gasms, & other fictional-totally-nonexistent things are on the menu. Where Extra Crispy is King but what is the Kernel hiding in his Southern plantation walls besides his herbs & spices? Two star-crossed lovers won't let crumbs like shackles, mercenaries, nor sexy chickens get in their special sauce. Will they ever smell freedom again before being overcome by the vapors?

Anthologies:
Error Code
Splatter Chatter Anthology